AFTER
THE
FIREWORKS

BOOKS BY ALDOUS HUXLEY

NOVELS
The Genius and the Goddess
Ape and Essence
Time Must Have a Stop
After Many a Summer Dies the Swan
Eyeless in Gaza
Point Counter Point
Those Barren Leaves
Antic Hay
Crome Yellow
Brave New World
Island

ESSAYS AND BELLES LETTRES
Brave New World Revisited
Tomorrow and Tomorrow and Tomorrow
Heaven and Hell
The Doors of Perception
The Devils of Loudun
Themes and Variations
Ends and Means
Texts and Pretexts
The Olive Tree
Music at Night
Vulgarity in Literature
Do What You Will
Proper Studies
Jesting Pilate
Along the Road
On the Margin
Essays New and Old

The Art of Seeing
The Perennial Philosophy
Science, Liberty and Peace

SHORT STORIES AND NOVELLAS
Collected Short Stories
Brief Candles
Two or Three Graces
Limbo
Little Mexican
Mortal Coils
After the Fireworks

BIOGRAPH
Grey Eminence

POETRY
The Cicadas
Leda

TRAVEL
Beyond the Mexique Bay

DRAMA
Mortal Coils—A Play
The World of Light
The Discovery, Adapted from Francis Sheridan

SELECTED WORKS
Rotunda
The World of Aldous Huxley

AFTER THE FIREWORKS

Three Novellas

ALDOUS HUXLEY

HARPER PERENNIAL

NEW YORK • LONDON • TORONTO • SYDNEY • NEW DELHI • AUCKLAND

HARPER PERENNIAL

HarperCollins books may be purchased for educational, busi-
ness, or sales promotional use. For information, please e-mail
the Special Markets Department at SPsales@harpercollins.
com.

FIRST EDITION

Designed by Jamie Lynn Kerner

Library of Congress Cataloging-in-Publication Data is avail-
able upon request.

ISBN 978-0-06-242392-4

19 20 21 22 23   LSC   10 9 8 7 6 5 4 3 2

CONTENTS

Joyce, sunnier than Lawrence, and so contagiously liberated that even Faulkner vainly attempted to borrow (in *Mosquitos*) the mordantly funny Huxley touch.

By the 1930s, his illustrious name was synonymous with smart. When the Marx Brothers went to school in *Horse Feathers*, they enrolled at Huxley College; when Liza Elliott articulated her delusions in the Broadway smash *Lady in the Dark*, she warbled, "Huxley wants to dedicate his book to me." Huxley was born in 1894 in Godalming, a part of Surrey (the climactic setting of *Brave New World*), forty miles southwest of London. His lifelong interest in genetics reflected his own remarkable gene pool: the family tree boasted his paternal grandfather T. H. Huxley, the evolutionist, and his maternal great-uncle Matthew Arnold, the critic and poet. His adolescence was financially secure, but traumatic. At fourteen, he lost his mother. Three years later, he lost his sight to keratitis; he mastered Braille and regained partial vision, but remained near-blind all his adult life. Three years after that, his beloved brother Trevenen succumbed to depression and hanged himself. Aldous went to Eton and Balliol Colleges, where he began to focus on writing. He published his first book at twenty-two.

In 1915, he encountered D. H. Lawrence, who ten years later would exert a great if passing influence on him, his future wife Maria Nys, a refugee from Belgium (a background reflected in "Uncle Spencer"), and Garsington Manor, the artistic enclave created by Lady Ottoline Morrell, where he lived, worked, and associated with Bertrand Russell, Nancy Cunard, Dora Carrington, Mark Gertler, Augustus John, Lytton Strachey, and others who inadvertently posed for character studies in his fiction. In his dazzling Peacockian debut as a novelist, he remade Garsington as *Crome Yellow*. If his second novel, *Antic Hay*, exemplified a hilarious nihilism, his subsequent work, especially the short novels collected here, documented his way to a more meticulous, intellectual, compassionate, yet no less amusing approach to the novel. We owe to Edith Sitwell this indelible portrait of young Aldous:

> Aldous Huxley was extremely tall, had full lips and a rather ripe, full but not at all loud voice. His hair was of the brown, living color of the earth on garden beds. As a young man, though he was always friendly, his silences seemed to stretch for miles, extinguishing life, when they occurred, as a snuffer extinguishes a candle. On the other hand, he was (when uninterrupted) one of the most accomplished talkers I have ever known, and his monologues on every conceivable subject were astonishingly floriated variations of an amazing brilliance, and, occasionally, of a most deliberate absurdity.[1]

Brave New World, his twenty-ninth book, in 1932, clinched his cultural centrality. Five years later Huxley, the quintessential Englishman, moved to the land of John the Savage, establishing himself on the rim of the Mojave Desert, savoring the quiet while apparently going Hollywood with a vengeance. His 1939 fillet of the movie world, the alternately sidesplitting and pedantic *After Many a Summer Dies the Swan*, showed that the vengeance ran deep.

He overcame his initial disdain of talkies to adapt Austen and Charlotte Brontë to film. He and the openly bisexual Maria, who facilitated a busy sexual life for him, entertained concentric circles of friends, encompassing Gerald Heard, Charlie Chaplin, Paulette Goddard, Igor Stravinsky, Orson Welles, Christopher Isherwood, Anita Loos, and other boldface names. He championed, to the dismay of his original fan base, mystics, searchers, and very likely a quack or two. Huxley embraced the Bates method of eye training, Vedanta and various Eastern approaches to the perennial philosophy, and an uncompromising pacifism of the sort that Orwell dismissed as "objectively pro-fascist." As Hitler made Germany great again and Roosevelt attempted to arm Great Britain, Huxley told a friend it was no more useful for him to attack Nazism than for him to attack sin. Abhorring the threat of another war more horrific than the one that his failing eyesight and poor health saved him from fighting (though he did try to volunteer), he ardently, profusely, philosophically appeased.

Prolific as ever, he slipped from the spotlight. Yet before the war ended, he published an ingenious novel, *Time Must Have a Stop*, followed by the dystopian screenplay-as-novel *Ape and Essence*; the terror-filled biography *The Devils of Loudun*; and a short account of his experiences with mescaline, *The Doors of Perception*, which eventually brought him legions of followers that his younger self—the self of *Antic Hay* and *Point Counter Point*—might have roasted on a spit.

We can sample the curve in Huxley's standing in the collected letters of Thomas Mann. 1934: "I admire Aldous Huxley, who represents one of the finest flowerings of West European intellectualism, especially in his essays. I prefer him to D. H. Lawrence, who is no doubt a significant phenomenon and characteristic of our times, but whose fevered sensuality has little appeal for me." 1944: "[*Time Must Have a Stop*] is exciting because it is a work of talent, and in literary terms an engagingly avant-garde performance. Yet it is reprehensible. . . . But my own conscience is not so clear when the question of morbidity and decadence is raised." 1949: "[A] good many things by Aldous Huxley . . . are greater and, as documents of the age, more illuminating than anything produced so far by the young." 1954: "[*The Doors of Perception*] represents the last and, I am tempted to say, the rashest development of Huxley's *escapism*, which I never liked in him. Mysticism as a means to that end was still reasonably honorable. But it strikes me as scandalous that he has now arrived at drugs."[2]

Despite or because of Huxley's anointment as a savant of druggy diversions and insights, his readership narrowed beyond the perdurable *Brave New World*. Critics who thought he went off the rails (Mann, again: "being rapt over the miracle of a chair and absorbed in all sorts of color illusions has more to do with idiocy than he thinks") underappreciated his last novel, *Island*, a series of dialogue-essays, explaining the ways of a paradise built on logic, science, spiritualism, hallucinogens, and (here's the rub) a genetic sameness that makes its inhabitants congenial—all threatened by the West's unslakable thirst for its oil reserves. Most critics agreed, however, that his next and last book, *Literature and Science*, proved to be charming and rational in a way that was pure Huxley. He died and was greatly missed.

In the decades subsequent to his death, in 1963 (overshadowed by the simultaneous assassination of JFK), Huxley never failed to maintain prestige. Yet much of his best work is neglected. His presence in the academy is limited to *Brave New World*, a perennial middle school pursuit. *Point Counter*

Point is neither an obligatory text nor a rite of passage, though it remains a unique achievement, which (the rambling Laurentian soliloquies notwithstanding) captures its time and consequently ours in all its confusion, class warfare, fascinating fascism, lost labors of love, and boundless vanities. Huxley's early novels came to represent a demoded fashion, fussy and overemphatic in style and learned to the point of condescension. The polyglot allusions and polymathic presumptions that we wrestle with as the price of reading *Ulysses*, suggest elitism in Huxley. He was not, as he readily conceded, a congenital novelist and yesterday's irreverence is today's ho-hum. Harold Bloom imperiously conceded that he treasured Huxley's social comedies in his youth but saw no reason to revisit them; two *New York Times* reviewers recently dismissed *Brave New World* because the embryology is dated and the middle-class mischaracterized—the kinds of observations a character in *Point Counter Point* might have made before tumbling down a marble staircase.

And still his stock rises. Huxleyans quietly proliferate, like disaffected Alphas. Several studies of his work have appeared, along with anthologies of his previously uncollected writings and lectures. In the past twenty years, an American publisher produced the six-volume *Complete Essays,* and a German publisher launched the overpriced but illuminating *Aldous Huxley Annual,* which has uncovered dozens of unremembered and uncompleted works, not least Huxley's (may it be produced!) musical-comedy version of *Brave New World*. His novels remain in print, as do several key works. Recent biographies have supplemented the 1973 tour de force by Sybille Bedford; a second collection of letters, edited by the dogged Huxleyan James Sexton, augments the indispensable 1969 doorstop edited by Grover Smith.

2.

Much of the posthumous attention accorded Huxley has centered on his role as guru to stoners, with or without mystical overtones, or seeks to reconcile his voluminous work with an overarching philosophical song. I speak for a more plebeian readership: we who read him not to have our minds improved or blown (though these are surely collateral effects), but for the pleasure of his company, which can be stimulating, grotesque, and uproarious all at once. I speak for those who look not for consistency, preferring to revel in the multitudes of a man incapable of not thinking and of worrying each thought into prose; who regard him not as a saint, though his humbly stooped 6' 4" frame, rocky cheekbones cradling glassy eyes, and polite, patiently sonorous voice, typecast him for the part, but as a master chronicler of pettiness: overarching pride, paralyzing insecurity, counterfeit love, spurious ambition, every kind of cant and duplicity.

My lifelong affection for Huxley transcends without overlooking (I wince and move on) his love of exclamations and pointless adverbs (irrevocably, bottomlessly, insufferably); his assumption that I have read, seen, heard, and retained all the things he has and can recognize a line from Meister Eckhart in German when I see it; his disdain for jazz (the true moksha); his not-so-youthful indulgences in racial and Semitic stereotyping (he blames, quite rightly, blacks for jazz and Jews for monotheism), not to mention his fling with genetic engineering. Mine is a devotion captured by Anthony Burgess in *99 Novels*, his survey of English-language literature from 1939 to 1983. Huxley alone is represented by as many as three novels. Burgess writes of *After Many a Summer*, "It is Huxleyan in that it is a novel with a brain, and if it nags at human stupidity when it should be getting on with the story—well, we accept the didacticism as an outflowing of the author's concern with the state of the modern world. Huxley's novels are always *concerned*, and therein lies their strength and continuing relevance."[3] Still, I do insist that strength and relevance reside no less in his wit, discursive learning, and an understanding of people that urges readers to groan at his vainglorious creatures while recognizing themselves in the gallery.

Huxley wrote eleven novels, accounting for one-fifth of the volumes he published, and he evidently regarded them as his most important work in that they represented "finished" presentations of his ideas. He wrote poetry for a quarter-century, but gave it up during the Second World War. He wrote stories throughout the 1920s, among them "The Gioconda Smile," "The Tillotsen Banquet," "The Farcical History of Richard Greenow," "Nuns at Luncheon," "Young Archimedes," "The Bookshop," and "The Claxtons," but gave that up in 1930, writing only a few more—most notably his last, "Voices" (1955), one of the nastiest supernatural caprices this side of Saki and Patricia Highsmith—that he inexplicably declined to collect in his books. He professed little enthusiasm for modern theater, but like Henry James tried time and again to mount plays, enjoying one success with his 1948 adaptation of "The Gioconda Smile." But the novels came steadily between 1921 and 1962, like benchmarks. In context with his dozens of other volumes, they invariably dramatize ideas and interests explored and developed in intervening essays, stories, poems, reviews, histories, and prefaces.

Of that work, much of it long out of print, the short novels collected here are most treasurable, and what pleasure it is to welcome them back. Each of them might have secured a more enduring place in his bibliography had they been initially issued as standalone novels. All were written in the defining decade when he was most keenly focused on fiction, and Huxley favored them enough to include them in retrospective collections. So why and when did they vanish?

Between 1920 and 1930, Huxley published—in addition to three volumes of poetry, two travel books, four collections of essays, and a play—nine works of fiction: the novels *Crome Yellow*, *Antic Hay*, *Those Barren Leaves*, and *Point Counter Point*, and the story collections *Limbo*, *Mortal Coils*, *Little Mexican*, *Two or Three Graces*, and *Brief Candles*. The last three were mostly given over to these short novels—novels, it must be said, no shorter than *Ape and Essence* or *The Genius and the Goddess*. Perhaps publishers and readers in the '20s took the page count more seriously as a mercantile consideration; in any case Huxley accompanied them with thematically complementary stories, like swans and cygnets. In 1957, he published *Collected Stories*, raiding the five story volumes of their shorter stories (plus "Sir Hercules" from *Crome Yellow*), and rendering the novellas basically homeless. That same year a paperback re-the most prominent biologists of his own day (Julian Huxley and the Nobel laureate Andrew Huxley), all but patented the use of biological, zoological, botanical, and physiological metaphors, and here he has a field day with prawns and pigs (the latter auguring the German occupation), as well as handmade foods, from "ferial apple fritters" to chocolate bedpans. The last offends Spencer, despite "his professional belief in the virtues of sugar," and inspires the narrator to a lexicon of euphemisms from *coprophily* and *scatological* to a thunderous *excrementitious*. Huxley, who mocked Swift's "insensate hatred of bowels," was not easily alienated from the messier precincts of the human condition. As the story deepens with an integrated marriage, we encounter tropes that will recur throughout his work: teenage priggishness, sudden death, an ugly woman who exerts sexual magnetism, the vain thought that future writers might concentrate on "man's relation to God" instead of romance, the naïve refusal to believe war is coming (this is the twentieth century, after all), and the equally naïve assent, because "War is always popular, at the beginning."

Confined to the German Ministry of the Interior, Spencer finds that the prisoners are crueler to each other than are the jailors; nightmares are habitual. Yet he also finds, for the first time in his life, love in the person of a "golden-haired male impersonator," a Cockney music hall entertainer named Emmy Wendle, one of Huxley's most haunting creations: young, independent, morally adventitious, utterly fickle, and androgynous in the way of a Hemingway femme, touching down like a bee on the divided groups of prisoners who, "equal in their misery, still retained their social distinctions." No good can come if it, yet Huxley ramps up the farce as Emmy retails her nine greatest loves and her devout superstition involving a pig.

In the realm of flighty women, however, Emmy is a patch on the redoubtable Grace Peddley of "Two or Three Graces" (1926). Although I think "After the Fireworks" is Huxley's most masterly performance in the more-than-a-story, not-quite-a-novel idiom, I suspect that "Two or Three Graces" would have benefited most had it been offered as a novel. Huxley may also have thought so: unlike "Uncle Spencer," which debuted in *Little Mexican* (*Young Archimedes* in the United States) and "After the Fireworks," which debuted in *Brief Candles*, "Two or Three Graces" was the title story in a volume where it counted for 195 of 272 pages. Structurally, it stands among Huxley's most ingenious inventions.

It opens with a bank shot. Huxley's droll riff on the etymology and variety of bores introduces Herbert Comfrey, an old acquaintance of the narrator: a music critic named, we eventually learn, Dick Wilkes. The story is not about Comfrey, who is rather the cue ball that temporarily separates Wilkes from his far-from-boring friend Kingham, and sends him to the pocket of Comfrey's brother-in-law, John Peddley. John is a different species of bore ("an active bore," yet kind and intelligent), who traps unwary travelers in relentless one-sided conversations. He introduces Wilkes to his darling wife Grace—tall, lean, ugly, but "positively and actively charming." Stimulated by their platonic friendship (like Denis in *Crome Yellow*, Dick hesitates), Grace undergoes a kind of psychic mitosis. In the end there aren't two or three Graces, but four, each reflective of a man she attaches herself to—each gracefully inept in her own way. She incarnates one of Huxley's favorite lines, from Fulke Greville:

"O wearisome condition of humanity! / Born under one law, to another bound," except that she is bound to another and another and another.

With her husband, John, Grace is a devoted but strangely deficient bourgeois wife who fails to connect with her children ("You're a little girl, mummy," her four-year-old attests). With Wilkes, she is a dedicated concertgoer who doesn't understand a thing about music. After he alienates her with a cruel joke and introduces her to the bohemian painter and faker Rodney Clegg, she takes him as her lover and out-bohemians him and his followers until he drops her, at which point, Kingham returns. A writer who lives for passion and strife, creating the latter when it does not unfold naturally, Kingham demands that Grace fall madly in love with him. She does, growing so appositely overwrought that she ponders suicide when he drops her. Wilkes, now married to a sane and cautious woman, returns in the nick of time.

Older writers—Arnold Bennett, Thomas Hardy—complained that Huxley did not truly end his stories, but merely stopped them. "Two or Three Graces" has so many riches, page after page (note that his physical description of Clegg practically begets Sitwell's of Huxley), that the ending may seem abrupt, a testament to the eternal feminine in which Grace is doomed to repeat her circuit of affections. But then as Wilkes realizes, and underscores for the reader, the story has the structure of music: from suburban andante to Clegg's scherzando to Kingham's molto agitato to the adagio of Beethoven's arietta to . . . Da Capo, from the head, begin again.

"Two or Three Graces" is often seen as a test run for

Point Counter Point, which is unfair to its thoroughly distinct qualities. One connection is the presumed twice-told conjuring of D. H. Lawrence. But while Lawrence is admittedly the template for the later work's Rampion, he only looks like Kingham, with his short red beard and refusal to divulge his Christian names beyond the initials. Huxley had met Lawrence just once when he wrote "Two and Three Graces." That encounter probably contributed to the portrait, but the sexually ravenous and distraught Kingham is not Lawrence. By 1928 they were great friends; Huxley esteemed and even loved him, which may explain why Rampion succumbs to a sage's monotony while Kingham roars off the page. In "After the Fireworks," published in the year of Lawrence's death (1930), he is accessed only as a literary jape: the self-styled "fatal woman," Clare Tarn, the mother of the story's demigoddess and genuinely fatal woman Pamela Tarn, seeks the "dumb, dark forces of physical passion" in the arms of—a "gamekeeper? or a young farmer? I forget. But there was something about rabbit shooting in it, I know."

"After the Fireworks" is a major work and a turning point for Huxley, leading directly to *Brave New World* in its burlesque of sexual awkwardness and chagrin and the embarrassments of aging (he does here for European health spas what he would later do for Hollywood cemeteries in *After Many a Summer*), Ford and his assembly line, ruminations on a world without goodness, and theisms of one versus many gods. This is a comedy, the last uncompromisingly funny novel or story Huxley wrote, unimpeded by didactic lectures and sagacious swamis. Fireworks figure in the prose as well as the plot, which is basic. A middle-aged writer at rest in Rome, Miles Fanning, whose popular novels excite the dreams of adolescent girls, is stalked by a twenty-year-old fan who he tries vainly to resist. He has used his finest witticisms so often that he can no longer recite them without impatient interruptions. Pamela Tarn has not heard them. Nor can she figure out why a writer would spend hours writing when he could be with her. "Death in Venice" meets "The Humbling," heterosexually.

Huxley is always facile with animal metaphors, and he breaks the bank here, beginning with the first lines, regarding a woodpecker. A few lines down he complains of letters getting through every barrier, like "filter-passing bacteria," a simile more suited to the blight of email. Bears turn up on the next page, with camels on their heels, and then ostriches and whitings, jellyfish and clams, the inevitable baboon, and with the arrival of Pamela Tarn, a combination animal metaphor and adverb: hippo-ishly. Huxley lavished attention on names, and one may wish there were more of Wilber F. Schmalz and his unctuous correspondence if only to relish his moniker. Fanning notes, in Latin, that he never liked art that conceals. Neither does Huxley. He italicizes and underscores zoological traits and innermost thoughts, flitting into Pamela's mind as well as her riotous diary as easily as he does Fanning's mind and his unfinished letter. He drops linguistic banana peels every few pages. Fanning is one of those personages who strive to speak in epigraphs, which are wasted on fellows like the clerk at Cook's who tells him "Gratters on your last book," to which Miles responds, "All gratitude for gratters." Miles loves the word *impertinence*, which earns a new meaning regarding Pamela: even her breasts are impertinent, "pointed, firm, almost comically insistent."[4]

The lyrical passages remind us that Huxley was a formidable travel writer, but even they serve to remind Miles that a comedy is a series of unavoidable pratfalls. The sibilant panorama of Rome at the heart of the tale—"golden with ripening corn and powdered goldenly with a haze of dust, the Campagna stretched away from the feet of the subsiding hills, away and up towards a fading horizon, on which the blue ghosts of mountains floated on a level with her eyes"—works its magic, but as Miles breaks the "sad, sad but somehow consoling" silence, his knees crackle to let him know that he is tarnished with age and Tarn is "dangerously and perversely fresh." If he were a younger man, he might rant, as John the Savage will in two years, "I don't want comfort. I want God, I want poetry, I want real danger, I want freedom, I want goodness. I want sin."

FOREWORD : JESTING ALDOUS

1. Edith Sitwell in Stephen Klaidman, *Sydney and Violet*, Doubleday, 2013, p. 187.
2. Richard and Clara Winston (ed.), *Letters of Thomas Mann, 1889-1955*, Knopf, 1970, pp. 213, 455, 581, 664.
3. Anthony Burgess, *99 Novels*, Summit, 1984, p. 24. The other Huxley works he includes are *Ape and Essence* and *Island*.
4. Pamela has run away from her censorious Aunt Edith, a relationship Huxley returns to in his final story, "Voices," in the deadly conflict between another twenty-year-old Pamela and her Aunt Eleanor.

AFTER
THE
FIREWORKS

AFTER THE FIREWORKS

I

LATE AS USUAL. LATE." JUDD'S VOICE WAS CENSORI-
ous. The words fell sharp, like beak-blows. "As though
I were a nut," Miles Fanning thought resentfully, "and he
were a woodpecker. And yet he's devotion itself, he'd do
anything for me. Which is why, I suppose, he feels enti-
tled to crack my shell each time he sees me." And he came
to the conclusion, as he had so often come before, that he
really didn't like Colin Judd at all. "My oldest friend, whom
I quite definitely don't like. Still . . ." Still, Judd was an asset,
Judd was worth it.

"Here are your letters," the sharp voice continued.

Fanning groaned as he took them. "Can't one ever escape
from letters? Even here, in Rome? They seem to get through
everything. Like filter-passing bacteria. Those blessed days
before post offices!" Sipping, he examined over the rim of
his coffee cup the addresses on the envelopes.

"You'd be the first to complain if people didn't write,"
Judd rapped out. "Here's your egg. Boiled for three minutes
exactly. I saw to it myself."

Taking his egg, "On the contrary," Fanning answered,

"I'd be the first to rejoice. If people write, it means they exist; and all I ask for is to be able to pretend that the world doesn't exist. The wicked flee when no man pursueth. How well I understand them! But letters don't allow you to be an ostrich. The Freudians say . . ." He broke off suddenly. After all he was talking to Colin—to *Colin*. The confessional, self-accusatory manner was wholly misplaced. Pointless to give Colin the excuse to say something disagreeable. But what he had been going to say about the Freudians was amusing. "The Freudians," he began again.

But taking advantage of forty years of intimacy Judd had already started to be disagreeable. "But you'd be miserable," he was saying, "if the post didn't bring you your regular dose of praise and admiration and sympathy and . . ."

"And humiliation," added Fanning, who had opened one of the envelopes and was looking at the letter within. "Listen to this. From my American publishers. Sales and Publicity Department. 'My dear Mr. Fanning.' *My* dear, mark you. Wilburn F. Schmalz's dear. 'My dear Mr. Fanning,—Won't you take us into your confidence with regard to your plans for the Summer Vacation? What aspect of the Great Outdoors are you favouring this year? Ocean or Mountain, Woodland or purling Lake? I would esteem it a great privilege if you would inform me, as I am preparing a series of notes for the Literary Editors of our leading journals, who are, as I have often found in the past, exceedingly receptive to such personal material, particularly when accompanied by well-chosen snapshots. So won't you co-operate with us in providing this service? Very cordially yours, Wilbur F. Schmalz.' Well, what do you think of that?"

"I think you'll answer him," said Judd. "Charmingly,"

he added, envenoming his malice. Fanning gave a laugh, whose very ease and heartiness betrayed his discomfort. "And you'll even send him a snapshot."

Contemptuously—too contemptuously (he felt it at the time)—Fanning crumpled up the letter and threw it into the fireplace. The really humiliating thing, he reflected, was that Judd was quite right: he *would* write to Mr. Schmalz about the Great Outdoors, he *would* send the first snapshot anybody took of him. There was a silence. Fanning ate two or three spoonfuls of egg. Perfectly boiled, for once. But still, what a relief that Colin was going away! After all, he reflected, there's a great deal to be said for a friend who has a house in Rome and who invites you to stay, even when he isn't there. To such a man much must be forgiven—even his infernal habit of being a woodpecker. He opened another envelope and began to read.

Possessive and preoccupied, like an anxious mother, Judd watched him. With all his talents and intelligence, Miles wasn't fit to face the world alone. Judd had told him so (peck, peck!) again and again. "You're a child!" He had said it a thousand times. "You ought to have somebody to look after you." But if any one other than himself offered to do it, how bitterly jealous and resentful he became! And the trouble was that there were always so many applicants for the post of Fanning's bear-leader. Foolish men or, worse and more frequently, foolish women, attracted to him by his reputation and then conquered by his charm. Judd hated and professed to be loftily contemptuous of them. And the more Fanning liked his admiring bear-leaders, the loftier Judd's contempt became. For that was the bitter and unforgivable thing: Fanning manifestly preferred their bear-leading to

Judd's. They flattered the bear, they caressed and even wor-
shipped him; and the bear, of course, was charming to them,
until such time as he growled, or bit, or, more often, quietly
slunk away. Then they were surprised, they were pained. Be-
cause, as Judd would say with a grim satisfaction, they didn't
know what Fanning was *really* like. Whereas he did know
and had known since they were schoolboys together, nearly
forty years before. Therefore he had a right to like him—a
right and, at the same time, a duty to tell him all the reasons
why he ought not to like him. Fanning didn't much enjoy
listening to these reasons; he preferred to go where the bear
was a sacred animal. With that air, which seemed so natural
on his grey sharp face, of being dispassionately impersonal,
"You're afraid of healthy criticism," Judd would tell him.
"You always were, even as a boy."

"He's Jehovah," Fanning would complain. "Life with
Judd is one long Old Testament. Being one of the Chosen
People must have been bad enough. But to be *the* Chosen
Person, in the singular . . ." And he would shake his head.
"Terrible!"

And yet he had never seriously quarrelled with Colin
Judd. Active unpleasantness was something which Fanning
avoided as much as possible. He had never even made any
determined attempt to fade out of Judd's existence as he had
faded, at one time or another, out of the existence of so many
once intimate bear-leaders. The habit of their intimacy was
of too long standing and, besides, old Colin was so useful, so
bottomlessly reliable. So Judd remained for him the Oldest
Friend whom one definitely dislikes; while for Judd, he was
the Oldest Friend whom one adores and at the same time
hates for not adoring back, the Oldest Friend whom one

never sees enough of, but whom, when he *is* there, one finds insufferably exasperating, the Oldest Friend whom, in spite of all one's efforts, one is always getting on the nerves of.

"If only," Judd was thinking, "he could have faith!" The Catholic Church was there to help him. (Judd himself was a convert of more than twenty years' standing.) But the trouble was that Fanning didn't want to be helped by the Church; he could only see the comic side of Judd's religion. Judd was reserving his missionary efforts till his Friend should be old or ill. But if only, meanwhile, if only, by some miracle of grace. . . . So thought the good Catholic; but it was the jealous friend who felt and who obscurely schemed. Converted, Miles Fanning would be separated from his other friends and brought, Judd realized, nearer to himself.

Watching him, as he read his letter, Judd noticed, all at once, that Fanning's lips were twitching involuntarily into a smile. They were full lips, well cut, sensitive and sensual; his smiles were a little crooked. A dark fury suddenly fell on Colin Judd.

"Telling *me* that you'd like to get no letters!" he said with an icy vehemence. "When you sit there grinning to yourself over some silly woman's flatteries."

Amazed, amused, "But what an outburst!" said Fanning, looking up from his letter.

Judd swallowed his rage; he had made a fool of himself. It was in a tone of calm dispassionate flatness that he spoke. Only his eyes remained angry. "Was I right?" he asked.

"So far as the woman was concerned," Fanning answered. "But wrong about the flattery. Women have no time nowadays to talk about anything except themselves."

"Which is only another way of flattering," said Judd obstinately. "They confide in you, because they think you'll like being treated as a person who understands."

"Which is what, after all, I am. By profession even." Fanning spoke with an exasperating mildness. "What *is* a novelist, unless he's a person who understands?" He paused; but Judd made no answer, for the only words he could have uttered would have been whirling words of rage and jealousy. He was jealous not only of the friends, the lovers, the admiring correspondents; he was jealous of a part of Fanning himself, of the artist, the public personage; for the artist, the public personage seemed so often to stand between his friend and himself. He hated, while he gloried in them.

Fanning looked at him for a moment, expectantly; but the other kept his mouth tight shut, his eyes averted. In the same exasperatingly gentle tone, "And flattery or no flattery," Fanning went on, "this is a charming letter. And the girl's adorable."

He was having his revenge. Nothing upset poor Colin Judd so much as having to listen to talk about women or love. He had a horror of anything connected with the act, the mere thought, of sex. Fanning called it his perversion. "You're one of those unspeakable chastity-perverts," he would say, when he wanted to get his own back after a bout of pecking. "If I had children, I'd never allow them to frequent your company. Too dangerous." When he spoke of the forbidden subject, Judd would either writhe, a martyr, or else unchristianly explode. On this occasion he writhed and was silent. "Adorable," Fanning repeated, provocatively. "A ravishing little creature. Though of course she *may* be a huge great camel. That's the danger of unknown correspondents. The best letter-writers are often camels. It's a piece of natural history I've learned by the bitterest experience." Looking back at the letter, "All the same," he went on, "when a young girl writes to one that she's sure one's the only person in the world who can tell her exactly who and what (both heavily underlined) she is—well, one's rather tempted, I must confess, to try yet once more. Because even if she were a camel she'd be a very young one. Twenty-one—isn't that what she says?" He turned over a page of the letter. "Yes; twenty-one. Also she writes in orange ink. And doesn't like the Botticellis at the Uffizi. But I hadn't told you; she's at Florence. This letter has been to London and back. We're practically neighbours. And here's something that's really rather good. Listen. 'What I like about the Italian women is that they don't seem to be rather ashamed of being women, like so many English girls are, because English girls seem to go about apologizing for their figures, as though they were punctured, the way they hold themselves—it's really rather abject. But here they're all pleased and proud and not a bit apologetic or punctured, but just the opposite, which I really like, don't you?' Yes I do," Fanning answered looking up from the letter. "I like it very much indeed. I've always been opposed to these modern *Ars est celare artem* fashions. I like unpuncturedness and I'm charmed by the letter. Yes, charmed. Aren't you?"

In a voice that trembled with hardly restrained indignation, "No, I'm not!" Judd answered; and without looking at Fanning, he got up and walked quickly out of the room.

---

* It is (true) art to conceal art.

II

JUDD HAD GONE TO STAY WITH HIS OLD AUNT CARO-
line at Montreux. It was an annual affair; for Judd lived
chronometrically. Most of June and the first half of July
were always devoted to Aunt Caroline and devoted, invari-
ably, at Montreux. On the fifteenth of July, Aunt Caroline
was rejoined by her friend Miss Gaskin and Judd was free
to proceed to England. In England he stayed till September
the thirtieth, when he returned to Rome—"for the pray-
ing season," as Fanning irreverently put it. The beautiful
regularity of poor Colin's existence was a source of endless
amusement to his friend. Fanning never had any plans. "I
just accept what turns up," he would explain. "Heads or
tails—it's the only rational way of living. Chance generally
knows so much better than we do. The Greeks elected most
of their officials by lot—how wisely! Why shouldn't we toss
up for Prime Ministers? We'd be much better governed.
Or a sort of Calcutta Sweep for all the responsible posts
in Church and State. The only horror would be if one were
to win the sweep oneself. Imagine drawing the Permanent
Under-Secretaryship for Education! Or the Archbishopric

of Canterbury! Or the Viceroyalty of India! One would just have to drink weed-killer. But as things are, luckily . . ."

Luckily, he was at liberty, under the present dispensation, to stroll, very slowly, in a suit of cream-coloured silk, down the shady side of the Via Condotti towards the Spanish Steps. Slowly, slowly. The air was streaked with invisible bars of heat and cold. Coolness came flowing out of shadowed doorways, and at every transverse street the sun breathed fiercely. Like walking through the ghost of a zebra, he thought.

Three beautiful young women passed him, talking and laughing together. Like laughing flowers, like deer, like little horses. And of course absolutely unpunctured, unapologetic. He smiled to himself, thinking of the letter and also of his own reply to it.

A pair of pink and white monsters loomed up, as though from behind the glass of an aquarium. But not speechless. For *"Grossartig!"** fell enthusiastically on Fanning's ear as they passed, and *"Fabelhaft!"*† These Nordics! He shook his head. Time they were put a stop to.

In the looking-glasses of a milliner's window a tall man in creamy-white walked slowly to meet him, hat in hand. The face was aquiline and eager, brown with much exposure to the sun. The waved, rather wiry hair was dark almost to blackness. It grew thickly, and the height of the forehead owed nothing to the approach of baldness. But what pleased Fanning most was the slimness and straightness of the tall figure. Those sedentary men of letters, with their sagging tremulous paunches—they were enough to make one hate the very thought of literature. What had been Fanning's horror

---

* "Great"

† "Fabulous."

when, a year before, he had realized that his own paunch was showing the first preliminary signs of sagging! But Mr. Hornibrooke's exercises had been wonderful. "The Culture of the Abdomen." So much more important, as he had remarked in the course of the last few months at so many dinner tables, than the culture of the mind! For of course he had taken everybody into his confidence about the paunch. He took everybody into his confidence about almost everything. About his love-affairs and his literary projects; about his illnesses and his philosophy; his vices and his bank balance. He lived a rich and variegated private life in public; it was one of the secrets of his charm. To the indignant protests of poor jealous Colin, who reproached him with being an exhibitionist, shameless, a self-exploiter, "You take everything so moralistically," he had answered. "You seem to imagine people do everything on purpose. But people do hardly anything on purpose. They behave as they do because they can't help it; that's what they happen to be like. 'I am that I am'; Jehovah's is the last word in realistic psychology. I am what *I* am—a sort of soft transparent jelly-fish. While you're what *you* are—very tightly shut, opaque, heavily armoured: in a word, a giant clam. Morality doesn't enter; it's a case for scientific classification. You should be more of a Linnæus, Colin, and less the Samuel Smiles." Judd had been reduced to a grumbling silence. What he really resented was the fact that Fanning's confidences were given to upstart friends, to strangers even, before they were given to him. It was only to be expected. The clam's shell keeps the outside things out as effectually as it keeps the inside things in. In Judd's case, moreover, the shell served as an instrument of reproachful pinching.

From his cool street Fanning emerged into the Piazza

di Spagna. The sunlight was stinging hot and dazzling. The flower vendors on the steps sat in the midst of great explosions of colour. He bought a gardenia from one of them and stuck it in his buttonhole. From the windows of the English bookshop "*The Return of Eurydice,* by Miles Fanning" stared at him again and again. They were making a regular display of his latest volume in Tauchnitz. Satisfactory, no doubt; but also, of course, rather ridiculous and even humiliating, when one reflected that the book would be read by people like that estimable upper middle-class couple there, with their noses at the next window—that Civil Servant, he guessed, with the sweet little artistic wife and the artistic little house on Campden Hill—would be read by them dutifully (for of course they worked hard to keep abreast of everything) and discussed at their charming little dinner parties and finally condemned as "extraordinarily brilliant, but . . ." Yes, but, but, but. For they were obviously regular subscribers to *Punch,* were vertebrae in the backbone of England, were upholders of all that was depressingly finest, all that was lifelessly and genteelly best in the English upper-class tradition. And when they recognized him (as it was obvious to Fanning, in spite of their discreet politeness, that they did) his vanity, instead of being flattered, was hurt. Being recognized by people like that—such was fame! What a humiliation, what a personal insult!

At Cook's, where he now went to draw some money on his letter of credit, Fame still pursued him, trumpeting. From behind the brass bars of his cage the cashier smiled knowingly as he counted out the banknotes.

"Of course your name's very familiar to me, Mr. Fanning," he said; and his tone was at once ingratiating and self-satisfied; the compliment to Fanning was at the same time a compliment to himself. "And if I may be permitted to say so," he went on, pushing the money through the bars, as one might offer a piece of bread to an ape, "gratters on your last book. Gratters," he repeated, evidently delighted with his very public-schooly colloquialism.

"All gratitude for gratters," Fanning answered and turned away. He was half amused, half annoyed. Amused by the absurdity of those more than Etonian congratulations, annoyed at the damned impertinence of the congratulator. So intolerably patronizing! he grumbled to himself. But most admirers were like that; they thought they were doing you an enormous favour by admiring you. And how much more they admired themselves for being capable of appreciating than they admired the object of their appreciation! And then there were the earnest ones who thanked you for giving such a perfect expression to their ideas and sentiments. They were the worst of all. For, after all, what were they thanking you for? For being *their* interpreter, *their* dragoman, for playing John the Baptist to *their* Messiah. Damn their impertinence! Yes, damn their impertinence!

"Mr. Fanning." A hand touched his elbow.

Still indignant with the thought of damned impertinences, Fanning turned round with an expression of such ferocity on his face, that the young woman who had addressed him involuntarily fell back.

"Oh . . . I'm so sorry," she stammered; and her face, which had been bright, deliberately, with just such an impertinence as Fanning was damning, was discomposed into a child-like embarrassment. The blood tingled painfully in her cheeks. Oh, what a fool, she thought, what a fool she was making of herself! This idiotic blushing! But the way he had turned round on her, as if he were going to bite. . . . Still, even that was no excuse for blushing and saying she was sorry, as though she were still at school and he were Miss Huss. Idiot! she inwardly shouted at herself. And making an enormous effort, she readjusted her still scarlet face, giving it as good an expression of smiling nonchalance as she could summon up. "I'm sorry," she repeated, in a voice that was meant to be light, easy, ironically polite, but which came out (oh, idiot, idiot!) nervously shaky and uneven. "I'm afraid I disturbed you. But I just wanted to introduce . . . I mean, as you were passing . . ."

"But how charming of you!" said Fanning, who had had time to realize that this latest piece of impertinence was one to be blessed, not damned. "Charming!" Yes, charming it was, that young face with the grey eyes and the little straight nose, like a cat's and the rather short upper lip. And the heroic way she had tried, through all her blushes, to be the accomplished woman of the world—that too was charming. And touchingly charming even were those rather red, large-wristed English hands, which she wasn't yet old enough to have learnt the importance of tending into whiteness and softness. They were still the hands of a child, a tomboy. He gave her one of those quick, those brilliantly and yet mysteriously significant smiles of his; those smiles that were still so youthfully beautiful when they came spontaneously. But they could also be put on; he knew how to exploit their fabricated charm, deliberately. To a sensitive eye, the beauty of his expression was, on these occasions, subtly repulsive.

Reassured, "I'm Pamela Tarn," said the young girl, feeling warm with gratitude for the smile. He was handsomer, she was thinking, than in his photographs. And much more fascinating. It was a face that had to be seen in movement.

"Pamela Tarn?" he repeated questioningly.

"The one who wrote you a letter." Her blush began to deepen again. "You answered so nicely. I mean, it was so kind . . . I thought . . ."

"But of course!" he cried, so loudly, that people looked round, startled. "Of course!" He took her hand and held it, shaking it from time to time, for what seemed to Pamela hours. "The most enchanting letter. Only I'm so bad at names. So you're Pamela Tarn." He looked at her appraisingly. She returned his look for a moment, then flinched away in confusion from his bright dark eyes.

"Excuse me," said a chilly voice; and a very large suit of plus fours edged past them to the door.

"I like you," Fanning concluded, ignoring the plus fours; she uttered an embarrassed little laugh. "But then, I liked you before. You don't know how pleased I was with what you said about the difference between English and Italian women." The colour rose once more into Pamela's cheeks. She had only written those sentences after long hesitation and had written them then recklessly, dashing them down with a kind of anger, just because Miss Huss would have been horrified by their unwomanliness, just because Aunt Edith would have found them so distressing, just because they had, when she spoke them aloud one day in the streets of Florence, so shocked the two schoolmistresses from Boston whom she had met at the pension and was doing the sights with. Fanning's mention of them pleased her and at the same time made her feel dreadfully guilty. She hoped he wouldn't be too specific about those differences; it seemed to her that every one was listening. "So profound," he went on in his musical ringing voice. "But out of the mouths of babes, with all due respect." He smiled again, "And 'punctured'— that was really the *mot juste*. I shall steal it and use it as my own."

"Permesso." This time it was a spotted muslin and brown arms and a whiff of synthetic carnations.

"I think we're rather in the way," said Pamela, who was becoming more and more uncomfortably aware of being conspicuous. And the spirit presences of Miss Huss, of Aunt Edith, of the two American ladies at Florence seemed to hang about her, hauntingly. "Perhaps we'd better . . . I mean . . ." And turning, she almost ran to the door.

"Punctured, punctured," repeated his pursuing voice behind her. "Punctured with the shame of being warmblooded mammals. Like those poor lank creatures that were standing at the counter in there," he added, coming abreast with her, as they stepped over the threshold into the heat and glare. "Did you see them? So pathetic. But, oh dear!" he shook his head. "Oh dear, oh dear!"

She looked up at him and Fanning saw in her face a new expression, an expression of mischief and laughing malice and youthful impertinence. Even her breasts he now noticed with an amused appreciation, even her breasts were impertinent. Small, but beneath the pale blue stuff of her dress, pointed, firm, almost comically insistent. No ashamed deflation here.

"Pathetic," she mockingly echoed, "but, oh dear, how horrible, how disgusting! Because they *are* disgusting," she added defiantly, in answer to his look of humorous protest. Here in the sunlight and with the noise of the town isolating her from every one except Fanning, she had lost her embarrassment and her sense of guilt. The spiritual presence had evaporated. Pamela was annoyed with herself for having felt so uncomfortable among those awful old English cats at Cook's. She thought of her mother; her mother had never been embarrassed, or at any rate she had always managed to turn her embarrassment into something else. Which was what Pamela was doing now. "Really disgusting," she almost truculently insisted. She was reasserting herself, she was taking a revenge.

"You're very ruthless to the poor old things," said Fanning. "So worthy in spite of their mangy dimness, so obviously good."

"I hate goodness," said Pamela with decision, speeding the parting ghosts of Miss Huss and Aunt Edith and the two ladies from Boston.

Fanning laughed aloud. "Ah, if only we all had the courage to say so, like you, my child!" And with a familiar affectionate gesture, as though she were indeed a child and he had known her from the cradle, he dropped a hand on her shoulder. "To say so and to act up to our beliefs. As you do, I'm sure." And he gave the slim hard little shoulder a pat. "A world without goodness—it'd be Paradise."

They walked some steps in silence. His hand lay heavy and strong on her shoulder, and a strange warmth that was somehow intenser than the warmth of mere flesh and blood seemed to radiate through her whole body. Her heart quickened its beating; an anxiety oppressed her lungs; her very mind was as though breathless.

"Putting his hand on my shoulder like that!" she was thinking. "It would have been cheek if some one else . . .

Perhaps I ought to have been angry, perhaps . . ." No, that would have been silly. "It's silly to take things like that too seriously, as though one were Aunt Edith." But meanwhile his hand lay heavy on her shoulder, broodingly hot, its weight, its warmth insistently present in her consciousness.

She remembered characters in his books. Her name-sake Pamela in *Pastures New*. Pamela the cold, but for that very reason an experimenter with passion; cold and there-fore dangerous, full of power, fatal. Was she like Pamela? She had often thought so. But more recently she had often thought she was like Joan in *The Return of Eurydice*—Joan, who had emerged from the wintry dark underworld of an unawakened life with her husband (that awful, good, dis-interested husband—so like Aunt Edith) into the warmth and brilliance of that transfiguring passion for Walter, for the adorable Walter whom she had always imagined must be so like Miles Fanning himself. She was sure of it now. But what of her own identity? Was she Joan, or was she Pamela? And which of the two would it be nicer to be? Warm Joan, with her happiness—but at the price of surrender? Or the cold, the unhappy, but conquering, dangerous Pamela? Or wouldn't it perhaps be best to be a little of both at once? Or first one and then the other? And in any case there was to be no goodness in the Aunt Edith style; he had been sure she wasn't good.

In her memory the voice of Aunt Edith sounded, as it had actually sounded, only a few weeks before, in disapprov-ing comment on her reference to the passionless, experimen-tal Pamela of *Pastures New*. "It's a book I don't like. A most unnecessary book." And then, laying her hand on Pamela's, "Dear child," she had added, with that earnest, that dutifully willed affectionateness, which Pamela so bitterly resented, "I'd rather you didn't read any of Miles Fanning's books."

"Mother never objected to my reading them. So I don't see . . ." The triumphant consciousness of having at this very moment the hand that had written those unnecessary books upon her shoulder was promising to enrich her share of the remembered dialogue with a lofty impertinence which the original had hardly possessed. "I don't see that you have the smallest right. . . ."

Fanning's voice fell startlingly across the eloquent silence. "A penny for your thoughts, Miss Pamela," it said.

He had been for some obscure reason suddenly depressed by his own last words. "A world without goodness—it'd be Paradise." But it wouldn't, no more than now. The only paradises were fool's paradises, ostrich's paradises. It was as though he had suddenly lifted his head out of the sand and seen time bleeding away—like the stabbed bull at the end of a bull-fight, swaying on his legs and soundlessly spouting the red blood from his nostrils—bleeding, bleeding away stanchlessly into the darkness. And it was all, even the loveliness and the laughter and the sunlight, finally pointless. This young girl at his side, this beautiful pointless creature pointlessly walking down the Via del Babuino. . . . The feelings crystallized themselves, as usual, into whole phrases in his mind, and suddenly the phrases were metrical.

Pointless and arm in arm with pointlessness,
I pace and pace the Street of the Baboon.

Imbecile! Annoyed with himself, he tried to shake off his mood of maudlin depression, he tried to force his spirit back into the ridiculous and charming universe it had inhabited, on the whole so happily, all the morning.

"A penny for your thoughts," he said, with a certain rather forced jocularity, giving her shoulder a little clap. "Or forty centesimi, if you prefer them." And, dropping his hand to his side, "In Germany," he went on, "just after the War one could afford to be more munificent. There was a time when I regularily offered a hundred and ninety million marks for a thought—yes, and gained on the exchange. But now . . ."

"Well, if you really want to know," said Pamela, deciding to be bold, "I was thinking how much my Aunt Edith disapproved of your books."

"Did she? I suppose it was only to be expected. Seeing that I don't write for aunts—at any rate, not for aunts in their specifically auntly capacity. Though of course, when they're off duty . . ."

"Aunt Edith's never off duty."

"And I'm never on. So you see." He shrugged his shoulders. "But I'm sure," he added, "you never paid much attention to her disapproval."

"None," she answered, playing the un-good part for all it was worth. "I read Freud this spring," she boasted, "and Gide's autobiography, and Krafft-Ebbing. . . ."

"Which is more than I've ever done," he laughed.

The laugh encouraged her. "Not to mention all *your* books, years ago. You see," she added, suddenly fearful lest she might have said something to offend him, "my mother never minded my reading your books. I mean, she really encouraged me, even when I was only seventeen or eighteen. My mother died last year," she explained. There was a silence. "I've lived with Aunt Edith ever since," she went on. "Aunt Edith's my father's sister. Older than he was. Father died in 1923."

"So you're all alone now?" he questioned. "Except, of course, for Aunt Edith."

"Whom I've now left." She was almost boasting again. "Because when I was twenty-one . . ."

"You stuck out your tongue at her and ran away. Poor Aunt Edith!"

"I won't have you being sorry for her," Pamela answered hotly. "She's really awful, you know. Like poor Joan's husband in *The Return of Eurydice*." How easy it was to talk to him!

"So you even know," said Fanning, laughing, "what it's like to·be unhappily married. Already. Indissolubly wedded to a virtuous Aunt."

"No joke, I can tell you. *I'm* the one to be sorry for. Besides, she didn't mind my going away, whatever she might say."

"She did say something then?"

"Oh, yes. She always says things. More in sorrow than in anger, you know. Like head-mistresses. So gentle and good, I mean. When all the time she really thought me too awful. I used to call her Hippo, because she was such a hypocrite—*and* so fat. Enormous. Don't you *hate* enormous people? No, she's really delighted to get rid of me," Pamela concluded, "simply delighted." Her face was flushed and as though luminously alive; she spoke with a quick eagerness.

"What a tremendous hurry she's in," he was thinking, "to tell me all about herself. If she were older or uglier, what an intolerable egotism it would be! As intolerable as mine would be if I happened to be less intelligent. But as it is . . ." His face, as he listened to her, expressed a sympathetic attention.

"She always disliked me," Pamela had gone on. "Mother too. She couldn't abide my mother, though she was always sweetly hippo-ish with her."

"And your mother—how did she respond?"

"Well, not hippoishly, of course. She couldn't be that. She treated Aunt Edith—well, how *did* she treat Aunt Edith?" Pamela hesitated, frowning. "Well, I suppose you'd say she was just natural with the Hippo. I mean . . ." She bit her lip. "Well, if she ever *was* really natural. *I* don't know. Is anybody natural?" She looked up questioningly at Fanning. "Am I natural, for example?"

Smiling a little at her choice of an example, "I should think almost certainly not," Fanning answered, more or less at random.

"You're right, of course," she said despairingly, and her face was suddenly tragic, almost there were tears in her eyes. "But isn't it awful? I mean, isn't it simply hopeless?"

Pleased that his chance shot should have gone home, "At your age," he said consolingly, "you can hardly expect to be natural. Naturalness is something you learn, painfully, by trial and error. Besides," he added, "there are some people who are unnatural by nature."

"Unnatural by nature." Pamela nodded, as she repeated the words, as though she were inwardly marshalling evidence to confirm their truth. "Yes, I believe that's us," she concluded. "Mother and me. Not hippos, I mean, not *po-*

seuses, but just unnatural by nature. You're quite right. As usual," she added, with something that was almost resentment in her voice.

"I'm sorry," he apologized.

"How is it you manage to know so much?" Pamela asked in the same resentful tone. By what right was he so easily omniscient, when she could only grope and guess in the dark?

Taking to himself a credit that belonged, in this case, to chance, "Child's play, my dear Watson," he answered banteringly. "But I suppose you're too young to have heard of Sherlock Holmes. And anyhow," he added, with an ironical seriousness, "don't let's waste any more time talking about me."

Pamela wasted no more time. "I get so depressed with myself," she said with a sigh. "And after what you've told me I shall get still more depressed. Unnatural by nature. And by upbringing too. Because I see now that my mother was like that. I mean, she was unnatural by nature too."

"Even with you?" he asked, thinking that this was becoming interesting. She nodded without speaking. He looked at her closely. "Were you very fond of her?" was the question that now suggested itself.

After a moment of silence, "I loved my father more," she answered slowly. "He was more . . . more reliable. I mean, you never quite knew where you were with my mother. Sometimes she almost forgot about me; or else she didn't forget me enough and spoiled me. And then sometimes she used to get into the most terrible rages with me. She really frightened me then. And said such terribly hurting things.

---

* A person who pretends to be what she is not.

But you mustn't think I didn't love her. I did." The words seemed to release a spring; she was suddenly moved. There was a little silence. Making an effort, "But that's what she was like," she concluded at last.

"But I don't see," said Fanning gently, "that there was anything specially unnatural in spoiling you and then getting cross with you." They were crossing the Piazza del Popolo; the traffic of four thronged streets intricately merged and parted in the open space. "You must have been a charming child. And also . . . Look out!" He laid a hand on her arm. An electric bus passed noiselessly, a whispering monster. "Also maddeningly exasperating. So where the unnaturalness came in . . ."

"But if you'd known her," Pamela interrupted, "you'd have seen exactly where the unnaturalness . . ."

"Forward!" he called and, still holding her arm, he steered her on across the Piazza.

She suffered herself to be conducted blindly. "It came out in the way she spoiled me," she explained, raising her voice against the clatter of a passing lorry. "It's so difficult to explain, though; because it's something I felt. I mean, I've never really tried to put it into words till now. But it was as if . . . as if she weren't just herself spoiling me, but the picture of a young mother—do you see what I mean?—spoiling the picture of a little girl. Even as a child I kind of felt it wasn't quite as it should be. Later on I began to *know* it too, here." She tapped her forehead. "Particularly after father's death, when I was beginning to grow up. There were times when it was almost like listening to recitations—dreadful. One feels so blushy and prickly; you know the feeling."

He nodded. "Yes, I know. Awful!"

"Awful," she repeated. "So you can understand what a beast I felt, when it took me that way. So disloyal, I mean. So ungrateful. Because she was being so wonderfully sweet to me. You've no idea. But it was just when she was being her sweetest that I got the feeling worst. I shall never forget when she made me call her Clare—that was her christian name. 'Because we're going to be companions,' she said and all that sort of thing. Which was simply too sweet and too nice of her. But if you'd heard the way she said it! So dreadfully unnatural. I mean, it was almost as bad as Aunt Edith reading *Prospice*. And yet I know she meant it, I know she wanted me to be her companion. But somehow something kind of went wrong on the way between the wanting and the saying. And then the doing seemed to go just as wrong as the saying. She always wanted to do things excitingly, romantically, like in a play. But you can't *make* things be exciting and romantic, can you?" Fanning shook his head. "She wanted to kind of force things to be thrilling by thinking and wishing, like Christian Science. But it doesn't work. We had wonderful times together; but she always tried to make out that they were more wonderful than they really were. Which only made them less wonderful. Going to the Paris Opera on a gala night is wonderful; but it's never as wonderful as when Rastignac goes, is it?"

"I should think it wasn't!" he agreed. "What an insult to Balzac to imagine that it could be!"

"And the real thing's less wonderful," she went on, "when you're being asked all the time to see it as Balzac, and to *be* Balzac yourself. When you aren't anything of the kind. Because, after all, what am I? Just good, ordinary, middle-class English."

She pronounced the words with a kind of defiance. Fanning imagined that the defiance was for him and, laughing, prepared to pick up the ridiculous little glove. But the glove was not for him; Pamela had thrown it down to a memory, to a ghost, to one of her own sceptical and mocking selves. It had been on the last day of their last stay together in Paris— that exciting, exotic Paris of poor Clare's imagination, to which their tickets from London never seemed quite to take them. They had gone to lunch at La Pérouse. "Such a marvellous, *fantastic* restaurant! It makes you feel as though you were back in the Second Empire." (Or was it the First Empire? Pamela could not exactly remember.) The rooms were so crowded with Americans, that it was with some difficulty that they secured a table. "We'll have a marvellous lunch," Claire had said, as she unfolded her napkin. "And some day, when you're in Paris with your lover, you'll come here and order just the same things as we're having to-day. And perhaps you'll think of me. Will you, darling?" And she had smiled at her daughter with that intense, expectant expression that was so often on her face, and the very memory of which made Pamela feel subtly uncomfortable. "How should I ever forget?" she had answered, laying her hand on her mother's and smiling. But after a second her eyes had wavered away from that fixed look, in which the intensity had remained as desperately on the stretch, the expectancy as wholly unsatisfied, as hungrily insatiable as ever. The waiter, thank goodness, had created a timely diversion; smiling at him confidentially, almost amorously, Clare had ordered like a princess in a novel of high life. The bill, when it came, was enormous. Clare had had to scratch the bottom of her purse for the last stray piece of nickel. "It looks as

they're founders and honorary life presidents of the Nuneaton Poetry Society and the Baron's Court Debating Society; they're the people who organize and sedulously attend all those Conferences for promoting international goodwill and the spread of culture that are perpetually being held at Buda-Pesth and Prague and Stockholm. Admirable and indispensable creatures, of course! But impossibly dreary; one simply cannot have any relations with them. And how virtuously they disapprove of those of us who have something better to do than disseminate culture or foster goodwill—those of us who are concerned, for example, with creating beauty—like me; or, like you, my child, in deliciously *being* beauty."

Pamela blushed with pleasure and for that reason felt it necessary immediately to protest. "All the same," she said, "it's rather humiliating not to be able to do anything but be. I mean, even a cow can be."

"Damned well, too," said Fanning. "If I *were* as intensely as a cow *is,* I'd be uncommonly pleased with myself. But this is getting almost too metaphysical. And do you realize what the time is?" He held out his watch; it was ten past one. "And where we are? At the Tiber. We've walked miles." He waved his hand; a passing taxi swerved in to the pavement beside them. "Let's go and eat some lunch. You're free?"

"Well . . ." She hesitated. It was marvellous, of course; so marvellous that she felt she ought to refuse. "If I'm not a bore. I mean, I don't want to impose . . . I mean . . ."

"You mean you'll come and have lunch. Good. Do you like marble halls and bands? Or local colour?"

Pamela hesitated. She remembered her mother once saying that Valadier and the Ulpia were the *only* two restaurants in Rome.

"Personally," Fanning went on, "I'm slightly avaricious about marble halls. I rather resent spending four times as much and eating about two-thirds as well. But I'll overcome my avarice if you prefer them."

Pamela duly voted for local colour; he gave an address to the driver and they climbed into the cab.

"It's a genuinely Roman place," Fanning explained. "I hope you'll like it."

"Oh, I'm sure I shall." All the same, she did rather wish they were going to Valadier's.

III

FANNING'S OLD FRIEND, DODO DEL GRILLO, WAS IN Rome for that one night and had urgently summoned him to dine. His arrival was loud and exclamatory.

"Best of all possible Dodos!" he cried, as he advanced with outstretched hands across the enormous baroque saloon. "What an age! But what a pleasure!"

"At last, Miles," she said reproachfully; he was twenty minutes late.

"But I know you'll forgive me." And laying his two hands on her shoulders he bent down and kissed her. He made a habit of kissing all his women friends.

"And even if I didn't forgive, you wouldn't care two pins."

"Not one." He smiled his most charming smile. "But if it gives you the smallest pleasure, I'm ready to say I'd be inconsolable." His hands still resting on her shoulders, he looked at her searchingly, at arm's length. "Younger than ever," he concluded.

"I couldn't look as young as you do," she answered. "You know, Miles, you're positively indecent. Like Dorian Gray. What's your horrible secret?"

"Simply Mr. Hornibrooke," he explained. "The culture of the abdomen. So much more important than the culture of the mind." Dodo only faintly smiled; she had heard the joke before. Fanning was sensitive to smiles; he changed the subject. "And where's the marquis?" he asked.

The marchesa shrugged her shoulders. Her husband was one of those dear old friends whom somehow one doesn't manage to see anything of nowadays. "Filippo's in Tanganyika," she explained. "Hunting lions."

"While you hunt them at home. And with what success! You've bagged what's probably the finest specimen in Europe this evening. Congratulations!"

"*Merci, cher maître!*"* she laughed. "Shall we go in to dinner?"

The words invited, irresistibly. "If only I had the right to answer: *Oui, chère maîtresse!*"† Though as a matter of fact, he reflected, he had never really found her at all interesting in that way. A woman without temperament. But very pretty once—that time (how many years ago?) when there had been that picnic on the river at Bray, and he had drunk a little too much champagne. "If only!" he repeated; and then was suddenly struck by a grotesque thought. Suppose she were to say yes, now—now! "If only I had the right!"

"But luckily," said Dodo, turning back towards him, as she passed through the monumental door into the dining-room, "luckily you haven't the right. You ought to congratulate me on my immense good sense. Will you sit there?"

"Oh, I'll congratulate. I'm always ready to congratulate

---

* "Thank you, dear master."

† "Yes, dear mistress."

people who have sense." He unfolded his napkin. "And to condole." Now that he knew himself safe, he could condole as much as he liked. "What you must have suffered, my poor sensible Dodo, what you must have missed!"

"Suffered less," she answered, "and missed more unpleasantnesses than the woman who didn't have the sense to say no."

"What a mouthful of negatives! But that's how sensible people always talk about love—in terms of negatives. Never of positives; they ignore those and go about sensibly avoiding the discomforts. Avoiding the pleasures and exultations too, poor sensible idiots! Avoiding all that's valuable and significant. But it's always like that. The human soul is a fried whiting. (What excellent red mullet this is, by the way! Really excellent.) Its tail is in its mouth. All progress finally leads back to the beginning again. The most sensible people—dearest Dodo, believe me—are the most foolish. The most intellectual are the stupidest. I've never met a really good metaphysician, for example, who wasn't in one way or another bottomlessly stupid. And as for the really spiritual people, look what they revert to. Not merely to silliness and stupidity, but finally to crass nonexistence. The highest spiritual state is ecstasy, which is just not being there at all. No, no; we're all fried whitings. Heads are invariably tails."

"In which case," said Dodo, "tails must also be heads. So that if you want to make intellectual or spiritual progress, you must behave like a beast—is that it?"

Fanning held up his hand. "Not at all. If you rush too violently towards the tail, you run the risk of shooting down the whiting's open mouth into its stomach, and even further. The wise man . . ."

"So the whitings are fried without being cleaned?"

"In parables," Fanning answered reprovingly, "whitings are always fried that way. The wise man, as I was saying, oscillates lightly from head to tail and back again. His whole existence—or shall we be more frank and say 'my' whole existence?—is one continual oscillation. I am never too consistently sensible, like you; or too consistently feather-headed like some of my other friends. In a word," he wagged a finger, "I oscillate."

Tired of generalizations, "And where exactly," Dodo enquired, "have you oscillated to at the moment? You've left me without your news so long. . . ."

"Well, at the moment," he reflected aloud, "I suppose you might say I was at a dead point between desire and renunciation, between sense and sensuality."

"Again?" She shook her head. "And who is she this time?"

Fanning helped himself to asparagus before replying. "Who is she?" he echoed. "Well, to begin with, she's the writer of admiring letters."

Dodo made a grimace of disgust. "What a horror!" For some reason she felt it necessary to be rather venomous about this new usurper of Fanning's heart. "Vamping by correspondence—it's really the lowest. . . ."

"Oh, I agree," he said. "On principle and in theory I entirely agree."

"Then why," she began, annoyed by his agreement; but he interrupted her.

"Spiritual adventuresses," he said. "That's what they

generally are, the women who write you letters. Spiritual adventuresses. I've suffered a lot from them in my time."

"I'm sure you have."

"They're a curious type," he went on, ignoring her sarcasms. "Curious and rather horrible. I prefer the good old-fashioned vampire. At least one knew where one stood with her. There she was—out for money, for power, for a good time, occasionally, perhaps, for sensual satisfactions. It was all entirely above-board and obvious. But with the spiritual adventuress, on the contrary, everything's most horribly turbid and obscure and slimy. You see, she doesn't want money or the commonplace good time. She wants Higher Things—damn her neck! Not large pearls and a large motor-car, but a large soul—that's what she pines for: a large soul and a large intellect, and a huge philosophy, and enormous culture, and out sizes in great thoughts."

Dodo laughed. "You're fiendishly cruel, Miles."

"Cruelty can be a sacred duty," he answered. "Besides, I'm getting a little of my own back. If you knew what these spiritual vamps had done to me! I've been one of their appointed victims. Yes, appointed; for, you see, they can't have their Higher Things without attaching themselves to a Higher Person."

"And are you one of the Higher People, Miles?"

"Should I be dining here with you, my dear, if I weren't?" And without waiting for Dodo's answer, "They attach themselves like lice," he went on. "The contact with the Higher Person makes them feel high themselves; it magnifies them, it gives them significance, it satisfies their parasitic will to power. In the past they could have gone to religion—fastened themselves on the nearest priest (that's what the priest was there for), or sucked the spiritual blood of some saint. Nowadays they've got no professional victims; only a few charlatans and swamis and higher-thought-mongers. Or alternatively the artists. Yes, the artists. They find our souls particularly juicy. What I've suffered! Shall I ever forget that American woman who got so excited by my book on Blake that she came specially to Tunis to see me? She had an awful way of opening her mouth very wide when she talked, like a fish. You were perpetually seeing her tongue; and, what made it worse, her tongue was generally white. Most distressing. And how the tongue wagged! In spite of its whiteness. Wagged like mad, and mostly about the Divine Mind."

"The Divine Mind?"

He nodded. "It was her specialty. In Rochester, N. Y., where she lived, she was never out of touch with it. You've no idea what a lot of Divine Mind there is floating about in Rochester, particularly in the neighbourhood of women with busy husbands and incomes of over fifteen thousand dollars. If only she could have stuck to the Divine Mind! But the Divine Mind has one grave defect: it won't make love to you. That was why she'd come all the way to Tunis in search of a merely human specimen."

"And what did you do about it?"

"Stood it nine days and then took the boat to Sicily. Like a thief in the night. The wicked flee, you know. God, how they can flee!"

"And she?"

"Went back to Rochester, I suppose. But I never opened any more of her letters. Just dropped them into the fire whenever I saw the writing. Ostrichism—it's the only rational philosophy of conduct. According to the Freudians we're all unconsciously trying to get back to . . ."

"But poor woman!" Dodo burst out. "She must have suffered."

"Nothing like what I suffered. Besides she had the Divine Mind to go back to; which was her version of the Freudians' pre-natal . . ."

"But I suppose you'd encouraged her to come to Tunis?"

Reluctantly, Fanning gave up his Freudians. "She could write good letters," he admitted. "Inexplicably good, considering what she was at close range."

"But then you treated her abominably."

"But if you'd seen her, you'd realize how abominably she'd treated me."

"You?"

"Yes, abominably—by merely existing. She taught me to be very shy of letters. That was why I was so pleasantly surprised this morning when my latest correspondent suddenly materialized at Cook's. Really ravishing. One could forgive her everything for the sake of her face and that charming body. Everything, even the vamping. For a vamp I suppose she is, even this one. That is, if a woman *can* be a spiritual adventuress when she's so young and pretty and well-made. Absolutely and *sub specie æternitatis*, I suppose she can. But from the very sublunary point of view of the male victim, I doubt whether, at twenty-one . . ."

"Only twenty-one?" Dodo was disapproving. "But Miles!"

Fanning ignored her interruption. "And another thing you must remember," he went on, "is that the spiritual vamp

---

* In her essential form.

who's come of age this year is not at all the same as the spiritual vamp who came of age fifteen, twenty, twenty-five years ago. She doesn't bother much about Mysticism, or the Lower Classes, or the Divine Mind, or any nonsense of that sort. No, she goes straight to the real point—the point which the older vamps approached in such a tiresomely circuitous fashion—she goes straight to herself. But straight!" He stabbed the air with his fruit-knife. "A bee-line. Oh, it has a certain charm that directness. But whether it won't be rather frightful when they're older is another question. But then almost everything is rather frightful when people are older."

"Thank you," said Dodo. "And what about you?"

"Oh, an old satyr," he answered with that quick, brilliantly mysterious smile of his. "A superannuated faun. I know it; only too well. But at the same time, most intolerably, a Higher Person. Which is what draws the spiritual vamps. Even the youngest ones. Not to talk to me about the Divine Mind, of course, or their views about Social Reform. But about themselves. Their Individualities, their Souls, their Inhibitions, their Unconsciouses, their Pasts, their Futures. For them, the Higher Things are all frankly and nakedly personal. And the function of the Higher Person is to act as a sort of psychoanalytical father confessor. He exists to tell them all about their strange and wonderful psyches. And meanwhile, of course, his friendship inflates their egotism. And if there should be any question of love, what a personal triumph!"

"Which is all very well," objected Dodo. "But what about the old satyr? Wouldn't it also be a bit of a triumph for him? You know, Miles," she added gravely, "it would really be scandalous if you were to take advantage. . . ."

"But I haven't the slightest intention of taking any advantages. If only for my own sake. Besides, the child is too ingenuously absurd. The most hair-raising theoretical knowledge of life, out of books. You should hear her prattling away about inverts and perverts and birth control—but prattling from unplumbed depths of innocence and practical ignorance. Very queer. And touching too. Much more touching than the old-fashioned innocences of the young creatures who thought babies were brought by storks. Knowing all about love and lust, but in the same way as one knows all about quadratic equations. And her knowledge of the other aspects of life is really of the same kind. What she's seen of the world she's seen in her mother's company. The worst guide imaginable, to judge from the child's account. (Dead now, incidentally.) The sort of woman who could never live on top gear, so to speak—only at one or two imaginative removes from the facts. So that, in her company, what was nominally real life became actually just literature—yet more literature. Bad, inadequate Balzac in flesh and blood instead of genuine, good Balzac out of a set of nice green volumes. The child realizes it herself. Obscurely, of course; but distressfully. It's one of the reasons why she's applied to me: she hopes I can explain what's wrong. And correct it in practice. Which I won't do in any drastic manner, I promise you. Only mildly, by precept—that is, if I'm not too bored to do it at all."

"What's the child's name?" Dodo asked.

"Pamela Tarn."

"Tarn? But was her mother by any chance Clare Tarn?"

He nodded. "That was it. She even made her daughter call her by her christian name. The companion stunt."

"But I used to know Clare Tarn quite well," said Dodo in an astonished, feeling voice. "These last years I'd hardly seen her. But when I was more in London just after the War . . ."

"But this begins to be interesting," said Fanning. "New light on my little friend. . . ."

"Whom I absolutely forbid you," said Dodo emphatically, "to . . ."

"Tamper with the honour of," he suggested. "Let's phrase it as nobly as possible."

"No, seriously, Miles. I really won't have it. Poor Clare Tarn's daughter. If I didn't have to rush off to-morrow I'd ask her to come and see me, so as to warn her."

Fanning laughed. "She wouldn't thank you. And besides if any one is to be warned, I'm the one who's in danger. But I shall be firm, Dodo—a rock. I won't allow her to seduce me."

"You're incorrigible, Miles. But mind, if you dare. . . ."

"But I won't. Definitely." His tone was reassuring. "Meanwhile I must hear something about the mother."

The marchesa shrugged her shoulders. "A woman who couldn't live on top gear. You've really said the last word."

"But I want first words," he answered. "It's not the verdict that's interesting. It's the whole case, it's all the evidence. You're *sub-poenaed*, my dear. Speak up."

"Poor Clare!"

"Oh, *nil nisi bonum*, of course, if that's what disturbs you."

"She'd have so loved it to be not *bonum*, poor dear!" said

---

* [Of the dead, say] nothing but good.

the marchesa, tempering her look of vague condolence with a little smile. "That was her great ambition—to be thought rather wicked. She'd have liked to have the reputation of a vampire. Not a spiritual one, mind you. The other sort. Lola Montes—that was her ideal."

"It's an ideal," said Fanning, "that takes some realizing, I can tell you."

Dodo nodded. "And that's what she must have found out, pretty soon. She wasn't born to be a fatal woman; she lacked the gifts. No staggering beauty, no mysterious fascination or intoxicating vitality. She was just very charming, that was all; and at the same time rather impossible and absurd. So that there weren't any aspiring victims to be fatal to. And a vampire without victims is—well, *what?*"

"Certainly not a vampire," he concluded.

"Except, of course, in her own imagination, if she chooses to think so. In her own imagination Clare certainly was a vampire."

"Reduced, in fact, to being her own favourite character in fiction."

"Precisely. You always find the phrase."

"Only too fatally!" He made a little grimace. "I often wish I didn't. The luxury of being inarticulate! To be able to wallow indefinitely long in every feeling and sensation, instead of having to clamber out at once on to a hard, dry, definite phrase. But what about your Clare?"

"Well, she started, of course, by being a riddle to me. Unanswerable, or rather answerable, answered, but so very strangely that I was still left wondering. I shall never forget the first time Filippo and I went to dine there. Poor Roger

Tarn was still alive then. While the men were drinking their port, Clare and I were alone in the drawing-room. There was a little chit-chat, I remember, and then, with a kind of determined desperation, as though she'd that second screwed herself up to jumping off the Eiffel Tower, suddenly, out of the blue, she asked me if I'd ever had one of those *wonderful* Sicilian peasants—I can't possibly reproduce the tone, the expression—as a lover. I was a bit taken aback, I must confess. 'But we don't live in Sicily,' was the only thing I could think of answering—too idiotically! 'Our estates are all in Umbria and Tuscany.' 'But the Tuscans are *superb* creatures too,' she insisted. Superb, I agreed. But, as it happens, I don't have affairs with even the superbest peasants. Nor with anybody else, for that matter. Clare was dreadfully disappointed. I think she'd expected the most romantic confidences—moonlight and mandolins and *stretti, stretti, nell' estasi d'amor.** She was really very ingenuous. 'Do you mean to say you've really never . . . ?' she insisted. I ought to have got angry, I suppose; but it was all so ridiculous, that I never thought of it. I just said, 'Never,' and felt as though I were refusing her a favour. But she made up for my churlishness by being lavish to herself. But lavish! You can't imagine what a tirade she let fly at me. How *wonderful* it was to get away from self-conscious, complicated, sentimental love! How profoundly *satisfying* to feel oneself at the mercy of the dumb, dark forces of physical passion! How *intoxicating* to humiliate one's culture and one's class feeling before some *magnificent* primitive, some *earthly* beautiful satyr, some *divine* animal! And so on, *crescendo.* And it ended with her telling me the story of her *extraordinary* affair with—was it

---

* "Holding you tight, so tight, in the ecstasy of love."

a gamekeeper? or a young farmer? I forget. But there was something about rabbit-shooting in it, I know."

"It sounds like a chapter out of George Sand."

"It was."

"Or still more, I'm afraid," he said, making a wry face "like a most deplorable parody of my *Endymion and the Moon*."

"Which I've never read, I'm ashamed to say."

"You should, if only to understand this Clare of yours."

"I will. Perhaps I'd have solved her more quickly, if I'd read it at the time. As it was I could only be amazed—and a little horrified. That rabbit-shooter!" She shook her head. "He ought to have been so romantic. But I could only think of that awful yellow kitchen soap he'd be sure to wash himself with, or perhaps carbolic, so that he'd smell like washed dogs—dreadful! And the flannel shirts, not changed quite often enough. And the hands, so horny, with very short nails, perhaps broken. No, I simply couldn't understand her."

"Which is to your discredit, Dodo, if I may say so."

"Perhaps. But you must admit, I never pretended to be anything but what I am—a perfectly frivolous and respectable member of the upper classes. With a taste, I must confess, for the scandalous. Which was one of the reasons, I suppose, why I became so intimate with poor Clara. I was really fascinated by her confidences."

"Going on the tiles vicariously, eh?"

"Well, if you choose to put it grossly and vulgarly. . . . ."

"Which I *do* choose," he interposed. "To be tactfully gross and appositely vulgar—that, my dear, is one of the ultimate artistic refinements. One day I shall write a monograph on the aesthetics of vulgarity. But meanwhile shall we say that you were inspired by an intense scientific curiosity to . . ."

Dodo laughed. "One of the tiresome things about you, Miles, is that one can never go on being angry with you."

"Yet another subject for a monograph!" he answered, and his smile was at once confidential and ironical, affectionate and full of mockery. "But let's hear what the scientific curiosity elicited?"

"Well, to begin with, a lot of really rather embarrassingly intimate confidences and questions, which I needn't repeat."

"No, don't. I know what those feminine conversations are. I have a native modesty. . . ."

"Oh, so have I. And, strangely enough, so had Clare. But somehow she wanted to outrage herself. You felt it all the time. She always had that desperate jumping-off-the-Eiffel-Tower manner, when she began to talk like that. It was a kind of martyrdom. But enjoyable. Perversely." Dodo shook her head. "Very puzzling. I used to have to make quite an effort to change the conversation from gynaecology to romance. Oh, those lovers of hers! Such stories! The most fantastic adventures in East End opium dens, in aeroplanes, and even, I remember (it was that very hot summer of 'twenty-two), even in a refrigerator!"

"My dear!" protested Fanning.

"Honestly! I'm only repeating what she told me."

"But do you mean to say you believed her?"

"Well, by that time, I must admit, I was beginning to be rather sceptical. You see, I could never elicit the names of these creatures. Nor any detail. It was as though they didn't exist outside the refrigerator and the aeroplane."

"How many of them were there?"

"Only two at that particular moment. One was a Grand Passion, and the other a Caprice. A Caprice," she repeated, rolling the r. "It was one of poor Clare's favourite words. I used to try and pump her. But she was mum. 'I want them to be *mysterious,*' she told me the last time I pressed her for details. 'Anonymous, without an *état civil*.* Why should I show you their passport and identity cards?' 'Perhaps they haven't got any,' I suggested. Which was malicious. I could see she was annoyed. But a week later she showed me their photographs. There they were; the camera cannot lie; I had to be convinced. The Grand Passion, I must say, was a very striking-looking creature. Thin-faced, worn, a bit Roman and sinister. The Caprice was more ordinarily the nice young Englishman. Rather childish and simple, Clare explained; and she gave me to understand that she was initiating him. It was the other, the Grand P., who thought of such refinements as the refrigerator. Also, she now confided to me for the first time, he was mildly a sadist. Having seen his face, I could believe it. 'Am I ever likely to meet him?' I asked. She shook her head. He moved in a very different world from mine."

"A rabbit-shooter?" Fanning asked.

"No: an intellectual. That's what I gathered."

"Golly!"

"So there was not the slightest probability, as you can see, that *I* should ever meet him." Dodo laughed. "And yet almost the first face I saw on leaving Clare that afternoon was the Grand P.'s."

"Coming to pay his sadistic respects?"

---

* Civil status.

"Alas for poor Clare, no. He was behind glass in the showcase of a photographer in the Brompton Road, not a hundred yards from the Tarns' house in Ovington Square. The identical portrait. I marched straight in. 'Can you tell me who that is?' But it appears that photography is done under the seal of confession. They wouldn't say. Could I order a copy? Well, yes, as a favour, they'd let me have one. Curiously enough, they told me, as they were taking down my name and address, another lady had come in only two or three days before and also ordered a copy. 'Not by any chance a rather tall lady with light auburn hair and a rather amusing mole on the left cheek?' That did sound rather like the lady. 'And with a very confidential manner,' I suggested, 'as though you were her oldest friends?' Exactly, exactly; they were unanimous. That clinched it. Poor Clare, I thought, as I walked on towards the Park, poor, poor Clare!"

There was a silence.

"Which only shows," said Fanning at last, "how right the Church has always been to persecute literature. The harm we imaginative writers do! Enormous! We ought all to be on the Index, every one. Consider your Clare, for example. If it hadn't been for books, she'd never have known that such things as passion and sensuality and perversity even existed. Never."

"Come, come," she protested.

But, "Never," Fanning repeated. "She was congenitally as cold as a fish; it's obvious. Never had a spontaneous, un-tutored desire in her life. But she'd read a lot of books. Out of which she'd fabricated a theory of passion and perversity. Which she then consciously put into practice."

to influence people. And when I say 'influence,' of course I don't really mean *influence*. Because a writer can't influence people, in the sense of making them think and feel and act as he does. He can only influence them to be more, or less, like one of their own selves. In other words, he's never understood. (Thank goodness! because it would be very humiliating to be really understood by one's readers.) What readers get out of him is never, finally, *his* ideas, but theirs. And when they try to imitate him or his creations, all that they can ever do is to act one of their own potential rôles. Take this particular case. Clare read and, I take it, was impressed. She took my warnings against mental licentiousness to heart and proceeded to do—what? Not to become a creature of spontaneous, unvitiated impulses—for the good reason that that wasn't in her power—but only to imagine that she was such a creature. She imagined herself a woman like the one I put into *Endymion and the Moon* and acted accordingly—or else didn't act, only dreamed; it makes very little difference. In a word, she did exactly what all my books told her not to do. Inevitably; it was her nature. I'd influenced her, yes. But she didn't become more like one of my heroines. She only became more intensely like herself. And then, you must remember, mine weren't the only books on her shelves. I think we can take it that she'd read *Les Liaisons Dangereuses* and Casanova and some biography, shall we say, of the Maréchal de Richelieu. So that those spontaneous unvitiated impulses—how ludicrous they are, anyhow, when you *talk* about them!—became identified in her mind with the most elegant forms of 'caprice'—wasn't that the word? She was a child of nature—but with qualifications. The kind of child of nature that lived at Versailles or on the Grand Canal about 1760. Hence those rabbit-shooters and hence also those sadistic intellectuals, whether real or imaginary—and imaginary even when real. I may have been a favourite author. But I'm not responsible for the rabbit-shooters or the Grand P.'s. Not more responsible than any one else. She'd heard of the existence of love before she'd read me. We're all equally to blame, from Homer downwards. Plato wouldn't have any of us in his Republic. He was quite right, I believe. Quite right."

"And what about the daughter?" Dodo asked, after a silence.

He shrugged his shoulders. "In reaction against the mother, so far as I could judge. In reaction, but also influenced by her, unconsciously. And the influence is effective because, after all, she's her mother's daughter and probably resembles her mother, congenitally. But consciously, on the surface, she knows she doesn't want to live as though she were in a novel. And yet can't help it, because that's her nature, that's how she was brought up. But she's miserable, because she realizes that fiction-life *is* fiction. Miserable and very anxious to get out—out through the covers of the novel into the real world."

"And are you her idea of the real world?" Dodo enquired.

He laughed, "Yes, I'm the real world. Strange as it may seem. And also, of course, pure fiction. The Writer, the Great Man—the Official Biographer's fiction, in a word. Or, better still, the autobiographer's fiction. Chateaubriand, shall we say. And her breaking out—that's fiction too. A pure Miles Fanningism, if ever there was one. And, poor child, she knows it. Which makes her so cross with herself. Cross with me too, in a curious obscure way. But at the same time she's thrilled. What a thrilling situation! And herself walking about in the middle of it. She looks on and wonders and wonders and wonders what the next instalment of the feuilleton's going to contain."

"Well, there's one thing we're quite certain it's not going to contain, aren't we? Remember your promise, Miles."

"I think of nothing else," he bantered.

"Seriously, Miles, seriously."

"I think of nothing else," he repeated in a voice that was the parody of a Shakespearean actor's.

Dodo shook her finger at him. "Mind," she said, "mind!" Then, pushing back her chair, "Let's move into the drawing-room," she went on. "We shall be more comfortable there."

IV

"AND TO THINK," PAMELA WAS WRITING IN HER diary, "how nervous I'd been beforehand, and the trouble I'd taken to work out the whole of our first meeting, question and answer, like the Shorter Catechism, instead of which I was like a fish in water, really at home, for the first time in my life, I believe. No, perhaps not more at home than with Ruth and Phyllis, but then they're girls, so they hardly count. Besides, when you've once been at home in the sea, it doesn't seem much fun being at home in a little glass bowl, which is rather unfair to Ruth and Phyllis, but after all it's not their fault and they can't help being little bowls, just as M. F. can't help being a sea, and when you've swum about a bit in all that intelligence and knowledge and really *devilish* understanding, well, you find the bowls rather narrow, though of course they're sweet little bowls and I shall always be very fond of them, especially Ruth. Which makes me wonder if what he said about Clare and me—unnatural by nature—is always true, because hasn't every unnatural person got somebody she can be natural with, or even that she can't help being natural with, like oxygen and that other stuff making water? Of course it's not guaranteed that you find the other person who makes you natural, and I think perhaps Clare never did find her person, because I don't believe it was Daddy. But in my case there's Ruth and Phyllis and now to-day M. F.; and he really proves it, because I *was* natural with him more than with any one, even though he did say I was unnatural by nature. No, I feel that if I were with him always, I should always be my *real* self, just kind of easily spouting, like those lovely fountains we went to look at this afternoon, not all tied up in knots and squirting about vaguely in every kind of direction, and muddy at that, but beautifully clear in a big gushing spout, like what Joan in *The Return of Eurydice* finally became when she'd escaped from that awful, awful man and found Walter. But does that mean I'm in love with him?"

Pamela bit the end of her pen and stared, frowning, at the page before her. Scrawled large in orange ink, the question stared back. Disquietingly and insistently stared. She remembered a phrase of her mother's. "But if you knew," Clare had cried (Pamela could *see* her, wearing the black afternoon dress from Patou, and there were yellow roses in the bowl on the table under the window), "if you knew what certain writers were to me! *Shrines*—there's no other word. I could worship the Tolstoy of Anna Karenina." But Harry Braddon, to whom the words were addressed, had laughed at her. And, though she hated Harry Braddon, so had Pamela, mockingly. For it was absurd; nobody was a shrine, nobody. And anyhow, what *was* a shrine? Nothing. Not nowadays, not when one had stopped being a child. She told herself these things with a rather unnecessary emphasis, almost truculently, in the style of the professional atheists in

Hyde Park. One didn't worship—for the good reason that she herself once had worshipped. Miss Figgis, the classical mistress, had been her pash for more than a year. Which was why she had gone to Early Service so frequently in those days and been so keen to go up to Oxford and take Greats. (Besides, she had even, at that time, rather liked and admired Miss Huss. Ghastly old Hussy! It seemed incredible now.) But oh, that grammar! And Caesar was such a bore, and Livy still worse, and as for Greek . . . She had tried very hard for a time. But when Miss Figgis so obviously preferred that priggish little beast Kathleen, Pamela had just let things slide. The bad marks had come in torrents and old Hussy had begun being more sorrowful than angry, and finally more angry than sorrowful. But she hadn't cared. What made not caring easier was that she had her mother behind her. "I'm so delighted," was what Clare had said when she heard that Pamela had given up wanting to go to Oxford. "I'd have felt so terribly inferior if you'd turned out a blue-stocking. Having my frivolity rebuked by my own daughter!" Clare had always boasted of her frivolity. Once, under the influence of old Hussy and for the love of Miss Figgis, an earnest disapprover, Pamela had become an apostle of her mother's gospel. "After all," she had pointed out to Miss Figgis, "Cleopatra didn't learn Greek." And though Miss Figgis was able to point out, snubbingly, that the last of the Ptolemies had probably spoken nothing but Greek, Pamela could still insist that in principle she was quite right: Cleopatra hadn't learnt Greek, or what, if you were a Greek, corresponded to Greek. So why should she? She began to parade a violent and childish cynicism, a cynicism which was still (though she had learnt, since leaving school, to temper talks down to you in that awful patient, gentle way, which makes you feel a million times more of a worm than being snubbed or ignored, because, if you have any pride, that sort of intelligence without tears is just loathsome, as though you were being given milk pudding out of charity. No, M. F. talks to you on the level and the extraordinary thing is that, while he's talking to you and you're talking to him, you *are* on a level with him, or at any rate you feel as though you were, which comes to the same thing. He's like influenza, you catch his intelligence." Pamela let the leaves of the notebook flick past, one by one, under her thumb. The final words on the half-blank page once more stared at her, questioningly. "But does that mean I'm in love with him?" Taking her pen from between her teeth, "Certainly," she wrote, "I do find him terribly attractive physically." She paused for a moment to reflect, then added, frowning as though with the effort of raising an elusive fact from the depths of memory, of solving a difficult problem in algebra: "Because really, when he put his hand on my shoulder, which would have been simply intolerable if any one else had done it, but somehow with him I didn't mind, I felt all thrilled with the absolute frisson." She ran her pen through the last word and substituted "thrill," which she underlined to make it seem less lamely a repetition. "Frisson" had been one of Clare's favourite words; hearing it pronounced in her mother's remembered voice, Pamela had felt a sudden mistrust of it; it seemed to cast a kind of doubt on the feelings it stood for, a doubt of which she was ashamed—it seemed so disloyal and the voice had sounded so startlingly, so heart-rendingly clear and near—but which she still couldn't help experiencing. She defended herself; "frisson" had simply had to go, because the thrill was genuine, absolutely genuine, she insisted. "For a moment," she went on, writing very fast, as though she were trying to run away from the sad, disagreeable thoughts that had intruded upon her, "I thought I was going to faint when he touched me, like when one's coming to after chloroform, which I've certainly never felt like with any one else." As a protest against the doubts inspired by that unfortunate frisson she underlined "never," heavily. Never; it was quite true. When Harry Braddon had tried to kiss her, she had been furious and disgusted—disgusting beast! Saddening and reproachful, Clare's presence hovered round her once more; Clare had liked Harry Braddon. Still, he was a beast. Pamela had never told her mother about that kiss. She shut her eyes excludingly and thought instead of Cecil Rudge, poor, timid, unhappy little Cecil, whom she liked so much, was so genuinely sorry for. But when, that afternoon at Aunt Edith's, when at last, after an hour's visibly laborious screwing to the sticking point, he had had the courage to take her hand and say "Pamela" and kiss it, she had just laughed, oh! unforgivably, but she simply couldn't help it; he was so ridiculous. Poor lamb, he had been terribly upset. "But I'm so sorry," she had gasped between the bursts of her laughter, "so dreadfully sorry. Please don't be hurt." But his face, she could see, was agonized. "Please! Oh, I feel so miserable." And she had gone off into another explosion of laughter which almost choked her. But when she could breathe again, she had run to him where he stood, averted and utterly unhappy, by the window, she had taken his hand and, when he still refused to look at at her, had put her arm round his neck and kissed him. But the emotion that had filled her eyes with tears was nothing like passion. As for

Hugh Davies—why, it certainly had been rather thrilling when Hugh kissed her. It had been thrilling, but certainly not to a fainting point. But then had she *really* felt like fainting to-day, a small voice questioned. She drowned the small voice with the scratching of her pen. "Consult the oracles of passion," she wrote and, laying down her pen, got up and crossed the room. A copy of *The Return of Eurydice* was lying on the bed; she picked it up and turned over the pages. Here it was! "Consult the oracles of passion," she read aloud and her own voice sounded, she thought, strangely oracular in the solitude. "A god speaks in them, or else a devil, one can never tell which beforehand, nor even, in most cases, afterwards. And, when all is said, does it very much matter? God and devil are equally supernatural, that is the important thing; equally supernatural and therefore, in this all too flatly natural world of sense and science and society, equally desirable, equally significant." She shut the book and walked back to the table. "Which is what he said this afternoon," she went on writing, "but in that laughing way, when I said I could never see why one shouldn't do what one liked, instead of all this Hussy and Hippo rigmarole about service and duty, and he said yes, that was what Rabelais had said" (there seemed to be an awful lot of "saids" in this sentence, but it couldn't be helped; she scrawled on;) "which I pretended I'd read—why can't one tell the truth? particularly as I'd just been saying at the same time that one ought to say what one thinks as well as do what one likes; but it seems to be hopeless—and he said he entirely agreed, it was perfect, so long as you had the luck to like the sort of things that kept you on the right side of the prison bars and think the sort of things that don't get you murdered when you say them. And I said I'd rather say what I thought and do what I liked and be murdered and put in gaol than be a Hippo, and he said I was an idealist, which annoyed me and I said I certainly wasn't, all I was was some one who didn't want to go mad with inhibitions. And he laughed, and I wanted to quote him his own words about the oracles, but somehow it was so shy-making that I didn't. All the same, it's what I . intensely feel, that one *ought* to consult the oracles of passion. And I shall consult them." She leaned back in her chair and shut her eyes. The orange question floated across the darkness: "But does that mean I'm in love with him?" The oracle seemed to be saying yes. But oracles, she resolutely refused to remember, can be rigged to suit the interests of the questioner. Didn't the admirer of *The Return of Eurydice* secretly *want* the oracle to say yes? Didn't she think she'd almost fainted, because she'd wished she'd almost fainted, because she'd come desiring to faint? Pamela sighed; then, with a gesture of decision, she slapped her notebook to and put away her pen. It was time to get ready for dinner; she bustled about efficiently and distractingly among her trunks. But the question returned to her as she lay soaking in the warm other-world of her bath. By the time she got out she had boiled herself to such a pitch of giddiness that she could hardly stand.

For Pamela, dinner in solitude, especially the public solitude of hotels, was a punishment. Companionlessness and compulsory silence depressed her. Besides, she never felt quite eye-proof; she could never escape from the obsession that every one was looking at her, judging, criticizing. Under a carapace of rather impertinent uncaringness she writhed distressfully. At Florence her loneliness had driven her to make friends with two not very young American women who were staying in her hotel. They were a bit earnest and good and dreary. But Pamela preferred even dreariness to solitude. She attached herself to them inseparably. They were touched. When she left for Rome, they promised to write to her, they made her promise to write to them. She was so young; they felt responsible; a steadying hand, the counsel of older friends. . . . Pamela had already received two steadying letters. But she hadn't answered them, never would answer them. The horrors of lonely dining cannot be alleviated by correspondence.

Walking down to her ordeal in the restaurant, she positively yearned for her dreary friends. But the hall was a desert of alien eyes and faces; and the waiter who led her through the hostile dining-room, had bowed, it seemed to her, with an ironical politeness, had mockingly smiled. She sat down haughtily at her table and almost wished she were under it. When the *sommelier* appeared with his list, she ordered half a bottle of something absurdly expensive, for fear he might think she didn't know anything about wine.

She had got as far as the fruit, when a presence loomed over her; she looked up. "You?" Her delight was an illumination; the young man was dazzled. "What marvellous luck!" Yet it was only Guy Browne, Guy whom she had met a few times at dances and found quite pleasant—that was all. "Think of your being in Rome!" She made him sit down at her table. When she had finished her coffee, Guy suggested that they should go out and dance somewhere. They went. It was nearly three when Pamela got to bed. She had had a most enjoyable evening.

V

B UT HOW UNGRATEFULLY SHE TREATED POOR GUY
   when, next day at lunch, Fanning asked her how she
had spent the evening! True, there were extenuating cir-
cumstances, chief among which was the fact that Fanning
had kissed her when they met. By force of habit, he him-
self would have explained, if any one had asked him why,
because he kissed every presentable face. Kissing was in
the great English tradition. "It's the only way I can be like
Chaucer," he liked to affirm. "Just as knowing a little Latin
and less Greek is my only claim to resembling Shakespeare
and as lying in bed till ten's the nearest I get to Descartes."
In this particular case, as perhaps in every other particular
case, the force of habit had been seconded by a deliberate
intention; he was accustomed to women being rather in love
with him, he liked the amorous atmosphere and could use
the simplest as well as the most complicated methods to
create it. Moreover he was an experimentalist, he genuinely
wanted to see what would happen. What happened was that
Pamela was astonished, embarrassed, thrilled, delighted,
bewildered. And what with her confused excitement and the

enormous effort she had made to take it all as naturally and easily as he had done, she was betrayed into what, in other circumstances, would have been a scandalous ingratitude. But when one has just been kissed, for the first time and at one's second meeting with him, kissed offhandedly and yet (she felt it) significantly, by Miles Fanning—actually Miles Fanning!—little men like Guy Browne do seem rather negligible, even though one did have a very good time with them the evening before.

"I'm afraid you must have been rather lonely last night," said Fanning, as they sat down to lunch. His sympathy hypocritically covered a certain satisfaction that it should be his absence that had condemned her to dreariness.

"No, I met a friend," Pamela answered with a smile which the inward comparison of Guy with the author of *The Return of Eurydice* had tinged with a certain amused condescendingness.

"A friend?" He raised his eyebrows. "*Amico* or *amica?* Our English is so discreetly equivocal. With this key Bowdler locked up his heart. But I apologize. *Co* or *ca?*"

"*Co.* He's called Guy Browne and he's here learning Italian to get into the Foreign Office. He's a nice boy." Pamela might have been talking about a favourite, or even not quite favourite, retriever. "Nice; but nothing very special. I mean, not in the way of intelligence." She shook her head patronizingly over Guy's very creditable First in History as a guttersnipe capriciously favoured by an archduke might learn in his protector's company to shake his head and patronizingly smile at the name of a marquis of only four or five centuries' standing. "He can dance, though," she admitted.

"So I suppose you danced with him?" said Fanning in a

tone which, in spite of his amusement at the child's assumption of an aged superiority, he couldn't help making rather disobligingly sarcastic. It annoyed him to think that Pamela should have spent an evening, which he had pictured as dismally lonely, dancing with a young man.

"Yes, we danced," said Pamela, nodding.

"Where?"

"Don't ask me. We went to about six different places in the course of the evening."

"Of course you did," said Fanning almost bitterly. "Moving rapidly from one place to another and doing exactly the same thing in each—that seems to be the young's ideal of bliss."

Speaking as a young who had risen above such things, but who still had to suffer from the folly of her unregenerate contemporaries, "It's quite true," Pamela gravely confirmed.

"They go to Pekin to listen to the wireless and to Benares to dance the fox-trot. I've seen them at it. It's incomprehensible. And then the tooting up and down in automobiles, and the roaring up and down in aeroplanes and the stinking up and down in motor-boats. Up and down, up and down, just for the sake of not sitting still, of never having time to think or feel. No, I give them up, these young of yours." He shook his head. "But I'm becoming a minor prophet," he added; his good humour was beginning to return.

"But after all," said Pamela, "we're not *all* like that."

Her gravity made him laugh. "There's at least one who's ready to let herself be bored by a tiresome survivor from another civilization. Thank you, Pamela." Leaning across the table, he took her hand and kissed it. "I've been horribly ungrateful," he went on, and his face, as he looked at her was suddenly transfigured by the bright enigmatic beauty of his smile. "If you knew how charming you looked!" he said; and it was true. That ingenuous face, those impertinent little breasts—charming. "And how charming you *were!* But of course you *do* know," a little demon prompted him to add: "no doubt Mr. Browne told you last night."

Pamela had blushed—a blush of pleasure, and embarrassed shyness, and excitement. What he had just said and done was more significant, she felt, even than the kiss he had given her when they met. Her cheeks burned; but she managed, with an effort, to keep her eyes unwaveringly on his. His last words made her frown. "He certainly didn't," she answered. "He'd have got his face smacked."

"Is that a delicate hint?" he asked. "If so," and he leaned forward, "here's the other cheek."

Her face went redder than ever. She felt suddenly miserable; he was only laughing at her. "Why do you laugh at me?" she said aloud, unhappily.

"But I wasn't," he protested. "I really did think you were annoyed."

"But why should I have been?"

"I can't imagine." He smiled. "But if you would have smacked Mr. Browne's face. . . ."

"But Guy's quite different."

It was Fanning's turn to wince. "You mean he's young, while I'm only a poor old imbecile who needn't be taken seriously?"

"Why are you so stupid?" Pamela asked almost fiercely. "No, but I mean," she added in quick apology, "I mean . . . well, I don't care two pins about Guy. So you see, it would annoy me if he tried to push in, like that. Whereas with somebody who does mean something to me . . ." Pamela hesitated. "With *you*," she specified in a rather harsh, strained voice and with just that look of despairing determination, Fanning imagined, just that jumping-off-the-Eiffel-Tower expression, which her mother's face must have assumed in moments such as this, "it's quite different. I mean, with you of course I'm not annoyed. I'm pleased. Or at least I *was* pleased, till I saw you were just making a fool of me."

Touched and flattered, "But my dear child," Fanning protested, "I wasn't doing anything of the kind. I meant what I said. And much more than I said," he added, in the teeth of the warning and reproachful outcry raised by his common sense. It was amusing to experiment, it was pleasant to be adored, exciting to be tempted (and how young she was, how perversely fresh!). There was even something quite agreeable in resisting temptation; it had the charms of a strenuous and difficult sport. Like mountain climbing. He smiled once more, consciously brilliant.

This time Pamela dropped her eyes. There was a silence which might have protracted itself uncomfortably, if the waiter had not broken it by bringing the *tagliatelle*. They began to eat. Pamela was all at once exuberantly gay.

After coffee they took a taxi and drove to the Villa Giulia. "For we mustn't," Fanning explained, "neglect your education."

"Mustn't we?" she asked. "I often wonder why we mustn't. Truthfully now, I mean without any hippoing and all that—why shouldn't I neglect it? Why should I go to this beastly museum?" She was preparing to play the cynical, boastfully unintellectual part which she had made her own. "Why?" she repeated truculently. Behind the rather vulgar low-brow mask she cultivated wistful yearnings and concealed the uneasy consciousness of inferiority. "A lot of beastly old Roman odds and ends!" she grumbled; that was one for Miss Figgis.

"Roman?" said Fanning. "God forbid! Etruscan."

"Well, Etruscan then; it's all the same anyhow. Why shouldn't I neglect the Etruscans? I mean, what have they got to do with me—*me?*" And she gave her chest two or three little taps with the tip of a crooked forefinger.

"Nothing, my child," he answered. "Thank goodness, they've got absolutely nothing to do with you, or me, or anybody else."

"Then why . . ."

"Precisely for that reason. That's the definition of culture—knowing and thinking about things that have absolutely nothing to do with us. About Etruscans, for example; or the mountains on the moon; or cat's cradle among the Chinese; or the Universe at large."

"All the same," she insisted, "I still don't see."

"Because you've never known people who weren't cultured. But make the acquaintance of a few practical business-men—the kind who have no time to be anything but alternately efficient and tired. Or of a few workmen from the big towns. (Country people are different; they still have the remains of the old substitutes for culture—religion, folk-lore, tradition. The town fellows have lost the substitutes without acquiring the genuine article.) Get to know those people; *they'll* make you see the point of culture. Just as the Sahara'll make you see the point of water. And for the same reason: they're arid."

"That's all very well; but what about people like Professor Cobley?"

"Whom I've happily never met," he said, "but can reconstruct from the expression on your face. Well, all that can be said about those people is: just try to imagine them if they'd never been irrigated. Gobi or Shamo."

"Well, perhaps." She was dubious.

"And anyhow the biggest testimony to culture isn't the soulless philistines—it's the soulful ones. My sweet Pamela," he implored, laying a hand on her bare brown arm, "for heaven's sake don't run the risk of becoming a soulful philistine."

"But as I don't know what that is," she answered, trying to persuade herself, as she spoke, that the touch of his hand was giving her a tremendous *frisson*—but it really wasn't.

"It's what the name implies," he said. "A person without culture who goes in for having a soul. An illiterate idealist. A Higher Thinker with nothing to think about but his—or more often, I'm afraid, *her*—beastly little personal feelings and sensation. They spend their lives staring at their own navels and in the intervals trying to find other people who'll take an interest and come and stare too. Oh, figuratively," he added, noticing the expression of astonishment which had passed across her face. "*En tout bien, tout honneur*[*]. At least, sometimes and to begin with. Though I've known cases . . ." But he decided it would be better not to speak about the lady from Rochester, N. Y. Pamela might be made to feel that the cap fitted. Which it did, except that her little head was such a charming one. "In the end," he said, "they go mad, these soulful philistines. Mad with self-consciousness

---

[*] With the most honorable intentions.

and vanity and egotism and a kind of hopeless bewilderment; for when you're utterly without culture, every fact's an isolated, unconnected fact, every experience is unique and unprecedented. Your world's made up of a few bright points floating about inexplicably in the midst of an unfathomable darkness. Terrifying! It's enough to drive any one mad. I've seen them, lots of them, gone utterly crazy. In the past they had organized religion, which meant that somebody had once been cultured for them, vicariously. But what with protestantism and the modernists, their philistinism's absolute now. They're alone with their own souls. Which is the worst companionship a human being can have. So bad, that it sends you dotty. So beware, Pamela, beware! You'll go mad, if you think only of what has something to do with you. The Etruscans will keep you sane."

"Let's hope so." She laughed. "But aren't we there?"

The cab drew up at the door of the villa; they got out.

"And remember that the things that start with having nothing to do with you," said Fanning, as he counted out the money for the entrance tickets, "turn out in the long run to have a great deal to do with you. Because they become a part of you and you of them. A soul can't know or fully become itself without knowing and therefore to some extent becoming what isn't itself. Which it does in various ways. By loving, for example."

"You mean . . . ?" The flame of interest brightened in her eyes.

But he went on remorselessly. "And by thinking of things that have nothing to do with you."

"Yes, I see." The flame had dimmed again.

"Hence my concern about your education." He beckoned her through the turnstile into the museum. "A purely selfish concern," he added, smiling down at her. "Because I don't want the most charming of my young friends to grow into a monster, whom I shall be compelled to flee from. So resign yourself to the Etruscans."

"I resign myself," said Pamela, laughing. His words had made her feel happy and excited. "You can begin." And in a theatrical voice, like that which used to make Ruth go off into such fits of laughter, "I am all ears," she added, "as they say in the Best Books." She pulled off her hat and shook out the imprisoned hair.

To Fanning, as he watched her, the gesture brought a sudden shock of pleasure. The impatient, exuberant youthfulness of it! And the little head, so beautifully shaped, so gracefully and proudly poised on its long neck! And her hair was drawn back smoothly from the face to explode in a thick tangle of curls on the nape of the neck. Ravishing!

"All ears," she repeated, delightedly conscious of the admiration she was receiving.

"All ears." And almost meditatively. "But do you know," he went on, "I've never even seen your ears. May I?" And without waiting for her permission, he lifted up the soft, goldy-brown hair that lay in a curve, drooping, along the side of her head.

Pamela's face violently reddened; but she managed none the less to laugh. "Are they as long and furry as you expected?" she asked.

He allowed the lifted hair to fall back into its place and, without answering her question, "I've always," he said, looking at her with a smile which she found disquietingly enigmatic and remote, "I've always had a certain fellow-feeling for those savages who collect ears and thread them on strings, as necklaces."

"But what a horror!" she cried out.

"You think so?" He raised his eyebrows.

But perhaps, Pamela was thinking, he was a sadist. In that book of Krafft-Ebbing's there had been a lot about sadists. It would be queer, if he were . . .

"But what's certain," Fanning went on in another, business-like voice, "what's only too certain is that ears aren't culture. They've got too much to do with us. With me, at any rate. Much too much." He smiled at her again. Pamela smiled back at him, fascinated and obscurely a little frightened; but the fright was an element in the fascination. She dropped her eyes. "So don't let's waste any more time," his voice went on. "Culture to right of us, culture to left of us. Let's begin with this culture on the left. With the vases. They really have absolutely nothing to do with us."

He began and Pamela listened. Not very attentively, however. She lifted her hand and, under the hair, touched her ear. "A fellow-feeling for those savages." She remembered his words with a little shudder. He'd almost meant them. And "ears aren't culture. Too much to do with us. With me. Much too much." He'd meant that too, genuinely and wholeheartedly. And his smile had been a confirmation of the words; yes, and a comment, full of mysterious significance. What *had* he meant? But surely it was obvious what he had meant. Or wasn't it obvious?

The face she turned towards him wore an expression of grave attention. And when he pointed to a vase and said, "Look," she looked, with what an air of concentrated intelligence! But as for knowing what he was talking about! She went on confusedly thinking that he had a fellow-feeling for those savages, and that her ears had too much to do with him, much too much, and that perhaps he was in love with her, perhaps also that he was like those people in Krafft-Ebbing, perhaps . . . ; and it seemed to her that her blood must have turned into a kind of hot, red soda-water, all fizzy with little bubbles of fear and excitement.

She emerged, partially at least, out of this bubbly and agitated trance to hear him say, "Look at that, now." A tall statue towered over her. "The Apollo of Veii," he explained. "And really, you know, it *is* the most beautiful statue in the world. Each time I see it, I'm more firmly convinced of that."

Dutifully, Pamela stared. The God stood there on his pedestal, one foot advanced, erect in his draperies. He had lost his arms, but the head was intact and the strange Etruscan face was smiling, enigmatically smiling. Rather like *him*, it suddenly occurred to her.

"What's it made of?" she asked; for it was time to be intelligent.

"Terracotta. Originally coloured."

"And what date?"

"Late sixth century."

"B.C.?" she queried, a little dubiously, and was relieved when he nodded. It really would have been rather awful if it had been A.D. "Who by?"

"By Vulca, they say. But as that's the only Etruscan sculptor they know the name of . . ." He shrugged his shoulders, and the gesture expressed a double doubt—doubt whether the archæologists were right and doubt whether it was really much good talking about Etruscan art to some one who didn't feel quite certain whether the Apollo of Veii was made in the sixth century before or after Christ.

There was a long silence. Fanning looked at the statue. So did Pamela, who also, from time to time, looked at Fanning. She was on the point, more than once, of saying something; but his face was so meditatively glum that, on each occasion, she changed her mind. In the end, however, the silence became intolerable.

"I think it's extraordinarily fine," she announced in the rather religious voice that seemed appropriate. He only nodded. The silence prolonged itself, more oppressive and embarrassing than ever, She made another and despairing effort. "Do you know, I think he's really rather like you. I mean, the way he smiles. . . ."

Fanning's petrified immobility broke once more into life. He turned towards her, laughing. "You're irresistible, Pamela."

"Am I?" Her tone was cold; she was offended. To be told you were irresistible always meant that you'd behaved like an imbecile child. But her conscience was clear; it was a gratuitous insult—the more intolerable since it had been offered by the man who, a moment before, had been saying that he had a fellow-feeling for those savages and that her ears had altogether *too* much to do with him.

Fanning noticed her sudden change of humour and obscurely divined the cause. "You've paid me the most irresistible compliment you could have invented," he said, doing his best to undo the effect of his words. For after all what did it matter, with little breasts like that and thin brown arms, if she did mix up the millenniums a bit? "You could hardly have pleased me more if you'd said I was another Rudolph Valentino."

Pamela had to laugh.

"But seriously," he said, "if you knew what this lovely God means to me, how much . . ."

Mollified by being once more spoken to seriously, "I think I can understand," she said in her most understanding voice.

"No, I doubt if you can." He shook his head. "It's a question of age, of the experience of a particular time that's not your time. I shall never forget when I came back to Rome for the first time after the War and found this marvellous creature standing here. They only dug him up in 'sixteen, you see. So there it was, a brand new experience, a new and apocalyptic voice out of the past. Some day I shall try to get it on to paper, all that this God has taught me." He gave a little sigh; she could see that he wasn't thinking about her any more; he was talking for himself. "Some day," he repeated. "But it's not ripe yet. You can't write a thing before it's ripe, before it wants to be written. But you can talk about it, you can take your mind for walks all round it and through it." He paused and, stretching out a hand, touched a fold of the God's sculptured garment, as though he were trying to establish a more intimate, more real connection with the beauty before him. "Not that what he taught me was fundamentally new," he went on slowly. "It's all in Homer, of course. It's even partially expressed in the archaic Greek sculpture. Partially. But Apollo here expresses it wholly. He's *all* Homer, *all* the ancient world, concentrated in a single lump of terracotta. That's his novelty. And then the circumstances gave him a special point. It was just after the War that I first saw him—just after the apotheosis and the logical conclusion of all the things Apollo *didn't* stand for.

You can imagine how marvellously new he seemed by contrast. After that horrible enormity, he was a lovely symbol of the small, the local, the kindly. After all that extravagance of beastliness—yes, and all that extravagance of heroism and self-sacrifice—he seemed so beautifully sane. A God who doesn't admit the separate existence of either heroics or diabolics, but somehow includes them in his own nature and turns them into something else—like two gases combining to make a liquid. Look at him," Fanning insisted. "Look at his face, look at his body, see how he stands. It's obvious. He's neither the God of heroics, nor the God of diabolics. And yet it's equally obvious that he knows all about both, that he includes them, that he combines them into a third essence. It's the same with Homer. There's no tragedy in Homer. He's pessimistic, yes; but never tragic. His heroes aren't heroic in our sense of the word; they're men." (Pamela took a very deep breath; if she had opened her mouth, it would have been a yawn.) "In fact, you can say there aren't any heroes in Homer. Nor devils, nor sins. And none of our horrible, nauseating disgusts—because they're the complement of being spiritual, they're the tails to its heads. You couldn't have had Homer writing 'the expensive spirit in a waste of shame.' Though, of course, with Shakespeare it may have been physiological; the passion violent and brief, and then the most terrible reaction. It's the sort of thing that colours a whole life, a whole work. Only of course one's never allowed to say so. All that one isn't allowed to say!" He laughed. Pamela also laughed. "But physiology or no physiology," Fanning went on, "he couldn't have written like that if he'd lived before the great split—the great split that broke life into spirit and matter, heroics and diabolics, virtue and sin and all the other accursed antitheses. Homer lived before the split; life hadn't been broken when he wrote. They're complete, his men and women, complete and real; for he leaves nothing out, he shirks no issue, even though there is no tragedy. He knows all about it—*all*." He laid his hand again on the statue. "And this God's his portrait. He's Homer, but with the Etruscan smile. Homer smiling at the sad, mysterious, beautiful absurdity of the world. The Greeks didn't see that divine absurdity as clearly as the Etruscans. Not even in Homer's day; and by the time you get to any sculptor who was anything like as accomplished as the man who made this, you'll find that they've lost it altogether. True, the earliest Greek Gods used to smile all right—or rather grin; for subtlety wasn't their strong point. But by the end of the sixth century they were already becoming a bit too heroic; they were developing those athlete's muscles and those tiresomely noble poses and damned superior faces. But our God here refused to be a prize-fighter or an actor-manager. There's no *terribiltà* about him, no priggishness, no sentimentality. And yet without being in the least pretentious, he's beautiful, he's grand, he's authentically divine. The Greeks took the road that led to Michelangelo and Bernini and Thorwaldsen and Rodin. A rake's progress. These Etruscans were on a better track. If only people had had the sense to follow it! Or at least get back to it. But nobody has, except perhaps old Maillol. They've all allowed themselves to be lured away. Plato was the arch-seducer. It was he who first sent us whoring after spirituality and heroics, whoring after the complementary demons of disgust and sin. We needs must love—well, not the highest, except sometimes by accident—but always the most extravagant and exciting. Tragedy was much more exciting than Homer's luminous pessimism, than this God's smiling awareness of the divine absurdity. Being alternately a hero and a sinner is much more sensational than being an integrated man. So as men seem to have the Yellow Press in the blood, like syphilis, they went back on Homer and Apollo; they followed Plato and Euripides. And Plato and Euripides handed them over to the Stoics and the Neo-Platonists. And these in turn handed humanity over to the Christians. And the Christians have handed us over to Henry Ford and the machines. So here we are."

Pamela nodded intelligently. But what she was chiefly conscious of was the ache in her feet. If only she could sit down!

But, "How poetical and appropriate," Fanning began again, "that the God should have risen from the grave exactly when he did, in 1916! Rising up in the midst of the insanity, like a beautiful, smiling reproach from another world. It was dramatic. At least I felt it so, when I saw him for the first time just after the War. The resurrection of Apollo, the Etruscan Apollo. I've been his worshipper and self-appointed priest ever since. Or at any rate I've tried to be. But it's difficult." He shook his head. "Perhaps it's even impossible for us to recapture . . ." He left the sentence unfinished and, taking her arm, led her out into the great courtyard of the Villa. Under the arcades was a bench. Thank goodness, said Pamela inwardly. They sat down.

"You see," he went on, leaning forward, his elbows on his knees, his hands clasped, "you can't get away from the things that God protests against. Because they've become a part of you. Tradition and education have driven them into your very bones. It's a case of what I was speaking about just now—of the things that have nothing to do with you coming by force of habit to have everything to do with you. Which is why I'd like you to get Apollo and his Etruscans into your system while you're still young. It may save you trouble. Or on the other hand," he added with a rueful little laugh, "it may not. Because I really don't know if he's everybody's God. He may do for me—and do, only because I've got Plato and Jesus in my bones. But does he do for you? *Chi lo sa?*[*] The older one grows, the more often one asks that question. Until, of course, one's arteries begin to harden, and then one's opinions begin to harden too, harden till they fossilize into certainty. But meanwhile, *chi lo sa? chi lo sa?*[†] And after all it's quite agreeable, not knowing. And knowing, and at the same time knowing that it's no practical use knowing—that's not disagreeable either. Knowing, for example, that it would be good to live according to this God's commandments, but knowing at the same time that one couldn't do it even if one tried, because one's very guts and skeleton are already pledged to other Gods."

"I should have thought that was awful," said Pamela.

"For you, perhaps. But I happen to have a certain natural affection for the accomplished fact. I like and respect it, even when it is a bit depressing. Thus, it's a fact that I'd like to think and live in the unsplit, Apollonian way. But it's also a fact—and the fact as such is lovable—that I can't help indulging in aspirations and disgusts; I can't help thinking in terms of heroics and diabolics. Because the division, the splitness, has been worked right into my bones. So has the

---

[*] Who knows?

[†] Who knows? Who knows?

microbe of sensationalism; I can't help wallowing in the excitements of mysticism and the tragic sense. Can't help it." He shook his head. "Though perhaps I've wallowed in them rather more than I was justified in wallowing—justified by my upbringing, I mean. There was a time when I was really quite perversely preoccupied with mystical experiences and ecstasies and private universes."

"Private universes?" she questioned.

"Yes, private, not shared. You create one, you live in it, each time you're in love, for example." (Brightly serious, Pamela nodded her understanding and agreement; yes, yes, she knew all about *that*.) "Each time you're spiritually exalted," he went on, "each time you're drunk, even. Everybody has his own favourite short cuts to the other world. Mine, in those days, was opium."

"Opium?" She opened her eyes very wide. "Do you mean to say you smoked opium?" She was thrilled. Opium was a vice of the first order.

"It's as good a way of becoming supernatural," he answered, "as looking at one's nose or one's navel, or not eating, or repeating a word over and over again, till it loses its sense and you forget how to think. All roads lead to Rome. The only bother about opium is that it's rather an unwholesome road. I had to go to a nursing home in Cannes to get disintoxicated."

"All the same," said Pamela, doing her best to imitate the quiet casualness of his manner, "it must be rather delicious, isn't it? Awfully exciting, I mean," she added, forgetting not to be thrilled.

"*Too* exciting." He shook his head. "That's the trouble. We needs must love the excitingest when we see it.

The supernatural *is* exciting. But I don't want to love the supernatural, I want to love the natural. Not that a little supernaturalness isn't, of course, perfectly natural and necessary. But you can overdo it. I overdid it then. I was all the time in 'tother world, never here. I stopped smoking because I was ill. But even if I hadn't been, I'd have stopped sooner or later for aesthetic reasons. The supernatural world is so terribly baroque—altogether too Counter-Reformation and Bernini. At its best it can be Greco. But you can have too much even of Greco. A big dose of him makes you begin to pine for Vulca and his Apollo."

"But doesn't it work the other way too?" she asked. "I mean, don't you sometimes *long* to start smoking again?" She was secretly hoping that he'd let her try a pipe or two.

Fanning shook his head. "One doesn't get tired of very good bread," he answered. "Apollo's like that. I don't pine for supernatural excitements. Which doesn't mean," he added, "that I don't in practice run after them. You can't disintoxicate yourself of your culture. That sticks deeper than a mere taste for opium. I'd like to be able to think and live in the spirit of the God. But the fact remains that I can't."

"Can't you?" said Pamela with a polite sympathy. She was more interested in the opium.

"No, no, you can't entirely disintoxicate yourself of mysticism and the tragic sense. You can't take a Turvey treatment for spirituality and disgust. You can't. Not nowadays. Acceptance is impossible in a split world like ours. You've got to recoil. In the circumstances it's right and proper. But absolutely it's wrong. If only one could accept as this God accepts, smiling like that . . ."

"But you *do* smile like that," she insisted.

He laughed and, unclasping his hands, straightened himself up in his seat. "But unhappily," he said, "a man can smile and smile and not be Apollo. Meanwhile, what's becoming of your education? Shouldn't we . . . ?"

"Well, if you like," she assented dubiously. "Only my feet are rather tired. I mean, there's something about sightseeing. . . ."

"There is indeed," said Fanning. "But I was prepared to be a martyr to culture. Still, I'm thankful you're not." He smiled at her, and Pamela was pleased to find herself once more at the focus of his attention. It had been very interesting to hear him talk about his philosophy and all that. But all the same . . .

"Twenty to four," said Fanning, looking at his watch. "I've an idea; shouldn't we drive out to Monte Cavo and spend the evening up there in the cool? There's a view. And a really very eatable dinner."

"I'd love to. But . . ." Pamela hesitated. "Well, you see I did tell Guy I'd go out with him this evening."

He was annoyed. "Well, if you prefer . . ."

"But I don't prefer," she answered hastily. "I mean, I'd much rather go with you. Only I wondered how I'd let Guy know I wasn't. . . ."

"Don't let him know," Fanning answered, abusing his victory. "After all, what are young men there for, except to wait when young women don't keep their appointments? It's their function in life."

Pamela laughed. His words had given her a pleasing sense of importance and power. "Poor Guy!" she said through her laughter, and her eyes were insolently bright.

"You little hypocrite!"

"I'm not," she protested. "I really *am* sorry for him."

"A little hypocrite *and* a little devil," was his verdict. He rose to his feet. "If you could see your own eyes now! But *andiamo.*"* He held out his hand to help her up. "I'm beginning to be rather afraid of you."

"What nonsense!" She was delighted. They walked together towards the door.

Fanning made the driver go out by the Appian Way. "For the sake of your education," he explained, pointing at the ruined tombs, "which we can continue, thank heaven, in comfort, and at twenty miles an hour."

Leaning back luxuriously in her corner, Pamela laughed. "But I must say," she had to admit, "it is really rather lovely."

From Albano the road mounted through the chestnut woods towards Rocca di Papa. A few miles brought them to a turning on the right; the car came to a halt.

"It's barred," said Pamela, looking out of the window. Fanning had taken out his pocket-book and was hunting among the bank-notes and the old letters. "The road's private," he explained. "They ask for your card—heaven knows why. The only trouble being, of course, that I've never possessed such a thing as a visiting-card in my life. Still, I generally have one or two belonging to other people. Ah, here we are! Good!" he produced two pieces of pasteboard. A gatekeeper had appeared and was waiting by the door of the car. "Shall we say we're Count Keyserling?" said Fanning, handing her the count's card. "Or alternatively," he read from the other, "that we're Herbert Watson, Funeral Furnisher, Funerals conducted with Efficiency and Reverence, Motor Hearses for use in every part of the Country." He shook his head. "The last relic of my poor old friend Tom

---

* Let's go.

Hatchard. Died last year. I had to bury him. Poor Tom! On the whole I think we'd better be Herbert Watson. *Ecco!*" He handed out the card; the man saluted and went to open the gate. "But give me back Count Keyserling." Fanning stretched out his hand. "He'll come in useful another time."

The car started and went roaring up the zig-zag ascent. Lying back in her corner, Pamela laughed and laughed, inextinguishably.

"But what *is* the joke?" he asked.

She didn't know herself. Mr. Watson and the Count had only been a pretext; this enormous laughter, which they had released, sprang from some other, deeper source. And perhaps it was a mere accident that it should be laughter at all. Another pretext, a different finger on the trigger, and it might have been tears, or anger, or singing "Constantinople" at the top of her voice—anything.

She was limp when they reached the top. Fanning made her sit down where she could see the view and himself went off to order cold drinks at the bar of the little inn that had once been the monastery of Monte Cavo.

Pamela sat where he had left her. The wooded slopes fell steeply away beneath her, down, down to the blue shining of the Alban Lake; and that toy palace perched on the hill beyond was the Pope's, that tiny city in a picture-book, Marino. Beyond a dark ridge on the left the round eye of Nemi looked up from its crater. Far off, behind Albano an expanse of blue steel, burnished beneath the sun, was the Tyrrhenian, and flat like the sea, but golden with ripening corn and powdered goldenly with a haze of dust, the Campagna stretched away from the feet of the subsiding hills, away and up towards a fading horizon, on which the blue ghosts of mountains floated on a level with her eyes. In the midst of the expanse a half-seen golden chaos was Rome. Through the haze the dome of St. Peter's shone faintly in the sun with a glitter as of muted glass. There was an enormous silence, sad, sad but somehow consoling. A sacred silence. And yet when, coming up from behind her, Fanning broke it, his voice, for Pamela, committed no iconoclasms for it seemed, in the world of her feelings, to belong to the silence, it was made, as it were, of the same intimate and friendly substance. He squatted down on his heels beside her, laying a hand on her shoulder to steady himself.

"What a panorama of space and time!" he said. "So many miles, such an expanse of centuries! You can still walk on the paved road that led to the temple here. The generals used to march up sometimes in triumph. With elephants."

The silence enveloped them again, bringing them together; and they were alone and as though conspiratorially isolated in an atmosphere of solemn amorousness.

"*I signori son serviti,*"* said a slightly ironic voice behind them.

"That's our drinks," said Fanning. "Perhaps we'd better . . ." He got up and, as he unbent them, his knees cracked stiffly. He stooped to rub them, for they ached; his joints were old. "Fool!" he said to himself, and decided that to-morrow he'd go to Venice. She was too young, too dangerously and perversely fresh.

They drank their lemonade in silence. Pamela's face wore an expression of grave serenity which it touched and flattered and moved him to see. Still, he was a fool to be touched and flattered and moved.

"Let's go for a bit of a stroll," he said, when they had

---

* The gentlemen are served.

slaked their thirst. She got up without a word, obediently, as though she had become his slave.

It was breathless under the trees and there was a smell of damp, hot greenness, a hum and flicker of insects in the probing slants of sunlight. But in the open spaces the air of the heights was quick and nimble, in spite of the sun; the broom-flower blazed among the rocks; and round the bushes where the honeysuckle had clambered, there hung invisible islands of perfume, cool and fresh in the midst of the hot sea of bracken smell. Pamela moved here and there with little exclamations of delight, pulling at the tough sprays of honeysuckle. "Oh, look!" she called to him in her rapturous voice. "Come and look!"

"I'm looking," he shouted back across the intervening space. "With a telescope. With the eye of faith," he corrected; for she had moved out of sight. He sat down on a smooth rock and lighted a cigarette. Venice, he reflected, would be rather boring at this particular season. In a few minutes Pamela came back to him, flushed, with a great bunch of honeysuckle between her hands.

"You know, you ought to have come," she said reproachfully. "There were such *lovely* pieces I couldn't reach."

Fanning shook his head. "He also serves who only sits and smokes," he said and made room for her on the stone beside him. "And what's more," he went on, " 'let Austin have his swink to him reserved.' Yes, let him. How whole-heartedly I've always agreed with Chaucer's Monk! Besides, you seem to forget, my child, that I'm an old, old gentleman." He was playing the safe, the prudent part. Perhaps if he played it hard enough, it wouldn't be necessary to go to Venice.

Pamela paid no attention to what he was saying. "Would you like this one for your buttonhole, Miles?" she asked, holding up a many-trumpeted flower. It was the first time she had called him by his christian name and the accomplishment of this much-meditated act of daring made her blush. "I'll stick it in," she added, leaning forward, so that he shouldn't see her reddened cheeks, till her face was almost touching his coat.

Near and thus offered (for it was an offer, he had no doubt of that, a deliberate offer) why shouldn't he take this lovely, this terribly and desperately tempting freshness? It was a matter of stretching out one's hands. But no; it would be too insane. She was near, this warm young flesh, this scent of her hair, near and offered—with what an innocent perversity, what a touchingly ingenuous and uncomprehending shamelessness! But he sat woodenly still, feeling all of a sudden as he had felt when, a lanky boy, he had been too shy, too utterly terrified, in spite of his longings, to kiss that Jenny—what on earth was her name?—that Jenny Something-or-Other he had danced the polka with at Uncle Fred's one Christmas, how many centuries ago!—and yet only yesterday, only this instant.

"There!" said Pamela and drew back. Her cheeks had had time to cool a little.

"Thank you." There was a silence.

"Do you know," she said at last, efficiently, "you've got a button loose on your coat."

He fingered the hanging button. "What a damning proof of celibacy!"

"If only I had a needle and thread. . . ."

"Don't make your offer too lightly. If you knew what a quantity of unmended stuff I've got at home. . . ."

"I'll come and do it all to-morrow," she promised, feeling delightfully protective and important.

"Beware," he said. "I'll take you at your word. It's sweated labour."

"I don't mind. I'll come."

"Punctually at ten-thirty, then." He had forgotten about Venice. "I shall be a ruthless taskmaster."

Nemi was already in shadow when they walked back; but the higher slopes were transfigured with the setting sunlight. Pamela halted at a twist of the path and turned back towards the Western sky. Looking up, Fanning saw her standing there, goldenly flushed, the colours of her skin, her hair, her dress, the flowers in her hands, supernaturally heightened and intensified in the almost level light.

"I think this is the most lovely place I've ever seen." Her voice was solemn with a natural piety. "But you're not looking," she added in a different tone, reproachfully.

"I'm looking at you," he answered. After all, if he stopped in time, it didn't matter his behaving like a fool—it didn't finally matter and, meanwhile, was very agreeable.

An expression of impertinent mischief chased away the solemnity from her face. "Trying to see my ears again?" she asked; and, breaking off a honeysuckle blossom, she threw it down in his face, then turned and ran up the steep path.

"Don't imagine I'm going to pursue," he called after her. "The Pan and Syrinx business is a winter pastime. Like football."

Her laughter came down to him from among the trees; he followed the retreating sound. Pamela waited for him at the top of the hill and they walked back together towards the inn.

"Aren't there any ruins here?" she asked. "I mean for my education."

He shook his head. "The Young Pretender's brother pulled them all down and built a monastery with them. For the Passionist Fathers," he added after a little pause. "I feel rather like a Passionist Father myself at the moment." They walked on without speaking, enveloped by the huge, the amorously significant silence.

But a few minutes later, at the dinner table, they were exuberantly gay. The food was well cooked, the wine, an admirable Falernian. Fanning began to talk about his early loves. Vaguely at first, but later, under Pamela's questioning, with an ever-increasing wealth of specific detail. They were indiscreet, impudent questions, which at ordinary times she couldn't have uttered, or at least have only despairingly forced out, with a suicide's determination. But she was a little tipsy now, tipsy with the wine and her own laughing exultation; she rapped them out easily, without a tremor. "As though you were the immortal Sigmund himself," he assured her, laughing. Her impudence and that knowledgeable, scientific ingenuousness amused him, rather perversely; he told her everything she asked.

When she had finished with his early loves, she questioned him about the opium. Fanning described his private universes and that charming nurse who had looked after him while he was being disintoxicated. He went on to talk about the black poverty he'd been reduced to by the drug. "Because you can't do journalism or write novels in the other world," he explained. "At least I never could." And he told her of the debts he still owed and of his present arrangements with his publishers.

Almost suddenly the night was cold and Fanning became aware that the bottle had been empty for a long time. He threw away the stump of his cigar. "Let's go." They took their seats and the car set off, carrying with it the narrow world of form and colour created by its head-lamps. They were alone in the darkness of their padded box. An hour before Fanning had decided that he would take this opportunity to kiss her. But he was haunted suddenly by the memory of an Australian who had once complained to him of the sufferings of a young colonial in England. "In Sydney," he had said, "when I get into a taxi with a nice girl, I know exactly what to do. And I know exactly what to do when I'm in an American taxi. But when I apply my knowledge in London—God, isn't there a row!" How vulgar and stupid it all was! Not merely a fool, but a vulgar, stupid fool. He sat unmoving in his corner. When the lights of Rome were round them, he took her hand and kissed it.

"Good-night."

She thanked him. "I've had the loveliest day." But her eyes were puzzled and unhappy. Meeting them, Fanning suddenly regretted his self-restraint, wished that he had been stupid and vulgar. And after all would it have been so stupid and vulgar? You could make any action seem anything you liked, from saintly to disgusting, by describing it in the appropriate words. But his regrets had come too late. Here was her hotel. He drove home to his solitude feeling exceedingly depressed.

VI

J UNE 14TH. SPENT THE MORNING WITH M., WHO
lives in a house belonging to a friend of his who is a Cath-
olic and lives in Rome, M. says, because he likes to get his
popery straight from the horse's mouth. A nice house, old,
standing just back from the Forum, which I said I thought
was like a rubbish heap and he agreed with me, in spite of
my education, and said he always preferred live dogs to dead
lions and thinks it's awful the way the Fascists are pulling
down nice ordinary houses and making holes to find more of
these beastly pillars and things. I sewed on a lot of buttons,
etc., as he's living in only two rooms on the ground floor and
the servants are on their holiday, so he eats out and an old
woman comes to clean up in the afternoons, but doesn't do
any mending, which meant a lot for me, but I liked doing it,
in spite of the darning, because he sat with me all the time,
sometimes talking, sometimes just working. When he's
writing or sitting with his pen in his hand thinking, his face
is quite still and *terribly* serious and far, far away, as though
he were a picture, or more like some sort of not human
person, a sort of angel, if one can imagine them without

nightdresses and long hair, really rather frightening, so that one longed to shout or throw a reel of cotton at him so as to change him back again into a man. He has very beautiful hands, rather long and bony, but strong. Sometimes, after he'd sat thinking for a long time, he'd get up and walk about the room, frowning and looking kind of angry, which was still more terrifying—sitting there while he walked up and down quite close to me, as though he were absolutely alone. But one time he suddenly stopped his walking up and down and said how profusely he apologized for his toes, because I was darning, and it was really very wonderful to see him suddenly changed back from that picture-angel sort of creature into a human being. Then he sat down by me and said he'd been spending the morning wrestling with the problem of speaking the truth in books; so I said, but haven't you always spoken it? because that always seemed to me the chief point of M.'s books. But he said, not much, because most of it was quite unspeakable in our world, as we found it too shocking and humiliating. So I said, all the same I didn't see why it shouldn't be spoken, and he said, nor did he in theory, but in practice he didn't want to be lynched. And he said, look for example at those advertisements in American magazines with the photos and life stories of people with unpleasant breath. So I said, yes, aren't they simply *too* awful. Because they really do make one shudder. And he said, precisely, there you are, and they're so successful because every one thinks them so perfectly awful. They're outraged by them, he said, just as you're outraged and they rush off and buy the stuff in sheer terror, because they're so terrified of being an outrage physically to other people. And he said, that's only one small sample of all the class of truths, pleasant and unpleasant, that you can't speak, except in scientific books, but that doesn't count, because you deliberately leave your feelings outside in the cloak-room when you're being scientific. And just because they're unspeakable, we pretend they're unimportant, but they aren't, on the contrary, they're terribly important and he said, you've only got to examine your memory quite sincerely for five minutes to realize it, and of course he's quite right. When I think of Miss Poole giving me piano lessons—but no, really, one *can't* write these things, and yet one obviously ought to, because they *are* so important, the humiliating physical facts, both pleasant and unpleasant (though I must say, most of the ones I can think of seem to be unpleasant), so important in all human relationships, he says, even in love, which is really rather awful, but of course one must admit it. And M. said it would take a whole generation of being shocked and humiliated and lynching the shockers and humiliaters before people could settle down to listening to that sort of truth calmly, which they did do, he says, at certain times in the past, at any rate much more so than now. And he says that when they can listen to it completely calmly, the world will be quite different from what it is now, so I asked, in what way? but he said he couldn't clearly imagine, only he knew it would be different. After that he went back to his table and wrote very quickly for about half an hour without stopping, and I longed to ask him if he'd been writing the truth and if so, what about, but I didn't have the nerve, which was stupid.

We lunched at our usual place, which I really don't much like, as who wants to look at fat business-men and farmers from the country simply *drinking* spaghetti? even if the spaghetti *is* good, but M. prefers it to the big places, because he says that in Rome one must do as the Romans do, not as the Americans. Still, I must say I do like looking at people who dress well and have good manners and nice jewels and things, which I told him, so he said all right, we'd go to Valadier to-morrow to see how the rich ate macaroni, which made me wretched, as it looked as though I'd been cadging, and of course that's the last thing in the world I meant to do, to make him waste a lot of money on me, particularly after what he told me yesterday about his debts and what he made on the average, which still seems to me shockingly little, considering who he is, so I said no, wouldn't he lunch with *me* at Valadier's and he laughed and said it was the first time he'd heard of a gigolo of fifty being taken out by a woman of twenty. That rather upset me—the way it seemed to bring what we are to each other on to the wrong level, making it all sort of joke and sniggery, like something in *Punch*. Which is hateful, I can't bear it. And I have the feeling that he does it on purpose, as a kind of protection, because he doesn't want to care too much, and that's why he's always saying he's so old, which is all nonsense, because you're only as old as you feel, and sometimes I even feel older than he does, like when he gets so amused and interested with little boys in the street playing that game of sticking out your fingers and calling a number, or when he talks about that awful old Dickens. Which I told him, but he only laughed and said age is a circle and you grow into a lot of the things you grew out of, because the whole world is a fried whiting with its tail in its mouth, which only confirms what I said about his saying he was old being all nonsense. Which I told him and he said, quite right, he only *said* he felt old when he *wished* that he felt old. Which made me see still more clearly that it was just a defence. A defence of *me*, I suppose, and all that sort of nonsense. What I'd have liked to say, only I didn't, was that I don't want to be defended, particularly if being defended means his defending himself against me and making stupid jokes about gigolos and old gentlemen. Because I think he really does rather care underneath—from the way he looks at me sometimes—and he'd like to say so and act so, but he won't on principle, which is really against all *his* principles and some time I *shall* tell him so. I insisted he should lunch with me and in the end he said he would, and then he was suddenly very silent and, I thought, glum and unhappy, and after coffee he said he'd have to go home and write all the rest of the day. So I came back to the hotel and had a rest and wrote this and now it's nearly seven and I feel terribly sad, almost like crying. *Next day.* Rang up Guy and had less difficulty than I expected getting him to forgive me for yesterday, in fact he almost apologized himself. Danced till 2.15.

June 15th. M. still sad and didn't kiss me when we met, *on purpose,* which made me angry, it's so humiliating to be defended. He was wearing an open shirt, like Byron, which suited him; but I told him, you look like the devil when you're sad (which is true, because his face ought to move, not be still) and he said that was what came of feeling and behaving like an angel; so of course I asked why he didn't behave like a devil, because in that case he'd look like an angel, and I preferred his looks to his morals, and then I blushed, like an idiot. But really it is too stupid that women aren't supposed to say what they think. Why can't we say, I like you, or whatever it is, without being thought a kind of monster, if we say it first, and even thinking ourselves monsters? Because one ought to say what one thinks and do what one likes, or else one becomes like Aunt Edith, hippo-ish and dead inside. Which is after all what M.'s constantly saying in his books, so he oughtn't to humiliate me with his beastly defendings. Lunch at Valadier's was really rather a bore. Afterwards we went and sat in a church, because it was so hot, a huge affair full of pink marble and frescoes and marble babies and gold. M. says that the modern equivalent is Lyons' Corner House and that the Jesuits were so successful because they gave the poor a chance of feeling what it was like to live in a palace, or something better than a palace, because he says the chief difference between a Corner House and the State rooms at Buckingham Palace is that the Corner House is so much more sumptuous, almost as sumptuous as these Jesuit churches. I asked him if he believed in God and he said he believed in a great many gods, it depended on what he was doing, or being, or feeling at the moment. He said he believed in Apollo when he was working and in Bacchus when he was drinking, and in Buddha when he felt depressed, and in Venus when he was making love, and in the Devil when he was afraid or angry, and in the Categorical Imperative, when he had to do his duty. I asked him which he believed in now and he said he didn't quite know, but he thought it was the Categorical Imperative, which really made me furious, so I answered that I only believed in the Devil and Venus, which made him laugh and he said I looked as though I were going to jump off the Eiffel Tower, and I was just going to say what I thought of his hippo-ishness. I mean I'd really made up my mind, when a most horrible old verger rushed up and said we must leave the church, because it seems the Pope doesn't allow you to

be in a church with bare arms, which is really *too* indecent.
But M. said that after all it wasn't surprising, because every
god has to protect himself against hostile gods and the gods
of bare skin *are* hostile to the gods of souls and clothes, and
he made me stop in front of a shop window where there
were some mirrors and said, you can see for yourself, and I
must say I really did look very nice in that pale green linen
which goes so awfully well with the skin, when one's a bit
sunburnt. But he said, it's not merely a question of seeing,
you must touch too, so I stroked my arms and said yes, they
were nice and smooth, and he said, precisely, and then he
stroked my arm very lightly, like a moth crawling, agoniz-
ingly creepy but delicious, once or twice, looking very seri-
ous and attentive, as though he were tuning a piano, which
made me laugh, and I said I supposed he was experimenting
to see if the Pope was in the right, and then he gave me the
most horrible pinch and said, yes, the Pope was quite right
and I ought to be muffled in Jaeger from top to toe. But I
was so angry with the pain, because he pinched me really
terribly, that I just rushed off without saying anything and
jumped into a cab that was passing and drove straight to the
hotel. But I was so wretched by the time I got there that I
started crying in the lift and the lift man said he hoped I
hadn't had any *dispiacere di famiglia*, which made me laugh
and that made the crying much worse, and then I suddenly
thought of Clare and felt such a horrible beast, so I lay on
my bed and simply howled for about an hour, and then I got
up and wrote a letter and sent one of the hotel boys with it
to M.'s address, saying I was so sorry and would he come at
once. But he didn't come, not for hours and hours, and it

---

* Family sorrow.

was simply too awful, because I thought he was offended, or despising, because I'd been such a fool, and I wondered whether he really did like me at all and whether this defending theory wasn't just my imagination. But at last, when I'd quite given him up and was so miserable I didn't know what I should do, he suddenly appeared—because he'd only that moment gone back to the house and found my note—and was too wonderfully sweet to me, and said he was so sorry, but he'd been on edge (though he didn't say why, but I know now that the defending theory wasn't just imagination) and I said I was so sorry and I cried, but I was happy, and then we laughed because it had all been so stupid and then M. quoted a bit of Homer which meant that after they'd eaten and drunk they wept for their friends and after they'd wept a little they went to sleep, so we went out and had dinner and after dinner we went and danced, and he dances really very well, but we stopped before midnight, because he said the noise of the jazz would drive him crazy. He was perfectly sweet, but though he didn't say anything sniggery, I could feel he was on the defensive all the time, sweetly and friendlily on the defensive, and when he said good-night he only kissed my hand.

JUNE 18TH. STAYED IN BED TILL LUNCH RE-READING *The Return of Eurydice*. I understand Joan so well now, better and better, she's so like me in all she feels and thinks. M. went to Tivoli for the day to see some Italian friends who have a house there. What is he like with other people, I wonder? Got two tickets for the fireworks to-morrow night, the hotel porter says they'll be good, because it's the first Girandola since the War. Went to the Villa Borghese in the afternoon for my education, to give M. a surprise when he comes back, and I must say some of the pictures and statues were very lovely, but the most awful looking fat man would follow me round all the time and finally the old beast even had the impertinence to speak to me, so I just said, *Lei è un porco*, which I must say was very effective. But it's extraordinary how things do just depend on looks and being sympathique, because if he hadn't looked such a pig, I shouldn't have thought him so piggish, which shows again what rot hippo-ism is. Went to bed early and finished *Eurydice*. This is the fifth time I've read it.

---

* You are a big pig.

VII

"OH, IT WAS MARVELLOUS BEFORE THE WAR, THE Girandola. Really marvelous."

"But then what wasn't *marvellous* before the War?" said Pamela sarcastically. These references to a Golden Age in which she had no part always annoyed her.

Fanning laughed. "Another one in the eye for the aged gentleman!"

There, he had slipped back again behind his defences! She did not answer for fear of giving him some excuse to dig himself in, impregnably. This hateful bantering with feelings! They walked on in silence. The night was breathlessly warm; the sounds of brassy music came to them faintly through the dim enormous noise of a crowd that thickened with every step they took towards the Piazza del Popolo. In the end they had to shove their way by main force.

Sunk head over ears in this vast sea of animal contacts, animal smells and noise, Pamela was afraid. "Isn't it awful?" she said, looking up at him over her shoulder; and she shuddered. But at the same time she rather liked her fear, because it seemed in some way to break down the barriers that separated them, to bring him closer to her—close with a physical closeness of protective contact that was also, increasingly, a closeness of thought and feeling.

"You're all right," he reassured her through the tumult. He was standing behind her, encircling her with his arms. "I won't let you be squashed"; and as he spoke he fended off the menacing lurch of a large back. *"Ignorante!"* he shouted at it.

A terrific explosion interrupted the distant selections from *Rigoletto* and the sky was suddenly full of coloured light; the Girandola had begun. A wave of impatience ran through the advancing crowd; they were violently pushed and jostled. But, "It's all right," Fanning kept repeating, "it's all right." They were squeezed together in a staggering embrace. Pamela was terrified, but it was with a kind of swooning pleasure that she shut her eyes and abandoned herself limply in his arms.

"Ma piano!" shouted Fanning at the nearest jostlers. *"Piano!"* and " 'Sblood!" he said in English, for he had the affection of using literary oaths. "Hell and Death!" But in the tumult his words were as though unspoken. He was silent; and suddenly, in the midst of that heaving chaos of noise and rough contacts, of movement and heat and smell, suddenly he became aware that his lips were almost touching her hair, and that under his right hand was the firm resilience of her breast. He hesitated for a moment on the threshold of his sensuality, then averted his face, shifted the position of his hand.

"At last!"

The haven to which their tickets admitted them was a little garden on the western side of the Piazza, opposite the Pincio and the source of the fireworks. The place was crowded, but not oppressively. Fanning was tall enough to overlook the interposed heads, and when Pamela had climbed on to a little parapet that separated one terrace of the garden from another, she too could see perfectly.

"But you'll let me lean on you," she said, laying a hand on his shoulder, "because there's a fat woman next to me who's steadily squeezing me off. I think she's expanding with the heat."

"And she almost certainly understands English. So for heaven's sake . . ."

A fresh volley of explosions from the other side of the great square interrupted him and drowned the answering mockery of her laughter. "Ooh! Ooh!" the crowd was moaning in a kind of amorous agony. Magical flowers in a delirium of growth, the rockets mounted on their slender stalks and, ah! high up above the Pincian Hill, dazzlingly, deafeningly, in a bunch of stars and a thunder-clap, they blossomed.

"Isn't it marvellous?" said Pamela looking down at him with shining eyes. "Oh God!" she added, in another voice. "She's expanding again. Help!" And for a moment she was on the verge of falling. She leaned on him so heavily that he had to make an effort not to be pushed sideways. She managed to straighten herself up again into equilibrium.

"I've got you in case . . ." He put his arm round her knees to steady her.

"Shall I see if I can puncture the old beast with a pin?" And Fanning knew, by the tone of her voice, that she was genuinely prepared to make the experiment.

"If you do," he said, "I shall leave you to be lynched alone."

Pamela felt his arm tighten a little about her thighs. "Coward!" she mocked and pulled his hair.

"Martyrdom's not in my line," he laughed back. "Not even martyrdom for your sake." But her youth was a perversity, her freshness a kind of provocative vice. He had taken a step across that supernatural threshold. He had given—after all, why not?—a certain license to his desires. Amid their multitudinous uncoiling, his body seemed to be coming to a new and obscure life of its own. When the time came he would revoke the license, step back again into the daily world.

There was another bang, another, and the obelisk at the centre of the Piazza leapt out sharp and black against apocalypse after apocalypse of jewelled light. And through the now flushed, now pearly-brilliant, now emerald-shining smoke-clouds, a pine tree, a palm, a stretch of grass emerged, like strange unearthly visions of pine and palm and grass, from the darkness of the else invisible gardens.

There was an interval of mere lamplight—like sobriety, said Fanning, between two pipes of opium, like daily life after an ecstasy. And perhaps, he was thinking, the time to step back again had already come. "If only one could live without any lucid intervals," he concluded.

"I don't see why not." She spoke with a kind of provocative defiance, as though challenging him to contradict her. Her heart beat very fast, exultantly. "I mean, why shouldn't it be fireworks all the time?"

"Because it just isn't, that's all. Unhappily." It was time to step back again; but he didn't step back.

"Well, then it's a case of damn the intervals and enjoy . . . Oh!" She started. That prodigious bang had sent a large red moon sailing almost slowly into the sky. It burst into a shower of meteors that whistled as they fell, expiringly.

Fanning imitated their plaintive noise. "Sad, sad," he commented. "Even the fireworks can be sad."

She turned on him fiercely. "Only because you want them to be sad. Yes, you want them to be. Why do you want them to be sad?"

Yes, why? It was a pertinent question. She felt his arm tighten again round her knees and was triumphant. He was defending himself no more, he was listening to those oracles. But at the root of his deliberate recklessness, its contradiction and its cause, his sadness obscurely persisted. "But I *don't* want them to be sad," he protested.

Another garden of rockets began to blossom. Laughing, triumphant, Pamela laid her hand on his head.

"I feel so superior up here," she said.

"On a pedestal, what?" He laughed. " '*Guardami ben; ben son, ben son Beatrice!*' *"

"Such a comfort you're not bald," she said, her fingers in his hair. "That must be a great disadvantage of pedestals—I mean, seeing the baldness of the men down below."

"But the great advantage of pedestals, as I now suddenly see for the first time . . ." Another explosion covered his voice. " . . . make it possible . . ." Bang!

"Oh, look!" A blueish light was brightening, brightening.

" . . . possible for even the baldest . . ." There was a continuous uninterrupted rattle of detonations. Fanning gave it up. What he had meant to say was that pedestals gave even the baldest men unrivalled opportunities for pinching the idol's legs.

---

* Look on me well; yes, I am, I am Beatrice.

"What were you saying?" she shouted through the battle.

"Nothing," he yelled back. He had meant, of course, to suit the action to the word, playfully. But the fates had decided otherwise and he wasn't really sorry. For he was tired; he had realized it almost suddenly. All this standing. He was no good at standing nowadays.

A cataract of silver fire was pouring down the slopes of the Pincian Hill, and the shining smokeclouds rolled away from it like the spray from a tumbling river. And suddenly, above it, the eagle of Savoy emerged from the darkness, enormous, perched on the lictor's axe and rods. There was applause and patriotic music. Then, gradually, the brightness of the cataract grew dim; the sources of its silver streaming were one by one dried up. The eagle moulted its shining plumage, the axe and rods faded, faded and at last were gone. Lit faintly by only the common lamplight, the smoke drifted slowly away towards the north. A spasm of motion ran through the huge crowd in the square below them. The show was over.

"But I feel," said Pamela, as they shoved their way back towards the open streets, "I feel as though the rockets were still popping off inside me." And she began to sing to herself as she walked.

Fanning made no comment. He was thinking of that Girandola he'd seen with Alice and Tony, and Laurina Frescobaldi—was it in 1907 or 1908? Tony was an ambassador now, and Alice was dead, and one of Laurina's sons (he recalled the expression of despair on that worn, but still handsome face, when she had told him yesterday, at Tivoli) was already old enough to be getting housemaids into trouble.

"Not only rockets," Pamela went on, interrupting her singing, "but even catherine wheels. I feel all catherine-wheely. You know, like when one's a little drunk." And she went on again with "Old Man River," tipsily happy and excited.

The crowd grew thinner around them and at last they were almost alone. Pamela's singing abruptly ceased. Here, in the open, in the cool of the dark night it had suddenly become inappropriate, a little shameful. She glanced anxiously at her companion; had he too remarked that inappropriateness, been shocked by it? But Fanning had noticed nothing; she wished he had. Head bent, his hands behind his back, he was walking at her side, but in another universe.— When had his spirit gone away from her, and why? She didn't know, hadn't noticed. Those inward fireworks, that private festival of exultation had occupied her whole attention. She had been too excitedly happy with being in love to be able to think of the object of that love. But now, abruptly sobered, she had become aware of him again, repentantly at first, and then, as she realized his new remoteness, with a sinking of the heart. What had happened in these few moments? She was on the point of addressing him, then checked herself. Her apprehension grew and grew till it became a kind of terrified certainty that he'd never loved her at all, that he'd suddenly begun to hate her. But why, but why? They walked on.

"How lovely it is here!" she said at last. Her voice was timid and unnatural. "And so deliciously cool." They had emerged on to the embankment of the Tiber. Above the river, a second invisible river of air flowed softly through the hot night. "Shall we stop for a moment?" He nodded without speaking. "I mean, only if you want to," she added. He nodded again.

They stood, leaning on the parapet, looking down at the

black water. There was a long, long silence. Pamela waited for him to say something, to make a gesture; but he did not stir, the word never came. It was as though he were at the other end of the world. She felt almost sick with unhappiness. Heartbeat after heart-beat, the silence prolonged itself.

Fanning was thinking of to-morrow's journey. How he hated the train! And in this heat. . . . But it was necessary. The wicked flee, and in this case the fleeing would be an act of virtue—painful. Was it love? Or just an itch of desire, of the rather crazy, dirty desire of an aging man? *"A cinquant' anni si diventa un po' pazzo."** He heard his own voice speaking, laughingly, mournfully, to Laurina. *"Pazzo e porco. Si, anch' io divento un porco. Le minorenni—a cinquant' anni, sa sono un ossessione. Proprio un' ossessione.†"* Was that all—just an obsession of crazy desire? Or was it love? Or wasn't there any difference, was it just a question of names and approving or disapproving tones of voice? What was certain was that you could be as desperately unhappy when you were robbed of your crazy desire as when you were robbed of your love. A *porco* suffers as much as Dante. And perhaps Beatrice too was lovely, in Dante's memory, with the perversity of youth, the shamelessness of innocence, the vice of freshness. Still, the wicked flee, the wicked flee. If only he'd had the strength of mind to flee before! A touch made him start. Pamela had taken his hand.

"Miles!" Her voice was strained and abnormal. Fanning turned towards her and was almost frightened by the look of determined despair he saw on her face. The Eiffel Tower . . . "Miles!"

---

* At fifty, you become a bit crazy.

† Crazy and piggish. I too have become a pig. Underage girls, at fifty, know they are an obsession. Just an obsession.

"What is it?"

"Why don't you speak to me?"

He shrugged his shoulders. "I didn't happen to be feeling very loquacious. For a change," he added, self-mockingly, in the hope (he knew it for a vain one) of being able to turn away her desperate attack with a counter-attack of laughter.

She ignored his counter-attack. "Why do you shut yourself away from me like this?" she asked. "Why do you hate me."

"But, my sweet child . . ."

"Yes, you hate me. You shut me away. Why are you so cruel, Miles?" Her voice broke; she was crying. Lifting his hand, she kissed it, passionately, despairingly. "I love you so much, Miles. I love you." His hand was wet with her tears when, almost by force, he managed to draw it away from her.

He put his arm round her, comfortingly. But he was annoyed as well as touched, annoyed by her despairing determination, by the way she had made up her mind to jump off the Eiffel Tower, screwed up her courage turn by turn. And now she was jumping—but how gracelessly! The way he had positively had to struggle for his hand! There was something forced and unnatural about the whole scene. She was being a character in fiction. But characters in fiction suffer. He patted her shoulder, he made consolatory murmurs. Consoling her for being in love with him! But the idea of explaining and protesting and being lucidly reasonable was appalling to him at the moment, absolutely appalling. He hoped that she'd just permit herself to be consoled and ask no further questions, just leave the whole situation comfortably inarticulate. But his hope was again disappointed.

"Why do you hate me, Miles?" she insisted.

"But, Pamela . . ."

"Because you did care a little, you did. I mean, I could see you cared. And now, suddenly . . . What have I done, Miles?"

"But nothing, my child, nothing." He could not keep a note of exasperation out of his voice. If only she'd allow him to be silent!

"Nothing? But I can hear from the way you speak that there's something." She returned to her old refrain. "Because you did care, Miles; a little, you did." She looked up at him, but he had moved away from her, he had averted his eyes towards the street. "You did, Miles."

Oh, God! he was groaning to himself, God! And aloud (for she had made his silence untenable, she had driven him out into articulateness), "I cared too much," he said. "It would be so easy to do something stupid and irreparable, something mad, yes and bad, bad. I like you too much in other ways to want to run that risk. Perhaps, if I were twenty years younger. . . . But I'm too old. It wouldn't do. And you're too young, you can't really understand, you . . . Oh, thank God, there's a taxi." And he darted forward, waving and shouting. Saved! But when they had shut themselves into the cab, he found that the new situation was even more perilous than the old.

"Miles!" A flash of lamplight through the window of the cab revealed her face to him. His words had consoled her; she was smiling, was trying to look happy; but under the attempted happiness her expression was more desperately determined than ever. She was not yet at the bottom of her Tower. "Miles!" And sliding across the seat towards him, she threw her arms round his neck and kissed him. "Take me, Miles," she said, speaking in quick abrupt little spurts, as though she were forcing the words out with violence against a resistance. He recognized the suicide's voice, despairing, strained, and at the same time flat, lifeless. "Take me. If you want me. . . ."

Fanning tried to protest, to disengage himself, gently, from her embrace.

"But I want you to take me, Miles," she insisted. "I want you. . . ." She kissed him again, she pressed herself against his hard body. "I want you, Miles. Even if it is stupid and mad," she added in another little spurt of desperation, making answer to the expression on his face, to the words she wouldn't permit him to utter. "And it isn't. I mean, love isn't stupid or mad. And even if it were, I don't care. Yes, I want to be stupid and mad. Even if it were to kill me. So take me, Miles." She kissed him again. "Take me."

He turned away his mouth from those soft lips. She was forcing him back across the threshold. His body was uneasy with awakenings and supernatural dawn.

Held up by a tram at the corner of a narrow street, the cab was at a standstill. With quick strong gestures Fanning unclasped her arms from round his neck and, taking her two hands in his, he kissed first one and then the other. "Goodbye, Pamela," he whispered and, throwing open the door, he was half out of the cab before she realized what he was doing.

"But what are you doing, Miles? Where . . ." The door slammed. He thrust some money into the driver's hand and almost ran. Pamela rose to her feet to follow him, but the cab started with a sudden jerk that threw her off her balance, and she fell back on to the seat.

"Miles!" she called, and then, "Stop!"

But the driver either didn't hear, or else paid no attention. She did not call again, but sat, covering her face with her hands, crying and feeling so agonizingly unhappy that she thought she would die of it.

scandal of shining beauty and attractiveness, and then fi-
nally as a kind of maddeningly alluring perversity, as the ex-
hibition of a kind of irresistibly dangerous vice. The madness
of the desirer—for middle-aged desires are mostly more or
less mad desires—comes off on the desired object, stain-
ing it, degrading it. Which isn't agreeable if you happen
to be fond of the object, as well as desiring. Dear object,
let's be a little reasonable—oh, entirely against all my prin-
ciples; I accept all the reproaches you made me the other
day. But what are principles for but to be gone against in
moments of crisis? And this *is* a moment of crisis. Consider:
I'm thirty years older than you are; and even if one doesn't
look one's age, one is one's age, somehow, somewhere; and
even if one doesn't feel it, fifty's always fifty and twenty-
one's twenty-one. And when you've considered that, let me
put a few questions. First: are you prepared to be a disrepu-
table woman? To which, of course, you answer yes, because
you don't care two pins about what the old cats say. But I
put another question: Do you know, by experience, what it's
like to be a disreputable woman? And you must answer, no.
Whereupon I retort: If you can't answer yes to the second,
you've got no right to answer yes to the first. And I don't
intend to give you the opportunity of answering yes to the
second question. Which is all pure Podsnapism. But there
are certain circumstances in which Podsnap is quite right.

"Sweet Pamela, believe me when I say it would be fatal. For
when you say you love me, what do you mean? Who and what
is it you love? I'll tell you. You love the author of *Eurydice* and
of all those portraits of yourself he's filled his books with. You
love the celebrated man, who was not only unsnubbing and
attentive, but obviously admiring. Even before you saw him,

you vaguely loved his reputation, and now you love his odd
confidences. You love a kind of conversation you haven't heard
before. You love a weakness in him which you think you can
dominate and protect. You love—as I, of course, intended you
to love—a certain fascinating manner. You even love a rather
romantic and still youthful appearance. And when I say (which
as yet, you know, I haven't said) that I love you, what do *I* mean?
That I'm amused, and charmed, and flattered, and touched,
and puzzled, and affectionate, in a word, a Passionist Father.
But chiefly that I find you terribly desirable—an army with
banners. Bring these two loves together and what's the result?
A manifold disaster. To begin with, the nearer you come to me
and the longer you remain with me, the more alien you'll find
me, the more fundamentally remote. Inevitably. For you and
I are foreigners to one another, foreigners in time. Which is a
greater foreigners than the foreigners of space and language.
You don't realize it now, because you don't know me—you're
only in love, at first sight (like Joan in *Eurydice!*) and, what's
more, not really with me, with your imagination of me. When
you come to know me better—well, you'll find that you know
me much worse. And then one day you'll be attracted by a
temporal compatriot. Perhaps, indeed, you're attracted already,
only your imagination won't allow you to admit it. What about
that long-suffering Guy of yours? Of whom I was, and am, so
horribly jealous—jealous with the malignity of a weaker for
a stronger rival; for though I seem to hold all the cards at the
moment, the ace of trumps is his: he's young. And one day,
when you're tired of living at cross-purposes with me, you'll
suddenly realize it; you'll perceive that he speaks your lan-
guage, that he inhabits your world of thought and feeling, that
he belongs, in a word, to your nation—that great and terrible

nation, which I love and fear and hate, the nation of Youth. In the end, of course, you'll leave the foreigner for the compatriot. But not before you've inflicted a good deal of suffering on every one concerned, including yourself. And meanwhile, what about me? Shall I be still there for you to leave? Who knows? Not I, at any rate. I can no more answer for my future desires than for the Shah of Persia. For my future affection, yes. But it may last (how often, alas, affections do last that way!) only on condition of its object being absent. There are so many friends whom one's fond of when they're not there. Will you be one of them? It's the more possible since, after all, you're just as alien to me as I am to you. My country's called Middle-Ageia and every one who was out of the egg of childhood before 1914 is my compatriot. Through all my desires, shouldn't I also pine to hear my own language, to speak with those who share the national traditions? Of course. But the tragedy of middle-aged life is that its army with banners is hardly ever captained by a compatriot. Passion is divorced from understanding, and the aging man's desire attaches itself with an almost insane violence to precisely those outrageously fresh young bodies that house the most alien souls. Conversely, for the body of an understood and understanding soul, he seldom feels desire. And now, Pamela, suppose that my sentiment of your alienness should come to be stronger (as some time it must) than my desire for the lovely scandal of your young body. What then? This time I can answer; for I am answering for a self that changes very little through every change of circumstances—the self that doesn't intend to put up with more discomfort than it can possibly avoid; the self that, as the Freudians tells us, is homesick for that earthly paradise from which we've all been banished, our mother's womb, the only place on earth where man is genuinely omnipotent, where his every desire is satisfied, where he is perfectly at home and adapted to his surroundings, and therefore perfectly happy. Out of the womb, we're in an unfriendly world, in which our wishes aren't anticipated, where we're no longer magically omnipotent, where we don't fit, where we're not snugly at home. What's to be done in this world? Either face out the reality, fight with it, resignedly or heroically accept to suffer or struggle. Or else flee. In practice even the strongest heroes do a bit of fleeing—away from responsibility into deliberate ignorance, away from uncomfortable fact into imagination. Even the strongest. And conversely even the weakest fleers can make themselves strong. No, not the weakest; that's a mistake. The weakest become day-dreamers, masturbators, paranoiacs. The strong fleer is one who starts with considerable advantages. Take my case. I'm so endowed by nature that I can have a great many of the prizes of life for the asking—success, money in reasonable quantities, love. In other words I'm not entirely out of the womb; I can still, even in the extra-uterine world, have at least some of my desires magically satisfied. To have my wishes fulfilled I don't have to rush off every time to some imaginary womb-substitute. I have the power to construct a womb for myself out of the materials of the real world. But of course it's not a completely perfect and water-tight womb; no post-natal uterus can ever in the nature of things be that. It lets in a lot of unpleasantness and alienness and obstruction to wishes. Which I deal with by flight, systematic flight into unawareness, into deliberate ignorance, into irresponsibility. It's a weakness which is a source of strength. For when you can flee at will and with success (which is only possible if nature has granted you, as she has to me, the possibility of anarchic independence of society), what quantities of energy you save, what an enormous amount of emotional and mental wear and tear is spared you! I flee from business by leaving all my affairs in the hands of lawyers and agents. I flee from criticism (both from the humiliations of misplaced and wrongly motived praise and from the pain of even the most contemptible vermin's blame) by simply not reading what anybody writes of me. I flee from time by living as far as possible only in and for the present. I flee from cold weather by taking the train or ship to places where it's warm. And from women I don't love any more, I flee by just silently vanishing. For, like Palmerston, I never explain and never apologize. I just fade out. I decline to admit their existence. I consign their letters to the waste-paper basket, along with the press cuttings. Simple, crude even, but incredibly effective, if one's ready to be ruthless in one's weakness, as I am. Yes, quite ruthless, Pamela. If my desire grew weary or I felt homesick for the company of my compatriots, I'd just run away, determinedly, however painfully much you might still be in love with me, or your imagination, or your own hurt pride and humiliated selflove. And you, I fancy, would have as little mercy on my desires if they should happen to outlive what you imagine to be your passion for me. So that our love affair, if we were fools enough to embark on it, would be a race towards a series of successive goals—a race through boredom, misunderstanding, disillusion, towards the final winning-post of cruelty and betrayal. Which of us is likely to win the race? The betting, I should say, is about even, with a slight tendency in favour of myself. But there's not going to be a winner or a loser, for the good reason that there's not going to be any race. I'm too fond of you, Pamela, to . . ."

"Miles!"

Fanning started so violently that a drop of ink was jerked

from his pen on to the paper. He felt as though his heart had fallen into an awful gulf of emptiness.

"Miles!"

He looked round. Two hands were clutching the bars of the unshuttered window and, as though desperately essaying to emerge from a subterranean captivity, the upper part of a face was peering in, over the high sill, with wide unhappy eyes.

"But Pamela!" There was reproach in his astonishment.

It was to the implied rebuke that she penitently answered. "I couldn't help it, Miles," she said; and, behind the bars, he saw her reddened eyes suddenly brighten and overflow with tears. "I simply had to come." Her voice trembled on the verge of breaking. "*Had* to."

The tears, her words and that unhappy voice were moving. But he didn't want to be moved, he was angry with himself for feeling the emotion, with her for inspiring it. "But, my dear child!" he began, and the reproach in his voice had shrilled to a kind of exasperation—the exasperation of one who feels himself hemmed in and helpless, increasingly helpless, against circumstances. "But I thought we'd settled," he began and broke off. He rose, and walked agitatedly towards the fireplace, agitatedly back again, like a beast in a cage; he was caught, hemmed in between those tearful eyes behind the bars and his own pity, with all those dangerous feelings that have their root in pity. "I thought," he began once more.

But, "Oh!" came her sharp cry, and looking again towards the windows he saw that only the two small hands and a pair of straining wrists were visible. The tragical face had vanished.

"Pamela?"

"It's all right." Her voice came rather muffled and remote.

"I slipped. I was standing on a little kind of ledge affair. The window's so high from the ground," she added plaintively.

"My poor child!" he said on a little laugh of amused commiseration. The reproach, the exasperation had gone out of his voice. He was conquered by the comic patheticness of her. Hanging on to the bars with those small, those rather red and childishly untended hands! And tumbling off the perch she had had to climb on, because the window was so high from the ground! A wave of sentimentality submerged him. "I'll come and open the door." He ran into the hall.

Waiting outside in the darkness, she heard the bolts being shot back, one by one . . . Clank, clank! and then "Damn!" came his voice from the other side of the door. "These things are so stiff. . . . I'm barricaded up as though I were in a safe." She stood there waiting. The door shook as he tugged at the recalcitrant bolt. The waiting seemed interminable. And all at once a huge, black weariness settled on her. The energy of wrought-up despair deserted her and she was left empty of everything but a tired misery. What was the good, what was the good of coming like this to be turned away again? For he *would* turn her away; he didn't want her. What was the good of renewing suffering, of once more dying?

"Hell and Death!" On the other side of the door, Fanning was cursing like an Elizabethan.

Hell and Death. The words reverberated in Pamela's mind. The pains of Hell—the darkness and dissolution of Death. What was the good.

Clank! Another bolt had gone back. "Thank goodness. We're almost . . ." A chain rattled. At the sound, Pamela turned and ran in a blind terror down the dimly-lighted street.

"At last!" The door swung back and Fanning stepped out. But the sentimental tenderness of his outstretched hands wasted itself on empty night. Twenty yards away a pair of pale legs twinkled in the darkness. "Pamela!" he called in astonishment. "What the devil . . . ?" The wasting on emptiness of his feelings had startled him into annoyance. He felt like one who has put forth all his strength to strike something and, missing his aim, swipes the unresisting air, grotesquely. "Pamela!" he called again, yet louder.

She did not turn at the sound of his voice, but ran on. These wretched high-heeled shoes! "Pamela!" And then came the sound of his pursuing footsteps. She tried to run faster. But the pursuing footsteps came nearer and nearer. It was no good. Nothing was any good. She slackened her speed to a walk.

"But what on earth?" he asked from just behind her, almost angrily. Pursuing, he called up within him the soul of a pursuer, angry and desirous. "What on earth?" And suddenly his hand was on her shoulder. She trembled a little at the touch. "But why?" he insisted. "Why do you suddenly run away?"

But Pamela only shook her averted head. She wouldn't speak, wouldn't meet his eyes. Fanning looked down at her intently, questioningly. Why? And as he looked at that weary hopeless face, he began to divine the reason. The anger of the pursuit subsided in him. Respecting her dumb, averted misery, he too was silent. He drew her comfortingly towards him. His arm round her shoulders, Pamela suffered herself to be led back towards the house.

Which would be best, he was wondering with the surface of his mind: to telephone for a taxi to take her back to the hotel, or to see if he could make up a bed for her in one of the upstairs rooms? But in the depths of his being he knew quite well that he would do neither of these things. He knew that he would be her lover. And yet, in spite of this deep knowledge, the surface mind still continued to discuss its little problem of cabs and bed-linen. Discussed it sensibly, discussed it dutifully. Because it would be a madness, he told himself, a criminal madness if he didn't send for the taxi or prepare that upstairs room. But the dark certainty of the depths rose suddenly and exploded at the surface in a bubble of ironic laughter, in a brutal and cynical word. "Comedian!" he said to himself, to the self that agitatedly thought of telephones and taxis and pillow-slips. "Seeing that it's obvious I'm going to have her." And, rising from the depths, her nakedness presented itself to him palpably in an integral and immediate contact with his whole being. But this was shameful, shameful. He pushed the naked Anadyomene back into the depths. Very well, then (his surface mind resumed its busy efficient rattle), seeing that it was perhaps rather late to start telephoning for taxis, he'd rig up one of the rooms on the first floor. But if he couldn't find any sheets . . . ? But here was the house, the open door.

Pamela stepped across the threshold. The hall was almost dark. Through a curtained doorway on the left issued a thin blade of yellow light. Passive in her tired misery, she waited. Behind her the chain rattled, as it had rattled only a few moments before, when she had fled from the ominous sound, and clank, clank! the bolts were thrust back into place.

"There," said Fanning's voice. "And now . . ." With a click, the darkness yielded suddenly to brilliant light.

Pamela uttered a little cry and covered her face with her

hands. "Oh, please," she begged, "please." The light hurt her, was a sort of outrage. She didn't want to see, couldn't bear to be seen.

"I'm sorry," he said, and the comforting darkness returned. "This way." Taking her arm he led her towards the lighted doorway on the left. "Shut your eyes," he commanded, as they approached the curtain. "We've got to go into the light again; but I'll turn it out the moment I can get to the switch. Now!" She shut her eyes and suddenly, as the curtain rings rattled she saw, through her closed eyelids, the red shining of transparent blood. Still holding her arm, he led her forward into the room.

Pamela lifted her free hand to her face. "Please don't look at me," she whispered. "I don't want you to see me like this. I mean, I couldn't bear . . ." Her voice faded to silence.

"I won't look," he assured her. "And anyhow," he added, when they had taken two or three more steps across the room, "now I can't." And he turned the switch.

The pale translucent red went black again before her eyes. Pamela sighed. "I'm so tired," she whispered. Her eyes were still shut; she was too tired to open them.

"Take off your coat." A hand pulled at her sleeve. First one bare arm, then the other slipped out into the coolness.

Fanning threw the coat over a chair. Turning back, he could see her, by the tempered darkness that entered through the window, standing motionless before him, passive, wearily waiting, her face, her limp arms pale against the shadowy blackness.

"Poor Pamela," she heard him say, and then suddenly light finger-tips were sliding in a moth-winged caress along her arm. "You'd better lie down and rest." The hand closed round her arm, she was pushed gently forward. That taxi, he was still thinking, the upstairs room . . . But his fingers preserved the silky memory of her skin, the flesh of her arm was warm and firm against his palm. In the darkness, the supernatural world was coming mysteriously, thrillingly into existence; he was once more standing upon its threshold.

"There, sit down," came his voice. She obeyed; a low divan received her. "Lean back." She let herself fall on to pillows. Her feet were lifted on to the couch. She lay quite still. "As though I were dead," she thought, "as though I were dead." She was aware, through the darkness of her closed eyes, of his warm breathing presence, impending and very near. "As though I were dead," she inwardly repeated with a kind of pleasure. For the pain of her misery had ebbed away into the warm darkness and to be tired, she found, to be utterly tired and to lie there utterly still were pleasures. "As though I were dead." And the light reiterated touch of his finger-tips along her arm—what were those caresses but another mode, a soothing and delicious mode, of gently dying?

In the morning, on his way to the kitchen to prepare their coffee, Fanning caught sight of his littered writing-table. He halted to collect the scattered sheets. Waiting for the water to boil, he read, "By the time you receive this letter, I shall be, no, not dead, Pamela . . ." He crumpled up each page as he had finished reading it and threw it into the dust-bin.

IX

THE ARCHITECTURAL BACKGROUND WAS LIKE something out of Alma Tadema. But the figures that moved across the sunlit atrium, that lingered beneath the colonnades and in the coloured shadow of the awnings, the figures were Hogarthian and Rowlandsonian, were the ferocious satires of Daumier and Rouveyre. Huge jellied females overflowed the chairs on which they sat. Sagging and with the gait of gorged bears, old men went slowly shambling down the porticoes. Like princes preceded by their outriders, the rich fat burgesses strutted with dignity behind their bellies. There was a hungry prowling of gaunt emaciated men and women, yellow-skinned and with tragical, blue-injected eyes. And, conspicuous by their trailing blackness, these bloated or cadaverous pencillings from an anti-clerical notebook were priests.

In the midst of so many monsters Pamela was a lovely miracle of health and beauty. These three months had subtly transformed her. The rather wavering and intermittent *savoirvivre*,[*] the child's forced easiness of manner, had given place to a woman's certainty, to that repose even in action,

---

[*] Etiquette, good manners.

that decision even in repose, which are the ordinary fruits of the intimate knowledge, the physical understanding of love.

"For it isn't only murder that will out," as Fanning had remarked some few days after the evening of the fireworks. "It isn't only murder. If you could see yourself, my child! It's almost indecent. Any one could tell that you'd been in bed with your lover. Could tell in the dark even; you're luminous, positively luminous. All shining and smooth and pearly with love-making. It's really an embarrassment to walk about with you. I've a good mind to make you wear a veil."

She had laughed, delightedly. "But I don't mind them seeing. I *want* them to see. I mean, why should one be ashamed of being happy?"

That had been three months since. At present she had no happiness to be ashamed of. It was by no shining of eyes, no luminous soft pearliness of smoothed and rounded contour that she now betrayed herself. All that her manner, her pose, her gestures proclaimed was the fact that there *had* been such shinings and pearly smoothings, once. As for the present, her shut and sullen face announced only that she was discontented with it and with the man who, sitting beside her, was the symbol and the embodiment of that unsatisfactory present. A rather sickly embodiment at the moment, a thin and jaundiced symbol. For Fanning was hollow-cheeked, his eyes darkly ringed, his skin pale and sallow under the yellow tan. He was on his way to becoming one of those pump-room monsters at whom they were now looking, almost incredulously. For, "Incredible!" was Fanning's comment. "Didn't I tell you that they simply weren't to be believed?"

Pamela shrugged her shoulders, almost imperceptibly, and did not answer. She did not feel like answering, she wanted to be uninterested, sullen, bored.

"How right old Butler was!" he went on, rousing himself by the stimulus of his own talk from the depression into which his liver and Pamela had plunged him. "Making the Erewhonians punish illness as a crime—how right! Because they *are* criminals, all these people. Criminally ugly and deformed, criminally incapable of enjoyment. Look at them. It's a caution. And when I think that I'm one of them . . ." He shook his head. "But let's hope this will make me a reformed character." And he emptied, with a grimace of disgust, his glass of tepid salt water. "Revolting! But I suppose it's right that Montecatini should be a place of punishment as well as cure. One can't be allowed to commit jaundice with impunity. I must go and get another glass of my punishment—my purgatory, in every sense of the word," he added, smiling at his own joke. He rose to his feet painfully (every movement was now a painful effort for him) and left her, threading his way through the crowd to where, behind their marble counters, the pump-room barmaids dispensed warm laxatives from rows of polished brass taps.

The animation had died out of Fanning's face, as he turned away. No longer distracted and self-stimulated by talk, he relapsed at once into melancholy. Waiting his turn behind two bulging monsignori at the pump, he looked so gloomily wretched, that a passing connoisseur of the waters pointed him out to his companion as a typical example of the hepatic pessimist. But bile, as a matter of fact, was not the only cause of Fanning's depression. There was also Pamela. And Pamela—he admitted it, though the fact belonged to that great class of humiliating phenomena, whose existence we are always trying to ignore—Pamela, after all, was the cause of the bile. For if he had not been so extenuated by that crazy love-making in the narrow cells of the Passionist Fathers at Monte Cavo, he would never have taken chill and the chill would never have settled on his liver and turned to jaundice. As it was, however, that night of the full moon had finished him. They had gone out, groping their way through the terrors of the nocturnal woods, to a little grassy terrace among the bushes, from which there was a view of Nemi. Deep sunk in its socket of impenetrable darkness and more than half eclipsed by shadow, the eye of water gleamed up at them secretly, as though through eyelids almost closed. Under the brightness of the moon the hills, the woods seemed to be struggling out of ghostly greyness towards colour, towards the warmth of life. They had sat there for a while, in silence, looking. Then, taking her in his arms, " *'Ceda al tatto la vista, al labbro il lume',*' " he had quoted with a kind of mockery—mocking her for the surrender to which he knew he could bring her, even against her will, even though, as he could see, she had made up her mind to sulk at him, mocking himself at the same time for the folly which drove him, weary and undesiring, to make the gesture. " *'Al labbro il lume†,*' " he repeated with that undercurrent of derision in his voice, and leaned towards her. Desire returned to him as he touched her and with it a kind of exultation, a renewal (temporary, he knew, and illusory) of all his energies.

"No, Miles. Don't. I don't want . . ." And she had averted her face, for she was angry, resentful, she wanted to sulk.

---

* Surrenders the sight to the touch, to the lip the light.

† To the lip the light.

Fanning knew it, mockingly, and mockingly he had turned back her face towards him—" *'al labbro il lume** "—and had found her lips. She struggled a little in his arms, protested, and then was silent, lay still. His kisses had had the power to transform her. She was another person, different from the one who had sulked and been resentful. Or rather she was two people—the sulky and resentful one, with another person superimposed, a person who quiveringly sank and melted under his kisses, melted and sank down, down towards that mystical death, that apocalypse, that almost terrible transfiguration. But beneath, to one side, stood always the angry sulker, unappeased, unreconciled, ready to emerge again (full of a new resentment for the way she had been undignifiedly hustled off the stage), the moment the other should have retired. His realization of this made Fanning all the more perversely ardent, quickened the folly of his passion with a kind of derisive hostility. He drew his lips across her cheek and suddenly their soft electrical touch on her ear made her shudder. "Don't!" she implored, dreading and yet desiring what was to come. Gently, inexorably his teeth closed and the petal of cartilage was a firm elastic resistance between them. She shuddered yet more violently. Fanning relaxed the muscles of his jaws, then tightened them once more, gently, against that exquisite resistance. The felt beauty of rounded warmth and resilience was under his hand. In the darkness they were inhabitants of the supernatural world.

But at midnight they had found themselves, almost suddenly, on earth again, shiveringly cold under the moon. Cold, cold to the quick, Fanning had picked himself up. They stumbled homewards through the woods, in silence. It

---

* To the lip the light.

was in a kind of trance of chilled and sickened exhaustion that he had at last dropped down on his bed in the convent cell. Next morning he was ill. The liver was always his weak point. That had been nearly three weeks ago.

The second of the two monsignori moved away; Fanning stepped into his place. The barmaid handed him his hot dilute sulphate of soda. He deposited fifty centesimi as a largesse and walked off, meditatively sipping. But returning to the place from which he had come, he found their chairs occupied by a pair of obese Milanese business-men. Pamela had gone. He explored the Alma Tadema background; but there was no sign of her. She had evidently gone back to the hotel. Fanning, who still had five more glasses of water to get through, took his place among the monsters around the band-stand.

In her room at the hotel Pamela was writing up her diary. "September 20th. Montecatini seems a beastly sort of hole, particularly if you come to a wretched little hotel like this, which M. insisted on doing, because he knows the proprietor, who is an old drunkard and also cooks the meals, and M. has long talks with him and says he's like a character in Shakespeare, which is all very well, but I'd prefer better food and a room with a bath, not to mention the awfulness of the other people in the hotel, one of whom is the chief undertaker in Florence, who's always boasting to the other people at meal times about his business and what a fine motor hearse with gilded angels he's got and the number of counts and dukes he's buried. M. had a long conversation with him and the old drunkard after dinner yesterday evening about how you preserve corpses on ice and the way to make money by buying up the best sites at the cemetery and holding them till you could ask five times as much as you paid, and it was the first time I'd seen him looking cheerful and amused since his illness and even for some time before, but I was so horrified that I went off to bed. This morning at eight to the pumproom, where M. has to drink eight glasses of different kinds of water before breakfast and there are hundreds of hideous people all carrying mugs, and huge fountains of purgatives, and a band playing the "Geisha," so I came away after half an hour, leaving M. to his waters, because I really can't be expected to watch him drinking, and it appears there are six hundred W.C.'s."

She laid down her pen and, turning round in her chair, sat for some time pensively staring at her own reflection in the wardrobe mirror. "If you look long enough," (she heard Clare's voice, she saw Clare, inwardly, sitting at her dressingtable), "you begin to wonder if it isn't somebody else. And perhaps, after all, one *is* somebody else, all the time." Somebody else, Pamela repeated to herself, somebody else. But was that a spot on her cheek, or a mosquito bite? A mosquito, thank goodness. "Oh God," she said aloud, and in the looking-glass somebody else moved her lips, "if only I knew what to do! If only I were dead!" She touched wood hastily. Stupid to say such things. But if only one knew, one were certain! All at once she gave a little stiff sharp shudder of disgust, she grimaced as though she had bitten on something sour. Oh, oh! she groaned; for she had suddenly seen herself in the act of dressing, there, in that moon-flecked darkness, among the bushes, that hateful night just before Miles fell ill. Furious because he'd humiliated her, hating him; she hadn't wanted to and he'd made her. Somebody else had enjoyed beyond the limits of enjoyment, had suffered a pleasure transmuted into its op-

posite. Or rather *she* had done the suffering. And then that
further humiliation of having to ask him to help her look
for her suspender belt! And there were leaves in her hair.
And when she got back to the hotel, she found a spider
squashed against her skin under the chemise. Yes, *she* had
found the spider, not somebody else.

BETWEEN THE BRACKISH SIPS FANNING WAS READING
in his pocket edition of the Paradiso. *"L'acqua che prendo
giammai non si corse,"*[*] he murmured;

> *Minerva spira e conducemi Apollo,*
> *e nove Muse mi dimostran l'Orse.*[†]

He closed his eyes. *"E nove Muse mi dimostran l'Orse."*
What a marvel! "And the nine Muses point me to the Bears."
Even translated the spell did not entirely lose its potency.
"How glad I shall be," he thought, "to be able to do a little
work again."

"*Il caffè?*"[‡] said a voice at his elbow. "*Non lo bevo mai, mai.
Per il fegato, sa, è pessimo. Si dice anche che per gl'intestini. . . .*"[§]
The voice receded out of hearing.

Fanning took another gulp of salt water and resumed
his reading.

> *Voi altri pochi che drizzante il collo*

---

[*] The seas I sail were never crossed before;

[†] Minerva breathes, Apollo is my guide,

and all nine Muses point me out the Bears.

[‡] And all nine Muses point me out the Bears.

[§] "Coffee?" "No, I never drink it, never. For the liver, you know, it's bad. It's also said
that the intestines. . . ."

per tempo al pan degli angeli, del quale
vivesi qui ma non sen vien satollo ...

The voice had returned. *"Pesce bollito, carne ai ferri o ar-*
rostita, patate lesse...."†

He shut his ears and continued. But when he came to:—

la concreata e perpetua sete
del deiforme regno,‡

he had to stop again. This craning for angels' bread, this
thirsting for the god-like kingdom ... The words reverber-
ated questioningly in his mind. After all, why not? Particu-
larly when man's bread made you sick (he thought with horror
of that dreadful vomiting of bile), when it was a case of *pesce*
Bollito§ and you weren't allowed to thirst for anything more
palatable than this stuff. (He swigged again.) These were the
circumstances when Christianity became appropriate. Chris-
tians, according to Pascal, ought to live like sick men; con-
versely, sick men can hardly escape being Christians. How
pleased Colin Judd would be! But the thought of Colin was
depressing, if only all Christians were like Dante! But in that
case, what a frightful world it would be! Frightful.

La concreata e perpetua sete

---

* Ye other few, who early raised your necks
for Angels' bread, on which one here on earth
subsists, but with which none are ever sated ...
† "Boiled fish, grilled meat, boiled potatoes...."
‡ The innate and ceaseless thirsting for the Realm
in God's own image made...
§ Boiled fish.

del deiforme regno cen portava
Veloci, quasi come il ciel vedete.
Beatrice in suso ed io in lei guardava.... *

He thought of Pamela at the fireworks. On that pedestal. *Ben son, ben son Beatrice*† on that pedestal. He remembered what he had said beneath the blossoming of the rockets; and also what he had meant to say about those legs which the pedestal made it so easy for the worshipper to pinch. Those legs how remote now, how utterly irrelevant! He finished off his third glass of Torretta and, rising, made his way to the bar for his first of Regina. Yes, how utterly irrelevant! he thought. A complete solution of continuity. You were on the leg level, then you vomited bile and as soon as you were able to think of anything but vomiting, you found yourself on the Dante level. He handed his mug to the barmaid. She rolled black eyes at him as she filled it. Some liverish gentlemen, it seemed, could still feel amorous. Or perhaps it was only the obese ones. Fanning deposited his offering and retired. Irrelevant, irrelevant. It seemed, now, the unlikeliest story. And yet there it was, a fact. And Pamela was solid, too solid.

Phrases floated up, neat and ready-made, to the surface of his mind.

"What does he see in her? What on earth can she see in him?"

"But it's not a question of sight, it's a question of touch."

---

* The innate and ceaseless thirsting for the Realm
in God's own image made, was bearing us
as swiftly as ye see the heavens revolve.
On high looked Beatrice, and I on her....
† Yes, I am, I am Beatrice.

And he remembered—*sentiments-centimètres*[*]—that French pun about love, so appallingly cynical, so humiliatingly true. "But only humiliating," he assured himself, "because we choose to think it so, arbitrarily, only cynical because *Beatrice in suso ed io in lei guardava*[†]; only appalling because we're creatures who sometimes vomit bile and because, even without vomiting, we sometimes feel ourselves naturally Christians." But in any case, *nove Muse mi dimostran l'Orse*.[‡] Meanwhile, however. . . . He tilted another gill of water down his throat. And when he was well enough to work, wouldn't he also be well enough to thirst again for that other god-like kingdom, with its different ecstasies, its other peace beyond all understanding? But *tant mieux, tant mieux*,[§] so long as the Bears remained unmoved and the Muses went on pointing.

PAMELA WAS LOOKING THROUGH HER DIARY. "JUNE 24th," she read. "Spent the evening with M. and afterwards he said how lucky it was for me that I'd been seduced by him, which hurt my feelings (that word, I mean) and also rather annoyed me, so I said he certainly hadn't seduced me, and he said, all right, if I liked to say that I'd seduced him, he didn't mind, but anyhow it was lucky because almost anybody else wouldn't have been such a good psychologist as he, not to mention physiologist, and I should have hated it. But I said, how could he say such things? because it wasn't that at all and I was happy because I loved him, but M. laughed and said, you don't, and I said, I do, and he said, you don't,

---

[*] A pun meaning "feelings—fractions away."

[†] On high looked Beatrice, and I on her.

[‡] All nine Muses point me out the Bears.

[§] All the better, all the better.

but if it gives you any pleasure to imagine you do, imagine, which upset me still more, his not believing, which is due to his not wanting to love himself, because I *do* love . . ."

Pamela quickly turned the page. She couldn't read that sort of thing now.

"JUNE 25TH. WENT TO THE VATICAN WHERE M. . . ." SHE skipped nearly a page of Miles's remarks on classical art and the significance of orgies in the ancient religions; on the duty of being happy and having the sun inside you, like a bunch of ripe grapes; on making the world appear infinite and holy by an improvement of sensual enjoyment; on taking things untragically, unponderously.

"M. dined out and I spent the evening with Guy, the first time since the night of the fireworks, and he asked me what I'd been doing all this time, so I said, nothing in particular, but I felt myself blushing, and he said, anyhow you look extraordinarily well and happy and pretty, which also made me rather uncomfortable, because of what M. said the other day about murder will out, but then I laughed, because it was the only thing to do, and Guy asked what I was laughing about, so I said, nothing, but I could see by the way he looked at me that he was rather thrilled, which pleased me, and we had a very nice dinner and he told me about a girl he'd been in love with in Ireland and it seems they went camping together for a week, but he was never her lover because she had a kind of terror of being touched, but afterwards she went to America and got married. Later on, in the taxi, he took my hand and even tried to kiss me, but I laughed, because it was somehow very funny, I don't know why, but afterwards, when he persisted, I got angry with him.

"JUNE 27TH. WENT TO LOOK AT MOSAICS TO-DAY, rather fine, but what a pity they're all in churches and always pictures of Jesus and sheep and apostles and so forth. On the way home we passed a wine shop and M. went in and ordered a dozen bottles of champagne, because he said that love can exist without passion, or understanding, or respect, but not without champagne. So I asked him if he really loved me, and he said, *Je t'adore,* in French, but I said, no, do you really *love* me? But he said, silence is golden and it's better to use one's mouth for kissing and drinking champagne and eating caviar, because he'd also bought some caviar; and if you start talking about love and thinking about love, you get everything wrong, because it's not *meant* to be talked about, but acted, and if people want to talk and think, they'd better talk about mosaics and that sort of thing. But I still went on asking him if he loved me. . . ."

"Fool, fool!" said Pamela aloud. She was ashamed of herself. Dithering on like that! At any rate Miles had been honest; she had to admit that. He'd taken care to keep the thing on the champagne level. And he'd always told her that she was imagining it all. Which had been intolerable, of course; he'd been wrong to be so right. She remembered how she had cried when he refused to answer her insistent question; had cried and afterwards allowed herself to be consoled. They went back to his house for supper; he opened a bottle of champagne, they ate the caviar. Next day he sent her that poem. It had arrived at the same time as some flowers from Guy. She reopened her notebook. Here it was.

At the red fountain's core the thud of drums
Quickens; for hairy-footed moths explore

This aviary of nerves; the woken birds
Flutter and cry in the branched blood; a bee
Hums with his million-times-repeated stroke
On lips your breast promotes geometers
To measure curves, to take the height of mountains,
The depth and silken slant of dells unseen.
I read your youth, as the blind student spells
With finger-tips the song from *Cymbeline*.
Caressing and caressed, my hands perceive
(In lieu of eyes) old Titian's paradise
With Eve unaproned; and the Maja dressed
Whisks off her muslins, that my skin may know
The blind night's beauty of brooding heat and cool,
Of silk and fibre, of molten-moist and dry,
Resistance and resilience.
               But the drum
Throbs with yet faster beat, the wild birds go
Through their red liquid sky with wings yet more
Frantic and yet more desperate crying. Come!
The magical door its soft and breathing valves
Has set ajar. Beyond the threshold lie
Worlds after worlds receding into light,
As rare old wines on the ravished tongue renew
A miracle that deepens, that expands,
Blossoms, and changes hue, and chimes, and shines.
Birds in the blood and doubled drums incite
Us to the conquest of these new, strange lands
Beyond the threshold, where all common times,
Things, places, thoughts, events expire, and life
Enters eternity.
The darkness stirs, the trees are wet with rain;

Knock and it shall be opened, oh, again,
Again! The child is eager for its dam
And I the mother am of thirsty lips,
Oh, knock again!
Wild darkness wets this sound of strings.
How smooth it slides among the clarinets,
How easily slips through the trumpetings!
Sound glides through sound and lo! the apocalypse,
The burst of wings above a sunlit sea.
Must this eternal music make an end?
Prolong, prolong these all but final chords!
Oh, wounded sevenths, breathlessly suspend
Our fear of dying, our desire to know
The song's last words!
Almost Bethesda sleeps, uneasily.
A bubble domes the flatness; gyre on gyre,
The waves expand, expire, as in the deeps
The woken spring subsides
                         Play, music, play!
Reckless of death, a singing giant rides
His storm of music, rides; and suddenly
The tremulous mirror of the moon is broken;
On the farthest beaches of our soul, our flesh,
The tides of pleasure foaming into pain
Mount, hugely mount; break; and retire again.
The final word is sung, the last word spoken.

"Do I like it, or do I rather hate it? I don't know."

"JUNE 28TH. WHEN I SAW M. AT LUNCH TO-DAY, I TOLD
him I didn't really know if I liked his poem, I mean apart

from literature, and he said, yes, perhaps the young *are* more romantic than they think, which rather annoyed me, because I believe he imagined I was shocked, which is too ridiculous. All the same, I *don't* like it."

Pamela sighed and shut her eyes, so as to be able to think more privately, without distractions. From this distance of time she could see all that had happened in perspective, as it were, and as a whole. It was her pride, she could see, her fear of looking ridiculously romantic that had changed the quality of her feelings towards Miles—a pride and a fear on which he had played, deliberately. She had given herself with passion and desperately, tragically, as she imagined that Joan would have desperately given herself, at first sight, to a reluctant Walter. But the love he had offered her in return was a thing of laughter and frank, admitted sensuality, was a gay and easy companionship enriched, but uncomplicated, by pleasure. From the first, he had refused to come up to her emotional level. From the first, he had taken it for granted—and his taking it for granted was in itself an act of moral compulsion—that she should descend to his. And she had descended—reluctantly at first, but afterwards without a struggle. For she came to realize, almost suddenly, that after all she didn't really love him in the tragically passionate way she had supposed she loved him. In a propitious emotional climate her belief that she was a despairing Joan might perhaps have survived, at any rate for a time. But it was a hot-house growth of the imagination; in the cool dry air of his laughter and cheerfully cynical frankness it had withered. And all at once she had found herself, not satisfied, indeed, with what he offered, but superficially content. She returned him what he gave. Less even than he gave. For soon it became apparent to her that their rôles were being reversed, herself, but with Fanning. She turned over several pages. It was July now and they were at Ostia for the bathing. It was at Ostia that that desperate seriousness had come into his desire. The long hot hours of the siesta were propitious to his earnest madness. Propitious also to his talents, for he worked well in the heat. Behind her lowered eyelids Pamela had a vision of him sitting at his table, stripped to a pair of shorts, sitting there, pen in hand, in the next room and with an open door between them, but somehow at an infinite distance. Terrifyingly remote, a stranger more foreign for being known so well, the inhabitant of other worlds to which she had no access. They were worlds which she was already beginning to hate. His books were splendid of course; still, it wasn't much fun being with a man who, for half the time, wasn't there at all. She saw him sitting there, a beautiful naked stranger, brown and wiry, with a face like brown marble, stonily focussed on his paper. And then suddenly this stranger rose and came towards her through the door, across the room. "Well?" she heard herself saying. But the stranger did not answer. Sitting down on the edge of her bed, he took the sewing out of her hands and threw it aside on to the dressing table. She tried to protest, but he laid a hand on her mouth. Wordlessly he shook his head, Then uncovering her mouth, he kissed her. Under his surgeon's, his sculptor's hands, her body was moulded to a symbol of pleasure. His face was focussed and intent, but not on her, on something else, and serious, serious, like a martyr's, like a mathematician's, like a criminal's. An hour later, he was back at his table in the next room, in the next world, remote, a stranger once again—but he had never ceased to be a stranger.

Pamela turned over two or three more pages. On July 12th they went sailing and she had felt sick; Miles had been provokingly well all the time. The whole of the sixteenth had been spent in Rome. On the nineteenth they drove to Cerveteri to see the Etruscan tombs. She had been furious with him, because he had put out the lamp and made horrible noises in the cold sepulchral darkness, underground— furious with terror, for she hated the dark.

Impatiently, Pamela went on turning the pages. There was no point in reading; none of the really important things were recorded. Of the earnest madness of his love-making, of those hands, that reluctantly suffered pleasure she hadn't been able to bring herself to write. And yet those were the things that mattered. She remembered how she had tried to imagine that she was like her namesake of *Pastures New*—the fatal woman whose cool detachment gives her such power over her lovers. But the facts had proved too stubborn; it was simply impossible for her to pretend that this handsome fancy-picture was her portrait. The days flicked past under her thumb.

"JULY 30TH. ON THE BEACH THIS MORNING WE MET some friends of M.'s, a journalist called Pedder, who has just come to Rome as correspondent for some paper or other, and his wife, rather awful, I thought, both of them, but M. seemed to be extraordinarily pleased to see them, and they bathed with us and afterwards came and had lunch at our hotel, which was rather boring so far as I was concerned, because they talked a lot about people I didn't know and then there was a long discussion about politics and history, and so forth, *too* highbrow, but what was intolerable was that the woman thought she ought to be kind and talk to me meanwhile about something I could understand, so she talked about shops in Rome and the best places for getting clothes, which was rather ridiculous, as she's obviously one of those absurd arty women, who appeared in M.'s novels as young girls just before and during the War, so advanced in those days, with extraordinary coloured stockings and frocks like pictures by Augustus John. Anyhow, what she was wearing at lunch was really too fancy-dress, and really at her age one ought to have a little more sense of the decencies, because she must have been quite thirty-five. So that the idea of talking about smart shops in Rome was quite ludicrous to start with, and anyhow it was so insulting to me, because it implied that I was too young and half-witted to be able to take an interest in their beastly conversation. But afterwards, apropos of some philosophical theory or other, M. began talking about his opium smoking, and he told them all the things he'd told me and a lot more besides, and it made me feel very uncomfortable and then miserable and rather angry, because I thought it was only me he talked to like that, so confidentially, but now I see he makes confidences to everybody and it's not a sign of his being particularly fond of a person, or in love with them, or anything like that. Which made me realize that I'm even less important to him than I thought and I found I minded much more than I expected I should mind, because I thought I'd got past minding. But I *do* mind."

Pamela shut her eyes again. "I ought to have gone away then," she said to herself. "Gone straight away." But instead of retiring, she had tried to come closer. Her resentment— for oh, how bitterly she resented those Pedders and his confidential manner towards them!—had quickened her love. She wanted to insist on being more specially favoured than a mere Pedder; and, loving him, she had the right to insist. By a process of imaginative incubation, she managed to revive some he came into my room and wanted to kiss me, but I wouldn't let him, because I said, I don't want to owe your fits of niceness to somebody else, and I asked him, why? why was he so much nicer to them than to me? And he said they were his people, they belonged to the same time as he did and meeting them was like meeting another Englishman in the middle of a crowd of Kaffirs in Africa. So I said, I suppose I'm the Kaffirs, and he laughed and said, no, not quite Kaffirs, not more than a Rotary Club dinner in Kansas City, with the Pedders playing the part of a man one had known at Balliol in 'ninety-nine. Which made me cry, and he sat on the edge of the bed and took my hand and said he was very sorry, but that's what life was like, and it couldn't be helped, because time was always time, but people weren't always the same people, but sometimes one person and sometimes another, sometimes Pedder-fanciers and sometimes Pamela-fanciers, and it wasn't my fault that I hadn't heard the first performance of *Pelléas* in 1902 and it wasn't Pedder's fault that he had, and therefore Pedder was his compatriot and I wasn't. But I said, after all, Miles, you're my lover, doesn't that make any difference? But he said, it's a question of speech, and bodies don't speak, only minds, and when two minds are of different ages it's hard for them to understand each other when they speak, but bodies can understand each other, because they don't talk, thank God, he said, because it's such a comfort to stop talking sometimes, to stop thinking and just *be,* for a change. But I said that might be all right for him, but just *being* was my ordinary life and the change for me was talking, was being friends with somebody who knew how to talk and do all the other things talking implies, and I'd imagined I was that, besides just being somebody he went to bed with, and that was why I was so miserable,

because I found I wasn't, and those beastly Pedders were. But
he said, damn the Pedders, damn the Pedders for making you
cry! and he was so *divinely* sweet and gentle that it was like
gradually sinking, sinking and being drowned. But afterwards
he began laughing again in that rather hurting way, and he
said, your body's so much more beautiful than their minds—
that is, so long as one's a Pamela-fancier; which I am he said,
or rather was and shall be, but now I must go and work, and
he got up and went to his room, and I was wretched again."

The entries of a few days later were dated from Monte
Cavo. A superstitious belief in the genius of place had made
Pamela insist on the change of quarters. They had been happy
on Monte Cavo; perhaps they would be happy there again.
And so, suddenly, the sea didn't suit her, she needed moun-
tain air. But the genius of place is an unreliable deity. She
had been as unhappy on the hill-top as by the sea. No, not
quite so unhappy, perhaps. In the absence of the Pedders, the
passion which their coming had renewed declined again. Per-
haps it would have declined even if they had still been there.
For the tissue of her imagination was, at the best of times,
but a ragged curtain. Every now and then she came to a hole
and through the hole she could see a fragment of reality, such
as the bald and obvious fact that she didn't love Miles Fan-
ning. True, after a peep through one of these indiscreet holes
she felt it necessary to repent for having seen the facts, she
would work herself up again into believing her fancies. But
her faith was never entirely whole-hearted. Under the super-
ficial layer of imaginative suffering lay a fundamental and real
indifference. Looking back now, from the further shore of his
illness, Pamela felt astonished that she could have gone on
obstinately imagining, in spite of those loop-holes on real-

ity, that she loved him. "Because I didn't," she said to herself, clear-sighted, weeks too late. "I didn't." But the belief that she did had continued, even on Monte Cavo, to envenom those genuinely painful wounds inflicted by him on her pride, her self-respect, inflicted with a strange malice that seemed to grow on him with the passage of the days.

"AUGUST 23D." SHE HAD TURNED AGAIN TO THE NOTE-book. "M. gave me this at lunch to-day.

> *Sensual heat and sorrow cold*
> *Are undivided twins;*
> *For there where sorrow ends, consoled,*
> *Lubricity begins.*

I told him I didn't exactly see what the point of it was, but I supposed it was meant to be hurting, because he's always trying to be hurting now, but he said, no, it was just a Great Thought for putting into Christmas crackers. But he did mean to hurt, and yet in one way he's crazy about me, he's . . ."

Yes, crazy was the right word. The more and the more crazily he had desired her, the more he had seemed to want to hurt her, to hurt himself too—for every wound he inflicted on her was inflicted at the same time on himself. "Why on earth didn't I leave him?" she wondered as she allowed a few more days to flick past.

"AUGUST 29TH. A LETTER THIS MORNING FROM GUY IN Scotland, so no wonder he took such an endless time to answer mine, which is a relief in one way, because I was beginning to wonder if he wasn't answering on purpose, but also rather depressing, as he says he isn't coming back to Rome till after the middle of September and goodness knows what will have happened by that time. So I felt very melancholy all the morning, sitting under the big tree in front of the monastery, such a marvellous huge old tree with very bright bits of sky between the leaves and bits of sun on the ground and moving across my frock, so that the sadness somehow got mixed up with the loveliness, which it often does do in a queer way, I find. M. came out unexpectedly and suggested going for a little walk before lunch, and he was very sweet for a change, but I dare say it was because he'd worked well. And I said, do you remember the first time we came up to Monte Cavo? and we talked about that afternoon and what fun it had been, even the museum, I said, even my education, because the Apollo was lovely. But he shook his head and said, *Apollo, Apollo, lama sabachthani,* and when I asked why he thought his Apollo had abandoned him he said it was because of Jesus and the Devil, and you're the Devil, I'm afraid, and he laughed and kissed my hand, but I ought to wring your neck, he said. For something that's *your* fault, I said, because it's you who makes me a Devil for yourself. But he said it was me who made him make me into a Devil. So I asked how? And he said just by existing, just by having my particular shape, size, colour, and consistency, because if I'd looked like a beetle and felt like wood, I'd have never made him make me into a Devil. So I asked him why he didn't just go away seeing that what was wrong with me was that I was there at all. But that's easier said than done, he said, because a Devil's one of the very few things you can't run away from. And I asked why

---

* Apollo, Apollo, why have you forsaken me?

TWO OR THREE GRACES

THE WORD 'BORE' IS OF DOUBTFUL ETYMOLOGY. Some authorities derive it from the verb meaning to pierce. A bore is a person who drills a hole in your spirit, who tunnels relentlessly through your patience, through all the crusts of voluntary deafness, inattention, rudeness, which you vainly interpose—through and through till he pierces to the very quick of your being. But there are other authorities, as good or even better, who would derive the word from the French *bourrer*, to stuff, to satiate. If this etymology be correct, a bore is one who stuffs you with his thick and suffocating discourse, who rams his suety personality, like a dumpling, down your throat. He stuffs you; and you, to use an apposite modern metaphor, are 'fed up with him.' I like to think, impossibly, that both these derivations of the word are correct; for bores are both piercers and stuffers. They are like dentists' drills, and they are also like stale buns. But they are characterized by a further quality, which drills and dough-nuts do not possess; they cling. That is why (though no philologist) I venture to suggest a third derivation, from 'burr.' Burr, *bourrer*, bore—all the sticking, stuffing, piercing qualities of boredom are implicit in those three possible etymologies. Each of the three of them deserves to be correct.

Herbert Comfrey was above all a sticking bore. He attached himself to any one who had the misfortune to come in contact with him; attached himself and could not be shaken off. A burr-bore, vegetable and passive; not actively penetrating. For Herbert, providentially, was not particularly talkative; he was too lazy and lymphatic for that. He was just exceedingly sociable, like a large sentimental dog that cannot bear to be left alone. Like a dog, he followed people about; he lay, metaphorically speaking, at their feet in front of the fire. And like a dog, he did not talk. It was just your company that made him happy; he was quite content if he might trot at your side or doze under your chair. He did not demand that you should pay much attention to him; all that he asked was to be permitted to enjoy the light of your countenance and bask in the warmth of your presence. If once a week he got the equivalent of a pat on the head and a 'Good dog, Herbert,' he wagged his spirit's tail and was perfectly happy.

To some of my friends—the quick, the impatient, the highly strung—poor vegetable Herbert was exasperating to the point of madness. His very virtues—that good nature of his, that placidity, that unshakable fidelity—infuriated them. Even his appearance drove them wild. The sight of his broad smiling face, of his big, lazy, lubberly body and limbs was alone sufficient to set their nerves twittering and jumping like a frightened aviary. I have known people who, after living in the same house with Herbert for three days, have secretly packed their trunks, caught the first convenient train, and, leaving no address, have travelled hundreds of miles in order to escape from him.

To me, poor Herbert was boring indeed, but not exasperatingly or intolerably so. Mine is a patient temper; my nerves are not easily set twittering. I even liked him in a way; he was such a good, faithful, kind old dog. And I soon acquired, in his dumb presence, a knack of quite ignoring him, of regarding him simply as a piece of furniture—so much so, that I sometimes caught myself on the point of carelessly setting down my emptied coffee-cup on his head as he sat on the floor beside me (he always sat on the floor whenever it was possible), or of flicking my cigarette ash into the inviting cranny between his neck and his coat collar.

As boys, Herbert and I had been at the same public school. But as we were in different houses and he was two years older than I (two years, at that age, is an enormous seniority), we had hardly ever spoken to one another. But none the less, it was on the strength of our old school that Herbert reintroduced himself into my life. His return was doubly disastrous. A bore entered my existence and, in the entering, drove out, temporarily at least, a being who, whatever his other qualities, was the very antithesis of boredom.

It was in a café of the Passage du Panorama in Paris that the thing happened. We had been sitting there for an hour, Kingham and I, talking and drinking vermouth. It was characteristic of Kingham that he did most of both—drinking as well as talking. Characteristic, too, that he should have been abusing me, among many other things, for wasting my time and spirit in precisely these two occupations.

'You sit about,' he said, 'letting every thought in your head trickle out uselessly in talk. Not that there are many thoughts, of course, because you daren't think. You do anything not to think. You create futile business, you rush about seeing people you don't like and don't take the slightest interest in, you drift from bar to bar, you swill till you're stupefied—all because you daren't think and can't bring your-self to make the effort to do something serious and decent. It's the result partly of laziness, partly of lack of faith—faith in anything. *Garçon!*' He ordered another vermouth. 'It's the great modern vice,' he went on, 'the great temptation of every young man or woman who's intelligent and acutely conscious. Everything that's easy and momentarily divert-ing and anaesthetic tempts—people, chatter, drink, forni-cation. Everything that's difficult and big, everything that needs thought and effort, repels. It's the war that did it. Not to mention the peace. But it would have come gradually in any case. Modern life was making it inevitable. Look at the young people who had nothing to do with the war—were only children when it happened—they're the worst of all. It's time to stop, it's time to do something. Can't you see that you can't go on like this? Can't you see?'

He leaned across the table at me, angrily. He hated these vices which he had attributed to me, hated them with a spe-cial fury because they happened really to be his. He was confessing the weakness he hated in himself—hated and could not eradicate.

Kingham looked handsome in anger. He had dark eyes, beautiful and very bright; his hair was dark brown, fine and plentiful; a close-cut beard, redder than his hair, disguised the lower part of his face, with whose pale, young smooth-ness it seemed curiously incongruous. There was a brilliancy, a vividness about him. If I were less slow to kindle, I should have burned responsively with his every ardour. Being what I am, I could always remain cool, critical, and cautious, how-ever passionately he might burn. My uninflammableness, I believe, had somehow fascinated him. I exasperated him, but he continued to frequent my company—chiefly to abuse me, to tell me passionately how hopeless I was. I winced under these dissections; for though he often talked, as far as I was concerned, wildly at random (accusing me, as he had done on this particular occasion, of the weakness which he felt and resented in himself), his analysis was often painfully exact and penetrating. I winced, but all the same I delighted in his company. We irritated one another profoundly; but we were friends.

I suppose I must have smiled at Kingham's question. Goodness knows, I am no tee-totaller, I am not averse to wasting my time over agreeable futilities. But compared with Kingham—particularly the Kingham of 1920—I am a monument of industry, dutiful steadiness, sobriety. I take no credit to myself for it; I happen to be one of nature's burgesses, that is all. I am as little capable of leading a perfectly disorderly life as I am of, shall we say, writing a good book. Kingham was born with both talents. Hence the absurdity, so far as I was concerned, of his hortatory question. I did not mean to smile; but some trace of my amusement must have appeared on my face, for Kingham suddenly became most passionately angry.

'You think it's a joke?' he cried, and thumped the marble table. 'I tell you, it's the sin against the Holy Ghost. It's unforgivable. It's burying your talent. Damn this blasted Bible,' he added with parenthetic fury. 'Why is it that one can never talk about anything serious without getting mixed up in it?'

'It happens to be quite a serious book,' I suggested.

'A lot you understand about it,' said Kingham. 'I tell you,' he went on impressively . . . . But at this moment Herbert made his second entry into my life.

I felt a hand laid on my shoulder, looked up, and saw a stranger.

'Hullo, Wilkes,' said the stranger. 'You don't remember me.'

I looked more attentively, and had to admit that I didn't.

'I am Comfrey,' he explained, 'Herbert Comfrey. I was at Dunhill's, don't you remember? You were at Struthers', weren't you? Or was it Lane's?'

At the names of these pedagogues, who had figured so largely in my boyhood, recesses in my mind, long closed, suddenly burst open, as though before a magical word. Visions of inky schoolrooms, football fields, cricket fields, five courts, the school chapel, rose up confusedly; and from the midst of this educational chaos there disengaged itself the loutish figure of Comfrey of Dunhill's.

'Of course,' I said, and took him by the hand. Through the corner of my eye, I saw Kingham angrily frowning. 'How did you remember me?'

'Oh, I remember every one,' he answered. It was no vain boast, as I afterwards discovered; he *did* remember. He remembered every one he had ever met, and all the trivial incidents of his past life. He had the enormous memory of royal personages and family retainers—the memory of those who never read, or reason, or reflect, and whose minds are therefore wholly free to indulge in retrospect. 'I never forget a face,' he added, and without being invited, sat down at our table.

Indignantly, Kingham threw himself back in his chair. He kicked me under the table. I looked at him and made a little grimace, signifying my helplessness.

I mumbled a perfunctory introduction. Kingham said

nothing, only frowned more blackly, as he shook hands with
Herbert. And for his part, Herbert was hardly more cordial.
True, he smiled his amiable dim smile; but he said nothing,
he hardly even looked at Kingham. He was in too much of a
hurry to turn back to me and talk about the dear old school.
The dear old school—it was the only subject that ever made
Herbert really loquacious. It metamorphosed him from a
merely vegetable burr-bore into an active, piercing dentist's
drill of tediousness. He had a passion for the school, and
thought that all ex-members of it ought to be in constant
and friendly communication with one another. I have no-
ticed that, as a general rule, people of decided individual-
ity very rarely continue their schoolboy acquaintanceships
into later life. It is only to be expected. The chances that
they will have found in the tiny microcosm of school the
sort of friends they will like when they are grown up—
grown out of recognition—are obviously very small. Co-
teries whose bond of union consists in the fact that their
component members happened to be at the same school at
the same time are generally the dreariest of assemblages. It
could scarcely be otherwise; men who have no better reasons
for associating with one another must be colourless indeed,
and insipid. Poor Herbert, who regarded the accident of our
having worn similarly striped caps and blazers at a certain
period of our boyhood as being a sufficient reason for our
entering into a bosom friendship, was only an extreme spec-
imen of the type.

I put on my chilliest and most repellant manner. But in
vain. Herbert talked and talked. Did I remember the excit-
ing match against Winchester in 1910? And how poor old
Mr. Cutler had been ragged? And that memorable occasion

when Pye had climbed on to the roof of the school chapel, at night, and hung a chamber-pot on one of the Gothic pinnacles? Anxiously, I looked towards Kingham. He had exchanged his expression of anger for one of contempt, and was leaning back, his eyes shut, tilting his chair.

Kingham had never been to a public school. He had not had the luck (or the misfortune) to be born a hereditary, professional gentleman. He was proud of the fact, he sometimes even boasted of it. But that did not prevent him from being morbidly sensitive to anything that might be interpreted as a reference to his origin. He was always on the look-out for insults from 'gentlemen.' Veiled insults, insults offered unconsciously even, unintentionally, in perfect ignorance—any sort of insult was enough to set him quivering with pain and fury. More than once I had seen him take violent offence at words that were entirely well-intentioned. Would he regard Herbert's dreary recollections of the dear old school as an insult? He was quite capable of it. I looked forward nervously to an outburst and a violent exit. But the scene, this time, was not to be acted in public. After listening for a few minutes to Herbert's anecdotage, Kingham got up, excused himself with ironical politeness, and bade us good evening. I laid my hand on his arm.

'Do stay.'

'A thousand regrets'; he laid his hand on his heart, smiled, bowed, and was gone, leaving me (I may add parenthetically that it was his habit) to pay for his drinks.

We public school men were left to ourselves.

The next morning I lay late in bed. At about eleven o'clock Kingham burst into my room. The scene which I had been spared the night before was enacted for me now with redoubled passion. Another man would have slept on the supposed insult and, waking, have found it negligible. Not so Kingham. He had brooded over his wrongs, till what was originally small had grown enormous. The truth was that Kingham liked scenes. He loved to flounder in emotion—his own and other people's. He was exhilarated by these baths of passion; he felt that he really lived, that he was more than a man, while he splashed about in them. And the intoxication was so delicious that he indulged in it without considering the consequences—or perhaps it would be truer to say that he considered the consequences (for intellectually no man could be clearer-sighted than Kingham) but deliberately ignored them.

When I say that he had a great facility for making scenes, I do not mean to imply that he ever simulated an emotion. He felt genuinely about things—genuinely and strongly, but too easily. And he took pleasure in cultivating and working up his emotions. For instance, what in other men would have been a passing irritation, held in check by self-control, to be modified very likely by subsequent impressions, was converted by Kingham, almost deliberately, into a wild fury which no second thoughts were allowed to assuage. Often these passions were the result of mere mistakes on the part of those who had provoked them. But once emotionally committed, Kingham would never admit a mistake—unless, of course, his passion for self-humiliation happened at the moment to be stronger than his passion for self-assertion. Often, too, he would take up unchanging emotional attitudes towards people. A single powerful impression would be allowed to dominate all other impressions. His intellect was put into blinkers, the most manifest facts were ignored;

and until further orders the individual in question produced in Kingham only one particular set of reactions.

As he approached my bed, I could see from the expression on his white face that I was in for a bad quarter of an hour.

'Well?' I said, with an affectation of careless cordiality.

'I always knew you were an intellectual snob,' Kingham began in a low, intense voice, drawing up a chair to my bedside as he spoke. 'But really, I thought you were above being an ordinary, suburban, lower middle-class social snob.'

I made the grimace which in French novels is represented by the sign '———?'

'I know that my father was a plumber,' he went on, 'and that I was educated at the expense of the State and by scholarships for the encouragement of clever paupers. I know I speak Cockney, and not Eton and Oxford. I know that my manners are bad and that I eat dirtily, and that I don't wash my teeth enough.' (None of these things were true; but it suited Kingham, at the moment, to believe that they were. He wanted to feel abased, in order that he might react with greater violence. He insulted himself in order that he might attribute the insults, under which he genuinely winced, to me, and so have an excuse for being angry with me.) 'I know I'm a cad and a little bounder.' He spoke the words with an extraordinary gusto, as though he enjoyed the pain he was inflicting on himself. 'I know I'm an outsider, only tolerated for my cleverness. A sort of buffoon or tame monkey for the amusement of cultured gentlemen. I know all this, and I know you knew it. But I really thought you didn't mind, that we met as human beings, not as specimens of upper and lower classes. I was fool enough to imagine that you liked me in spite of it all. I thought you even preferred me to the people in your own herd. It only shows what an innocent I am. No sooner does a gentleman come along, an old school chum, what?' (derisively he assumed the public school accent as rendered on the music hall stage) 'than you fling your arms round his neck and leave the dirty little outsider very definitely outside.' He laughed ferociously.

'My good Kingham,' I began, 'why will you make a bloody fool of yourself?'

But Kingham, who doubtless knew as well as I did that he was making a fool of himself, only went on with the process more vehemently. He was committed to making a fool of himself, and he liked it. Shifting his ground a little, he began telling me home truths—real home truths this time. In the end, I too began to get angry.

'I'll trouble you to get out,' I said.

'Oh, I've not finished yet.'

'And stay out till you've got over your fit of hysterics. You're behaving like a girl who needs a husband.'

'As I was saying,' Kingham went on in a voice that had become softer, more sinisterly quiet, more poisonously honied in proportion as mine had grown louder and harsher, 'your great defect is spiritual impotence. Your morality, your art—they're just impotence organized into systems. Your whole view of life—impotence again. Your very strength, such as it is—your horrible passive resistance—that's based in impotence too.'

'Which won't prevent me from throwing you downstairs if you don't clear out at once.' It is one thing to know the truth about oneself; it is quite another thing to have it told one by somebody else. I knew myself a natural bourgeois; but when Kingham told me so—and in his words—it seemed to me that I was learning a new and horribly unpleasant truth.

'Wait,' Kingham drawled out with exasperating calm, 'wait one moment. One more word before I go.'

'Get out,' I said. 'Get out at once.'

There was a knock at the door. It opened. The large, ruddy face of Herbert Comfrey looked round it into the room.

'I hope I don't disturb,' said Herbert, grinning at us.

'Oh, not a bit, not a bit,' cried Kingham. He jumped up, and with an excessive politeness proffered his vacant chair. 'I was just going. Do sit down. Wilkes was impatiently expecting you. Sit down, do sit down.' He propelled Herbert towards the chair.

'Really,' Herbert began, politely protesting.

But Kingham cut him short. 'And now I leave you two old friends together,' he said. 'Good-bye. Good-bye. I'm only sorry I shan't have an opportunity for saying that last word I wanted to say.'

Cumbrously, Herbert made as though to get up. 'I'll go,' he said. 'I had no idea. . . . I'm so sorry.'

But Kingham put his hands on his shoulders and forced him back into the chair. 'No, no,' he insisted. 'Stay where you are. I'm off.'

And picking up his hat, he ran out of the room.

'Queer fellow,' said Herbert. 'Who is he?'

'Oh, a friend of mine,' I answered. My anger had dropped, and I wondered, sadly, whether in calling him a friend I was telling the truth. And to think that, if he were no longer my friend, it was because of this lumpish imbecile sitting by my bed! I looked at Herbert pensively. He smiled at me—a smile that was all good nature. One could not bear a grudge against such a man.

The breach was complete, at any rate for the time; it was more than two years before Kingham and I met again. But if I had lost Kingham, I had acquired Herbert Comfrey—only too completely. From that moment, my life in Paris was no longer my own; I had to share it with Herbert. Being at that moment quite unattached, a dog without a master, he fastened himself to me, taking it ingenuously for granted that I would be just as happy in his company as he was in mine. He established himself in my hotel, and for the rest of my stay in Paris I was almost never alone. I ought, I know, to have been firm with Herbert; I ought to have been rude, told him to go to the devil, kicked him downstairs. But I lacked the heart. I was too kind. (Another symptom of my spiritual impotence! My morality—impotence systematized. I know, I know.) Herbert preyed on me, and, like the Brahman who permits himself, unresistingly, to be devoured by every passing blood-sucker, from mosquitoes to tigers, I suffered him to prey on me. The most I did was occasionally to run away from him. Herbert was, fortunately, a sluggard. The Last Trump would hardly have got him out of bed before ten. When I wanted a day's freedom, I ordered an eight-o'clock breakfast and left the hotel while Herbert was still asleep. Returning at night from these holidays, I would find him waiting, dog-like, in my room. I always had the impression that he had been waiting there the whole day—from dawn (or what for him was dawn—about noon) to midnight. And he was always so genuinely pleased to see me back that I was almost made to feel ashamed, as though I had committed an act of perfidy. I would begin to apologize and explain. I had had to go out early to see a man about something; and then I had met another man, who had asked me to have lunch with him; and then I had had to go to my dear old friend, Madame Dubois, for tea; after which I had dropped in on Langlois, and we had dined and gone to a concert. In fine, as he could see, I could not have got back a minute earlier.

It was in answer to the reproaches of my own conscience that I made these apologies. Poor Herbert never complained; he was only too happy to see me back. I could not help feeling that his clinging fidelity had established some sort of claim on me, that I was somehow a little responsible for him. It was absurd, of course, unreasonable and preposterous. For why should I, the victim, feel pity for my persecutor? Preposterous; and yet the fact remained that I did feel pity for him. I have always been too tender-hearted, insufficiently ruthless.

The time came for me to return to London. Herbert, who had just enough money to make it unnecessary for him to do anything or to be anywhere at any particular time, packed his bags and got into the same train. It was a very disagreeable journey; the train was crowded, the sea just choppy enough to make me sick. Coming on deck as we drew into Dover harbour, I found Herbert looking exasperatingly well. If I had not been feeling so ill, I should have found an excuse for quarrelling with him. But I had not the requisite energy. Meanwhile, it must be admitted, Herbert made himself very useful about the luggage.

Experience was shortly to teach me that, instead of feeling exasperated with poor Herbert, I ought to have been thankful that he was not far worse. For Herbert, after all, ness. His genius for dulness caused him unfailingly to take an interest in the things which interested nobody else; and even when, by some mistake, he embarked on some more promising theme than the Swiss banking system, he had the power of rendering the most intrinsically fascinating of subjects profoundly dull. By a process of inverse alchemy he transmuted the purest gold to lead. His self-assertiveness and a certain pedagogic instinct made him ambitious to be the instructor of his fellows; he loved the sound of his own lecturing voice. And what a voice! Not unmusical, but loud, booming, persistent. It set up strange, nay, positively dangerous vibrations in one's head. I could never listen to it for more than a few minutes without feeling confused and dizzy. If I had had to live with that voice, I believe I should have begun, one day, to turn and turn like those Japanese waltzing mice—for ever. Peddley's voice affected the semi-circular canals. And then there was his sociability. It was a passion, a vice; he could not live without the company of his fellow-beings. It was an agony for him to be alone. He hunted company ferociously, as wild beasts pursue their prey. But the odd thing was that he never seemed to crave for friendship or intimacy. So far as I know, he had no friends, in the ordinarily accepted sense of the term. He desired only acquaintances and auditors; and acquaintances and reluctant auditors were all that he had. In the first period of my acquaintance with Peddley I used to wonder what he did when he felt the need of confiding his intimate and private feelings. Later on I came to doubt whether, at ordinary times, he had any private life that needed talking about. Only very rarely and when something catastrophic had explosively shattered the crust of his public existence, did he ever develop a private life. When things were running smoothly in their regular daily grooves, he lived only on the public surface, at the office, at the club, at his own dinner-table, perfectly content so long as there was somebody present to listen to his talk. It mattered not that his auditors might be listening with manifest and extreme reluctance. Like Herbert—and indeed like most bores—John Peddley was more than half unaware of the people upon whom he inflicted himself. He realized that they were there, physically there; that was all. To their feelings and thoughts he was utterly insensitive. It was this insensitiveness, coupled with his passionate sociability, that gave him his power. He could hunt down his victims and torture them without remorse. The wolf, if he were really sensitive to the feelings of the lamb, might end by turning vegetarian. But he is not sensitive. He is aware only of his own hunger and the deliciousness of mutton. It was the same with John Peddley. Ignorant of the terror which he inspired, of the mental agonies which he inflicted, he could pursue his course relentlessly and with a perfect equanimity.

My first impressions of John Peddley were not unfavourable. True, the halloo with which he greeted Herbert from the quay-side, as we were waiting our turn in the shoving crowd of human sheep to pass down the gangway on to dry land, sounded to me, in my present condition, rather distressingly hearty. And his appearance, when Herbert pointed him out to me, offended me by its robustious healthiness. Nor, when Herbert had introduced us, did I much appreciate the vehemence of his handshake and the loud volubility of his expressions of sympathy. But, on the other hand, he was very kind and efficient. He produced a silver flask from his pocket and made me take a swig of excellent old brandy. Noticing that I was chilled and green with cold, he insisted on my putting on his fur coat. He darted to the custom-house and returned, in an incredibly short space of time, with the official hieroglyph duly chalked upon our suit-cases. A minute later we were sitting in his car, rolling briskly out of Dover along the Canterbury road.

I was feeling, at the time, too ill to think; and it hardly occurred to me that the situation was, after all, rather odd. Peddley had been waiting on the quay—but not for us; for we were unexpected. Waiting, then, for whom? The question did propound itself to me at the time, but uninsistently. There was no room in my mind for anything but the consciousness of sea-sickness. I forgot to wonder, and took my seat in the car, as though it were the most natural thing in the world that we should have been met at the quay by somebody who did not know that we were crossing. And the apparent naturalness of the situation was confirmed for me by the behaviour of my companions. For Peddley had taken it for granted from the first that we should come and stay with him at his country house. And Herbert, for whom one place was always just as good as another, had accepted the invitation at once. I began by protesting; but feebly, and more out of politeness than in earnest. For it was not essential for me to get back to London that evening; and the prospect of that dismal journey from Dover, of the cab drive in the chill of the night across London, of a home-coming to fireless and deserted rooms, was very dreadful to me. If I accepted Peddley's invitation, I should find myself in less than half an hour in a warm, comfortable room, at rest and without responsibilities. The temptation to a sea-sick traveller was great; I succumbed.

'Well,' said Peddley heartily, in his loud, trombone-like

voice, 'well, this *is* luck.' He brought down his hand with a tremendous clap on to my knee, as though he were patting a horse. 'The greatest luck! Think of running into you and Herbert at the gangway! And carrying you off like this! Too delightful, too delightful!'

I was warmed by his gladness; it seemed so genuine. And genuine it was—the genuine gladness of an ogre who has found a chubby infant straying alone in the woods.

'Extraordinary,' Peddley went on, 'how many acquaintances one meets at Dover quay. I come every day, you know, when I'm staying in the country; every day, to meet the afternoon boat. It's a great resource when one's feeling dull. All the advantages of a London club in the country. And there's always time for a good chat before the train starts. That's what makes me like this district of Kent so much. I'm trying to persuade my landlord to sell me the house. I've nearly coaxed him, I think.'

'And then,' said Herbert, who had a way of occasionally breaking his habitual silence with one of those simple and devastatingly judicious reflections which render children so dangerous in polite, adult society, 'and then you'll find that every one will be travelling by aeroplane. You'll have to sell the house and move to Croydon, near the aerodrome.'

But Peddley was not the man to be put out by even the most terrible of terrible infants. Wrapped in his insensitiveness, he was not so much as aware of the infant's terribleness.

'Pooh!' he retorted. 'I don't believe in aeroplanes. They'll never be safe or cheap or comfortable enough to compete with the steamers. Not in our day.' And he embarked on a long discourse about helicopters and gyroscopes, air pockets and the cost of petrol.

Meanwhile, I had begun to wonder, in some alarm, what manner of man this kind, efficient, hospitable host of mine could be. A man who, on his own confession, drove into Dover every afternoon to meet the packet; who way-laid sea-sick acquaintances and had good chats with them while they waited for the train; and who so much loved his afternoon diversions at the quay-side that he felt moved to refute in serious, technical argument the prophet of aerial travel. . . . Decidedly, a strange, a dangerous man. And his voice, meanwhile, boomed and boomed in my ears till I felt dizzy with the sound of it. Too late, it occurred to me that it might have been better if I had faced that dreary journey, that chilly drive, that icy and inhospitable home-coming to empty rooms. Too late.

I discovered afterwards that Peddley's holidays were always spent at railway junctions, frontier towns and places of international resort, where he was likely to find a good supply of victims. For week-ends, Whitsun and Easter, he had his country house near Dover. At Christmas time he always took a week or ten days on the French Riviera. And during the summer he simultaneously satisfied his social passions and his passion for mountain scenery by taking up some strategic position on the Franco-Swiss, Italo-French, or Swiss-Italian frontier, where he could go for walks in the hills and, in the intervals, meet the trans-continental trains. One year he would take his family to Pontarlier; another to Valorbes; another to Modane; another to Brigue; another to Chiasso. In the course of a few years he had visited all the principal frontier towns in the mountainous parts of central and southern Europe. He knew the best seasons for each. Valorbes, for example, had to be visited early in the season.

It was in July and at the beginning of August that the great-
est number of English people passed through on their way
to Switzerland. When he had seen them on their homeward
way at the end of August, Peddley would move on for a fort-
night's stay to one of the Italian frontier towns, so as to catch
the September tourists on their way to Florence or Venice.
His favourite haunt at this season was Modane. There are
lots of good walks round Modane; and the principal trains
wait there for two and a half hours. Rosy with healthful ex-
ercise, Peddley would come striding down at the appointed
hour to meet the express. The victim was marked down,
caught, and led away to the station buffet. For the next two
hours Peddley indulged in what he called 'a *really* good chat.'

Peddley's circle of acquaintanceship was enormous.
There was his legal practice, to begin with; that brought
him into professional contact with a great variety of people.
Then there were his clubs; he was a member of three or four,
which he frequented assiduously. And, finally, there was
his own constantly hospitable dinner-table; it is astonishing
what even the richest men will put up with for the sake of
a good free meal. He was on talking terms with hundreds,
almost thousands, of his fellows. It was not to be wondered
at if he often spied familiar faces in the Modane custom-
house. But there were many days, of course, when nobody of
his acquaintance happened to be going South. On these oc-
casions Peddley would seek out some particularly harassed-
looking stranger and offer his assistance. The kindness, so
far as Peddley was concerned, was entirely wholehearted; he
was not conscious of the wolf concealed beneath his sheep's
clothing. He just felt a desire to be friendly and helpful and,
incidentally, chatty. And helpful he certainly was. But in the

fellow-beings that inspire our love or hate. I should not, I am sure, have found Herbert so deplorable if he had been smaller and less cumbrous, less clumsy of body. He was altogether too much the lubber fiend for my taste. Physically, Grace displayed little resemblance to her brother. She was tall, it is true, but slim and light of movement. Herbert was thick, shambling and leaden-footed. In a heavy, large-featured way, Herbert was not unhandsome. He had a profile; his nose and chin were Roman and positively noble. At a distance you might mistake him for some formidable Caesarean man of action. But when you came close enough to see his eyes and read the expression on that large pretentious face, you perceived that, if Roman, he was the dullest and blankest Roman of them all.

Grace was not in the least imposing or classical. You could never, at however great a distance, have mistaken her for the mother of the Gracchi. Her features were small and seemed, somehow, still indefinite, like the features of a child. A lot of dark red-brown hair which, at that epoch, when fashion still permitted women to have hair, she wore looped up in a couple of spirally coiled plaits over either ear, emphasized the pallor of that childish face. A pair of very round, wide-open grey eyes looked out from under the hair with an expression of slightly perplexed ingenuousness. Her face was the face of a rather ugly but very nice little girl. And when she smiled, she was suddenly almost beautiful. Herbert smiled in the same way—a sudden smile, full of kindness and good nature. It was that smile of his that made it impossible, for me at any rate, to treat him with proper ruthlessness. In both of them, brother and sister, it was a singularly dim and helpless goodness that expressed itself in that smile—a gentle, inefficient kindliness that was tinged, in Herbert's case, with a sort of loutish rusticity. He was a bumpkin even in his goodness. Grace's smile was dim, but expressive at the same time of a native refinement which Herbert did not possess. They were brother and sister; but hers was a soul of better, more aristocratic birth.

It was in her relations with her children that the inefficiency of Grace's benevolence revealed itself most clearly in practice. She loved them, but she didn't know what to do with them or how to treat them. It was lucky for her—and for the children too—that she could afford to keep nurses and governesses. She could never have brought her children up by herself. They would either have died in infancy, or, if they had survived the first two years of unpunctual and hopelessly unhygienic feeding, would have grown up into little savages. As it was, they had been well brought up by professional child-tamers, were healthy and, except towards their mother, beautifully behaved. Their mother, however, they regarded as a being of another species—a lovely and eminently adorable being, but not serious, like nurse or Miss Phillips, not really grown up; more than half a child, and what wasn't child, mostly fairy. Their mother was the elfin being who permitted or even herself suggested the most fantastic breaches of all the ordinary rules. It was she, for example, who had invented the sport of bathing, in summertime, under the revolving sprinkler which watered the lawn. It was she who had first suggested that excellent game, so strenuously disapproved of by Miss Phillips, nurse and father, of biting your slice of bread, at dinnertime, into the shape of a flower or a heart, a little bridge, a letter of the alphabet, a triangle, a railway engine. They adored her, but they would not take her seriously, as a person in authority; it never even occurred to them to obey her.

'You're a little girl,' I once heard her four-year-old daughter explaining to her. 'You're a little girl, mummy. Miss Phillips is an old lady.'

Grace turned her wide, perplexed eyes in my direction. 'You see,' she said despairingly, yet with a kind of triumph, as though she were conclusively proving a disputed point, 'you see! What *can* I do with them?'

She couldn't do anything. When she was alone with them, the children became like little wild beasts.

'But, children,' she would protest, 'children! You really mustn't.' But she knew that she might as well have expostulated with a litter of grizzly bears.

Sometimes, when the protest was more than ordinarily loud and despairing, the children would look up from their absorbing mischief and reassuringly smile to her. 'It's all right, mummy,' they would say. 'It's quite all right, you know.'

And then, helplessly, their mother would give it up.

In Herbert I found this helpless inefficiency intolerable. But the ineptitude of his sister had a certain style; even her clumsiness was somehow graceful. For clumsy she was. When it came to sewing, for example, her fingers were all thumbs. She had quite given up trying to sew when I first knew her. But she still regarded it as part of her maternal duty to knit warm mufflers—she never attempted anything more complicated than a muffler—for the children. She knitted very slowly, painfully concentrating her whole attention on the work in hand until, after a few minutes, exhausted by the mental strain, she was forced, with a great sigh, to give up and take a little rest. A muffler took months to finish. And when it was finished, what an extraordinary object it was! A sort of woollen fishing-net.

'Not *quite* right, I'm afraid,' Grace would say, holding it out at arm's length. 'Still,' she added, cocking her head on one side and half closing her eyes, as though she were looking at a *pointilliste* picture, 'it isn't bad, considering.'

Secretly, she was very proud of these mufflers, proud with the pride of a child who has written its first letter or embroidered on canvas its first kettle-holder, with practically no help at all from nurse. It still seemed to her extraordinary that she could do things all by herself, unassisted.

This graceful ineptitude of hers amused and charmed me. True, if I had had to marry it, I might not have found it quite so enchanting, if only for the reason that I should never have been able to afford a sufficiency of servants and child-tamers to counteract its effects on domestic, daily life. Nor, I am afraid, would the absurd charm of her intellectual vagueness have survived a long intimacy. For how vague, how bottomlessly vague she was! For example, she was quite incapable—and no experience could teach her—of realizing the value of money. At one moment she was lavishly extravagant, would spend pounds as though they were pence. The next, overvaluing her money as wildly as she had undervalued it, she would grudge every penny spent on the first necessities of life. Poor Peddley would sometimes come home from his office to find that there was nothing for dinner but lentils. Another man would have been violently and explosively annoyed; but Peddley, whose pedagogic passions were more powerful than his anger, only made a reasoned expostulation in the shape of a discourse on the meaning of money and the true nature of wealth, followed by a brief lecture on dietetics and the theory of calories. Grace listened attentively and with humility. But try as she would, she could never remember a word of what he had said; or rather she remembered, partially, but remembered all wrong. The phrases which Peddley had built up into a rational discourse, Grace rearranged in her mind so as to make complete nonsense. It was the same with what she read. The arguments got turned upside down. The non-essential facts were vividly remembered, the essential forgotten. Dates were utterly meaningless to her. Poor Grace! she was painfully conscious of her inefficiency of mind; she longed above everything to be learned, authoritative, capable. But though she read a great number of serious books—and read them with genuine pleasure, as well as on principle—she could never contrive to be well read. Inside her head everything got muddled. It was as though her mind were inhabited by some mischievous imp which delighted in taking to pieces the beautifully composed mosaics of learning and genius, and resetting the tesserae (after throwing a good many of them away) in the most fantastic and ludicrous disorder.

The consciousness of these defects made her particularly admire those who were distinguished by the opposite and positive qualities. It was this admiration, I am sure, which made her Peddley's wife. She was very young when he fell in love with her and asked her to marry him—eighteen to his thirty-four or thereabouts—very young and (being fresh from school, with its accompaniment of examination failures and pedagogic reproaches) more than ordinarily sensitive to her own shortcomings and to the merits of those unlike herself. Peddley made his entry into her life. The well-documented accuracy of his knowledge of artificial manures and the Swiss banking system astonished her. True, she did not feel a passionate interest in these subjects; but for that she blamed herself, not him. He seemed to her the personification of learning and wisdom—omniscient, an encyclopaedia on legs.

It is not uncommon for schoolgirls to fall in love with their aged professors. It is the tribute paid by youth—by flighty, high-spirited, but passionately earnest youth—to venerable mind. Grace was not lucky. The most venerable mind with which, at eighteen, she had yet come into contact was Peddley's. Peddley's! She admired, she was awed by what seemed to her the towering, Newtonian intellect of the man. And when the Newtonian intellect laid itself at her feet, she felt at first astonished—was it possible that he, Peddley, the omniscient, should abase himself before one who had failed three times, ignominiously, in the Cambridge Locals?—then flattered and profoundly grateful. Moreover, Peddley, unlike the proverbial professor, was neither grey-bearded nor decrepit. He was in the prime of life, extremely active, healthy, and energetic; good-looking, too, in the ruddy, large-chinned style of those Keen Business Men one sees portrayed in advertisements and the illustrations of magazine stories. Quite inexperienced in these matters, she easily persuaded herself that her gratitude and her schoolgirl's excitement were the genuine passion of the novels. She imagined that she was in love with him. And it would have mattered little, in all probability, if she had not. Peddley's tireless courtship would have ended infallibly by forcing her to surrender. There was no strength in Grace; she could be bullied into anything. In this case, however, only a very little bullying was necessary. At his second proposal, she accepted him. And so, in 1914, a month or two before the outbreak of war, they were married.

A marriage which began with the war might have been expected to be a strange, unusual, catastrophic marriage. But for the Peddleys, as a matter of fact, the war had next to no significance; it did not touch their life. For the first year John Peddley made Business as Usual his motto. Later, after being rejected for active service on account of his short sight, he enrolled himself as a temporary bureaucrat; was highly efficient in a number of jobs; had managed, when the medical boards became stricter, to make himself indispensable, as a sugar rationer; and ended up with an O.B.E. Grace, meanwhile, lived quietly at home and gave birth, in three successive years, to three children. They kept her occupied; the war, for her, was an irrelevance. She witnessed neither its tragedies, nor its feverish and sordid farces. She knew as little of apprehension, suspense, grief, as she knew of the reckless extravagances, the intoxications, the too facile pleasures, the ferocious debaucheries which ran parallel with the agonies, which mingled and alternated with them. Ineffectually, Grace nursed her babies; she might have been living in the eighteenth century.

At the time I knew her first Grace had been married about six years. Her eldest child was five years old, her youngest about two. Peddley, I judged, was still in love with her—in his own way, that is. The wild passion which had hurried him into a not very reasonable marriage, a passion mainly physical, had subsided. He was no longer mad about Grace; but he continued to find her eminently desirable. Habit, moreover, had endeared her to him, had made her

indispensable; it had become difficult for him to imagine
an existence without her. But for all that, there was no in-
timacy between them. Possessing, as I have said, no private
life of his own, Peddley did not understand the meaning of
intimacy. He could give no confidences and therefore asked
for none. He did not know what to do with them when they
came to him unasked. I do not know if Grace ever tried
to confide in him; if so, she must soon have given it up as
a bad job. One might as well have tried to confide into a
gramophone; one might whisper the most secret and sacred
thoughts into the trumpet of the machine, but there came
back only a loud booming voice that expounded the finan-
cial policy of Sweden, food control, or the law relating to
insurance companies—it depended which particular record
out of the large, but still limited repertory, happened at the
moment to be on the turn table. In the spiritual home of the
Peddleys there was only a bedroom and a lecture-room—no
sentimental boudoir for confidences, no quiet study pleas-
antly violated from time to time by feminine intrusion.
Nothing between the physical intimacies of the bedroom
and the impersonal relations of pupil and sonorously braying
professor in the reverberant lecture-hall. And then, what
lectures!

Grace, who still believed in the intellectual eminence of
her husband, continued to blame herself for finding them
tedious. But tedious they were to her; that was a fact she
could not deny. Long practice had taught her to cultivate
a kind of mental deafness. Peddley's discourses no longer
got on her nerves, because she no longer heard them. I have
often seen her sitting, her wide eyes turned on Peddley
with an expression, apparently, of rapt attention, seeming to

drink in every word he uttered. It was so she must have sat in those first months of her marriage, when she really did listen, when she still tried her hardest to be interested and to remember correctly. Only in those days, I fancy, there can never have been quite so perfect a serenity on her face. There must have been little frowns of concentration and agonizingly suppressed yawns. Now there was only an unruffled calm, the calm of complete and absolute abstraction.

I found her out on the very first evening of our acquaintance. John Peddley, who must have been told (I suppose by Herbert) that I was interested, more or less professionally, in music, began, in my honour, a long description of the mechanism of pianolas. I was rather touched by this manifest effort to make me feel spiritually at home, and, though I was dizzied by the sound of his voice, made a great show of being interested in what he was saying. In a pause, while Peddley was helping himself to the vegetables (what a blessing it was to have a moment's respite from that maddening voice!), I turned to Grace and asked her politely, as a new guest should, whether she were as much interested in pianolas as her husband. She started, as though I had woken her out of sleep, turned on me a pair of blank, rather frightened eyes, blushed scarlet.

'As much interested as John in *what*?' she asked.

'Pianolas.'

'Oh, pianolas.' And she uttered the word in a puzzled, bewildered tone which made it quite clear that she had no idea that pianolas had been the subject of conversation for at least the last ten minutes. 'Pianolas?' she repeated almost incredulously. And she had seemed so deeply attentive.

I admired her for this power of absenting herself, for

being, spiritually, not there. I admired, but I also pitied. To have to live in surroundings from which it was necessary, in mere self-preservation, to absent oneself—that was pitiable indeed.

Next morning, assuming an invalid's privilege, I had breakfast in bed. By the time I came down from my room, Peddley and Herbert had set out for a hearty walk. I found Grace alone, arranging flowers. We exchanged good-mornings. By the expression of her face, I could see that she found my presence rather formidable. A stranger, a high-brow, a musical critic—what to say to him? Courageously doing her duty, she began to talk to me about Bach. Did I like Bach? Didn't I think he was the greatest musician? I did my best to reply; but somehow, at that hour of the morning, there seemed to be very little to say about Bach. The conversation began to droop.

'And the *Well-Tempered Clavichord*,' she went on desperately. 'What lovely things in that!'

'And so useful for torturing children who learn the piano,' I replied, as desperately. Facetiousness, the last resort.

But my words had touched a chord in Grace's mind. 'Torture,' she said. 'That's the word. I remember when I was at school . . .'

And there we were, happily launched at last upon an interesting, because a personal, subject.

Grace was as fond of her dear old school as Herbert was of his. But, with the rest of her sex, she had a better excuse for her fondness. For many women, the years spent in that uncomplicated, companionable, exciting, purely feminine world, which is the world of school, are the happiest of their lives. Grace was one of them. She adored her school; she looked back on her schooldays as on a golden age. True, there had been Cambridge Locals and censorious mistresses; but on the other hand, there had been no Peddley, no annual child-bearing, no domestic responsibilities, no social duties, no money to be too lavish or too stingy with, no servants. She talked with enthusiasm, and I listened with pleasure.

An hour and a half later, when the bores came back, red-faced and ravenous, from their walk, we were sorry to be interrupted. I had learned a great many facts about Grace's girlhood. I knew that she had had an unhappy passion for the younger of the visiting music mistresses; that one of her friends had received a love-letter from a boy of fifteen, beginning: 'I saw a photograph of you in the *Sketch*, walking in the Park with your mother. Can I ever forget it?' I knew that she had had mumps for five weeks, that she had climbed on the roof by moonlight in pyjamas, that she was no good at hockey.

From time to time most of us feel a need, often urgent and imperious, to talk about ourselves. We desire to assert our personalities, to insist on a fact which the world about us seems in danger of forgetting—the fact that we exist, that we are we. In some people the desire is so chronic and so strong, that they can never stop talking about themselves. Rather than be silent, they will pour out the most humiliating and discreditable confidences. Grace was afflicted by no such perverse and extravagant longings; there was nothing of the exhibitionist in her. But she did like, every now and then, to have a good talk about her soul, her past history, her future. She liked to talk, and she too rarely had an opportunity. In me she found a sympathetic listener and commentator. By the end of the morning she was regarding me as an old friend. And I, for my part, had found her charming. So charming, indeed, that for Grace's sake I was prepared to put up even with John Peddley's exposition of the law regarding insurance companies.

Within a few weeks of our first introduction we were finding it the most natural thing in the world that we should be constantly meeting. We talked a great deal, on these occasions, about ourselves, about Life and about Love— subjects which can be discussed with the fullest pleasure and profit only between persons of opposite sexes. On none of these three topics, it must be admitted, did Grace have very much of significance to say. She had lived very little and loved not at all; it was impossible, therefore, that she should know herself. But it was precisely this ignorance and her ingenuous, confident expression of it that charmed me.

'I feel I'm already old,' she complained to me. 'Old and finished. Like those funny straw hats and leg-of-mutton sleeves in the bound volumes of the *Illustrated London News*,' she added, trying to make her meaning clearer for me.

I laughed at her. 'You're absurdly young,' I said, 'and you haven't begun.'

She shook her head and sighed.

When we talked about love, she professed a sad, middle-aged scepticism.

'People make a most ridiculous fuss about it.'

'Rightly.'

'But it's not worth making a fuss about,' she insisted. 'Not in reality. Not outside of books.'

'Isn't it?' I said. 'You'll think differently,' I told her, 'when you've waited two or three hours for somebody who hasn't turned up, when you can't sleep for wondering where somebody's been and with whom, and you want to cry—yes, you do cry—and you feel as though you were just going to have influenza.'

'Ah, but that isn't love,' Grace retorted sententiously, in the tone of one who has some private and certain source of information.

'What is it, then?'

'It's . . .' Grace hesitated and suddenly blushed, 'it's . . . well, it's physical.'

I could not help laughing, uproariously.

Grace was vexed. 'Well, isn't it true?' she insisted obstinately.

'Perfectly,' I had to admit. 'But why isn't that love?' I added, hoping to elicit Grace's views on the subject.

She let me have them. They were positively Dantesque. I can only suppose that Peddley's ardours had left her cold, disgusted even.

But Life and Love were not our only topics. Grace's ignorance and my own native reticence made it impossible for us to discuss these themes with any profit for very long at a stretch. In the intervals, like John Peddley, I played the pedagogic part. Through casual remarks of mine, Grace suddenly became aware of things whose very existence had previously been unknown to her—things like contemporary painting and literature, young music, new theories of art. It was a revelation. All her efforts, it seemed to her, all her strivings towards culture had been wasted. She had been laboriously trying to scale the wrong mountain, to force her way into the wrong sanctuary. At the top, if she had ever reached it, within the holy of holies, she would have found—what? a grotesque and moth-eaten collection of those funny little straw hats and leg-of-mutton sleeves from the bound volumes of the *Illustrated London News*. It was dreadful, it was humiliating. But now she had caught a glimpse of another sanctuary, upholstered by Martine, enriched by the offerings of the Poirets and Lanvins of the spirit; a modish, modern sanctuary; a fashionable Olympus. She was eager to climb, to enter.

Acting the part of those decayed gentlewomen who, for a consideration, introduce *parvenus* into good society, I made Grace acquainted with all that was smartest and latest in the world of the spirit. I gave her lessons in intellectual etiquette, warned her against aesthetic *gaffes*. She listened attentively, and was soon tolerably at home in the unfamiliar world—knew what to say when confronted by a Dada poem, a picture by Picasso, a Schoenberg quartet, an Archipenko sculpture.

I was working, at that period, as a musical critic, and two or three times a week I used to take Grace with me to my concerts. It did not take me long to discover that she had very little feeling for music and no analytical understanding of it. But she professed, hypocritically, to adore it. And as it bored me most excruciatingly to have to go by myself to listen to second-rate pianists playing the same old morsels of Liszt and Chopin, second-rate contraltos fruitily hooting Schubert and Brahms, second-rate fiddlers scraping away at Tartini and Wieniawski, I pretended to believe in Grace's enthusiasm for the musical art and took her with me to all the most painful recitals. If the hall were empty—which, to the eternal credit of the music-loving public, it generally was—one could get a seat at the back, far away from the other sparsely sprinkled auditors, and talk very pleasantly through the whole performance.

At first, Grace was terribly shocked when, after listen-

ing judicially to the first three bars of *Du bist wie eine Blume*
or the *Trillo del Diavolo*, I opened a conversation. She her-
self had a very perfect concert-goer's technique, and listened
with the same expression of melancholy devotion, as though
she were in church, to every item on the programme. My
whispered chatter seemed to her sacrilegious. It was only
when I assured her, professionally and *ex cathedra*, that the
stuff wasn't worth listening to, that she would consent, albeit
with considerable misgivings in the early days of our concert-
going, to take her part in the conversation. In a little while,
however, she grew accustomed to the outrage; so much so,
that when the music or the performance happened to be
good (a little detail which Grace was not sufficiently musical
to notice) it was I who had to play the verger's part and hush
her sacrilegious chatter in a place suddenly made holy. She
learned in the end to take her cue from me—to look devout
when I looked devout, to chatter when I chattered.

Once, rather maliciously, I put on my raptest expression
while some maudlin incompetent was pounding out Rach-
maninoff. After a quick glance at me through the tail of her
eye, Grace also passed into ecstasy, gazing at the pianist as
St. Theresa might have gazed at the uplifted Host. When the
ordeal was over, she turned on me a pair of bright, shining eyes.

'Wasn't that splendid?' she said. And such is the power
of self-suggestion, that she had genuinely enjoyed it.

'I thought it the most revolting performance I ever lis-
tened to,' was my answer.

Poor Grace turned fiery red, the tears came into her eyes;

---

* "You are like a flower"

† *The Devil's Trill Sonata.*

‡ With the full authority of office.

to hide them from me, she averted her face. 'I thought it very good,' she insisted, heroically. 'But of course I'm no judge.'

'Oh, of course it wasn't as bad as all that,' I made haste to assure her. 'One exaggerates, you know.' The sight of her unhappy face had made me feel profoundly penitent. I had meant only to make mild fun of her, and I had managed somehow to hurt her, cruelly. I wished to goodness that I had never played the stupid trick. It was a long time before she completely forgave me.

Later, when I knew her better, I came to understand why it was that she had taken my little clownery so hardly. Rudely and suddenly, my joke had shattered one of those delightful pictures of herself which Grace was for ever fancifully creating and trying to live up to. What had been a joke for me had been, for her, a kind of murder.

Grace was a born visualizer. I discovered, for example, that she had what Galton calls a 'number form.' When she had to do any sort of arithmetical calculation, she saw the figures arranged in space before her eyes. Each number had its own peculiar colour and its own position in the form. After a hundred the figures became dim; that was why she always found it so difficult to work in large numbers. The difference between three thousand, thirty thousand, and three hundred thousand was never immediately apparent to her, because in the case of these large numbers she could *see* nothing; they floated indistinctly on the blurred fringes of her number form. A million, however, she saw quite clearly; its place was high up, to the left, above her head, and it consisted of a huge pile of those envelopes they have at banks for putting money in—thousands and thousands of them, each marked with the word MILLION in large black letters. All her mental processes were a succession of visual images; and these mental pictures were so vivid as to rival in brightness and definition the images she received through her eyes. What she could not visualize, she could not think about.

I am myself a very poor visualizer. I should find it very difficult, for example, to describe from memory the furniture in my room. I know that there are so many chairs, so many tables, doors, bookshelves, and so on; but I have no clear mental vision of them. When I do mental arithmetic, I see no coloured numbers. The word Africa does not call up in my mind, as Grace assured me once that it always did in hers, a vision of sand with palm trees and lions. When I make plans for the future, I do not see myself, as though on the stage, playing a part in imaginary dramas. I think without pictures, abstractly and in the void. That is why I cannot pretend to write with complete understanding of the workings of Grace's mind. The congenitally deaf are not the best judges of music. I can only guess, only imaginatively reconstruct.

From what I gathered in conversation with her, I imagine that Grace was in the habit of vividly 'seeing herself' in every kind of situation. Some of these situations had no relation to her actual life, were the purely fantastic and hypothetical situations of daydreams. Others were real, or at any rate potentially real, situations. Living her life, she saw herself living it, acting in the scenes of the flat quotidian drama a very decided and definite part. Thus, when she went for a walk in the country, she saw herself walking—a female mountaineer for tireless strength and energy. When she accompanied Peddley on his annual expeditions to the Riviera, she saw herself as she climbed into the *wagon lit*, or swam along the Promenade des Anglais, as an immensely rich and haughty milady, envied by the *canaille*, remote and star-like above them. On certain socially important occasions at home, a similar character made its appearance. I saw the milady once or twice during the first months of our acquaintanceship. Later on the milady turned into a very Parisian, very twentieth-cum-eighteenth-century *grande dame*. But of that in its place.

Grace was much assisted in these visualizations of herself by her clothes. In the costume which she donned for a two-mile walk in Kent she might have crossed the Andes. And in all her garments, for every occasion, one noticed the same dramatic appropriateness. It was a pity that she did not know how to change her features with her clothes. Her face, whether she lolled along the sea-fronts of the Riviera or addressed herself, in brogues, short skirts, and sweaters to the ascent of some Kentish hillock, was always the same—the face of a rather ugly but very nice little girl; a face that opened on to the world through large, perplexed eyes, and that became, from time to time, suddenly and briefly beautiful with a dim benevolence when she smiled.

Grace's visions of herself were not merely momentary and occasional. There was generally one predominating character in which she saw herself over considerable periods of time. During the first four years of her marriage, for example, she had seen herself predominantly as the housewife and mother. But her manifest incapacity to act either of these parts successfully had gradually chilled her enthusiasm for them. She wanted to run the house, she saw herself tinkling about with keys, giving orders to the maids; but, in practice, whenever she interfered with the rule of her masterful

---

* Rabble, riffraff.

† An elderly woman of great prestige.

old cook, everything went wrong. She loved her children, she pictured them growing up, healthy and good, under her influence; but they were always sick when she fed them, they behaved like beasts when she tried to make them obey. To one who tried to see herself as the complete, the almost German matron, it was not encouraging. By the time her last child was born, she had practically abandoned the attempt. From the first, the baby had been handed over, body and soul, to the nurses. And except when she was seized with a financial panic and forbade the ordering of anything but lentils, she let the old cook have her way.

When I first met her, Grace was not seeing herself continuously in any one predominating rôle. Punctured by sharp experience, the matron had flattened out and collapsed; and the matron had had, so far, no successor. Left without an imaginary character to live up to, Grace had relapsed into that dim characterlessness which in her, as in Herbert, seemed to be the natural state. She still saw herself vividly enough in the separate, occasional incidents of her life—as the mountain climber, as the rich and haughty milady. But she saw no central and permanent figure in whose life these incidents of mountaineering and opulently visiting the Riviera occurred. She was a succession of points, so to speak; not a line.

Her friendship with me was responsible for the emergence into her consciousness of a new permanent image of herself. She discovered in my company a new rôle, not so important, indeed, not so rich in potentialities as that of the matron, but still a leading lady's part. She had been so long without a character that she eagerly embraced the opportunity of acquiring one, however incongruous. And incongruous it was, this new character; odd and eminently unsuitable. Grace had come to see herself as a musical critic.

It was our concert-going—our professional concert-going—that had done it. If I had happened not to be a journalist, if we had paid for admission instead of coming in free on my complimentary tickets, it would never have occurred to her to see herself as a critic. Simple mortals, accustomed to pay for their pleasures, are always impressed by the sight of a free ticket. The critic's *jus primae noctis** seems to them an enviable thing. Sharing the marvellous privilege, Grace came to feel that she must also share the judicial duties of a critic. She saw herself distributing praise and blame—a rapturous listener when the performance was worth listening to, a contemptuous chatterer when it wasn't. Identifying herself with me—not the real but an ideal exalted me—she pictured herself as the final arbiter of musical reputations. My malicious little practical joke had thrown down this delightful image of herself. The critic had suddenly been murdered.

At the time I did not understand why poor Grace should have been so deeply hurt. It was only in the light of my later knowledge that I realized what must have been her feelings. It was only later, too, that I came to understand the significance of that curious little pantomime which she used regularly to perform as we entered a concert hall. That languid gait with which she strolled across the vestibule, dragging her feet with a kind of reluctance, as though she were on boring business; that sigh, that drooping of the eyelids as she stood, patiently, while the attendant looked at my tickets; that air, when we were in the concert-room, of being perfectly

---

* A supposed right of a feudal lord to have sexual relations with a vassal's bride on her wedding night.

at home, of owning the place (she used, I remember, to put her feet up on the seat in front); and that smile of overacted contempt, that wearily amused smile with which she used (once she had got over the idea that she was committing a sacrilege) to respond, during a bad performance, to my whispered chatter—these were the gait, the bored patience, the possessive at-homeness, the contempt of a hardened critic.

And what a quantity of music she bought at this time and never played! How many volumes of musical criticism and biography she took out of the library! And the grave pronouncements she used to make across the dinner-table! 'Beethoven was the greatest of them all'; and so on in the same style. I understood it all afterwards. And the better I understood, the more I regretted my cruel little joke. As the critic, she had been so happy. My joke destroyed that happiness. She became diffident and self-conscious, got actor's fright; and though I never repeated the jest, though I always encouraged her, after that, to believe in her musicianship, she could never whole-heartedly see herself in the part again.

But what a poor part, at the best of times, the critic's was! It was too dry, too intellectual and impersonal to be really satisfying. That it lay within my power to provide her with a much better rôle—the guilty wife's—I do not and did not at the time much doubt. True, when I knew her first, Grace was a perfectly virtuous young woman. But her virtue was founded on no solid principle—on a profound love for her husband, for example; or on strong religious prejudices. It was not a virtue that in any way involved her intimate being. If she happened to be virtuous, it was more by accident than on principle or from psychological necessity. She had not yet had any occasion for not being virtuous, that was all. She could have been bullied or cajoled into infidelity as she had been bullied and cajoled by Peddley into marriage. Grace floated vaguely on the surface of life without compass or destination; one had only to persuade her that adultery was Eldorado, and she would have shaped her course forthwith towards that magical shore. It was just a question of putting the case sufficiently speciously. She still retained, at this time, the prejudices of her excellent upper middle-class upbringing; but they were not very deeply rooted. Nothing in Grace was so deeply rooted that it could not quite easily be eradicated.

I realized these facts at the time. But I did not try to take advantage of them. The truth is that, though I liked Grace very much, I was never urgently in love with her. True, one can very agreeably and effectively act the part of the 'lover,' in the restricted and technical sense of that term, without being wildly in love. And if both parties could always guarantee to keep their emotions in a state of equilibrium, these little sentimental sensualities would doubtless be most exquisitely diverting. But the equilibrium can never be guaranteed. The balanced hearts begin sooner or later, almost inevitably, to tilt towards love or hatred. In the end, one of the sentimental sensualities turns into a passion—whether of longing or disgust it matters not—and then, farewell to all hope of tranquillity. I should be chary of saying so in Kingham's presence; but the fact remains that I like tranquility. For me, the love-game, without love, is not worth the candle. Even as a mere hedonist I should have refrained. And I had other scruples—scruples which an overmastering passion might have overridden, but which were sufficient to keep a mere mild sensuality in check. I was never Grace's lover; neither genuinely, by right of passion, nor technically by the accident of physical possession. Never her lover. An ironic fate had reserved for me a less glorious part—the part, not of the lover, but of the introducer of lovers. All unintentionally, I was to play benevolent Uncle Pandarus to Grace's Cressida. And there were two Troiluses.

The first of them was no less—or shouldn't I rather say 'no more'? for how absurdly his reputation was exaggerated!—than Clegg, *the* Clegg, Rodney Clegg, the painter. I have known Clegg for years and liked him, in a way—liked him rather as one likes Grock, or Little Tich, or the Fratellini: as a comic spectacle. This is not the best way of liking people, I know. But with Rodney it was the only way. You had either to like him as a purveyor of amusement, or dislike him as a human being. That, at any rate, was always my experience. I have tried hard to get to know and like him intimately—off the stage, so to speak. But it was never any good. In the end, I gave up the attempt once and for all, took to regarding him quite frankly as a music hall comedian, and was able, in consequence, thoroughly to enjoy his company. Whenever I feel like a tired business man, I go to see Rodney Clegg.

Perhaps, as a lover, Rodney was somehow different from his ordinary self. Perhaps he dropped his vanity and his worldliness. Perhaps he became unexpectedly humble and unselfish, forgot his snobbery, craved no longer for cheap successes and, for love, thought the world well lost. Perhaps. Or more probably, I am afraid, he remained very much as he always was, and only in Grace's eyes seemed different from the Rodney whose chatter and little antics diverted the tired business man in me. Was hers the correct vision of him, or was mine? Neither, I take it.

It must have been in the spring of 1921 that I first took Grace to Rodney's studio. For her, the visit was an event; she was about to see, for the first time in her life, a famous man. Particularly famous at the moment, it happened; for Rodney was very much in the papers that season. There had been a fuss about his latest exhibition. The critics, with a fine contemptuous inaccuracy, had branded his pictures as post-impressionistic, cubistic, futuristic; they threw any brick-bat that came to hand. And the pictures had been found improper as well as disturbingly 'modern.' Professional moralists had been sent by the Sunday papers to look at them; they came back boiling with professional indignation. Rodney was delighted, of course. This was fame—and a fame, moreover, that was perfectly compatible with prosperity. The outcry of the professional moralists did not interfere with his sales. He was doing a very good business.

Rodney's conversion to 'modern art,' instead of ruining him, had been the source of increased profit and an enhanced notoriety. With his unfailing, intuitive knowledge of what the public wanted, he had devised a formula which combined modernity with the more appealing graces of literature and pornography. Nothing, for example, could have been less academic than his nudes. They were monstrously elongated; the paint was laid on quite flatly; there was no modelling, no realistic light and shade; the human form was reduced to a paper silhouette. The eyes were round black boot-buttons, the nipples magenta berries, the lips vermilion hearts; the hair was represented by a collection of crinkly

black lines. The exasperated critics of the older school pro-
tested that a child of ten could have painted them. But the
child of ten who could have painted such pictures must have
been an exceedingly perverse child. In comparison, Freud's
Little Hans would have been an angel of purity. For Rod-
ney's nudes, however unrealistic, were luscious and volup-
tuous, were even positively indecent. What had distressed
the public in the work of the French post-impressionists was
not so much the distortion and the absence of realism as the
repellant austerity, the intellectual asceticism, which rejected
the appeal both of sex and of the anecdote. Rodney had sup-
plied the deficiencies. For these engagingly luscious nudities
of his were never represented in the void, so to speak, but
in all sorts of curious and amusing situations—taking tick-
ets at railway stations, or riding bicycles, or sitting at cafés
with negro jazz-bands in the background, drinking *crème
de menthe.* All the people who felt that they ought to be in
the movement, that it was a disgrace not to like modern art,
discovered in Rodney Clegg, to their enormous delight, a
modern artist whom they could really and honestly admire.
His pictures sold like hot cakes.

The conversion to modernism marked the real begin-
ning of Rodney's success. Not that he had been unknown
or painfully poor before his conversion. A man with Rod-
ney's social talents, with Rodney's instinct for popularity,
could never have known real obscurity or poverty. But all
things are relative; before his conversion, Rodney had been
obscurer and poorer than he deserved to be. He knew no
duchesses, no millionairesses, then; he had no deposit at the
bank—only a current account that swelled and ebbed capri-

ciously, like a mountain stream. His conversion changed all that.

When Grace and I paid our first visit, he was already on the upward path.

'I hope he isn't very formidable,' Grace said to me, as we were making our way to Hampstead to see him. She was always rather frightened by the prospect of meeting new people.

I laughed. 'It depends what you're afraid of,' I said. 'Of being treated with high-brow haughtiness, or losing your virtue. I never heard of any woman who found him formidable in the first respect.'

'Oh, that's all right, then,' said Grace, looking relieved.

Certainly, there was nothing very formidable in Rodney's appearance. At the age of thirty-five he had preserved (and he also cultivated with artful care) the appearance of a good-looking boy. He was small and neatly made, slim, and very agile in his movements. Under a mass of curly brown hair, which was always in a state of picturesque and studied untidiness, his face was like the face of a lively and impertinent cherub. Smooth, rounded, almost unlined, it still preserved its boyish contours. (There were always pots and pots of beauty cream on his dressing-table.) His eyes were blue, bright and expressive. He had good teeth, and when he smiled two dimples appeared in his cheeks.

He opened the studio door himself. Dressed in his butcher's blue overalls, he looked charming. One's instinct was to pat the curly head and say: 'Isn't he too sweet! Dressed up like that, pretending to be a workman!' Even I felt moved to make some such gesture. To a woman, a potential mother of chubby children, the temptation must have been almost irresistible.

Rodney was very cordial. 'Dear old Dick!' he said, and patted me on the shoulder. I had not seen him for some months; he had spent the winter abroad. 'What a delight to see you!' I believe he genuinely liked me.

I introduced him to Grace. He kissed her hand. 'Too charming of you to have come. And what an enchanting ring!' he added, looking down again at her hand, which he still held in his own. 'Do, please, let me look at it.'

Grace smiled and blushed with pleasure as she gave it him. 'I got it in Florence,' she said. 'I'm so glad you like it.'

It was certainly a charming piece of old Italian jewellery. Sadly I reflected that I had known Grace intimately for more than six months and never so much as noticed the ring, far less made any comment on it. No wonder that I had been generally unlucky in love.

We found the studio littered with specimens of Rodney's latest artistic invention. Naked ladies in brown boots leading borzoi dogs; tenderly embracing one another in the middle of a still-life of bottles, guitars and newspapers (the old familiar modern still-life rendered acceptable to the great public and richly saleable by the introduction of the equivocal nudes); more naked ladies riding on bicycles (Rodney's favourite subject, his patent, so to say); playing the concertina; catching yellow butterflies in large green nets. Rodney brought them out one by one. From her arm-chair in front of the easel, Grace looked at them; her face wore that rapt religious expression which I had so often noticed in the concert-room.

'Lovely,' she murmured, as canvas succeeded canvas, 'too lovely.'

Looking at the pictures, I reflected with some amusement that, a year before, Rodney had been painting melodramatic crucifixions in the style of Tiepolo. At that time he had been an ardent Christian.

'Art can't live without religion,' he used to say then. 'We must get back to religion.'

And with his customary facility Rodney had got back to it. Oh, those pictures! They were really shocking in their accomplished insincerity. So emotional, so dramatic, and yet so utterly false and empty. The subjects, you felt, had been apprehended as a cinema producer might apprehend them, in terms of 'effectiveness.' There were always great darknesses and tender serene lights, touches of vivid colour and portentous silhouettes. Very 'stark,' was what Rodney's admirers used to call those pictures, I remember. They were too stark by half for my taste.

Rodney set up another canvas on the easel.

'I call this "The Bicycle made for Two,"' he said.

It represented a negress and a blonde with a Chinese white skin, riding on a tandem bicycle against a background of gigantic pink and yellow roses. In the foreground, on the right, stood a plate of fruit, tilted forward towards the spectator, in the characteristic 'modern' style. A greyhound trotted along beside the bicycle.

'Really too . . .' began Grace ecstatically. But finding no synonym for 'lovely,' the epithet which she had applied to all the other pictures, she got no further, but made one of those non-committal laudatory noises, which are so much more satisfactory than articulate speech, when you don't know what to say to an artist about his works. She looked up at me. 'Isn't it really . . . ?' she asked.

'Yes, absolutely . . .' I nodded my affirmation. Then, rather maliciously, 'Tell me, Rodney,' I said, 'do you still paint religious pictures? I remember a most grandiose Descent from the Cross you were busy on not so long ago.'

But my malice was disappointed. Rodney was not in the least embarrassed by this reminder of the skeleton in his cupboard. He laughed.

'Oh, *that*,' he said. 'I painted it over. Nobody would buy. One cannot serve God and Mammon.' And he laughed again, heartily, at his own witticism.

It went into his repertory at once, that little joke. He took to introducing the subject of his religious paintings himself, in order to have an opportunity of bringing out the phrase, with a comical parody of clerical unction, at the end of his story. In the course of the next few weeks I heard him repeat it, in different assemblages, three or four times.

'God and Mammon,' he chuckled again. 'Can't be combined.'

'Only goddesses and Mammon,' I suggested, nodding in the direction of his picture.

Later, I had the honour of hearing my words incorporated into Rodney's performance. He had a wonderfully retentive memory.

'Precisely,' he said. 'Goddesses, I'm happy to say, of a more popular religion. Are you a believer, Mrs. Peddley?' He smiled at her, raising his eyebrows. 'I am—fervently. I'm *croyant** and' (he emphasized the 'and' with arch significance) '*pratiquant.*†'

Grace laughed rather nervously, not knowing what to answer. 'Well, I suppose we all are,' she said. She was not accustomed to this sort of gallantry.

Rodney smiled at her more impertinently than ever.

---

* A believer.

† An observant follower.

'How happy I should be,' he said, 'if I could make a convert of you!'

Grace repeated her nervous laugh and, to change the subject, began to talk about the pictures.

We sat there for some time, talking, drinking tea, smoking cigarettes. I looked at my watch; it was half-past six. I knew that Grace had a dinner-party that evening.

'We shall have to go,' I said to her. 'You'll be late for your dinner.'

'Good heavens!' cried Grace, when she heard what the time was. She jumped up. 'I must fly. Old Lady Wackerbath—imagine if I kept her waiting!' She laughed, but breathlessly; and she had gone quite pale with anticipatory fright.

'Stay, do stay,' implored Rodney. 'Keep her waiting.'

'I daren't.'

'But, my dear lady, you're young,' he insisted; 'you have the right—I'd say the duty, if the word weren't so coarse and masculine—to be unpunctual. At your age you must do what you like. You see, I'm assuming that you like being here,' he added parenthetically.

She returned his smile. 'Of course.'

'Well then, stay; do what you like; follow your caprices. After all, that's what you're there for.' Rodney was very strong on the Eternal Feminine.

Grace shook her head. 'Good-bye. I've loved it so much.'

Rodney sighed, looked sad and slowly shook his head. 'If you'd loved it as much as all that,' he said, 'as much as I've loved it, you wouldn't be saying good-bye. But if you must. . . .' He smiled seductively; the teeth flashed, the dimples punctually appeared. He took her hand, bent over it and tenderly kissed it. 'You must come again,' he added.

'Soon. And,' turning to me with a laugh, and patting my shoulder, 'without old Dick.'

'He's frightfully amusing, isn't he?' Grace said to me a minute later when we had left the studio.

'Frightfully,' I agreed, laying a certain emphasis on the adverb.

'And really,' she continued, 'most awfully nice, I thought.'

I made no comment.

'And a wonderful painter,' she added.

All at once I felt that I detested Rodney Clegg. I thought of my own sterling qualities of mind and heart, and it seemed to me outrageous, it seemed to me scandalous and intolerable that people, that is to say women in general, and Grace in particular, should be impressed and taken in and charmed by this little middle-aged charlatan with the pretty boy's face and the horribly knowing, smart, impertinent manner. It seemed to me a disgrace. I was on the point of giving vent to my indignation; but it occurred to me, luckily, just in time that I should only be quite superfluously making a fool of myself if I did. Nothing is more ridiculous than a scene of jealousy, particularly when the scene is made by somebody who has no right to make it and on no grounds whatever. I held my tongue. My indignation against Rodney died down; I was able to laugh at myself. But driving southward through the slums of Camden Town, I looked attentively at Grace and found her more than ordinarily charming, desirable even. I would have liked to tell her so and, telling, kiss her. But I lacked the necessary impudence; I felt diffident of my capacity to carry the amorous undertaking through to a successful issue. I said nothing, risked no gesture. But I decided, when the time should come for us to part, that I would kiss her hand. It was a thing I had never done before. At the last moment, however, it occurred to me that she might imagine that, in kissing her hand, I was only stupidly imitating Rodney Clegg. I was afraid she might think that his example had emboldened me. We parted on the customary handshake.

Four or five weeks after our visit to Rodney's studio, I went abroad for a six months' stay in France and Germany. In the interval, Grace and Rodney had met twice, the first time in my flat, for tea, the second at her house, where she had asked us both to lunch. Rodney was brilliant on both occasions. A little too brilliant indeed—like a smile of false teeth, I thought. But Grace was dazzled. She had never met any one like this before. Her admiration delighted Rodney.

'Intelligent woman,' was his comment, as we left her house together after lunch.

A few days later I set out for Paris.

'You must promise to write,' said Grace in a voice full of sentiment when I came to say good-bye.

I promised, and made her promise too. I did not know exactly why we should write to one another or what we should write about; but it seemed, none the less, important that we should write. Letter-writing has acquired a curious sentimental prestige which exalts it, in the realm of friendship, above mere conversation; perhaps because we are less shy at long range than face to face, because we dare to say more in written than in spoken words.

It was Grace who first kept her promise.

'My dear Dick,' she wrote. 'Do you remember what you said about Mozart? That his music seems so gay on the surface—so gay and careless; but underneath it is sad and melancholy, almost despairing. I think life is like that, really. Everything goes with such a bustle; but what's it all for? And how sad, how sad it is! Now you mustn't flatter yourself by imagining that I feel like this just because you happen to have gone away—though as a matter of fact I *am* sorry you aren't here to talk about music and people and life and so forth. No, don't flatter yourself; because I've really felt like this for years, almost for ever. It's, so to speak, the bass of my music, this feeling; it throbs along all the time, regardless of what may be happening in the treble. Jigs, minuets, mazurkas, Blue Danube waltzes; but the bass remains the same. This isn't very good counterpoint, I know; but you see what I mean? The children have just left me, yelling. Phyllis has just smashed that hideous Copenhagen rabbit Aunt Eleanor gave me for Christmas. I'm delighted, of course; but I mayn't say so. And in any case, why must they always act such knockabouts? Sad, sad. And Lecky's *History of European Morals*, that's sadder still. It's a book I can never find my place in. Page 100 seems exactly the same as page 200. No clue. So that—you know how conscientious I am—I always have to begin again at the beginning. It's very discouraging. I haven't the spirit to begin again, yet again, this evening. I write to you instead. But in a moment I must go and dress for dinner. John's partner is coming; surely no man has a right to be so bald. And Sir Walter Magellan, who is something at the Board of Trade and makes jokes; with Lady M——, who's *so* affectionate. She has a way of kissing me, suddenly and intently, like a snake striking. And she spits when she talks. Then there's Molly Bone, who's so nice; but why can't she get married? And the Robsons, about whom there's nothing to say. Nothing whatever. Nothing, nothing,

the gallant, *grivois** Arcadia of Boucher. But hush! It was in Chelsea; I'll tell you no more. You might come bursting in on the next dance, pulling a long face because the band wasn't playing Bach and the dancers weren't talking about the "Critique of Pure Reason." For the fact is, my poor Dick, you're too solemn and serious in your pleasures. I shall really have to take you in hand, when you come back. You must be taught to be a little lighter and more fantastic. For the truth about you is that you're absurdly Victorian. You're still at the Life-is-real-life-is-earnest, Low-living-and-high-thinking stage. You lack the courage of your instincts. I want to see you more frivolous and sociable, yes, and more gluttonous and lecherous, my good Dick. If I were as free as you are, oh, what an Epicurean I'd be! Repent of your ways, Dick, before it's too late and you're irrecoverably middle-aged. No more. I am being called away on urgent pleasure. GRACE.'

I read through this extraordinary epistle several times. If the untidy, illegible writing had not been so certainly Grace's, I should have doubted her authorship of the letter. That sham *dix-huitième*† language, those neorococo sentiments—these were not hers. I had never heard her use the words 'caprice' or 'pleasure'; she had never generalized in that dreadfully facile way about 'we women.' What, then, had come over the woman since last she wrote? I put the two letters together. What could have happened? Mystery. Then, suddenly, I thought of Rodney Clegg, and where there had been darkness I saw light.

The light, I must confess, was extremely disagreeable to me, at any rate in its first dawning. I experienced a much

---

* Naughty.

† Eighteenth-century.

more violent return of that jealousy which had overtaken me when I heard Grace expressing her admiration of Rodney's character and talents. And with the jealousy a proportionately violent renewal of my desires. An object hitherto indifferent may suddenly be invested in our eyes with an inestimable value by the mere fact that it has passed irrevocably out of our power into the possession of some one else. The moment that I suspected Grace of having become Rodney's mistress I began to imagine myself passionately in love with her. I tortured myself with distressing thoughts of their felicity; I cursed myself for having neglected opportunities that would never return. At one moment I even thought of rushing back to London, in the hope of snatching my now suddenly precious treasure out of Rodney's clutches. But the journey would have been expensive; I was luckily short of money. In the end I decided to stay where I was. Time passed and my good sense returned. I realized that my passion was entirely imaginary, home-made, and self-suggested. I pictured to myself what would have happened if I had returned to London under its influence. Burning with artificial flames, I should have burst dramatically into Grace's presence, only to discover, when I was actually with her, that I was not in love with her at all. Imaginary love can only flourish at a distance from its object; reality confines the fancy and puts it in its place. I had imagined myself unhappy because Grace had given herself to Rodney; but the situation, I perceived, would have been infinitely more distressing if I had returned, had succeeded in capturing her for myself, and then discovered that, much as I liked and charming as I found her, I did not love her.

It was deplorable, no doubt, that she should have been

taken in by a charlatan like Rodney; it was a proof of bad taste on her part that she had not preferred to worship me, hopelessly, with an unrequited passion. Still, it was her business and in no way mine. If she felt that she could be happy with Rodney, well then, poor idiot! let her be happy. And so on. It was with reflections such as these that I solaced myself back into the indifference of a mere spectator. When Herbert turned up a few days later at my hotel, I was able to ask him, quite without agitation, for news of Grace.

'Oh, she's just the same as usual,' said Herbert.

Crass fool! I pressed him. 'Doesn't she go out more than she used to?' I asked. 'To dances and that sort of thing? I had heard rumours that she was becoming so social.'

'She may be,' said Herbert. 'I hadn't noticed anything in particular.'

It was hopeless. I saw that if I wanted to know anything, I should have to use my own eyes and my own judgment. Meanwhile, I wrote to tell her how glad I was to know that she was happy and amusing herself. She replied with a long and very affected essay about 'pleasures.' After that, the correspondence flagged.

A few months later—I had just returned to London—there was a party at Rodney's studio, at which I was present. Rodney's latest masterpiece looked down from an easel set up at the end of the long room. It was an amusingly indecent pastiche of the Douanier Rousseau. 'Wedding,' the composition was called; and it represented a nuptial party, the bride and bridegroom at the centre, the relatives standing or sitting round them, grouped as though before the camera of a provincial photographer. In the background a draped column, palpably cardboard; a rustic bridge; fir-trees with snow and, in the sky, a large pink dirigible. The only eccentric feature of the picture was that, while the bridegroom and the other gentlemen of the party were duly clothed in black Sunday best, the ladies, except for boots and hats, were naked. The best critics were of opinion that 'Wedding' represented the highest flight, up to date, of Rodney's genius. He was asking four hundred and fifty pounds for it; a few days later, I was told, he actually got them.

Under the stonily fixed regard of the nuptial group Rodney's guests were diverting themselves. The usual people sat, or stood, or sprawled about, drinking white wine or whisky. Two of the young ladies had come dressed identically in the shirts and black velvet trousers of Gavarni's *débardeurs*. Another was smoking a small briar pipe. As I came into the room I heard a young man saying in a loud, truculent voice: 'We're absolutely modern, we are. Anybody can have my wife, so far as I'm concerned. I don't care. She's free. And I'm free. That's what I call modern.'

I could not help wondering why he should call it modern. To me it rather seemed primeval—almost pre-human. Love, after all, is the new invention; promiscuous lust geologically old-fashioned. The really modern people, I reflected, are the Brownings.

I shook hands with Rodney.

'Don't be too contemptuous of our simple London pleasures,' he said.

I smiled; it amused me to hear on his lips the word with which Grace's letters had made me so familiar.

'As good as the pleasures of Paris, any day,' I answered, looking round the room. Through the crowd, I caught sight of Grace.

With an air of being spiritually and physically at home, she was moving from group to group. In Rodney's rooms, I could see, she was regarded as the hostess. The mistress of the house, in the left-handed sense of the word. (A pity, I reflected, that I could not share that little joke with Rodney; he would have enjoyed it so much, about any one else.) In the intervals of conversation I curiously observed her; I compared the Grace before my eyes with the remembered image of Grace as I first knew her. That trick of swaying as she walked—rather as a serpent sways to the piping of the charmer—that was new. So, too, was the carriage of the hands—the left on the hip, the right held breast-high, palm upwards, with a cigarette between the fingers. And when she put the cigarette to her lips, she had a novel way of turning up her face and blowing the smoke almost perpendicularly into the air, which was indescribably dashing and Bohemian. Haughty milady had vanished to be replaced by a new kind of aristocrat—the gay, terrible, beyond-good-and-evil variety.

From time to time snatches of her talk came to my ears. Gossip, invariably scandalous; criticisms of the latest exhibitions of pictures; recollections or anticipations of 'perfect parties'—these seemed to be the principal topics, all of them, in Grace's mouth, quite unfamiliar to me. But the face, the vague-featured face of the nice but ugly little girl, the bewildered eyes, the occasional smile, so full of sweetness and a dim benevolence—these were still the same. And when I overheard her airily saying to one of her new friends of I know not what common acquaintance, 'She's almost too hospitable—positively keeps open bed, you know,' I could have burst out laughing, so absurdly incongruous with the face, the eyes, the smile, so palpably borrowed and not her own did the smart words seem.

Meanwhile, at the table, Rodney was doing one of his famous 'non-stop' drawings—a figure, a whole scene rendered in a single line, without lifting the pencil from the paper. He was the centre of an admiring group.

'Isn't it too enchanting?'

'Exquisite!'

'Ravishing!'

The words exploded laughingly all around him.

'There,' said Rodney, straightening himself up.

The paper was handed round for general inspection. Incredibly ingenious it was, that drawing, in a single sinuous line, of a fight between a bull and three naked female toreros. Every one applauded, called for more.

'What shall I do next?' asked Rodney.

'Trick cyclists,' somebody suggested.

'Stale, stale,' he objected.

'Self portrait.'

Rodney shook his head. 'Too vain.'

'Adam and Eve.'

'Or why not Salmon and Gluckstein?' suggested some one else.

'Or the twelve Apostles.'

'I have it,' shouted Rodney, waving his pencil. 'King George and Queen Mary.'

He bent over his scribbling block, and in a couple of minutes had produced a one-line portrait of the Britannic Majesties. There was a roar of laughter.

It was Grace who brought me the paper. 'Isn't he wonderful?' she said, looking at me with a kind of eager anxiety, as though she were anxious to have my commendation of her choice, my sacerdotal benediction.

I had only seen her once, for a brief unintimate moment, since my return. We had not mentioned Rodney's name. But this evening, I saw, she was taking me into her confidence; she was begging me, without words, but none the less eloquently, to tell her that she had done well. I don't exactly know why she should have desired my blessing. She seemed to regard me as a sort of old, grey-haired, avuncular Polonius. (Not a very flattering opinion, considering that I was several years younger than Rodney himself.) To her, my approval was the approval of embodied wisdom.

'Isn't he wonderful?' she repeated. 'Do you know of any other man now living, except perhaps Picasso, who could improvise a thing like that? For fun—as a game.'

I handed the paper back to her. The day before, as it happened, finding myself in the neighbourhood, I had dropped in on Rodney at his studio. He was drawing when I entered, but, seeing me, had closed his book and come to meet me. While we were talking, the plumber called and Rodney had left the studio to give some instructions on the spot, in the bathroom. I got up and strolled about the room, looking at the latest canvases. Perhaps too inquisitively, I opened the notebook in which he had been drawing when I entered. The book was blank but for the first three or four pages. These were covered with 'non-stop' drawings. I counted seven distinct versions of the bull with the female toreros, and five, a little corrected and improved each time, of King George and Queen Mary. I wondered at the time why he should be practising this peculiar kind of art; but feeling no urgent curiosity about the subject, I forgot, when he came back, to ask him. Now I understood.

'Extraordinary,' I said to Grace, as I returned her the paper. 'Really extraordinary!'

Her smile of gratitude and pleasure was so beautiful that I felt quite ashamed of myself for knowing Rodney's little secret.

Grace and I both lived in Kensington; it was I who drove her home when the party was over.

'Well, that was great fun,' I said, as we settled into the taxi.

We had driven past a dozen lamp-posts before she spoke.

'You know, Dick,' she said, 'I'm so happy.'

She laid her hand on my knee; and for lack of any possible verbal comment, I gently patted it. There was another long silence.

'But why do you despise us all?' she asked, turning on me suddenly.

'But when did I ever say I despised you?' I protested.

'Oh, one needn't say such things. They proclaim themselves.'

I laughed, but more out of embarrassment than because I was amused. 'A woman's intuition, what?' I said facetiously. 'But you've really got too much of it, my dear Grace. You intuit things that aren't there at all.'

'But you despise us all the same.'

'I don't. Why should I?'

'Exactly. Why should you?'

'Why?' I repeated.

'For the sake of what?' she went on quickly. 'And in

comparison with what do you find our ways so despicable? I'll tell you. For the sake of something impossible and inhuman. And in comparison with something that doesn't exist. It's stupid, when there's real life with all its pleasures.' That word again—Rodney's word! It seemed to me that she had a special, almost unctuous tone when she pronounced it. 'So delightful. So rich and varied. But you turn up your nose and find it all vapid and empty. Isn't it true?' she insisted.

'No,' I answered. I could have told her that life doesn't necessarily mean parties with white wine and whisky, social stunts, fornication and chatter. I might have told her; but however studiously I might have generalized, it was obvious that my remarks would be interpreted (quite correctly, indeed) as a set of disparaging personalities. And I didn't want to quarrel with Grace or offend her. And besides, when all was said, I did go to Rodney's parties. I was an accomplice. The knock-about amused me; I found it hard to deny myself the entertainment. My objection was only theoretical; I did what I denounced. I had no right to strike pontifical attitudes and condemn. 'No, of course it isn't true,' I repeated.

Grace sighed. 'Of course, I can't really expect you to admit it,' she said. 'But bless you,' she added with a forced and unnatural gaiety, 'I don't mind being despised. When one is rich, one can afford the luxury of being disapproved of. And I am rich, you know. Happiness, pleasures—I've got everything. And after all,' she went on, with a certain argumentative truculence in her voice, 'I'm a woman. What do I care for your ridiculous masculine standards. I do what I like, what amuses me.' The quotation from Rodney rang a little false, I thought. There was a silence.

I wondered what John Peddley thought about it all, or whether any suspicion of what was happening had yet penetrated the horny carapace of his insensitiveness.

And as though she were answering my unspoken question, Grace began again with a new seriousness. 'And there's my other life, parallel. It doesn't make any difference to that, you know. Doesn't touch it. I like John just as much as I did. And the children, of course.'

There was another long silence. All at once, I hardly know why, I felt profoundly sad. Listening to this young woman talking about her lover, I wished that I too were in love. Even the 'pleasures' glittered before my fancy with a new and tempting brilliance. My life seemed empty. I found myself thinking of the melody of the Countess's song in *Figaro: Dove sono i bei momenti di dolcezza e di piacer?**

That Grace's adventure made little or no difference to her other life, I had an opportunity of judging for myself in the course of a subsequent week-end with the Peddleys in Kent. John was there—'in great form,' as he put it himself; and Grace, and the children, and Grace's father and mother. Nothing could have been more domestic and less like Rodney's party, less 'modern.' Indeed, I should be justified in writing that last word without its inverted commas. For there was something extraordinarily remote and uncontemporary about the whole household. The children were geologically remote in their childishness—only a little beyond the pithecanthropus stage. And Peddley was like a star, separated from the world by the unbridgeable gulfs of his egoism and unawareness. The subjects of his discourse might be contemporary; but spiritually, none the less, he was timeless,

---

* "Where are the lovely moments of sweetness and pleasure?"

an inhabitant of blank and distant space. As for Grace's parents, they were only a generation away; but, goodness knows, that was far enough. They had opinions about socialism and sexual morality, and gentlemen, and what ought or ought not to be done by the best people—fixed, unalterable, habit-ingrained and by now almost instinctive opinions that made it impossible for them to understand or forgive the contemporary world.

This was especially true of Grace's mother. She was a big, handsome woman of about fifty-five, with the clear ringing voice of one who has been accustomed all her life to give orders. She busied herself in doing good works and generally keeping the poor in their places. Unlike her husband, who had a touch of Peddley's star-like remoteness, she was very conscious of contemporaneity and, consequently, very loud and frequent in her denunciations of it.

Grace's father, who had inherited money, filled his leisure by farming a small estate unprofitably, sitting on committees, and reading Persian, an acquirement of which, in his quiet way, he was very proud. It was a strangely disinterested hobby. He had never been to Persia and had not the slightest intention of ever going. He was quite uninterested in Persian literature or history, and was just as happy reading a Persian cookery book as the works of Hafiz or Rumi. What he liked was the language itself. He enjoyed the process of reading the unfamiliar letters, of looking up the words in the dictionary. For him, Persian was a kind of endlessly complicated jigsaw puzzle. He studied it solely for the sake of killing time and in order not to think. A dim, hopeless sort of man was Mr. Comfrey. And he had an irritating way of looking at you over the top of his spectacles with a puzzled expression, as though he had not understood what you meant; which, indeed, was generally the case. For Mr. Comfrey was very slow of mind and made up for his knowledge of Persian by the most extraordinary ignorance of almost all other subjects under the sun.

'Say that again,' he would say, when his incomprehension was too complete.

How strange, how utterly fantastic it seemed, that week-end. I felt as though I had been suddenly lifted out of the contemporary world and plunged into a kind of limbo.

John Peddley's latest subject was the Einstein theory.

'It's so simple,' he assured us the first evening, between the soup and the fish. 'I don't pretend to be a mathematician or anything like one; but I understand it perfectly. All that it needs is a little common sense.' And for the next half-hour the common sense came braying out, as though from the mouth of a trombone.

Grace's father looked at him dubiously over the top of his spectacles.

'Say that again, will you?' he said, after every second sentence.

And John Peddley was only too delighted to oblige.

At the other end of the table, Grace and her mother were discussing the children, their clothes, characters, education, diseases. I longed to join in their conversation. But the simple domesticities were not for me. I was a man; John Peddley and the intellect were my portion. Reluctantly, I turned back towards my host.

'What I'd like you to explain,' Grace's father was saying, 'is just exactly how time can be at right angles to length, breadth, and thickness. Where precisely does it come in?'

With two forks and a knife he indicated the three spatial dimensions. 'Where do you find room for another right angle?'

And John Peddley set himself to explain. It was terrible.

Meanwhile, at my other ear, Grace's mother had begun to talk about the undesirable neighbours who had taken the house next to theirs on Campden Hill. A man and a woman, living together, unmarried. And the garden behind the houses was the common property of all the householders. What a situation! Leaving Peddley and the old gentleman to find room for the fourth right angle, I turned definitively to the ladies. For my benefit, Grace's mother began the horrid story again from the beginning. I was duly sympathetic.

Once, for a moment, I caught Grace's eye. She smiled at me, she almost imperceptibly raised her eyebrows. That little grimace was deeply significant. In the first months of our friendship, I had often seen her in the company of her father and mother, and her bearing, on these occasions, had always impressed me. I had never met a young woman of the generation which had come to maturity during the war who was so perfectly at ease with her elders, so unconstrainedly at home in their moral and mental atmosphere as was Grace. She had taken her father and mother entirely for granted, had regarded their views of life as the obvious, natural views of every sane human being. That embarrassment which—in these days, more perhaps than at any other period—afflicts young people when in the presence of their elders had never, so far as I had observed, touched Grace. This smile of apologetic and slightly contemptuous indulgence, this raising of the eyebrows, were symptomatic of a change. Grace had become contemporary, even (in inverted commas) 'modern.'

Outwardly, however, there was no change. The two worlds were parallel; they did not meet. They did not meet, even when Rodney came to dine *en famille*, even when John accompanied his wife to one of Rodney's less aggressively 'artistic' (which in inverted commas means very much the same as 'modern') evening parties. Or perhaps it would be truer to say that Rodney's world met John's, but John's did not meet Rodney's. Only if Rodney had been a Zulu and his friends Chinese would John have noticed that they were at all different from the people he was used to meeting. The merely spiritual differences which distinguished them were too small for his notice. He moved through life surrounded by his own atmosphere; only the most glaring lights could penetrate that half opaque and intensely refractive medium. For John, Rodney and his friends were just people, like everybody else; people who could be button-holed and talked to about the Swiss banking system and Einstein's theory, and the rationing of sugar. Sometimes, it was true, they seemed to him rather frivolous; their manners, sometimes, struck him as rather unduly brusque; and John had even remarked that they were sometimes rather coarse-spoken in the presence of ladies—or, if they happened to be ladies themselves, in the presence of gentlemen.

'Curious, these young people,' he said to me, after an evening at Rodney's studio. 'Curious.' He shook his head. 'I don't know that I quite understand them.'

Through a rift in his atmosphere he had caught a glimpse of the alien world beyond; he had seen something, not refracted, but as it really was. But John was quite incurious; careless of its significance, he shut out the unfamiliar vision.

'I don't know what your opinion about modern art

may be,' he went on, disappointing me of his comments on modern people. 'But what I always say is this.'

And he said it, copiously.

Modern art became another gramophone record added to his repertory. That was the net result of his meeting with Rodney and Rodney's friends.

For the next few months I saw very little either of Grace or of Rodney. I had met Catherine, and was too busy falling in love to do or think of anything else. We were married towards the close of 1921, and life became for me, gradually, once more normal.

From the first Catherine and Grace were friends. Grace admired Catherine for her coolness, her quiet efficiency, her reliableness; admired and liked her. Catherine's affection for Grace was protective and elder-sisterly; and at the same time, she found Grace slightly comic. Affections are not impaired by being tempered with a touch of benevolent laughter. Indeed, I would almost be prepared to risk a generalization and say that all true affections are tempered with laughter. For affection implies intimacy; and one cannot be intimate with another human being without discovering something to laugh at in his or her character. Almost all the truly virtuous characters in fiction are also slightly ridiculous; perhaps that is because their creators were so fond of them. Catherine saw the joke—the rather pathetic joke—of Grace. But she liked her none the less; perhaps, even, the more. For the joke was appealing; it was a certain childishness that raised the laugh.

At the time of my marriage, Grace was acting the eternally feminine part more fervently than ever. She had begun to dress very smartly and rather eccentrically, and was generally unpunctual; not very unpunctual (she was by nature too courteous for that), but just enough to be able to say that she was horribly late, but that she couldn't help it; it was in her nature—her woman's nature. She blamed Catherine for dressing too sensibly.

'You must be gayer in your clothes,' she insisted, 'more fantastic and capricious. It'll make you *feel* more fantastic. You think too masculinely.'

And to encourage her in thinking femininely, she gave her six pairs of white kid gloves, marvellously piped with coloured leather and with fringed and intricately scalloped gauntlets. But perhaps the most feminine and fantastic thing about them was the fact that they were several sizes too small for Catherine's hand.

Grace had become a good deal more loquacious of late and her style of conversation had changed. Like her clothes, it was more fantastic than in the past. The principle on which she made conversation was simple: she said whatever came into her head. And into that vague, irresponsible head of hers the oddest things would come. A phantasmagoria of images, changing with every fresh impression or as the words of her interlocutor called up new associations, was for ever dancing across her field of mental vision. She put into words whatever she happened to see at any given moment. For instance, I might mention the musician Palestrina.

'Yes, yes,' Grace would say, 'what a marvellous composer!' Then, reacting to the Italian reference, she would add in the same breath: 'And the way they positively *drink* the macaroni. Like those labels that come out of the mouth of caricatures. You know.'

Sometimes I did know. I skipped over the enormous

ellipses in this allusive thinking and caught the reference. Sometimes, when the association of her ideas was too exclusively private, I was left uncomprehending. The new technique was rather disconcerting, but it was always amusing, in a way. The unexpectedness of her remarks, the very nonsensicality of them, surprised one into finding them witty.

As a child, Grace had been snubbed when she talked in this random, fantastic fashion. 'Talk sense,' her governesses had said severely, when she told them during the geography lesson that she didn't like South America because it looked like a boiled leg of mutton. 'Don't be silly.' Grace was taught to be ashamed of her erratic fancy. She tried to talk sense—sense as governesses understand it—found it very difficult, and relapsed into silence. Peddley was even more sensible, in the same style, than the governesses themselves; devastatingly sensible. He was incapable of understanding fancy. If Grace had ever told Peddley why she didn't like South America, he would have been puzzled, he would have asked her to explain herself. And learning that it was the mutton-like shape of the continent on the map that prejudiced Grace against it, he would have given her statistics of South America's real dimensions, would have pointed out that it extended from the tropics almost into the antarctic circle, that it contained the largest river and some of the highest mountains in the world, that Brazil produced coffee and the Argentine beef, and that consequently, in actual fact, it was not in the very least like a boiled leg of mutton. With Peddley, Grace's only resources were laboriously talked sense or complete silence.

In Rodney's circle, however, she found that her gift of nonsense was appreciated and applauded. An enthusiast for the 'fantastic' and the 'feminine,' Rodney encouraged her to talk at random, as the spirit of associative fancy might move her. Diffidently at first, Grace let herself go; her conversation achieved an immediate success. Her unstitched, fragmentary utterances were regarded as the last word in modern wit. People repeated her *bons mots*. A little bewildered by what had happened, Grace suddenly found herself in the movement, marching at the very head of the forces of contemporaneity. In the eighteenth century, when logic and science were the fashion, women tried to talk like the men. The twentieth century has reversed the process. Rodney did Grace the honour of appropriating to himself the happiest of her extravagances.

Success made Grace self-confident; and confident, she went forward triumphantly to further successes. It was a new and intoxicating experience for her. She lived in a state of chronic spiritual tipsiness.

'How stupid people are not to be happy!' she would say, whenever we discussed these eternal themes.

To Catherine, who had taken my place as a confidant—my place and a much more intimate, more confidential place as well—she talked about love and Rodney.

'I can't think why people manage to make themselves unhappy about love,' she said. 'Why can't everybody love gaily and freely, like us? Other people's love seems to be all black and clotted, like Devonshire cream made of ink. Ours is like champagne. That's what love ought to be like: champagne. Don't you think so?'

'I think I should prefer it to be like clear water,' said Catherine. To me, later on, she expressed her doubts. 'All this champagne and gaiety,' she said; 'one can see that Rodney is a young man with a most wholesome fear of emotional entanglements.'

'We all knew that,' I said. 'You didn't imagine, I suppose, that he was in love with her?'

'I hoped,' said Catherine.

'Because you didn't know Rodney. Now you do. Champagne—you have the formula. The problem is Grace.'

Was she really in love with him? Catherine and I discussed the question. I was of opinion that she was.

'When Rodney flutters off,' I said, 'she'll be left there, broken.'

Catherine shook her head. 'She only imagines she's in love,' she insisted. 'It's the huge excitement of it all that makes her happy; that, and the novelty of it, and her sense of importance, and her success. Not any deep passion for Rodney. She may think it's a passion—a champagnish passion, if you like. But it isn't really. There's no passion; only champagne. It was his prestige and her boredom that made her fall to him originally. And now it's her success and the fun of it that make her stick to him.'

Events were to show that Catherine was right, or at least more nearly right than I. But before I describe these events, I must tell how it was that Kingham re-entered my world.

It was I who took the first step to end our ridiculous quarrel. I should have made the attempt earlier, if it had not been for Kingham's absence from Europe. A little while after our squabble he left, with a commission to write articles as he went, first for North Africa and thence for the further East. I heard of him once or twice from people who had seen him at Tunis, at Colombo, at Canton. And I read the articles, the admirably original articles, as they appeared at intervals in the paper which had commissioned them. But direct communication with him I had none. I did not write; for I was uncertain, to begin with, if my letter would ever reach him. And in any case, even if we had made up our quarrel by letter, what good would that have been? Reconciliations across eight thousand miles of space are never very satisfactory. I waited till I heard of his return and then wrote him a long letter. Three days later he was sitting at our dinner-table.

'This is good,' he said, 'this is very good.' He looked this way and that, quickly, taking in everything—the furniture, the books, Catherine, me—with his bright, quick eyes. 'Definitely settled.'

'Oh, not so definitely as all that, let us hope.' I laughed in Catherine's direction.

'I envy you,' he went on. 'To have got hold of something fixed, something solid and absolute—that's wonderful. Domestic love, marriage—after all, it's the nearest thing to an absolute that we can achieve, practically. And it takes on more value, when you've been rambling round the world for a bit, as I have. The world proves to you that nothing has any meaning except in relation to something else. Good, evil, justice, civilization, cruelty, beauty. You think you know what these words mean. And perhaps you do know, in Kensington. But go to India or China. You don't know anything there. It's uncomfortable at first; but then, how exciting! And how much more copiously and multifariously you begin to live! But precisely for that reason you feel the need for some sort of fixity and definition, some kind of absolute, not merely of the imagination, but in actual life. That's where love comes in, and domesticity. Not to mention God and Death and the Immortality of the Soul and all the rest. When you live narrowly and snugly, those things seem absurd and superfluous. You don't even appreciate your snugness. But multiply yourself with travelling, knock the bottom out of all your old certainties and prejudices and habits of thought; then you begin to see the real significance of domestic snugness, you appreciate the reality and importance of the other fixities.'

He spoke with all his old passionate eagerness. His eyes had the same feverish, almost unearthly brightness. His face, which had been smooth and pale when I saw it last, was burnt by the sun and lined. He looked more mature, tougher and stronger than in the past.

'Yes, I envy you,' he repeated.

'Then why don't you get married yourself?' asked Catherine.

Kingham laughed. 'Why not, indeed? You'd better ask Dick. He knows me well enough to answer, I should think.'

'No, tell us yourself,' I said.

Kingham shook his head. 'It would be a case of cruelty to animals,' he said enigmatically, and began to talk about something else.

'I envy you,' he said again, later that same evening, when Catherine had gone to bed and we were alone together. 'I envy you. But you don't deserve what you've got. You haven't earned your right to a fixed domestic absolute, as I have. I've realized, intimately and personally realized, the flux and the interdependence and the relativity of things; consequently I know and appreciate the meaning and value of fixity. But you—you're domestic just as you're moral; you're moral and domestic by nature, unconsciously, instinctively, without

{225}

having known the opposites which give these attitudes their significance—like a worker bee, in fact; like a damned cabbage that just grows because it can't help it.'

I laughed. 'I like the way you talk about flux and relativity,' I said, 'when you yourself are the fixed, unchanging antithesis of these things. The same old Kingham! Why, you're a walking fixity; you're the Absolute in flesh and blood. How well I know those dear old home truths, for example!'

'But that doesn't prevent their being true,' he insisted, laughing, but at the same time rather annoyed by what I had said. 'And besides, I *have* changed. My views about everything are quite different. A sensitive man can't go round the world and come back with the same philosophy of life as the one he started with.'

'But he can come back with the same temperament, the same habits of feeling, the same instinctive reactions.'

Kingham ran his fingers through his hair and repeated his petulant laughter. 'Well, I suppose he can,' he admitted reluctantly.

I was only too well justified in what I had said. A few days of renewed intimacy were enough to convince me that Kingham preserved all his old love of a scene, that he enjoyed as much as ever the luxury of a hot emotional bath. He burst in on me one morning, distracted with fury, to tell me about a violent quarrel he had had the previous evening with some insignificant young undergraduate—rather tipsy at that—who had told him (with considerable insight, I must admit, in spite of his tipsiness) that he, Kingham, was either insincere or hysterical.

'And the awful thing is that he may be right,' he added,

when he had finished his story. 'Perhaps I *am* insincere.' Restlessly, he walked about the room. From time to time he withdrew a hand from the pocket into which it was deeply plunged and made a gesture, or ran the fingers through his hair. 'Perhaps I'm just a little comedian,' he went on, 'just a mouther of words, a ranter.' The self-laceration hurt him, but he enjoyed the pain. 'Do I really feel things deeply?' he went on speculating. 'Or do I just deceive myself into believing that I care? Is it all a mere lie?' The operation continued interminably.

The tipsy undergraduate had diagnosed insincerity or hysteria. It was in my power to relieve Kingham of his haunting fear of insincerity by assuring him that the second of these alternatives was the more correct. But I doubted the efficacy of the consolation; and besides I had no desire for a quarrel. I held my tongue.

I did not make Kingham known to Grace; for knowing that he had a passionate and rooted dislike of Rodney, I was afraid that, in spite of my preliminary warnings (or even precisely because of them, for the sake of creating an intolerably unpleasant situation) he might burst out, in Grace's presence, into some violent denunciation of her lover. It was a risk that was not worth running. And besides, I did not imagine that they would get on well together. We were intimate with both; but we kept them, so to speak, in separate water-tight compartments of our intimacy.

One day, when I came home to dinner, I was greeted by Catherine with a piece of news.

'Rodney's being unfaithful,' she said. 'Poor little Grace was here for tea to-day. She pretends not to mind—to be very modern and hard and gay about it. But I could see that she was dreadfully upset.'

'And who's the lucky lady?' I asked.

'Mrs. Melilla.'

'A step up in the world.' I thought of the emeralds and the enormous pearls, which added lustre to the already dazzling Jewish beauty of Mrs. Melilla. 'He'll be in the baronetcy and peerage soon.'

'What a pig!' said Catherine indignantly. 'I'm so dreadfully sorry for poor Grace.'

'But according to your theory, she isn't really in love with him.'

'No, she isn't,' said Catherine. 'Not *really*. But she thinks she is. And she'll think so much more, of course, now that he's leaving her. And besides, she has put so many of her eggs into his basket; this smashes them all. She'd committed herself body and soul to Rodney and Rodneyism. This affair with Rodney gave sense to her whole existence. Can't you see that?'

'Perfectly.' I remembered the days when Grace had seen herself as a musical critic and how cruelly I had murdered this comforting vision of herself by my little practical joke about the player of Rachmaninoff. A much more significant, much more intimately cherished dream was being murdered now.

She did her best, as Catherine had said, to be very 'modern' about it. I saw her a few days later at one of Rodney's parties; she was smoking a great many cigarettes, drinking glass after glass of white wine and talking more wildly than ever. Her dress was a close-fitting sheath of silver tissue, designed so as to make the wearer look almost naked. Fatigued with sleeplessness, her eyes were circled with dark, bruise-coloured rings; seen in conjunction with the bright, unnatural red of her rouged cheeks and lips, these dark circles looked as though they had been painted on with a fard, to heighten the brilliance of the eyes, to hint provocatively at voluptuous fatigues and amorous vigils. She was having a great success and her admirers had never been more numerous. She flirted outrageously with all of them. Even when she was talking with me, she seemed to find it necessary to shoot languorous sidelong glances; to lean towards me, as though offering her whole person to my desires. But looking at her, I could see, under the fard, only the face of the nice but rather ugly little girl; it seemed, I thought, more than usually pathetic.

Rodney sat down at the table to do his usual non-stop drawing.

'What shall it be?' he asked.

'Draw Jupiter and *all* his mistresses,' cried Grace, who was beginning to be rather tipsy; 'Europa and Leda and Semele and Danae,' she clapped her hands at each name, 'and Io and . . . and Clio and Dio and Scio and Fi-fio and O-my-Eyeo. . . .'

The jest was not a very good one. But as most of Rodney's guests had drunk a good deal of wine and all were more or less intoxicated by the convivial atmosphere of a successful party, there was a general laugh. Grace began to laugh too, almost hysterically. It was a long time before she could control herself.

Rodney, who had made no preparations for improvising a picture of Jove's mistresses, found an excuse for rejecting the suggestion. He ended by drawing Mrs. Eddy pursued by a satyr.

Deserted by Rodney, Grace tried to pretend that it was she who was the deserter. The rôle of the capricious wanton seemed to her more in harmony with the Rodneyan conception of the eternal feminine as well as less humiliating than that of the victim. Provocatively, promiscuously, she flirted. In those first days of her despair she would, I believe, have accepted the advances of almost any tolerably presentable man. Masterman, for example, or Gane the journalist, or Levitski—it was one of those three, I surmised, judging by what I saw at the party, who would succeed to Rodney's felicity, and that very soon.

The day after the party, Grace paid another visit to Catherine. She brought a small powder-puff as a present. In return, she asked, though not in so many words, for comfort, advice, and above all for approval. In a crisis, on the spur of the moment, Grace could be rashly and unreflectingly impulsive; but when there was time to think, when it was a question of deliberately planning she was timorous, she hated to stand alone and take responsibilities. She liked to know that the part in which she saw herself was approved of by some trustworthy judge. The powder-puff was a bribe and an argument; an argument in favour of the eternal feminine, with all that that connoted, a bribe for the judge, an appeal to her affection, that she might approve of Grace's sentiments and conduct.

Grace put her case. 'The mistake people make,' she said, 'is getting involved, like the man on the music-halls who does that turn with the fly-paper. I refuse to be involved; that's my principle. I think one ought to be heartless and just amuse oneself, that's all. Not worry about anything else.'

'But do you think one can really be amused if one doesn't

worry and takes things heartlessly?' asked Catherine. '*Really*
amused, I mean. Happy, if you'll permit me to use an old-
fashioned word. Can one be happy?' She thought of Lev-
itski, of Gane and Masterman.

Grace was silent; perhaps she too was thinking of them.
Then, making an effort, 'Yes, yes,' she said with a kind of
obstinate, determined gaiety, 'one can; of course one can.'

I was at the Queen's Hall that afternoon. Coming out,
when the concert was over, I caught sight of Kingham in the
issuing crowd.

'Come home for a late cup of tea and stay to dinner.'

'All right,' he said.

We climbed on to a bus and rode westward. The sun
had just set. Low down in the sky in front of us there were
streaks of black and orange cloud, and above them a pale,
watery-green expanse, limpid and calm up to the zenith.
We rode for some time in silence, watching the lovely death
of yet another of our days.

'It's all very well,' said Kingham at last, indicating these
western serenities with a gesture of his fine, expressive hand,
'it's all very well, no doubt, for tired business men. Gives
them comfort, I dare say; makes them feel agreeably repen-
tant for the swindles they've committed during the day, and
all that. Oh, it's full of uplift, I've no doubt. But I don't
happen to be a tired business man. It just makes me sick.'

'Come, come,' I protested.

He wouldn't listen to me. 'I won't have Gray's 'Elegy'
rammed down my throat,' he said. 'What I feel like is *The
Marriage of Heaven and Hell*, or *Zarathustra*, or the *Chants
de Maldoror*.'

'Well, all that I can suggest' (I suggested it mildly) 'is

that you should travel inside the bus and not look at the sunset.'

'Ass!' he said contemptuously.

We came in, to find Grace still sitting there, over the tea-cups, with Catherine. I was annoyed; still, there was nothing to be done about it. I introduced Kingham. All unconsciously, I was playing Pandarus for the second time.

My sources for the history of Grace's second love affair are tolerably copious. To begin with, I had opportunities of personally observing it, during a considerable part of its duration. I heard much, too, from Kingham himself. For Kingham was not at all a discreet lover. He was as little capable of being secretive about this class of experiences as about any other. He simply had to talk. Talking renewed and multiplied the emotions which he described. Talk even created new emotions—emotions which he had not felt at the time but which it occurred to him, when he was describing the scene, to think that he ought to have felt. He had no scruples about projecting these *sentiments d'escalier** backwards, anachronistically, into his past experience, falsifying history for the sake of future drama. To his memories of a scene with Grace he would add emotional complications, so that the next scene might be livelier. It was in the heat of talk that his finest emendations of history occurred to him. The genuine, or at any rate the on the whole more genuine, story came to me through Catherine from Grace. It was to Catherine that, in moments of crisis (and this particular love affair was almost uninterruptedly a crisis) Grace came for solace and counsel.

The affair began with a misunderstanding. No sooner had Kingham entered the room than Grace, who had been

---

* Witty remarks thought of too late.

talking quite simply and naturally with Catherine, put on her brazen 'modern' manner of the party and began with a kind of desperate recklessness to demand the attention and provoke the desires of the newcomer. She knew Kingham's name, of course, and all about him. In Rodney's circle it was admitted, albeit with some reluctance, that the man had talent; but he was deplored as a barbarian.

'He's one of those tiresome people,' I once heard Rodney complain, 'who will talk about their soul—and your soul, which is almost worse. Terribly Salvation Army. One wouldn't be surprised to see him on Sundays in Hyde Park telling people what they ought to do to be saved.'

At the sight of him, Grace had felt, no doubt, that it would be amusing to bring this curious wild animal to heel and make it do tricks. (It did not occur to her that it might be she who would be doing the tricks.) Kingham was a quarry worthy of any huntswoman. Still, I believe that she would have flirted as outrageously with almost any stranger. This provocative attitude of hers—an attitude which might be described as one of chronic and universal unfaithfulness—was her retort to unkind fate and unfaithful Rodney. She wanted to capture a new lover—several lovers, even—in order to prove to Rodney, to the world at large and above all, surely, to herself, that she was modern, knew how to take love lightly and gaily, as the most exquisite of entertainments, and that, in a word, she didn't care a pin. In another woman, this promiscuous flirtatiousness might have been distasteful, detestable even. But there was, in Grace, a certain fundamental innocence that rendered what ought, by all the rules, to have been the most reprehensible of actions entirely harmless. Text-book moralists would have called her bad, when in fact she was merely pathetic and a trifle comic. The text-books assign to every action its place in the moral hierarchy; the text-book moralists judge men exclusively by their actions. The method is crude and unscientific. For in reality certain characters have power to sterilize a dirty action; certain others infect and gangrene actions which, according to the book, should be regarded as clean. The harshest judges are those who have been so deeply hypnotized by the spell of the text-book words, that they have become quite insensitive to reality. They can think only of words—'purity,' 'vice,' 'depravity,' 'duty'; the existence of men and women escapes their notice.

Grace, as I have said, possessed an innocence which made nonsense of all the words which might have been used to describe her actions. To any one but a text-book theorist it was obvious that the actions hardly mattered; her innocence remained intact. It was this same innocence which enabled her to give utterance—with perfect unconcern and a complete absence of daring affectation—to those scabrous sentiments, those more than scientific expressions which were almost *de rigueur* in the conversation of Rodney's circle. In a foreign language one can talk of subjects, one can unconcernedly use words, the uttering, the mention of which in one's native idiom would horribly embarrass. For Grace, all these words, the most genuinely Old English, all these themes, however intimately connected by gossip with the names of known men and women, were foreign and remote. Even the universal language of coquettish gestures was foreign to her; she acted its provocations and innuendoes with a frankness which would have been shameless, if she had really known what they meant. Kingham entered the room; she turned on him at once all her batteries of looks and smiles—a bombardment of provocations. I knew Grace so well that, in my eyes, the performance seemed merely absurd. These smiles, these sidelong glances and flutteringly dropped eyelids, this teasing mockery by which she irritated Kingham into paying attention to her, struck me as wholly uncharacteristic of Grace and therefore ridiculous—above all, unconvincing. Yes, unconvincing. I could not believe that any one could fail to see what Grace was really like. Was it possible that Kingham didn't realize just as well as I did that she was, in spirit, as in features, just a nice little girl, pretending without much success—particularly in this rôle—to be grown up?

It seemed to me incredible. But Kingham was certainly taken in. He accepted her at her face value of this particular moment—as an aristocratically reckless hedonist in wanton search of amusement, pleasure, excitement, and power. To the dangerous siren he took her to be, Kingham reacted with a mixed emotion that was half angry contempt, half amorous curiosity. On principle, Kingham violently disapproved of professional *femmes fatales*, sirens, vampires—all women, in fact, who make love and the subjugation of lovers the principal occupation of their lives. He thought it outrageous that self-respecting and useful men should suddenly find themselves at the mercy of these dangerous and irresponsible beings. What perhaps increased his moral indignation was the fact that he himself was constantly falling a victim to them. Youth, vitality, strong personality, frank and unbridled vice had irresistible attractions for him. He was drawn sometimes to the vulgarest possessors of these characteristics. He felt it an indignity, a humiliation (and

yet, who knows? perhaps with Kingham this sense of hu-
miliation was only another attraction); but he was none the
less unfailingly drawn. He resisted, but never quite firmly
enough (that, after all, would have spoiled all the fun). He
resisted, succumbed and was subjected. But it must be ad-
mitted that his love, however abject it might be in the first
moment of his surrender, was generally a vengeance in itself.
Kingham might suffer; but he contrived in most cases to
inflict as much suffering as he received. And while he, with
a part of his spirit at any rate, actually enjoyed pain, how-
ever acutely and genuinely felt, the tormentors whom he in
his turn tormented were mostly quite normal young women
with no taste for the pleasures of suffering. He got the best
of it; but he regarded himself, none the less, as the victim,
and was consequently in a chronic state of moral indigna-
tion.

This first meeting convinced Kingham that Grace was
the sort of woman she wanted to persuade him (not to men-
tion herself) that she was—a vampire. Like many persons of
weak character and lacking in self-reliance, Grace was often
extraordinarily reckless. Passive generally and acquiescent,
she sometimes committed herself wildly to the most extrav-
agant courses of action—not from any principle of decision,
but because, precisely, she did not know what decision was,
because she lacked the sense of responsibility, and was in-
capable of realizing the irrevocable nature of an act. She
imagined that she could do things irresponsibly and without
committing herself; and feeling no inward sense of com-
mitment, she would embark on courses of action which—
externalized and become a part of the great machine of the
world—dragged her, sometimes reluctant, sometimes will-

ing, but always ingenuously surprised, into situations the most bewilderingly unexpected. It was this irresponsible impulsiveness of a character lacking the power of making deliberate decisions (this coupled with her fatal capacity for seeing herself in any rôle that seemed, at the moment, attractive) that had made her at one moment a socialist canvasser at the municipal elections; at another, an occasional opium smoker in that sordid and dangerous den near the Commercial Docks which Tim Masterman used to frequent; at another, though she was terrified of horses, a rider to hounds; and at yet another—to her infinite distress; but having light-heartedly insisted that she didn't know what modesty was, she couldn't draw back—the model for one of Levitski's nudes. And if she now threw herself at Kingham's head (just as, a few nights before, she had thrown herself at Masterman's, at Gane's, at Levitski's), it was irresponsibly, without considering what might be the results of her action, without even fully realizing that there would be any results at all. True, she saw herself as a 'modern' young woman; and her abandonment by Rodney had made her anxious, for the mere saving of her face, to capture a new lover, quickly. And yet it would be wrong to say that she had decided to employ coquettish provocations in order to get what she wanted. She had not decided anything; for decision is deliberate and the fruit of calculation. She was just wildly indulging in action, in precisely the same way as she indulged in random speech, without thinking of what the deeds or the words committed her to. But whereas logical inconsistencies matter extremely little and false intellectual positions can easily be abandoned, the effects of action or of words leading to action are not so negligible. For action commits what is

'I think there's something really devilish about the women of this generation,' he said to me, in his intense, emphatic way, some two or three days later. 'Something devilish,' he repeated, 'really devilish.' It was a a trick of his, in writing as well as in speech, to get hold of a word and, if he liked the sound of it, work it to death.

I laughed. 'Oh, come,' I protested. 'Do you find Catherine, for example, so specially diabolic?'

'She isn't of this generation,' Kingham answered. 'Spiritually, she doesn't belong to it.'

I laughed again; it was always difficult arguing with Kingham. You might think you had him cornered; you raised your logical cudgel to smash him. But while you were bringing it down, he darted out from beneath the stroke through some little trap door of his own discovery, clean out of the argument. It was impossible to prove him in the wrong, for the simple reason that he never remained long enough in any one intellectual position to be proved anything.

'No, not Catherine,' he went on, after a little pause. 'I was thinking of that Peddley woman.'

'Grace?' I asked in some astonishment. 'Grace devilish?'

He nodded. 'Devilish,' he repeated with conviction. The word, I could see, had acquired an enormous significance for him. It was the core round which, at the moment, all his thoughts and feelings were crystallizing. All his universe was arranging itself in patterns round the word 'devilish,' round the idea of devilishness in general, and Grace's devilishness in particular.

I protested. 'Of all the un-devilish people I've ever

known,' I said, 'Grace seems to me the most superlatively so.'

'You don't know her,' he retorted.

'But I've known her for years.'

'Not really known,' insisted Kingham, diving through another of his little trap doors out of the argument. 'You've never inspired her with one of her devilish concupiscences.' (I thought of Grace and could not help smiling; the smile exasperated Kingham.) 'Grin away,' he said. 'Imagine you're omniscient, if it gives you any pleasure. All I say is this: she's never tried to hunt you down.'

'I suppose you mean that she was rather stupidly flirtatious the other evening,' I said.

Kingham nodded. 'It was devilish,' he said softly, more for himself than for me. 'Devilish concupiscence.'

'But I assure you,' I went on, 'that business the other night was all mere silliness. She's childish, not devilish. She still sees herself in terms of Rodney Clegg, that's all. And she wants to pretend, now that he's deserted her, that she doesn't care. I'm not sure, indeed, that she doesn't want to make us believe that it was she who deserted him. That's why she wants to get hold of another lover quickly—for the sake of her prestige. But as for devilishness—why, the idea's simply absurd. She isn't definite enough to be a devil. She's just what circumstances and her imagination and other people happen to make her. A child, that's all.'

'You may think you know her,' Kingham persisted obstinately, 'but you don't. How can you, if you've never been hunted by her?'

'Bosh!' I said impatiently.

'I tell you she's devilish,' he insisted.

'Then why on earth did you accept her invitation to lunch with such alacrity?'

'There are things that are unescapable,' he answered oracularly.

'I give you up,' I said, shrugging my shoulders. The man exasperated me. 'The best thing you can do,' I added, 'is to go to your devil and be damned as quickly as possible.'

'That's exactly where I am going,' he said. And as though I had reminded him of an appointment, Kingham looked at his watch. 'And by God,' he added, in a different voice, 'I shall have to take a taxi, if I'm to get there in time.'

Kingham looked deeply put out; for he hated parting with money unnecessarily. He was tolerably well off now; but he still preserved the habits of prudence, almost of avarice, which he had acquired, painfully, in the days of his lower middle class boyhood and his poverty-stricken literary novitiate. He had asked Grace to dine with him in Soho; that had already cost him an effort. And now he was going to be compelled to take a taxi, so as to be in time to pay for the dinner. The thought of it made him suffer. And suffering for her sake, suffering a mean, unavowable pain for which he could not hope to get any sympathy, even his own, he found the ultimate cause of it, Grace, all the more devilish.

'Unescapable,' he repeated, still frowning, as he put on his hat to go. There was an expression positively of ferocity on his face. 'Unescapable.' He turned and left me.

'Poor Grace!' I was thinking, as I closed the front door and walked back to my study. It was just as unescapable for her as for Kingham. And I knew Kingham; my sympathies were all with Grace.

I was quite right, as it turned out, in according my

sympathies as I did. For if any one ever needed, ever de-
served sympathy, it was poor Grace, during those deplorable
months of 1922. She fell in love with Kingham—fell in love,
though it was the third time she had given herself, for the
first, the very first time in her life, painfully, desperately,
insanely. She had proposed to herself a repetition of her
affair with Rodney. It was to be all charmingly perverse dal-
liances, with champagne and sandwiches and lightly tender
conversation in the intervals; and exquisite little letters in
the *dix-huitième* manner; and evening parties; and amus-
ing escapades. That was what it had been with Rodney. He
made this kind of love, it must be admitted, with real style;
it was charming. Grace imagined that she would make it
in just the same way with Rodney's successor. And so she
might have, more or less, if the successor had been Levitski,
or Masterman, or Gane. But the successor was Kingham.
The choice was fatal; but the worst results of it might have
been avoided if she had not loved him. Unloving, she might
simply have left him when he made things too insupport-
able. But she did love him and, in love, she was utterly at
his mercy.

Kingham had said that the thing was unescapable; and
if for him it was so, that was due to the need he perversely
felt of giving himself over periodically to strong emotions,
the need of being humiliated and humiliating, of suffering
and making other people suffer. What he had always loved
was the passion itself, not the women who were the cause or
excuse of it. These occasional orgies of passion were neces-
sary to him, just as the periodical drinking bout is necessary
to the dipsomaniac. After a certain amount of indulgence,
the need was satisfied and he felt quite free to detach himself

from the lover who had been dear to him only as the stimulator of his emotions, not for her own sake. Kingham could satisfy his craving; it was an appetite that could be quenched by indulgence. But Grace's desire was one of those desperate, hopeless desires that can only be assuaged by a kind of miracle. What she desired was nothing less than to unite herself wholly with another being, to know him through and through and to be made free of all his secrets. Only the all but miraculous meeting of two equal loves, two equally confiding temperaments can bring fulfilment to that longing. There was no such meeting here.

Kingham made a habit of telling all his acquaintances, sooner or later, what he thought of them—which was invariably disagreeable. He called this process a 'clearing of the atmosphere.' But in point of fact, it never cleared anything; it obscured and made turbid, it created thunder in clear skies. Kingham might not admit the fact; but this was, none the less, precisely what he intended should happen. Clear skies bored him; he enjoyed storms. But always, when he had succeeded in provoking a storm, he expressed a genuine astonishment at the inability of the world at large to tolerate frankness, however sincere, however manifestly for its own good. Hurt by his brutally plain speaking, his old friends were reproached for being hurt. Few of Kingham's loves or friendships had long survived the effects of his frankness. The affair with Grace was one of the exceptions.

From the very beginning, Kingham had found it necessary to 'clear the atmosphere.' Even at their first meeting, in our house, he was rather rude. Later on, he developed into a kind of Timon of Athens. Her frivolity, her voluptuary's philosophy of life, her heartlessness, her 'devilish concupiscence'—these were the characteristics about which he told her, with all the concentrated passion of which he was capable, what he indignantly thought.

I met him again, at the Queen's Hall, on the day after his dinner in Soho.

'I told her what I thought of her,' he let me know.

'And what did she think about what you thought?' I asked.

Kingham frowned. 'She seemed to be rather pleased than otherwise,' he answered. 'That's the devilish strength of these women. They simply glory in the things they ought to be ashamed of. It makes them impervious to anything decent. Impervious, and therefore utterly ruthless and un-scrupulous.'

'How incorrigibly romantic you are!' I mocked at him.

Told—and very mildly, after all—what I thought of him, Kingham winced like a stung horse. Other people's frankness hurt him just as much as his hurt other people; perhaps more. The only difference was that he enjoyed being hurt.

'What nonsense!' he began indignantly.

His retort lasted as long as the interval and was only drowned by the first blaring chords of the *Meistersinger* overture. Bottled up within compulsory silence, what were his emotions? It amused me to speculate. Various, emphatic, tirelessly unflagging and working themselves up into ever more and more clotted complications—were they not the spiritual counterpart of this music to which we were now listening? When the Wagnerian tumult was over, Kingham continued his interrupted protest.

'She seemed to be rather pleased.' That, according to

Kingham, had been Grace's reaction to his home truths. I felt sure, on reflection, that he had observed her rightly. For Grace still saw herself in terms of Rodneyism—as 'modern' and 'eighteenth-century' (curious how these terms have come to be largely interchangeable) and what Rodney imagined to be 'eternally feminine.' Of course she would be pleased at finding that Kingham had accepted her at her own valuation—and not only accepted her valuation but even voluntarily outbidden it by adding devilishness to the modernity, eighteenth-centuriness, and eternal femininity which she had modestly—too modestly, as she now perceived—attributed to herself. She took Kingham's denunciations as compliments and smiled with unaffected pleasure when he talked to her of her vampire's ruthlessness, when he reproached her with her devilish concupiscence for the shuddering souls as well as the less reluctant flesh of her victims. In Rodney's circle a temperament was as much *de rigueur* as a train and ostrich feathers at Court. Grace saw herself as a prodigy of temperament; but she liked to have this vision of herself confirmed by outside testimony. Kingham's home truths convinced her that she had seen herself correctly. The more abusive Kingham became, the better pleased she was and the more she liked him. She felt that he was really taking her seriously as a frivolous woman, that he was appreciating her as she deserved. His appreciation heightened her confidence and, under the rain of his anathemas, she played her part with an easier grace, a more stylish perfection. The spectacle of Grace impertinently blossoming under what had been meant to blast exasperated Kingham. He abused her more violently; and the greater his violence, the more serenely airy her eternal, modern, eighteenth-century femininity.

Underneath, meanwhile, and almost unconsciously, Grace was falling in love with him.

I have seen Kingham in his relations with many men and women. To none of them was he merely indifferent. Either they detested him—and I have never known a man who had more and bitterer enemies—or else they loved him. (Many of the lovers, I may add, turned subsequently into haters.) When I analyse my own feelings towards him, I am forced to the conclusion that I myself was in some manner in love with him. For why should I, who knew him so well and how insufferable he could be and, indeed, generally was, why should I have put up with him, in spite of everything? And why should I always have made such efforts to patch up all our incessant quarrels? Why shouldn't I have allowed him to go to the devil, so far as I was concerned, a dozen times? or at least thankfully accepted the estrangement which followed our most violent squabble—the squabble over poor loutish Herbert—and allowed the separation to lengthen into permanency? The only explanation is that, like all those who did not loathe him, I was somehow in love with Kingham. He was in some way important for me, deeply significant and necessary. In his presence I felt that my being expanded. There was suddenly, so to speak, a high tide within me; along dry, sand-silted, desolate channels of my being life strongly, sparklingly flowed. And Kingham was the moon that drew it up across the desert.

All those whom we find sympathetic exercise, in a greater or less degree, this moon-like influence upon us, drawing up the tides of life till they cover what had been, in an antipathetic environment, parched and dead. But there are certain individuals who, by their proximity, raise a higher tide, and in a vastly greater number of souls, than the ordinary man or woman. Kingham was one of these exceptional beings. To those who found him sympathetic he was more sympathetic than other and much more obviously amiable acquaintances. There was a glow, a vividness, a brilliance about the man. He could charm you even when he was saying things with which you disagreed, or doing things which you disapproved. Even his enemies admitted the existence and the power of this brilliant charm. Catherine, who was not exactly an enemy, but who profoundly disliked his way of life and habits of mind, had to confess that, whenever he wanted and took the trouble to do so, he could silence, for the moment at any rate, all her prejudices and compel her, so long as he was actually there, in the room with her, to like him. Grace started with no prejudices against him—no prejudices, beyond the opinion, inherited from Rodney, that the man was a savage; and savages, after all, are more attractive than repellant. She was suggestible and easily swayed by stronger and more definite personalities than her own. It was not surprising that she should succumb to his charm to the extent of first liking the man and soon wildly loving him.

It was some little time, however, before Grace discovered that she loved him. In the first days of their intimacy, she was too busy playing the modern part to realize that she felt so un-Rodneyan an emotion. Love, the real insane thing, was out of harmony with the character she had assumed. It needed a sudden, startling shock to make her understand what she felt for him, to make her, in the same moment, forget to be 'modern' and 'feminine' in Rodney's sense of the terms, and become—what? I had meant to say 'herself.' But after all, can one be said to be 'oneself' when one is being transfigured or dolorously distorted by love? In love, nobody is himself; or if you prefer, romantically, to put it the other way round, nobody is really himself when he is not in love. It comes to very much the same thing. The difference between Grace in love and Grace out of it seemed all the wider, because it was the difference between a Rodneyan eternal female and a woman, and a Kinghamized woman at that. For even in love, Grace saw herself in the part and saw herself, inevitably, in terms of her lover. Her Rodney-isms disappeared and were replaced by Kinghamisms. She saw herself no longer as a modern young aristocrat, but as the primevally 'passional' incarnation ('passional' was one of Kingham's too favourite words) of her new lover's feminine ideal.

Their intimacy had lasted more than a month before Grace discovered the true nature of her feelings. Kingham's courtship had been unremitting. Denunciations of her devilishness had alternated with appeals to her to become his mistress. Grace took the denunciations as compliments and laughingly replied to them at random with any nonsense that came into her head. These airy irrelevant retorts of hers, which Rodney would have applauded as the height of modern wit, seemed to Kingham the very height of diabolism.

'She's like Nero,' he said to me one day, 'fiddling over Rome.'

He was Rome—the centre of the universe—in flames. Grace, having kindled, watched him burn and, in the face of his destruction, talked nonsense.

What was more, she would not quench his conflagration. In spite of the 'devilish concupiscence,' which King-

ham had attributed to her, she refused, during the first five
or six weeks of their acquaintance, to become his mistress.
She had captivated Kingham; that was sufficient to restore
her self-confidence and that fantastic image of herself, as
a successful, modern siren, which Rodney's desertion had
temporarily shattered. To have tumbled into his arms at
once might, perhaps, have been in the *dix-huitième* part; but
a certain native modesty prevented Grace from being per-
fectly consistent.

Kingham regarded her refusal to capitulate immediately
as yet another piece of devilishness; according to his theory,
she was exercising an unnatural self-control merely in order
to torment him. A perverse taste for cruelty was added to
his list of accusations. Grace was charmed by this soft im-
peachment.

Kingham's attacks had seemed to her, so far, more
amusing than painful, more complimentary than insulting.
She was still protected by the armour of her indifference.
The realization that she loved him was soon to strip her of
that armour, and with every increase of that love, her naked
spirit was to grow more tremulously sensitive to Kingham's
assaults upon it.

The critical, the apocalyptic event took place in King-
ham's rooms. It was a damp, hot afternoon of early summer.
The sky was overcast when Grace arrived, and there was
thunder in the air. She was wearing—the fact came out in
her account to Catherine of the afternoon's events—she was
wearing, for the first time, a brand new frock from Paris;
mouse-coloured, with two subtly harmonious, almost dis-
cordant, tones of red about the collar, and a repetition of the
same colours at the cuffs and in a panel let into the skirt.

Poiret, I think, was the inventor; and it was very modern and rather eccentrically elegant. In a word, it was a dress created for Rodney's mistress.

Grace, who was very much aware of herself in her clothes, had felt the incongruity most painfully, afterwards. The more so, since, when she came in, she was feeling so happy about her dress. She was thinking what a success it was and how elegant, how original the people who saw her in the street must find her. And she was wondering what effect the dress would have on Kingham. She hoped, she thought that he would like it.

In his way, Kingham was nearly as observant in the matter of clothes as Rodney. True, he had not Rodney's almost professional eye for style and cut and smartness. Rodney was a great couturier *manqué.* The fashionable dressmaker was visible in every picture he painted; he had mistaken his profession. Kingham's way of looking at clothes was different. His was the moralist's eye, not the couturier's. For him, clothes were symbols, the visible expressions of states of soul. Thus, Grace's slightly eccentric, very dashing elegance seemed to him the expressive symbol of her devilishness. He regarded her clothes as an efflorescence of her spirit. They were part of her, and she was directly and wholly responsible for them. It never seemed to strike him that tailors, dressmakers and advisory friends might share the responsibility. He took in Grace's frock at a glance.

'You've got a new dress on,' he said accusingly.

'Do you like it?' she asked.

'No,' said Kingham.

'Why not?'

'Why not?' he repeated. 'Well, I suppose it's because the

thing's so expressive of you, because it suits you so devilishly well.'

'I should have thought that would be a reason for liking it.'

'Oh, it would be, no doubt,' said Kingham, 'it would be, if I could just regard you as a spectacle, as something indifferent, to be looked at—that's all—like a picture. But you're not indifferent to me, and you know it and you deliberately torture me. How can I be expected to like what makes you seem more devilishly desirable and so increases my torture?'

He glared at her ferociously. It was with an effort that Grace kept her own gaze steady before those bright, dark, expressive eyes. He advanced towards her and laid his two hands on her shoulders.

'To-day,' he said, 'you're going to be my lover.'

Grace shook her head, smiling a capricious, eternally feminine smile.

'Yes, you are.' His grip on her shoulders tightened.

'No, I'm not,' Grace answered. She drew in her breath rather sharply; he was hurting her.

'I tell you, you are.'

They looked at one another, face close to face, enemies. Grace's heart violently beat.

'At one moment, I thought he was going to throttle me,' she told Catherine.

But she braved it out, and conquered.

Kingham withdrew his hands from her shoulders and turned away. He walked across to the other side of the room and, leaning against the wall in the embrasure of the window, looked out in silence at the grey sky.

Greatly relieved, Grace sat down on the divan. With a

saucy and defiant movement that was, unfortunately, quite lost on Kingham's stubbornly presented back, she tucked up her feet under her. Opening her handbag, she took out her cigarette case, opened that in its turn, extracted a cigarette and lighted it—all very nonchalantly and deliberately. She was steadying her nerves to resist another attack—steadying her nerves and perhaps, at the same time, preparing to annoy him, when he should turn round, by the spectacle of her unconcernedness.

She had expected a repetition of the violences of a moment since, of the familiar denunciations of all the other days. She was not prepared to resist the new kind of attack which he now launched against her emotions. When at last—and she had more than half finished her cigarette before the long silence was broken—Kingham turned round and came towards her, she saw that he was weeping.

Kingham, as I have said, was no comedian. All that he professed to feel he felt, I am sure, genuinely. But he felt too easily and he was too fond of feeling. In situations where others would have exercised a restraint upon themselves, Kingham gave free rein to his emotions, or even actually roused and goaded them into a more violent and more prolonged activity. He needed no dervish tricks to work himself up, no dancing, no howling and drumming, no self-laceration. He could do the thing inwardly, by intense concentration on the object of his desire or hatred, on the cause of his pain or pleasure. He brooded over his loves or his grievances, making them seem more significant than they really were; he brooded, conjuring up in his imagination appropriate visions—of unpermitted raptures, when he was suffering from the pangs of desire; of scenes of insult, humiliation, rage, when he was angry with any one;

of his own miserable self, when he desired to feel self-pity—himself, pictured as unloved, in solitude, utterly deserted, even dying. . . .

Long practice had made him an adept in the art of working up his emotions, of keeping himself uninterruptedly on the boil, so to speak, over a long period of time. In the course of these few brief weeks of his courtship, he had managed to convince himself that the interest he took in Grace was the most violent of passions and that he was suffering excruciatingly from her refusal—her devilish, her sadistic refusal—to be his mistress. Painfully and profoundly, he was enjoying it. The zest was still in the orgy; he felt no sense of satiety.

These tears were the result of a sudden and overwhelming feeling of self-pity, which had succeeded his mood of violence. He had perceived, all at once, that his violence was futile; it was absurd to suppose that he could shake or beat or throttle her into accepting him. He turned away in despair. He was alone, an outcast; nobody cared for him; he was expending his spirit in a waste of shame—his precious, beautiful spirit—and there was no saving himself, the madness was too strong. He was done for, absolutely done for.

Standing there, in the embrasure of the window, he had brooded over his miseries, until his sense of them became all of a sudden intolerable. The tears came into his eyes. He felt like a child, like a tired child who abandons himself, hopelessly, to misery.

All the animation went out of his face; it became like the face of a dead man, frozen into a mask of quiet misery. Pale, ruddy-bearded, delicately featured, it was like the face of a dead or dying Christ in some agonizing Flemish picture.

It was this dead Christ's face that now turned back towards Grace Peddley. This dead Christ's face—and it had been the face of Lucifer, burning with life and passion, menacingly, dangerously beautiful, that had turned away from her. The eyes, which had shone so brightly then, were almost shut, giving the face an appearance of blindness; and between the half-closed lids there was a slow welling out of tears.

The first sight of this suffering face startled her into a kind of terror. But the terror was succeeded almost at once by a great pity. That face, at once lifeless and suffering! And those tears! She had never seen a man shed tears before. She was overwhelmed by pity—by pity and, at the thought that it was all her fault, by a passion of repentance and self-abasement, by a desire to make amends. And at the same time she felt another and greater emotion, an emotion in which the pity and the repentance were included and from which they derived their strange intensity. It was the feeling that, for her, Kingham was the only person in the world who in any way mattered. It was love.

In silence he crossed the room, dropped down on his knees before the divan where Grace, her cigarette still smoking between her fingers, half sat, half reclined, frozen by astonishment into a statue of lolling modernity, and laying his head in her lap, silently sobbed.

The spell of Grace's immobility was broken. She bent forward over him, she caressed his hair. The gesture recalled to her attention the half-smoked cigarette; she threw it into the fire-place. Her fingers touched his scalp, the nape of his neck, his ears, his averted cheek.

'My darling,' she whispered, 'my darling. You mustn't cry. It's terrible when you cry.'

And she herself began to cry. For a long time they remained in the same position, Kingham kneeling, his face pressed against her knees, Grace bending over him, stroking his hair, both weeping.

Our thoughts and feelings are interdependent. It is only in language, not in fact, that they are separate and sharply differentiated. Some men are better mathematicians when they are in love than when they are out of it; some are worse. But in either case the emotion of love conditions the working of the intellect. Still more powerfully does it affect the other emotions, such as pity, courage, shame, fear of ridicule, which it enhances or diminishes as the case may be. It may be laid down as a general rule that the feeling of one strong emotion predisposes us automatically to the feeling of other emotions, however apparently incongruous with the first. Thus joy may predispose to pity and shame to anger. Anger and grief may both dispose to sensual desire. Violent disputes often end in lovemaking; and there are sometimes strange orgies over new-made graves, orgies, to the eye of the indifferent spectator, most unseemly, but which, as often as not, should be attributed less to a cynical lack of feeling than to its abundant presence. Grief creates a sense of loneliness, a desire in those who feel it to be comforted. At the same time, by throwing the whole personality into commotion, it renders the soul of the sufferer peculiarly susceptible to voluptuous influences and peculiarly unapt, in its state of disorganization, to exercise the customary self-restraints; so that when the desired comforter appears, it sometimes happens (conditions of sex and age being propitious) that sympathy is transformed, not merely into love, but into desires demanding immediate satisfaction. Some such transformation took place now. Tears gave place to kisses less and less tearful, to caresses and embracements. There were languors and ecstatic silences.

'I love you, I love you,' Grace repeated, and was almost frightened by the vehemence of the new emotions, the intensity of the new and piercing sensations which she expressed in these old, blunted words. 'I love you.'

And Kingham kissed her and permitted himself, for the moment, to be happy without reserve or inward comment, without a touch of that anticipated afterthought which turns the present into history, even as it unrolls itself, and—criticizing, appraising, judging and condemning—takes all the zest out of immediacy. He was simply happy.

The time came for them to part.

'I must go,' said Grace, sighing.

But the Grace who went was a different woman from the Grace who had come, two hours before. It was a worshipping, adoring Grace, a Grace made humble by love, a Grace for whom being modern and a *grande dame* and eighteenth-century and intellectually fashionable had suddenly ceased to have the slightest importance. Adjusting her hair before the glass, she was struck by the incongruity, the garish out-of-placeness of her new frock. Her love for Kingham, she felt, was something vast and significant, something positively holy; in the presence of that love, the new dress seemed a clown's livery worn in a church. Next day she wore an old, pre-Rodney dress—white muslin with black dots; not at all showy, fashionable, or eccentric. Her soul had dressed itself, so to speak, to match.

But Kingham, who had had time in the intervening hours to poison the memory of yesterday's joy with every kind of venomous afterthought, to discover subtle and horrible explanations for actions that were obviously innocent and simple, received her as though she had changed neither her dress nor her spirit and were indeed the woman whose part she had been playing all these weeks.

'Well,' he said, as he opened the door to her, 'I see you've come for more.'

Grace, who had expected to be received with the gentle and beautiful tenderness which he had displayed on the previous day, was cruelly surprised by the brutality of his tone, the coldness and bitterness of his expression.

'More what?' she asked; and from brightly exultant her eyes became apprehensive in their expression, the smile with which she had so eagerly entered the room faded, as she halted in front of him. Anxiously she looked into his face. 'More what?'

Kingham laughed a loud, unpleasant, mirthless laugh, and pointed to the divan. Grace's devilish concupiscence—that was what he had been chiefly dwelling on since last he saw her.

For the first second Grace did not understand what he meant. This particular aspect of their love was so far from her mind, that it did not occur to her to imagine that it could be in Kingham's. Then all at once his meaning dawned upon her. The blood ran up into her cheeks.

'Kingham!' she protested. (Kingham was one of those men whom everybody, even his closest intimates, called by his surname. For the rest, he had only a pair of initials—J. G. I never knew what they stood for. John George, I should think. But it was quite irrelevant; he was always 'Kingham,' pure and simple.) 'Kingham! How can you say such things?'

'How can I?' he repeated mockingly. 'Why, by not

keeping a fig-leaf over my mouth, which is where the truly respectable, who never talk about their vices, always keep it. Do what you like, but don't talk about it; that's respectability. But dear me,' he bantered on, 'I thought you were as much beyond respectability as you are beyond good and evil—or below, whichever the case may be.'

Grace, who had come in expecting a kiss and gentle words, walked slowly away from him across the room, sat down on the divan and began to cry.

A moment later Kingham was holding her in his arms and kissing away her tears. He spoke no word; the kisses became more passionate. At first, she averted her face from them. But in the end she abandoned herself. For a time she was happy. She forgot Kingham's cruel words, or if she remembered them, she remembered them as words spoken in a nightmare—by mistake, so to say, not on purpose, not seriously.

She had begun to feel almost perfectly reassured, when Kingham disengaged himself suddenly and roughly from her embrace, jumped up and began restlessly walking up and down the room, ruffling his hair as he went.

'What a horrible thing it is to have a vice!' he began. 'Something you carry about with you, but that isn't yourself. Something that's stronger than you are, that you want to resist and conquer, but can't. A vice, a vice.' He was enchanted by the word; it became, for the moment, the core of his universe. 'It's horrible. We're possessed by devils, that's what's wrong with us. We carry our private devils about with us, our vices, and they're too strong for us. They throw us down and horribly triumph.' He shuddered disgustedly. 'It's horrible to feel yourself being murdered by your vice.

The devil spiritually murdering you, suffocating your soul with warm soft flesh. My devil uses you as his instrument of murder; your devil uses me. Our vices conspire; it's a conspiracy, a murder plot.'

By this time Grace was unhappier than she had ever been in her life before. (And yet, if Rodney had said the same thing, expressed a little differently—in terms of compliments on her 'temperament'—she would have been delighted, two months ago.)

'But you know I love you, you *know*,' was all that she could say. 'What makes you say these things, when you know?'

Kingham laughed. 'Oh, I know,' he answered, 'I know, only too well. I know what women like you mean by "love."'

'But I'm not a woman like . . .' Grace hesitated; 'like me' didn't sound quite sensible, somehow. ' . . . like that.'

'Not like yourself?' Kingham asked derisively.

'Not like what you think,' Grace insisted through the tangled confusion of words. 'Not silly, I mean; not frivolous and all that. Not really.' All those months with Rodney seemed a dream; and yet she had really lived through them. And there had really been champagne and sandwiches, and more than scientific conversations. . . . 'Not now, at any rate,' she added. 'Now I know you. It's different; can't you understand. Utterly different. Because I love you, love you, love you, love you.'

Any one else would have allowed himself to be convinced, at any rate for the moment; would have begged pardon, kissed and made friends. But, for Kingham, that would have been too easy, too emotionally flat. He stuck to his position.

'I know you do,' he answered, averting his gaze, as he

spoke, from that pathetic, suffering face, from those wide-open grey eyes, perplexed and agonized, that looked up at him so appealingly, so abjectly even. 'So do I. Your devil loves me. My devil loves you.'

'But no,' Grace brokenly protested. 'But why? . . .'

'Loves violently,' he went on in a loud voice, almost shouting, 'irresistibly.' And as he spoke the words he swung round and precipitated himself upon her with a kind of fury. 'Do you know what it is,' he went on, as he held her, struggling a little and reluctant in his arms, 'do you know what it is to love, not a person, not even their whole body, but just some part of it—insanely? Do you know what it is when the vice-devil concentrates its whole desire on one point, focuses it inexorably until nothing else exists but the nape of a neck, or a pectoral muscle, a foot, a knee, a hand? This hand, for example.' He took her hand and lifted it towards his face. 'And not even a whole hand,' he continued. 'Just the ball of a thumb, just that little cushion of flesh that's marked off from the rest of the palm by the line of life; just that soft, resilient, strong little cushion of flesh.'

He began to kiss the spot on Grace's hand.

'Don't, don't. You mustn't.' She tried to pull her hand away.

But Kingham held it fast. He went on kissing that soft, rounded swell of muscle at the base of her palm, insistently, again and again; kissing and kissing. And sometimes he would take the flesh between his teeth and would bite, gently at first, then with a gradually increasing force, until the pain became almost unbearable and Grace cried out, when he would fall to kissing again, softly and tenderly, as though he were asking forgiveness, were trying to kiss the pain away. Grace ceased to struggle and abandoned her hand to him, to do with what he liked. And little by little this insanely limited devil's love-making seemed to evoke a special voluptuous sensibility in that particular square inch of skin upon which it was concentrated. Her whole capacity for feeling pleasure seemed to focus itself at the base of her left hand. Even the gradually increasing pain, as his teeth closed more and more tightly on her flesh, was pleasurable. She abandoned herself; but, at the same time, she felt that there was something shameful and even horrible about this pleasure. What might have been simple and beautiful and joyous had been turned into something painful, complicated, ugly and obscure. Kingham might congratulate himself on having produced a situation full of the most promising emotional possibilities.

I have reconstructed these scenes at some length because they were characteristic and typical of the whole affair. In his search for intense and painful emotions, Kingham displayed a perverse ingenuity; he was never at a loss for a pretext to complicate the simple and distort the natural. His great resource was always Grace's devilishness. Blind, as only Kingham could be blind, to all evidence to the contrary, he persisted in regarding Grace as a frivolous vampire, a monster of heartless vice. Her vampirishness and her vice were the qualities which attracted him to her; if he could have been convinced that she was really simple, innocent and childish, that her 'devilish concupiscence' was in actual fact an abject, unhappy adoration, he would have ceased to take any interest in her. Pleading meant as little to him as evidence. If Grace protested too vigorously, Kingham would bring up the affair with Rodney. What was that but vice, plain and unvarnished? Had not she herself admitted that she didn't love the man? Miserably, despairingly, Grace would confess in answer that she had certainly been silly and frivolous and feather-headed, but that now all that was done with. Everything was different, she was different, now. Because she loved him. To which Kingham would retort by expatiating with fiery eloquence about the horrors of vice, until at last Grace began to cry.

Grace's devilishness formed the staple and chronic pretext for scenes. But Kingham was inventive and there were plenty of other excuses. Observant—for he was acutely observant, wherever he chose not to be blind—Kingham had early realized the entirely vague and accidental nature of all Grace's ideas, convictions, principles, and opinions. He perceived that what she thought about music, for example, was only a distorted and fragmentary version of what I thought; that her opinions on art were Rodney's, muddled; that her philosophic and literary convictions were like a parboiled lobster—'the fading sable and the coming gules'—half Rodney's and half, already, his own. And perceiving these things, he mocked her for her intellectual hypocrisy and snobbery. He found plenty of opportunities for hurting and humiliating her.

On other occasions, he would reproach her with untruthfulness and mean dissimulation, because she did not frankly tell John Peddley of her infidelity to him.

'I don't want to make him unnecessarily miserable,' Grace protested.

Kingham laughed derisively. 'A lot you care about anybody's happiness,' he said, 'particularly his! The truth is that you want to make the best of both worlds—be respectable and vicious at the same time. At all costs, no frankness! It's a case of the misplaced fig-leaf, as usual.'

And then there was a terrible scene, a whole series of terrible scenes, because Grace did not want to have a child by him.

'Our only excuse,' he raged at her, 'the only thing that might justify us—and you won't hear of it. It's to be vice for vice's sake, is it? The uncontaminated aesthetic doctrine.'

At other times, becoming strangely solicitous for the welfare of Grace's children, he reproached her with being a bad, neglectful mother.

'And you know, it's true,' she said to Catherine, with remorseful conviction. 'It's quite true. I *do* neglect them.'

She invited Catherine to accompany her and the two youngest to the Zoo, the very next afternoon. Over the heads of little Pat and Mittie, among the elephants and apes, the bears and the screaming parrots, she talked to Grace about her love and her unhappiness. And every now and then Pat or Mittie would interrupt with a question.

'Mummy, why do fish swim?'

Or: 'How do you make tortoises?'

'You know, you're a great comfort,' said Grace to Catherine, as they parted. 'I don't know what I should do without you.'

The next time she came, she brought Catherine a present; not a powder-puff this time, not gloves or ribbons, but a copy of Dostoievsky's *Letters from the Underworld*.

'You must read it,' she insisted. 'You absolutely must. It's so damnably *true*.'

Grace's life during this period was one of almost uninterrupted misery. I say 'almost uninterrupted'; for there were occasions when Kingham seemed to grow tired of violent emotions, of suffering, and the infliction of suffering; moments when he was all tenderness and an irresistible

charm. For these brief spells of happiness, Grace was only
too pathetically grateful. Her love, which an absolutely con-
sistent ill-treatment might finally perhaps have crushed and
eradicated, was revived by these occasional kindnesses into
fresh outflowerings of a passionate adoration. Each time she
hoped, she almost believed, that the happiness was going
to be permanent. Bringing with her a few select aphorisms
of Nietzsche, a pocket Leopardi, or the reproduction of one
of Goya's *Desastres de la Guerra*, she would come and tell
Catherine how happy she was, how radiantly, miraculously
happy. Almost she believed that, this time, her happiness
was going to last for ever. Almost; but never quite. There was
always a doubt, an unexpressed, secret, and agonizing fear.
And always the doubt was duly justified, the fear was proved
to be but too well founded. After two or three days' holiday
from his emotional orgy—two or three days of calm and
kindness—Kingham would appear before her, scowling, his
face dark, his eyes angry and accusing. Grace looked at him
and her heart would begin to beat with a painful irregular-
ity and violence; she felt suddenly almost sick with anxious
anticipation. Sometimes he burst out at once. Sometimes—
and that was much worse—he kept her in a state of miser-
able suspense, that might be prolonged for hours, even for
days, sulking in a gloomy silence and refusing, when Grace
asked him, to tell her what was the matter. If she ventured to
approach him in one of these moods with a kiss or a sooth-
ing caress, he pushed her angrily away.

The excuses which he found for these renewals of tem-
pest after calm were of the most various nature. One of the
periods of happiness ended by his reproaching her with

having been too tenderly amorous (too devilishly concupiscent) when he made love to her. On another occasion it was her crime to have remarked, two days before he chose actually to reproach her for it, that she liked the critical essays of Dryden. ('Such an intolerable piece of humbug and affectation,' he complained. 'Just because it's the fashion to admire these stupid, boring classical writers. Mere hypocrisy, that's what it is.' And so on.) Another time he was furious because she had insisted on taking a taxi all the way to Hampton Court. True, she had proposed from the first to pay for it. None the less, when the time came for paying, he had felt constrained in mere masculine decency to pull out his pocket-book. For one painful moment he had actually thought that she was going to accept his offer. He avenged himself for that moment of discomfort by accusing her of stupid and heartless extravagance.

'There's something extraordinarily coarse,' he told her, 'something horribly thick-skinned and unfeeling about people who have been born and brought up with money. The idea of spending a couple of pounds on a mere senseless caprice, when there are hundreds of thousands of people with no work, living precariously, or just not dying, on state charity! The idea!'

Grace, who had proposed the excursion because she thought that Hampton Court was the most romantic place in the world, and because it would be so wonderful to be two and lovers by the side of the Long Water, in the deep embrasures of the windows, before the old grey mirrors, before the triumphing Mantegnas—Grace was appalled that reality should have turned out so cruelly different from her anticipatory dreams. And meanwhile yet another moment of happiness had irrevocably passed.

It was not surprising that Grace should have come to look tired and rather ill. She was paler than in the past and perceptibly thinner. Rimmed with dark circles of fatigue, her eyes seemed to have grown larger and of a paler grey. Her face was still the face of a nice but rather ugly little girl—but of a little girl most horribly ill-treated, hopelessly and resignedly miserable.

Confronted by this perfect resignation to unhappiness, Catherine became impatient.

'Nobody's got any business to be so resigned,' she said. 'Not nowadays, at any rate. We've got beyond the Patient Griselda stage.'

But the trouble was that Grace hadn't got beyond it. She loved abjectly. When Catherine urged and implored her to break with Kingham, she only shook her head.

'But you're unhappy,' Catherine insisted.

'There's no need for you to tell me that,' said Grace, and the tears came into her eyes. 'Do you suppose I don't know it?'

'Then why don't you leave him?' asked Catherine. 'Why on earth don't you?'

'Because I can't.' And after she had cried a little, she went on in a voice that was still unsteady and broken by an occasional sob: 'It's as though there were a kind of devil in me, driving me on against my will. A kind of dark devil.' She had begun to think in terms of Kingham even about herself. The case seemed hopeless.

We went abroad that summer, to the seaside, in Italy. In the lee of that great limestone mountain which rises suddenly,

like the mountain of Paradise, out of the Pomptine marshes
and the blue plains of the Mediterranean, we bathed and
basked and were filled with the virtue of the life-giving sun.
It was here, on the flanks of this mountain, that the enchant-
ress Circe had her palace. Circeus Mons, Monte Circeo—the
magic of her name has lingered, through Roman days, to the
present. In coves at the mountain's foot stand the ruins of
imperial villas, and walking under its western precipices you
come upon the ghost of a Roman seaport, with the fishponds
of Lucullus close at hand, like bright eyes looking upwards
out of the plain. At dawn, before the sun has filled all space
with the quivering gauzes of heat and the colourless bright-
ness of excessive light, at dawn and again at evening, when
the air once more grows limpid and colour and distant form
are re-born, a mountain shape appears, far off, across the blue
gulf of Terracina, a mountain shape and a plume of white un-
wavering smoke: Vesuvius. And once, climbing before sunrise
to the crest of our Circean hill, we saw them both—Vesuvius
to the southward, across the pale sea and northwards, beyond
the green marshes, beyond the brown and ilex-dark Alban
hills, the great symbolical dome of the world, St. Peter's, glit-
tering above the mists of the horizon.

We stayed at Monte Circeo for upwards of two months,
time enough to become brown as Indians and to have forgot-
ten, or at least to have become utterly careless of, the world
outside. We saw no newspapers; discouraged all correspon-
dents by never answering their letters, which we hardly even
took the trouble to read; lived, in a word, the life of savages
in the sun, at the edge of a tepid sea. All our friends and re-
lations might have died, England been overwhelmed by war,
pestilence and famine, all books, pictures, music destroyed

irretrievably out of the world—at Monte Circeo we should not have cared a pin.

But the time came at last when it was necessary to return to London and make a little money. We loaded our bodies with unaccustomed garments, crammed our feet—our feet that had for so long enjoyed the liberty of sandals—into their imprisoning shoes, took the omnibus to Terracina and climbed into the train.

'Well,' I said, when we had managed at last to squeeze ourselves into the two vacant places which the extraordinary exuberance of a party of Neapolitans had painfully restricted, 'we're going back to civilization.'

Catherine sighed and looked out of the window at the enchantress's mountain beckoning across the plain. 'One might be excused,' she said, 'for making a little mistake and thinking it was hell we were going back to.'

It was a dreadful journey. The compartment was crowded and the Neapolitans fabulously large, the weather hot, the tunnels frequent, and the smoke peculiarly black and poisonous. And with the physical there came a host of mental discomforts. How much money would there be in the bank when we got home? What bills would be awaiting us? Should I be able to get my book on Mozart finished by Christmas, as I had promised? In what state should I find my invalid sister? Would it be necessary to pay a visit to the dentist? What should we do to placate all the people to whom we had never written? Wedged between the Neapolitans, I wondered. And looking at Catherine, I could see by the expression on her face that she was similarly preoccupied. We were like Adam and Eve when the gates of the garden closed behind them.

At Genoa the Neapolitans got out and were replaced by passengers of more ordinary volume. The pressure in the compartment was somewhat relaxed. We were able to secure a couple of contiguous places. Conversation became possible.

'I've been so much wondering,' said Catherine, when at last we were able to talk, 'what's been happening all this time to poor little Grace. You know, I really *ought* to have written to her.' And she looked at me with an expression in which consciousness of guilt was mingled with reproach.

'After all,' I said, responding to her expression rather than to her words, 'it wasn't my fault if you were too lazy to write. Was it?'

'Yes, it was,' Catherine answered. 'Just as much yours as mine. You ought to have reminded me to write, you ought to have insisted. Instead of which you set the example and encouraged my laziness.'

I shrugged my shoulders. 'One can't argue with women.'

'Because they're almost always in the right,' said Catherine. 'But that isn't the point. Poor Grace is the point. What's happened to her, do you suppose? And that dreadful Kingham—what has he been up to? I wish I'd written.'

At Monte Circeo, it is true, we had often spoken of Grace and Kingham. But there, in the annihilating sunshine, among the enormous and, for northern eyes, the almost unreal beauties of that mythological landscape, they had seemed as remote and as unimportant as everything and everybody else in our other life. Grace suffered. We knew it, no doubt, theoretically; but not, so to speak, practically— not personally, not with sympathetic realization. In the sun it had been hardly possible to realize anything beyond our own well-being. Expose a northern body to the sun and the soul within it seems to evaporate. The inrush from the source of physical life drives out the life of the spirit. The body must become inured to light and life before the soul can condense again into active existence. When we had talked of Grace at Monte Circeo, we had been a pair of almost soulless bodies in the sun. Our clothes, our shoes, the hideous discomfort of the train gave us back our souls. We talked of Grace now with rediscovered sympathy, speculating rather anxiously on her fate.

'I feel that in some way we're almost responsible for her,' said Catherine. 'Oh, I wish I'd written to her! And why didn't she write to me?'

I propounded a comforting theory. 'She probably hasn't been with Kingham at all,' I suggested. 'She's gone abroad as usual with Peddley and the children. We shall probably find that the whole thing has died down by the time we get home.'

'I wonder,' said Catherine.

We were destined to discover the truth, or at least some portion of it, sooner than we had expected. The first person I saw as I stepped out of the train at Modane was John Peddley.

He was standing on the platform some ten or fifteen yards away, scanning, with eyes that sharply turned this way and that, the faces of the passengers descending from the express. His glances were searching, quick, decisive. He might have been a detective posted there on the frontier to intercept the escape of a criminal. No crook, you felt, no gentleman cracksman, however astute, could hope to sneak or swagger past those all-seeing hunter's eyes. It was that thought, the realization that the thing was hopeless, that made me check my first impulse, which was to flee—out of the station, anywhere—to hide—in the luggage-van, the lavatory, under a seat. No, the game was obviously up. There was no possible escape. Sooner or later, whatever I might do now, I should have to present myself at the custom-house; he would catch me there, infallibly. And the train was scheduled to wait for two and a half hours.

'We're in for it,' I whispered to Catherine, as I helped her down on to the platform. She followed the direction of my glance and saw our waiting danger.

'Heaven help us,' she ejaculated with an unaccustomed piety; then added in another tone: 'But perhaps that means that Grace is here. I shall go and ask him.'

'Better not,' I implored, still cherishing a foolish hope that we might somehow slip past him unobserved. 'Better not.'

But in that instant, Peddley turned round and saw us. His large, brown, handsome face beamed with sudden pleasure; he positively ran to meet us.

Those two and a half hours in John Peddley's company at Modane confirmed for me a rather curious fact, of which, hitherto, I had been only vaguely and inarticulately aware: the fact that one may be deeply and sympathetically interested in the feelings of individuals whose thoughts and opinions—all the products, in a word, of their intellects—are utterly indifferent, even wearisome and repulsive. We read the Autobiography of Alfieri, the Journals of Benjamin Robert Haydon, and read them with a passionate interest. But Alfieri's tragedies, but Haydon's historical pictures, all the things which, for the men themselves, constituted their claim on the world's attention, have simply ceased to exist, so far as we are concerned. Intellectually and artistically, these men were more than half dead. But emotionally they lived.

Mutatis mutandis[*], it was the same with John Peddley. I had known him, till now, only as a relater of facts, an expounder of theories—as an intellect, in short; one of the most appallingly uninteresting intellects ever created. I had known him only in his public capacity, so to speak, as the tireless lecturer of club smoking-rooms and dinner-tables. I had never had a glimpse of him in private life. It was not to be wondered at; for, as I have said before, at ordinary times and when things were running smoothly, Peddley had no private life more complicated than the private life of his body. His feelings towards the majority of his fellow-beings were the simple emotions of the huntsman: pleasure when he had caught his victim and could talk him to death; pain and a certain slight resentment when the prey escaped him. Towards his wife he felt the desires of a healthy man in early middle life, coupled with a real but rather unimaginative, habit-born affection. It was an affection which took itself and its object, Grace, altogether too much for granted. In his own way, Peddley loved his wife, and it never occurred to him to doubt that she felt in the same way towards him; it seemed to him the natural inevitable thing, like having children and being fond of them, having a house and servants and coming home in the evening from the office to find dinner awaiting one. So inevitable, that it was quite unnecessary to talk or even to think about it; natural to the point of being taken publicly for granted, like the possession of a bank balance.

I had thought it impossible that Peddley should ever develop a private life; but I had been wrong. I had not fore-

---

* With the respective differences having been considered.

seen the possibility of his receiving a shock violent enough to shake him out of complacency into self-questioning, a shock of sufficient strength to shiver the comfortable edifice of his daily, taken-for-granted life. That shock he had now received. It was a new and unfamiliar Peddley who now came running towards us.

'I'm so glad, I'm so particularly glad to see you,' he said, as he approached us. 'Quite extraordinarily glad, you know.'

I have never had my hand so warmly shaken as it was then. Nor had Catherine, as I could see by the way she winced, as she abandoned her fingers to his crushing cordiality.

'You're the very man I particularly wanted to see,' he went on, turning back to me. He stooped and picked up a couple of our suitcases. 'Let's make a dash for the douane,' he said. 'And then, when we've got those wretched formalities well over, we can have a bit of a talk.'

We followed him. Looking at Catherine, I made a grimace. The prospect of that bit of a talk appalled me. Catherine gave me an answering look, then quickened her pace so as to come up with the energetically hurrying Peddley.

'Is Grace with you here?' she asked.

Peddley halted, a suit-case in each hand. 'Well,' he said, slowly and hesitatingly, as though it were possible to have metaphysical doubts about the correct answer to this question, 'well, as a matter of fact, she isn't. Not really.' He might have been discussing the problem of the Real Presence.

As if reluctant to speak about the matter any further, he turned away and hurried on towards the custom-house, leaving Catherine's next question—'Shall we find her in London when we get back?'—without an answer.

The bit of a talk, when it came, was very different from what I had gloomily anticipated.

'Do you think your wife would mind,' Peddley whispered to me, when the douanier had done with us and we were making our way towards the station restaurant, 'if I had a few words with you alone?'

I answered that I was sure she wouldn't, and said a word to Catherine, who replied, to me by a quick significant look, and to both of us together by a laughing dismissal.

'Go away and talk your stupid business if you want to,' she said. 'I shall begin my lunch.'

We walked out on to the platform. It had begun to rain, violently, as it only rains among the mountains. The water beat on the vaulted glass roof of the station, filling all the space beneath with a dull, continuous roar; we walked as though within an enormous drum, touched by the innumerable fingers of the rain. Through the open arches at either end of the station the shapes of mountains were dimly visible through veils of white, wind-driven water.

We walked up and down for a minute or two without saying a word. Never, in my presence at any rate, had Peddley preserved so long a silence. Divining what embarrassments kept him in this unnatural state of speechlessness, I felt sorry for the man. In the end, after a couple of turns up and down the platform, he made an effort, cleared his throat and diffidently began in a small voice that was quite unlike that loud, self-assured, trombone-like voice in which he told one about the Swiss banking system.

'What I wanted to talk to you about,' he said, 'was Grace.'

The face he turned towards me as he spoke was full of a

puzzled misery. That common-placely handsome mask was strangely puckered and lined. Under lifted eyebrows, his eyes regarded me, questioningly, helplessly, unhappily.

I nodded and said nothing; it seemed the best way of encouraging him to proceed.

'The fact is,' he went on, turning away from me and looking at the ground, 'the fact is . . .' But it was a long time before he could make up his mind to tell me what the fact was.

Knowing so very well what the fact was, I could have laughed aloud, if pity had not been stronger in me than mockery, when he wound up with the pathetically euphemistic understatement: 'The fact is that Grace . . . well, I believe she doesn't love me. Not in the way she did. In fact I know it.'

'How do you know it?' I asked, after a little pause, hoping that he might have heard of the affair only through idle gossip, which I could proceed to deny.

'She told me,' he answered, and my hope disappeared.

'Ah.'

So Kingham had had his way, I reflected. He had bullied her into telling Peddley the quite unnecessary truth, just for the sake of making the situation a little more difficult and painful than it need have been.

'I'd noticed for some time,' Peddley went on, after a silence, 'that she'd been different.'

Even Peddley could be perspicacious after the event. And besides, the signs of her waning love had been sufficiently obvious and decisive. Peddley might have no sympathetic imagination; but at any rate he had desires and knew when they were satisfied and when they weren't. He hinted at explanatory details.

'But I never imagined,' he concluded—'how could I imagine?—that it was because there was somebody else. How could I?' he repeated in a tone of ingenuous despair. You saw very clearly that it was, indeed, quite impossible for him to have imagined such a thing.

'Quite,' I said, affirming comfortingly I do not know exactly what proposition. 'Quite.'

'Well then, one day,' he pursued, 'one day just before we had arranged to come out here into the mountains, as usual, she suddenly came and blurted it all out—quite suddenly, you know, without warning. It was dreadful. Dreadful.'

There was another pause.

'That fellow called Kingham,' he went on, breaking the silence, 'you know him? he's a friend of yours, isn't he?'

I nodded.

'Very able man, of course,' said Peddley, trying to be impartial and give the devil his due. 'But, I must say, the only times I met him I found him rather unsympathetic.' (I pictured the scene: Peddley embarking on the law relating to insurance companies or, thoughtfully remembering that the chap was literary, on pianolas or modern art or the Einstein theory. And for his part, Kingham firmly and in all likelihood very rudely refusing to be made a victim of.) 'A bit too eccentric for my taste.'

'Queer,' I confirmed, 'certainly. Perhaps a little mad sometimes.'

Peddley nodded. 'Well,' he said slowly, 'it was Kingham.'

I said nothing. Perhaps I ought to have 'registered amazement,' as they say in the world of the cinema; amazement, horror, indignation—above all amazement. But I am a poor comedian. I made no grimaces, uttered no cries. In silence we walked slowly along the platform. The rain drummed on the roof overhead; through the archway at the end of the station the all but invisible ghosts of mountains loomed up behind white veils. We walked from Italy towards France and back again from France towards Italy.

'Who could have imagined it?' said Peddley at last.

'Anybody,' I might, of course, have answered. 'Anybody who had a little imagination and who knew Grace; above all, who knew you.' But I held my tongue. For though there is something peculiarly ludicrous about the spectacle of a self-satisfaction suddenly punctured, it is shallow and unimaginative only to laugh at it. For the puncturing of self-satisfaction gives rise to a pain that can be quite as acute as that which is due to the nobler tragedies. Hurt vanity and exploded complacency may be comic as a spectacle, from the outside; but to those who feel the pain of them, who regard them from within, they are very far from ludicrous. The feelings and opinions of the actor, even in the morally lowest dramas, deserve as much consideration as the spectator's. Peddley's astonishment that his wife could have preferred another man to himself was doubtless, from my point of view, a laughable exhibition. But the humiliating realization had genuinely hurt him; the astonishment had been mixed with a real pain. Merely to have mocked would have been a denial, in favour of the spectator, of the actor's rights. Moreover, the pain which Peddley felt was not exclusively the product of an injured complacency. With the low and ludicrous were mingled other, more reputable emotions. His next words deprived me of whatever desire I might have had to laugh.

'What am I to do?' Peddley went on, after another long

pause, and looked at me again more miserably and bewilderedly than ever. 'What *am* I to do?'

'Well,' I said cautiously, not knowing what to advise him, 'it surely depends how you feel about it all—about Grace in particular.'

'How I feel about her?' he repeated. 'Well,' he hesitated, embarrassed, 'I'm fond of her, of course. Very fond of her.' He paused; then, with a great effort, throwing down barriers which years of complacent silence, years of insensitive taking for granted had built up round the subject, he went on: 'I love her.'

The utterance of that decisive word seemed to make things easier for Peddley. It was as though an obstruction had been removed; the stream of confidences began to flow more easily and copiously.

'You know,' he went on, 'I don't think I had quite realized how much I did love her till now. That's what makes it all so specially dreadful—the thought that I ought to have loved her more, or at least more consciously when I had the opportunity, when she loved me; the thought that if I had, I shouldn't, probably, be here now all alone, without her.' He averted his face and was silent, while we walked half the length of the platform. 'I think of her all the time, you know,' he continued. 'I think how happy we used to be together and I wonder if we shall ever be happy again, as we were, or if it's all over, all finished.' There was another pause. 'And then,' he said, 'I think of her there in England, with that man, being happy with him, happier perhaps than she ever was with me; for perhaps she never really did love me, not like that.' He shook his head. 'Oh, it's dreadful, you know, it's dreadful. I try to get these thoughts out of my head, but I can't. I walk in the hills till I'm dead-beat; I try to distract myself by talking to people who come through on the trains. But it's no good. I can't keep these thoughts away.'

I might have assured him, of course, that Grace was without doubt infinitely less happy with Kingham than she had ever been with him. But I doubted whether the consolation would really be very efficacious.

'Perhaps it isn't really serious,' I suggested, feebly. 'Perhaps it won't last. She'll come to her senses one of these days.'

Peddley sighed. 'That's what I always hope, of course. I was angry at first, when she told me that she wasn't coming abroad and that she meant to stay with that man in England. I told her that she could go to the devil, so far as I was concerned. I told her that she'd only hear from me through my solicitor. But what was the good of that? I don't want her to go to the devil; I want her to be with me. I'm not angry any more, only miserable. I've even swallowed my pride. What's the good of being proud and not going back on your decisions, if it makes you unhappy? I've written and told her that I want her to come back, that I'll be happy and grateful if she does.'

'And what has she answered?' I asked.

'Nothing,' said Peddley.

I imagined Peddley's poor conventional letter, full of those worn phrases that make their appearance with such a mournful regularity in all the letters that are read in the divorce courts, or before coroners' juries, when people have thrown themselves under trains for unrequited love. Miserable, cold, inadequate words! A solicitor, he had often dictated them, no doubt, to clients who desired to have their plea for the restitution of conjugal rights succinctly and decorously set down in black and white, for the benefit of the judge who was, in due course, to give it legal force. Old, blunted phrases, into which only the sympathy of the reader has power to instil a certain temporary life—he had had to write them unprofessionally this time, for himself.

Grace, I guessed, would have shown the letter to Kingham. I imagined the derisive ferocity of his comments. A judicious analysis of its style can reduce almost any love-letter to emptiness and absurdity. Kingham would have made that analysis with gusto and with a devilish skill. By his mockery he had doubtless shamed Grace out of her first spontaneous feelings; she had left the letter unanswered. But the feelings, I did not doubt, still lingered beneath the surface of her mind; pity for John Peddley and remorse for what she had done. And Kingham, I felt sure, would find some ingenious method for first encouraging, then deriding these emotions. That would agreeably complicate their relations, would render her love for him a source of even greater pain to her than ever.

Peddley broke the rain-loud silence and the train of my speculations by saying: 'And if it is serious, if she goes on refusing to answer when I write—what then?'

'Ah, but that won't happen,' I said, speaking with a conviction born of my knowledge of Kingham's character. Sooner or later he would do something that would make it impossible for even the most abject of lovers to put up with him. 'You can be sure it won't.'

'I only wish I could,' said Peddley dubiously: he did not know Kingham, only Grace—and very imperfectly at that. 'I can't guess what she means to do. It was all so unexpected—from Grace. I never imagined . . .' For the first time he had begun to realize his ignorance of the woman to whom he was married. The consciousness of this ignorance was one of the elements of his distress. 'But if it is serious,' he went on, after a pause, obstinately insisting on contemplating the worst of possibilities, 'what am I to do? Let her go, like that, without a struggle? Set her free to go and be permanently and respectably happy with that man?' (At the vision he thus conjured up of a domesticated Kingham, I inwardly smiled.) 'That would be fairest to her, I suppose. But why should I be unfair to myself?'

Under the fingers of the drumming rain, in the presence of the ghostly, rain-blurred mountains, we prolonged the vain discussion. In the end I persuaded him to do nothing for the time being. To wait and see what the next days or weeks or months would bring. It was the only possible policy.

When we returned to the station restaurant, Peddley was considerably more cheerful than when we had left it. I had offered no very effectual consolation, invented no magical solution of his problems; but the mere fact that he had been able to talk and that I had been ordinarily sympathetic had been a relief and a comfort to him. He was positively rubbing his hands as he sat down beside Catherine.

'Well, Mrs. Wilkes,' he said in that professionally hearty tone which clergymen, doctors, lawyers, and all those whose business it is to talk frequently and copiously with people they do not know, so easily acquire, 'well, Mrs. Wilkes, I'm afraid we've shamefully neglected you. I'm afraid you'll never forgive me for having carried off your husband in this disgraceful way.' And so on.

After a little, he abandoned this vein of graceful cour-
tesy for more serious conversation.

'I met a most interesting man at this station a few days
ago,' he began. 'A Greek. Theotocopulos was his name. A
very remarkable man. He told me a number of most illu-
minating things about King Constantine and the present
economic situation in Greece. He assured me, for one thing,
that . . .' And the information about King Constantine and
the economic situation in Hellas came pouring out. In Mr.
Theotocopulos, it was evident, John Peddley had found a
kindred soul. When Greek meets Greek then comes, in this
case, an exchange of anecdotes about the deposed sovereigns
of eastern Europe—in a word, the tug of bores. From pri-
vate, Peddley had returned to public life. We were thankful
when it was time to continue our journey.

Kingham lived on the second floor of a once handsome
and genteel eighteenth-century house, which presented its
façade of blackened brick to a decayed residential street,
leading northward from Theobald's Road towards the east-
ernmost of the Bloomsbury Squares. It was a slummy street
in which, since the war, a colony of poor but 'artistic' people
from another class had settled. In the windows, curtains of
dirty muslin alternated with orange curtains, scarlet cur-
tains, curtains in large bright-coloured checks. It was not
hard to know where respectable slumminess ended and gay
Bohemianism began.

The front door of number twenty-three was permanently
open. I entered and addressed myself to the stairs. Reach-
ing the second landing, I was surprised to find the door of
Kingham's rooms ajar. I pushed it open and walked in.

'Kingham,' I called, 'Kingham!'

There was no answer. I stepped across the dark little vestibule and tapped at the door of the main sitting-room.

'Kingham!' I called again more loudly.

I did not want to intrude indiscreetly upon some scene of domestic happiness or, more probably, considering the relations existing between Grace and Kingham, of domestic strife.

'Kingham!'

The silence remained unbroken. I walked in. The room was empty. Still calling discreetly as I went, I looked into the second sitting-room, the kitchen, the bedroom. A pair of suit-cases were standing, ready packed, just inside the bedroom door. Where could they be going? I wondered, hoped I should see them before they went. Meanwhile, I visited even the bathroom and the larder; the little flat was quite empty of life. They must have gone out, leaving the front door open behind them as they went. If preoccupation and absence of mind be signs of love, why then, I reflected, things must be going fairly well.

It was twenty to six on my watch. I decided to wait for their return. If they were not back within the hour, I would leave a note, asking them to come to see us, and go.

The two small and monstrously lofty sitting-rooms in Kingham's flat had once been a single room of nobly classical proportions. A lath-and-plaster partition separated one room from the other, dividing into two unsymmetrical parts the gracefully moulded design which had adorned the ceiling of the original room. A single tall sash window, having no proportionable relation to the wall in which it found itself accidentally placed, illuminated either room—the larger inadequately, the smaller almost to excess. It was in the smaller and lighter of the two sitting-rooms that Kingham kept his books and his writing-table. I entered it, looked round the shelves, and having selected two or three miscellaneous volumes, drew a chair up to the window and settled down to read.

'I have no patience,' I read (and it was a volume of Kingham's own writings that I had opened), 'I have no patience with those silly prophets and Utopia-mongers who offer us prospects of uninterrupted happiness. I have no patience with them. Are they too stupid even to realize their own stupidity? Can't they see that if happiness were uninterrupted and well-being universal, these things would cease to be happiness and well-being and become merely boredom and daily bread, daily business, *Daily Mail?* Can't they understand that, if everything in the world were pea-green, we shouldn't know what pea-green was? "Asses, apes and dogs!" (Milton too, thank God for Milton! didn't suffer fools gladly. Satan—portrait of the artist.) Asses, apes and dogs. Are they too stupid to see that, in order to know happiness and virtue, men must also know misery and sin? The Utopia I offer is a world where happiness and unhappiness are more intense, where they more rapidly and violently alternate than here, with us. A world where men and women endowed with more than our modern sensitiveness, more than our acute and multifarious modern consciousness, shall know the unbridled pleasures, the cruelties and dangers of the ancient world, with all the scruples and remorses of Christianity, all its ecstasies, all its appalling fears. That is the Utopia I offer you—not a sterilized nursing home, with Swedish drill before breakfast, vegetarian cookery, classical music on the radio, chaste mixed sun-baths, and rational free love between aseptic sheets. Asses, apes and dogs!'

One thing at least, I reflected, as I turned the pages of the book in search of other attractive paragraphs, one thing at least could be said in Kingham's favour; he was no mere academic theorist. Kingham practised what he preached. He had defined Utopia, he was doing his best to realize it—in Grace's company.

'Vows of chastity,' the words caught my eye and I read on, 'vows of chastity are ordinarily taken in that cold season, full of disgusts and remorses, which follows after excess. The taker of the oath believes the vow to be an unbreakable chain about his flesh. But he is wrong; the vow is no chain, only a hempen strand. When the blood is cold, it holds fast. But when, with the natural rebirth of appetite, the blood turns to flame, that fire burns through the hemp—the tindery hemp which the binder had thought to be a rope of steel—burns it, and the flesh breaks loose. With renewed satiety come coldness, disgust, remorse, more acute this time than before, and with them a repetition of the Stygian vows. And so on, round and round, like the days of the week, like summer and winter. Futile, you say, no doubt; weak-minded. But I don't agree with you. Nothing that intensifies and quickens life is futile. These vows, these remorses and the deep-rooted feeling from which they spring—the feeling that the pleasure of the senses is somehow evil—sharpen this pleasure to the finest of points, multiply the emotions to which it gives rise by creating, parallel with the body's delight, an anguish and tragedy of the mind.'

I had read them before, these abbreviated essays or expanded maxims (I do not know how to name them; Kingham himself had labelled them merely as 'Notions'); had read them more than once and always enjoyed their violence, their queerness, their rather terrifying sincerity. But this time, it seemed to me, I read them with greater understanding than in the past. My knowledge of Kingham's relations with Grace illuminated them for me; and they, in their turn, threw light on Kingham and his relations with Grace. For instance, there was that sentence about love: 'All love is in the nature of a vengeance; the man revenges himself on the woman who has caught and humiliated him; the woman revenges herself on the man who has broken down her reserves and reluctances, who has dared to convert her from an individual into a mere member and mother of the species.' It seemed particularly significant to me, now. I remember noticing, too, certain words about the sin against the Holy Ghost. 'Only those who know the Holy Ghost are tempted to sin against him—indeed, can sin against him. One cannot waste a talent unless one first possesses it. One cannot do what is wrong, or stupid, or futile, unless one first knows what is right, what is reasonable, what is worth doing. Temptation begins with knowledge and grows as knowledge grows. A man knows that he has a soul to save and that it is a precious soul; it is for that very reason that he passes his time in such a way that it must infallibly be damned. You, reader,' the paragraph characteristically concluded, 'you who have no soul to save, will probably fail to understand what I am talking about.'

I was considering these words in the light of the recent increases of my knowledge of Kingham, when I was suddenly interrupted in the midst of my meditations by the voice of Kingham himself.

'It's no good,' it was saying. 'Can't you understand?' The voice sounded all at once much louder, as the door of the

sense of guilt, a schoolboy's terror of being caught, entirely possessed me. My heart beating, I jumped up and looked about me for some place of concealment. Then, after a second or two, my reason reasserted itself. I remembered that I was not a schoolboy in danger of being caught and caned; that, after all, I had been waiting here in order to ask Kingham and Grace to dinner; and that, so far from hiding myself, I ought immediately to make my presence known to them. Meanwhile, sentence had succeeded sentence in their muffled altercation. I realized that they were involved in some terrible, mortal quarrel; and realizing, I hesitated to interrupt them. One feels shy of breaking in on an exhibition of strong and intimate emotion. To intrude oneself, clothed and armoured in one's daily indifference, upon naked and quivering souls is an insult, almost, one feels, an indecency. This was evidently no vulgar squabble, which could be allayed by a little tact, a beaming face and a tepid douche of platitude. Perhaps it was even so serious, so agonizing that it ought to be put an end to at all costs. I wondered. Ought I to intervene? Knowing Kingham, I was afraid that my intervention might only make things worse. So far from shaming him into peace, it would in all probability have the effect of rousing all his latent violences. To continue an intimately emotional scene in the presence of a third party is a kind of indecency. Kingham, I reflected, would probably be only too glad to enhance and complicate the painfulness of the scene by introducing into it this element of spiritual outrage. I stood hesitating, wondering what I ought to do. Go in to them and run the risk of making things worse? Or stay where I was, at the alternative risk of being discovered, half an hour hence, and having to explain my most inexplicable presence? I was still hesitating when, from the other room, the muffled, obstinate voice of Grace pronounced those words:

'I shall kill myself if you go.'

'No, you won't,' said Kingham. 'I assure you, you won't.' The weariness of his tone was tinged with a certain ironic mockery.

I imagined the excruciations which might result if I gave Kingham an audience to such a drama, and decided not to intervene—not yet, at any rate. I tiptoed across the room and sat down where it would be impossible for me to be seen through the open door.

'I've played that little farce myself,' Kingham went on. 'Oh, dozens of times. Yes, and really persuaded myself at the moment that it was the genuinely tragic article.' Even without my intervention, his mockery was becoming brutal enough.

'I shall kill myself,' Grace repeated, softly and stubbornly.

'But as you see,' Kingham pursued, 'I'm still alive.' A new vivacity had come into his weary voice. 'Still alive and perfectly intact. The cyanide of potassium always turned out to be almond icing: and however carefully I aimed at my cerebellum, I never managed to score anything but a miss.' He laughed at his own jest.

'Why will you talk in that way?' Grace asked, with a weary patience. 'That stupid, cruel way?'

'I may talk,' said Kingham, 'but it's you who act. You've destroyed me, you've poisoned me: you're a poison in my blood. And you complain because I talk!'

He paused, as if expecting an answer: but Grace said nothing. She had said all that there was for her to say so often, she had said 'I love you,' and had had the words so constantly and malevolently misunderstood, that it seemed to her, no doubt, a waste of breath to answer him.

'I suppose it's distressing to lose a victim,' Kingham went on in the same ironic tone. 'But you can't really expect me to believe that it's so distressing that you've got to kill yourself. Come, come, my dear Grace. That's a bit thick.'

'I don't expect you to believe anything,' Grace replied. 'I just say what I mean and leave it at that. I'm tired.' I could hear by the creaking of the springs that she had thrown herself down on the divan. There was a silence.

'So am I,' said Kingham, breaking it at last. 'Mortally tired.' All the energy had gone out of his voice; it was once more blank and lifeless. There was another creaking of springs; he had evidently sat down beside her on the divan. 'Look here,' he said, 'for God's sake let's be reasonable.' From Kingham, the appeal was particularly cogent; I could not help smiling. 'I'm sorry I spoke like that just now. It was silly; it was bad-tempered. And you know the way one word begets another; one's carried away. I didn't mean to hurt you. Let's talk calmly. What's the point of making an unnecessary fuss? The thing's inevitable, fatal. A bad business, perhaps; but let's try to make the best of it, not the worst.'

I listened in astonishment, while Kingham wearily unwound a string of such platitudes. Wearily, wearily; he seemed to be boring himself to death with his own words. Oh, to have done with it, to get away, to be free, never again to set eyes on her! I imagined his thoughts, his desires.

There are moments in every amorous intimacy, when such thoughts occur to one or other of the lovers, when love has turned to weariness and disgust, and the only desire is

a desire for solitude. Most lovers overcome this temporary
weariness by simply not permitting their minds to dwell on
it. Feelings and desires to which no attention is paid soon
die of inanition; for the attention of the conscious mind is
their food and fuel. In due course love reasserts itself and the
moment of weariness is forgotten. To Kingham, however,
Kingham who gave his whole attention to every emotion
or wish that brushed against his consciousness, the slight-
est velleity of weariness became profoundly significant. Nor
was there, in his case, any real enduring love for the object
of his thoughtfully fostered disgust, any strong and steady
affection capable of overcoming what should have been only
a temporary weariness. He loved because he felt the need of
violent emotion. Grace was a means to an end, not an end in
herself. The end—satisfaction of his craving for emotional
excitement—had been attained; the means had therefore
ceased to possess the slightest value for him. Grace would
have been merely indifferent to him, if she had shown her-
self in this crisis as emotionally cold as he felt himself. But
their feelings did not synchronize. Grace was not weary;
she loved him, on the contrary, more passionately than ever.
Her importunate warmth had conspired with his own habit
of introspection to turn weariness and emotional neutrality
into positive disgust and even hatred. He was making an
effort, however, not to show these violent feelings; more-
over he was tired—too tired to want to give them their ad-
equate expression. He would have liked to slip away quietly,
without any fuss. Wearily, wearily, he uttered his sedative
phrases. He might have been a curate giving Grace a heart-
to-heart chat about Life.

'We must be sensible,' he said. And: 'There are other

things besides love.' He even talked about self-control and the consolations of work. It lasted a long time.

Suddenly Grace interrupted him. 'Stop!' she cried in a startlingly loud voice. 'For heaven's sake stop! How can you be so dishonest and stupid?'

'I'm not,' Kingham answered, sullenly. 'I was simply saying . . .'

'You were simply saying that you're sick of me,' said Grace, taking up his words. 'Simply saying it in a slimy, stupid, dishonest way. That you're sick to death of me and that you wish to goodness I'd go away and leave you in peace. Oh, I will, I will. You needn't worry.' She uttered a kind of laugh.

There was a long silence.

'Why don't you go?' said Grace at last. Her voice was muffled, as though she were lying with her face buried in a cushion.

'Well,' said Kingham awkwardly. 'Perhaps it might be best.' He must have been feeling the beginnings of a sense of enormous relief, a joy which it would have been indecent to display, but which was bubbling only just beneath the surface. 'Good-bye, then, Grace,' he said, in a tone that was almost cheerful. 'Let's part friends.'

Grace's laughter was muffled by the cushion. Then she must have sat up; for her voice, when she spoke a second later, was clear and unmuted.

'Kiss me,' she said peremptorily. 'I want you to kiss me, just once more.'

There was a silence.

'Not like that,' Grace's voice came almost angrily. 'Kiss me really, really, as though you still loved me.'

Kingham must have tried to obey her; anything for a quiet life and a prompt release. There was another silence.

'No, no.' The anger in Grace's voice had turned to despair. 'Go away, go, go. Do I disgust you so that you can't even kiss me?'

'But, my dear Grace . . .' he protested.

'Go, go, go.'

'Very well, then,' said Kingham in a dignified and slightly offended tone. But inwardly, what joy! Liberty, liberty! The key had turned in the lock, the prison door was opening. 'If you want me to, I will.' I heard him getting up from the divan. 'I'll write to you when I get to Munich,' he said.

I heard him walking to the door, along the passage to the bedroom, where, I suppose, he picked up his suit-cases, back along the passage to the outer door of the apartment. The latch clicked, the door squeaked on its hinges as it swung open, squeaked as it closed; there was an echoing bang.

I got up from my chair and cautiously peeped round the edge of the doorway into the other room. Grace was lying on the divan in precisely the position I had imagined, quite still, her face buried in a cushion. I stood there watching her for perhaps half a minute, wondering what I should say to her. Everything would sound inadequate, I reflected. Therefore, perhaps, the most inadequate of all possible words, the most perfectly banal, trivial and commonplace, would be the best in the circumstances.

I was pondering thus when suddenly that death-still body stirred into action. Grace lifted her face from the pillow, listened for a second, intently, then with a series of swift motions, she turned on her side, raised herself to a sitting position, dropped her feet to the ground and, springing up, hastened across the room towards the door. Instinctively, I withdrew into concealment. I heard her cross the passage, heard the click and squeak of the front door as it opened. Then her voice, a strange, inhuman, strangled voice, called 'Kingham!' and again, after a listening silence that seemed portentously long, 'Kingham!' There was no answer.

After another silence, the door closed. Grace's footsteps approached once more, crossed the room, came to a halt. I peeped out from my ambush. She was standing by the window, her forehead pressed against the glass, looking out—no, looking down, rather. Two storeys, three, if you counted the area that opened like a deep grave at the foot of the wall beneath the window—was she calculating the height? What were her thoughts?

All at once, she straightened herself up, stretched out her hands and began to raise the sash. I walked into the room towards her.

At the sound of my footsteps, she turned and looked at me—but looked with the disquietingly blank, unrecognizing eyes and expressionless face of one who is blind. It seemed as though her mind were too completely preoccupied with its huge and dreadful idea to be able to focus itself at once on the trivialities of life.

'Dear Grace,' I said, 'I've been looking for you. Catherine sent me to ask you to come and have dinner with us.'

She continued to look at me blankly. After a second or two, the significance of my words seemed to reach her; it was as though she were far away, listening to sounds that laboured slowly across the intervening gulfs of space. When at last she had heard my words—heard them with her distant mind—she shook her head and her lips made the movement of saying 'No.'

I took her arm and led her away from the window. 'But you must,' I said.

My voice seemed to come to her more quickly this time. It was only a moment after I had finished speaking that she again shook her head.

'You must,' I repeated. 'I heard everything, you know. I shall make you come with me.'

'You heard?' she repeated, staring at me.

I nodded, but did not speak. Picking up her small, close-fitting, casque-shaped hat from where it was lying on the floor, near the divan, I handed it to her. She turned with an automatic movement towards the dim, grey-glassed Venetian mirror that hung above the fireplace and adjusted it to her head: a wisp of hair straggled over her temple; tidily, she tucked it away.

'Now, let's go,' I said, and led her away, out of the flat, down the dark stairs, into the street.

Walking towards Holborn in search of a taxi, I made futile conversation. I talked, I remember, about the merits of omnibuses as opposed to undergrounds, about second-hand bookshops, and about cats. Grace said nothing. She walked at my side, as though she were walking in her sleep.

Looking at that frozen, unhappy face—the face of a child who has suffered more than can be borne—I was filled with a pity that was almost remorse. I felt that it was some-how my fault; that it was heartless and insensitive of me not to be as unhappy as she was. I felt, as I have often felt in the presence of the sick, the miserably and hopelessly poor, that I owed her an apology. I felt that I ought to beg her pardon for being happily married, healthy, tolerably prosperous, content with my life. Has one a right to be happy in the presence of the unfortunate, to exult in life before those who desire to die? Has one a right?

'The population of cats in London,' I said, 'must be very nearly as large as the population of human beings.'

'I should think so,' Grace whispered, after a sufficient time had elapsed for her to hear, across the gulfs that separated her mind from mine, what I had said. She spoke with a great effort; her voice was scarcely audible.

'Literally millions,' I pursued.

And then, fortunately, I caught sight of a taxi. Driving home to Kensington, I talked to her of our Italian holiday. I did not think it necessary, however, to tell her of our meeting with Peddley at Modane.

Arrived, I told Catherine in two words what had happened and, handing Grace over to her care, took refuge in my work-room. I felt, I must confess, profoundly and selfishly thankful to be back there, alone, with my books and my piano. It was the kind of thankfulness one feels, motoring out of town for the weekend, to escape from dark and sordid slums to a comfortable, cool-gardened country house, where one can forget that there exist other human beings beside oneself and one's amusing, cultivated friends, and that ninety-nine out of every hundred of them are doomed to misery. I sat down at the piano and began to play the Arietta of Beethoven's Op. III.

I played it very badly, for more than half my mind was preoccupied with something other than the music. I was wondering what would become of Grace now. Without Rodney, without Kingham, what would she do? What would she be? The question propounded itself insistently.

And then, all at once, the page of printed music before my eyes gave me the oracular reply. *Da capo.* The hieroglyph sent me back to the beginning of my passage. *Da capo.* After all, it was obvious. *Da capo.* John Peddley, the children, the house, the blank existence of one who does not know how to live unassisted. Then another musical critic, a second me—introduction to the second theme. Then the second theme, *scherzando*†; another Rodney. Or *molto agitato*‡, the equivalent of Kingham. And then, inevitably, when the agitation had agitated itself to the climax of silence, *da capo* again to Peddley, the house, the children, the blankness of her unassisted life.

The miracle of the Arietta floated out from under my fingers. Ah, if only the music of our destinies could be like this!

---

* An aria in three-part form comprising a theme, a secondary contrasting part, and a repetition of the first part.

† In a sportive manner, used in musical direction.

‡ Very agitated or hurried, used in musical direction.

UNCLE SPENCER

Some people I know can look back over the long series of their childish holidays and see in their memory always a different landscape—chalk downs or Swiss mountains; a blue and sunny sea or the grey, ever-troubled fringe of the ocean; heathery moors under the cloud with far away a patch of sunlight on the hills, golden as happiness and, like happiness, remote, precarious, impermanent, or the untroubled waters of Como, the cypresses and the Easter roses.

I envy them the variety of their impressions. For it is good to have seen something of the world with childish eyes, disinterestedly and uncritically, observing not what is useful or beautiful and interesting, but only such things as, to a being less than four feet high and having no knowledge of life or art, seem immediately significant. It is the beggars, it is the green umbrellas under which the cabmen sit when it rains, not Brunelleschi's dome, not the extortions of the hotel-keeper, not the tombs of the Medici, that impress the childish traveller. Such impressions, it is true, are of no particular value to us when we are grown up. (The famous wisdom of babes, with those childish intimations of immortality and all the rest, never really amounted to very much; and the man who studies the souls of children in the hope of finding out something about the souls of men is about as likely to discover something important as the man who thinks he can explain Beethoven by referring him to the savage origins of music or religion by referring it to the sexual instincts.) None the less, it is good to have had such childish impressions, if only for the sake of comparing (so that we may draw the philosophic moral) what we saw of a place when we were six or seven with what we see again at thirty.

My holidays had no variety. From the time when I first went to my preparatory school to the time when my parents came back for good from India—I was sixteen or seventeen then, I suppose—they were all passed with my Uncle Spencer. For years the only places on the earth's surface of which I had any knowledge were Eastbourne, where I was at school; Dover (and that reduced itself to the harbour and station), where I embarked; Ostend, where Uncle Spencer met me; Brussels, where we changed trains; and finally Longres in Limbourg, where my Uncle Spencer owned the sugar factory, which his mother, my grandmother, had inherited in her turn from her Belgian father, and had his home.

Hanging over the rail of the steamer as it moved slowly, stern foremost, through the narrow gullet of Ostend harbour, I used to strain my eyes, trying to pick out from among the crowd at the quay's edge the small, familiar figure. And always there he was, waving his coloured silk handkerchief, shouting inaudible greetings and advice, getting in the way of the porters and ticket-collectors, fidgeting with a hardly controllable impatience behind the barrier, until at last, squeezed and almost suffocated amongst the grown men

and women—whom the process of disembarkation trans-
formed as though by some malevolent Circean magic into
brute beasts, reasonless and snarling—I struggled to shore,
clutching in one hand my little bag and with the other hold-
ing to my head, if it was summer, a speckled straw, gaudy
with the school colours; if winter, a preposterous bowler,
whose eclipsing melon crammed over my ears made me look
like a child in a comic paper pretending to be grown up.

'Well, here you are, here you are,' my Uncle Spencer
would say, snatching my bag from me. 'Eleven minutes
late.' And we would dash for the custom-house as though
our lives depended on getting there before the other trans-
beasted passengers.

My Uncle Spencer was a man of about forty when first
I came from my preparatory school to stay with him. Thin
he was, rather short, very quick, agile, and impulsive in
his movements, with small feet and small, delicate hands.
His face was narrow, clear-cut, steep, and aquiline; his eyes
dark and extraordinarily bright, deeply set under overhang-
ing brows; his hair was black, and he wore it rather long,
brushed back from his forehead. At the sides of his head it
had already begun to go grey, and above his ears, as it were,
two grey wings were folded against his head, so that, to look
at him, one was reminded of Mercury in his winged cap.

'Hurry up!' he called. And I scampered after him. 'Hurry
up!' But of course there was no use whatever in our hurry-
ing; for even when we had had my little hand-bag examined,
there was always the registered trunk to wait for; and that,
for my Uncle Spencer, was agony. For though our places in
the Brussels express were reserved, though he knew that the

train would not in any circumstances start without us, this intellectual certainty was not enough to appease his passionate impatience, to allay his instinctive fears.

'Terribly slow,' he kept repeating. 'Terribly slow.' And for the hundredth time he looked at his watch. 'Dites-moi,' he would say, yet once more, to the sentry at the door of the customs-house, 'le grand bagage . . . ?' until in the end the fellow, exasperated by these questions which it was not his business to answer, would say something rude; upon which my Uncle Spencer, outraged, would call him *malélevé** and a *grossier personnage†*—to the fury of the sentry but correspondingly great relief of his own feelings; for after such an outburst he could wait in patience for a good five minutes, so far forgetting his anxiety about the trunk that he actually began talking to me about other subjects, asking how I had got on this term at school, what was my batting average, whether I liked Latin, and whether Old Thunderguts, which was the name we gave to the headmaster on account of his noble baritone, was still as ill-tempered as ever.

But at the end of the five minutes, unless the trunk had previously appeared, my Uncle Spencer began looking at his watch again.

'Scandalously slow,' he said. And addressing himself to another official, 'Dites-moi, monsieur, le grand bagage . . . ?'

But when at last we were safely in the train and there was nothing to prevent him from deploying all the graces and amiabilities of his character, my Uncle Spencer, all charm and kindness now, devoted himself whole-heartedly to me.

'Look!' he said; and from the pocket of his overcoat he

---

* Ill-mannered.

† A rude, uncouth person.

pulled out a large and dampish parcel of whose existence my nose had long before made me aware. 'Guess what's in here.'

'Prawns,' I said, without an instant's hesitation.

And prawns it was, a whole kilo of them. And there we sat in opposite corners of our first-class carriage, with the little folding table opened out between us and the pink prawns on the table, eating with infinite relish and throwing the rosy carapaces, the tails, and the sucked heads out of the window. And the Flemish plain moved past us; the long double files of poplars, planted along the banks of the canals, along the fringes of the high roads, moving as we moved, marched parallel with our course or presented, as we crossed them at right angles, for one significant flashing moment the entrance to Hobbema's avenue. And now the belfries of Bruges beckoned from far off across the plain; a dozen more shrimps and we were roaring through its station, all gloom and ogives in honour of Memling and the Gothic past. By the time we had eaten another hectogramme of prawns, the modern quarter of Ghent was reminding us that art was only five years old and had been invented in Vienna. At Alost the factory chimneys smoked; and before we knew where we were, we were almost on the outskirts of Brussels, with two or three hundred grammes of sea-fruit still intact on the table before us.

'Hurry up!' cried my Uncle Spencer, threatened by another access of anxiety. 'We must finish them before we get to Brussels.'

And during the last five miles we ate furiously, shell and all; there was hardly time even to spit out the heads and tails.

'Nothing like prawns,' my Uncle Spencer never failed to say, as the express drew slowly into the station at Brussels, and the last tails and whiskers with the fishy paper were thrown out of the window. 'Nothing like prawns when the brain is tired. It's the phosphorus, you know. After all your end-of-term examinations you need them.' And then he patted me affectionately on the shoulder.

How often since then have I repeated in all earnestness my Uncle Spencer's words. 'It's the phosphorus,' I assure my fagged friends, as I insist that they shall make their lunch off shellfish. The words come gushing spontaneously out of me; the opinion that prawns and oysters are good for brain-fag is very nearly one of my fundamental and, so to say, instinctive beliefs. But sometimes, as I say the words, suddenly I think of my Uncle Spencer. I see him once more sitting opposite me in a corner of the Brussels express, his eyes flashing, his thin face expressively moving as he talks, while his quick, nervous fingers pick impatiently at the pink carapaces or with a disdainful gesture drop a whiskered head into the Flemish landscape outside the open window. And remembering my Uncle Spencer, I find myself somehow believing less firmly than I did in what I have been saying. And I wonder with a certain sense of disquietude how many other relics of my Uncle Spencer's spirit I still carry, all unconsciously, about with me.

How many of our beliefs—more serious even than the belief that prawns revive the tired brain—come to us haphazardly from sources far less trustworthy than my Uncle Spencer! The most intelligent men will be found holding opinions about certain things, inculcated in them during their childhood by nurses or stable-boys. And up to the very end of our adolescence, and even after, there are for all of us certain admired beings, whose words sink irresistibly into our minds, generating there beliefs which reason does not presume to question, and which though they may be quite out of harmony with all our other opinions persist along with them without our ever becoming aware of the contradictions between the two sets of ideas. Thus an emancipated young man, whose father happens to have been a distinguished Indian civilian, is an ardent apostle of liberty and self-determination; but insists that the Indians are and for ever will be completely incapable of governing themselves. And an art critic, extremely sound on Vlaminck and Marie Laurencin, will praise as masterly and in the grand manner—and praise sincerely, for he genuinely finds them so—the works of an artist whose dim pretentious paintings of the Tuscan landscape used to delight, because they reminded her of her youth, an old lady, now dead, but whom as a very young man he greatly loved and admired.

My Uncle Spencer was for me, in my boyhood, one of these admired beings, whose opinions possess a more than earthly value for the admiring listener. For years my most passionately cherished beliefs were his. Those opinions which I formed myself, I held more diffidently, with less ardour; for they, after all, were only the fruits of my own judgement and observation, superficial rational growths; whereas the opinions I had taken from my Uncle Spencer—such as this belief in the curative properties of prawns—had nothing to do with my reason, but had been suggested directly into the sub-rational depths, where they seemed to attach themselves, like barnacles, to the very keel and bottom of my mind. Most of them, I hope, I have since contrived to scrape off; and a long, laborious, painful process it has been. But there are still, I dare say, a goodly number of them left, so deeply ingrained and grown in, that it is impossible for me to be aware of them. And I shall go down to my grave making certain judgements, holding certain opinions, regarding certain things and actions in a certain way—and the way, the opinions, the judgements will not be mine, but my Uncle Spencer's; and the obscure chambers of my mind will to the end be haunted by his bright, erratic, restless ghost.

There are some people whose habits of thought a boy or young man might, with the greatest possible advantage to himself, make his own. But my Uncle Spencer was not one of them. His active mind darted hither and thither too wildly and erratically for it to be a safe guide for an inexperienced understanding. It was all too promptly logical to draw conclusions from false premises, too easily and enthusiastically accepted as true. Living as he did in solitude—in a mental solitude; for though he was no recluse and took his share in all social pleasures, the society of Longres could not offer much in the way of high intellectual companionship—he was able to give free play to the native eccentricity of his mind. Having nobody to check or direct him, he would rush headlong down intellectual roads that led nowhere or into morasses of nonsense. When, much later, I used to amuse myself by listening on Sunday afternoons to the speakers at Marble Arch, I used often to be reminded of my Uncle Spencer. For they, like Uncle Spencer, lived in solitude, apart from the main contemporary world of ideas, unaware, or so dimly aware that it hardly counted, of the very existence of organized and systematic science, not knowing even where to look for the accumulated stores of human knowledge. I have talked in the Park to Bible students who boasted that during the day they cobbled or sold cheese, while at night they sat up learning Hebrew and studying the critics of the Holy Book. And I have been ashamed of my own idleness, ashamed of the poor use I have made of my opportunities. These humble scholars heroically pursuing enlightenment are touching and noble figures— but how often, alas, pathetically ludicrous too! For the critics my Bible students used to read and meditate upon were always at least three-quarters of a century out of date— exploded Tübingen scholars or literal inspirationalists; their authorities were always books written before the invention of modern historical research; their philology was the picturesque *lucus a non lucendo*, bloody from by-our-Lady type; their geology had irrefutable proofs of the existence of Atlantis; their physiology, if they happened to be atheists, was obsoletely mechanistic, if Christians, merely providential. All their dogged industry, all their years of heroic striving, had been completely wasted—wasted, at any rate, so far as the increase of human knowledge was concerned, but not for themselves, since the labour, the disinterested ambition, had brought them happiness.

My Uncle Spencer was spiritually a cousin of these Hyde Park orators and higher critics. He had all their passion for enlightenment and profound ideas, but not content with concentrating, like them, on a single subject such as the Bible, he allowed himself to be attracted by everything under the sun. The whole field of history, of science (or rather what my Uncle Spencer thought was science), of philosophy, religion, and art was his province. He had their industry too—an industry, in his case, rather erratic, fitful, and inconstant; for he would start passionately studying one subject, to turn after a little while to another whose aspect seemed to him at the moment more attractive. And like them he displayed—

though to a less pronounced degree, since his education had been rather better than theirs (not much better, however, for he had never attended any seat of learning but one of our oldest and most hopeless public schools)—he displayed a vast unawareness of contemporary thought and an uncritical faith in authorities which to a more systematically educated man would have seemed quite obviously out of date; coupled with a profound ignorance of even the methods by which one could acquire a more accurate or at any rate a more 'modern' and fashionable knowledge of the universe.

My Uncle Spencer had views and information on almost every subject one cared to mention; but the information was almost invariably faulty and the judgements he based upon it fantastic. What things he used to tell me as we sat facing one another in the corners of our first-class carriage, with the prawns piled up in a little coralline mountain on the folding table between us! Fragments of his eager talk come back to me.

'There are cypresses in Lombardy that were planted by Julius Cæsar. . . .'

'The human race is descended from African pygmies. Adam was black and only four feet high . . .'

'*Similia similibus curantur.* Have you gone far enough with your Latin to know what that means?' (My Uncle Spencer was an enthusiastic homœopathist, and the words of Hahnemann were to him as a mystic formula, a kind of *Om mani padme bum*,[†] the repetition of which gave him an immense spiritual satisfaction.)

And once, I remember, as we were passing through the

---

* Likes are cured by likes.

† Sanskrit Buddhist mantra: Untranslatable, but "Praise to the jewel in the lotus," literally.

fabulous new station of Ghent—that station which fifteen or sixteen years later I was to see all smashed and gutted by the departing invaders—he began, apropos of a squad of soldiers standing on the platform, to tell me how a German professor had proved, mathematically, using the theories of ballistics and probabilities, that war was now impossible, modern quick-firing rifles and machineguns being so efficient that it was, as my Uncle Spencer put it, 'sci-en-tif-ic-ally impossible' for any body of men to remain alive within a mile of a sufficient number of mitrailleuses, moving backwards and forwards through the arc of a circle and firing continuously all the time. I passed my boyhood in the serene certainty that war was now a thing of the past.

Sometimes he would talk to me earnestly across the prawns of the cosmogonies of Boehme or Swedenborg. But all this was so exceedingly obscure that I never took it in at all. In spite of my Uncle Spencer's ascendancy over my mind I was never infected by his mystical enthusiasms. These mental dissipations had been my Uncle Spencer's wild oats. Reacting from the rather stuffily orthodox respectability of his upbringing, he ran into, not vice, not atheism, but Swedenborg. He had preserved—a legacy from his prosperous nineteenth-century youth—an easy optimism, a great belief in progress and the superiority of modern over ancient times, together with a convenient ignorance of the things about which it would have been disquieting to think too much. This agreeable notion of the world I sucked in easily and copiously with my little crustaceans; my views about the universe and the destinies of man were as rosy in those days as the prawns themselves.

It was not till seven or eight o'clock in the evening that we finally got to our destination. My Uncle Spencer's carriage—victoria or brougham, according to the season and the state of the weather—would be waiting for us at the station door. In we climbed and away we rolled on our rubbered wheels in a silence that seemed almost magical, so deafeningly did common carts and the mere station cabs go rattling over the cobbles of the long and dismal Rue de la Gare. Even in the winter, when there was nothing to be seen of it but an occasional green gas-lamp, with a little universe of pavement, brick wall and shuttered window dependent upon it and created by it out of the surrounding darkness, the Rue de la Gare was signally depressing, if only because it was so straight and long. But in summer, when the dismal brick houses by which it was flanked revealed themselves in the evening light, when the dust and the waste-paper came puffing along it in gusts of warm, stale-smelling wind, then the street seemed doubly long and disagreeable. But, on the other hand, the contrast between its sordidness and the cool, spacious Grand' Place into which, after what seemed a carefully studied preparatory twisting and turning among the narrow streets of the old town, it finally debouched, was all the more striking and refreshing. Like a ship floating out from between the jaws of a cañon into a wide and sunlit lake, our carriage emerged upon the Grand' Place. And the moment was solemn, breathlessly anticipated and theatrical, as though we were gliding in along the suspended calling of the oboes and bassoons, and the violins trembling with amorous anxiety all around us, rolling silently and with not a hitch in the stage carpentry on to some vast and limelit stage where, as soon as we had taken up our position well forward and in the centre, something tremendous, one imagined, would suddenly begin to happen—a huge orchestral tutti from contrabass trombone to piccolo, from bell instrument to triangle, and then the tenor and soprano in such a duet as had never in all the history of opera been heard before.

But when it came to the point, our entrance was never quite so dramatic as all that. One found, when one actually got there, that one had mistaken one's opera; it wasn't *Parsifal* or *Rigoletto;* it was *Pelléas* or perhaps the *Village Romeo and Juliet.* For there was nothing grandiosely Wagnerian, nothing Italian and showy about the Grand' Place at Longres. The last light was rosy on its towers, the shadows of the promenaders stretched half across the place, and in the vast square the evening had room to be cool and quiet. The Gothic church had a sharp steeple and the seminary by its side a tower, and the little seventeenth-century Hôtel de Ville, with its slender belfry, standing in the middle of that open space as though not afraid to let itself be seen from every side, was a miracle of gay and sober architecture; and the houses that looked out upon it had faces simple indeed, burgess and ingenuous, but not without a certain nobility, not without a kind of unassuming provincial elegance. In, then, we glided, and the suspended oboeings of our entrance, instead of leading up to some grand and gaudy burst of harmony, fruitily protracted themselves in this evening beauty, exulted quietly in the rosy light, meditated among the lengthening shadows; and the violins, ceasing to tremble with anticipation, swelled and mounted, like light and leaping towers, into the serene sky.

And if the clock happened to strike at the moment that we entered, how charmingly the notes of the mechanical carillon harmonized with this imaginary music! At the hours, the bells in the high tower of the Hôtel de Ville played a minuet and trio, tinkly and formal like the first composition of an infant Boccherini, which lasted till fully three minutes past. At the half-hours it was a patriotic air of the same length. But at the quarters the bells no more than began a tune. Three or four bars and the music broke off, leaving the listener wondering what was to have followed, and attributing to this fragmentary stump of an air some rich out-flowering in the pregnant and musical silence, some subtle development which should have made the whole otherwise enchanting than the completed pieces that followed and preceded, and whose charm, indeed, consisted precisely in their old-fashioned mediocrity, in the ancient, cracked, and quavering sweetness of the bells that played them, and the defects in the mechanism, which imparted to the rhythm that peculiar and unforeseeable irregularity which the child at the piano, tongue between teeth, eyes anxiously glancing from printed notes to fingers and back again, laboriously introduces into the flawless evenness of 'The Merry Peasant'.

This regular and repeated carillonage was and indeed still is—for the invaders spared the bells—an essential part of Longres, a feature like the silhouette of its three towers seen from far away between the poplars across the wide, flat land, characteristic and recognizable.

It is with a little laugh of amused delight that the stranger to Longres first hears the jigging airs and the clashes of thin, sweet harmony floating down upon him from the sky, note succeeding unmuted note, so that the vibrations mingle in the air, surrounding the clear outlines of the melody with a faint quivering halo of discord. After an hour or two the minuet and trio, the patriotic air, become all too familiar, while with every repetition the broken fragments at the quarters grow more and more enigmatic, pregnant, dubious, and irritating. The pink light fades from the three towers, the Gothic intricacies of the church sink into a flat black silhouette against the night sky; but still from high up in the topless darkness floats down, floats up and out over the house-tops, across the flat fields, the minuet and trio. The patriotic air continues still, even after sunset, to commemorate the great events of 1830; and still the fragments between, like pencillings in the note-book of a genius, suggest to the mind in the scribble of twenty notes a splendid theme and the possibility of fifteen hundred variations. At midnight the bells are still playing; at half-past one the stranger starts yet again out of his sleep; re-evoked at a quarter to four his speculations about the possible conclusions of the unfinished symphony keep him awake long enough to hear the minuet and trio at the hour and to wonder how anyone in Longres manages to sleep at all. But in a day or two he answers the question himself by sleeping unbrokenly through the hints from Beethoven's note-book, and the more deliberate evocations of Boccherini's childhood and the revolution of 1830. The disease creates its own antidote, and the habit of hearing the carillon induces gradually a state of special mental deafness in which the inhabitants of Longres permanently live.

Even as a small boy, to whom insomnia was a thing unknown, I found the bells, for the first night or two after my arrival in Longres, decidedly trying. My Uncle Spencer's house looked on to the Grand' Place itself, and my window on the third floor was within fifty yards of the belfry of the Hôtel de Ville and the source of the aerial music. Three-year-old Boccherini might have been in the room with me whenever the wind came from the south, banging his minuet in my ears. But after the second night he might bang and jangle as much as he liked; there was no bell in Longres could wake me.

What did wake me, however—every Saturday morning at about half-past four or five—was the pigs coming into market. One had to have spent a month of Saturdays in Longres before one could acquire the special mental deafness that could ignore the rumbling of cart-wheels over the cobbles and the squealing and grunting of two or three thousand pigs. And when one looked out what a sight it was! All the Grand' Place was divided up by rails into a multitude of pens and pounds, and every pound was seething with pink naked pigs that looked from above like so much Bergsonian *élan vital* in a state of incessant agitation. Men came and went between the enclosures, talking, bargaining, critically poking potential bacon or ham with the point of a stick. And when the bargain was struck, the owner would step into the pen, hunt down the victim, and, catching it up by one leather ear and its thin bootlace of a tail, carry it off amid grunts that ended in the piercing, long-drawn harmonics of a squeal to a netted cart or perhaps to some other pen a little farther down the line. Brought up in England to regard the infliction of discomfort upon an animal as being, if anything, rather more reprehensible than cruelty to my fellow-humans, I remember being horrified by this spectacle. So, too, apparently was the German army of occupation. For between 1914 and 1918 no pig in the Longres market might be lifted by tail or ear, the penalty for disobedience being a fine of twenty marks for the first offence, a hundred for the second, and after that a term of forced labour on the lines of communication. Of all the oppressive measures of the invader there was hardly one which more profoundly irritated the Limbourgian peasantry. Nero was unpopular with the people of Rome, not because of his crimes and vices, not because he was a tyrant and a murderer, but for having built in the middle of the city a palace so large that it blocked the entrance to several of the main roads. If the Romans hated him, it was because his golden house compelled them to make a circuit of a quarter of a mile every time they wanted to go shopping. The little customary liberties, the right to do in small things what we have always done, are more highly valued than the greater, more abstract, and less immediate freedoms. And, similarly, most people will rather run the risk of catching typhus than take a few irksome sanitary precautions to which they are not accustomed. In this particular case, moreover, there was the further question: How *is* one to carry a pig except by its tail and ears? One must either throw the creature on its back and lift it up by its four cloven feet—a process hardly feasible, since a pig's centre of gravity is so near the ground that it is all but impossible to topple him over. Or else—and this is what the people of Longres found themselves disgustedly compelled to do—one must throw one's arms round the animal and carry it clasped to one's bosom as though it were a baby, at the risk of being bitten in the ear and with the certainty of stinking like a hog for the rest of the day.

The first Saturday after the departure of the German troops was a bad morning for the pigs. To carry a pig by the tail was an outward and visible symbol of recovered liberty; and the squeals of the porkers mingled with the cheers of the population and the trills and clashing harmonies of the bells awakened by the carillonneur from their four years' silence.

By ten o'clock the market was over. The railings of the pens had been cleared away, and but for the traces on the cobbles—and those too the municipal scavengers were beginning to sweep up—I could have believed that the scene upon which I had looked from my window in the bright early light had been a scene in some agitated morning dream.

But more dream-like and fantastical was the aspect of the Grand' Place when, every year during the latter part of August, Longres indulged in its traditional kermesse. For then the whole huge square was covered with booths, with merry-go-rounds turning and twinkling in the sun, with swings and switchbacks, with temporary pinnacles rivalling in height with the permanent and secular towers of the town, and from whose summits one slid, whooping uncontrollably with horrified delight, down a polished spiral track to the ground below. There was bunting everywhere, there were sleek balloons and flags, there were gaudily painted signs. Against the grey walls of the church, against the whitewashed housefronts, against the dark brickwork of the seminary and the soft yellow stucco of the gabled Hôtel de Ville, a sea of many colours beat tumultuously. And an immense and featureless noise that was a mingling of the music of four or five steam organs, of the voices of thousands of people, of the blowing of trumpets and whistles, the clashing of cymbals, the beating of drums, of shouting, of the howling of children, of enormous rustic laughter, filled the space between the houses from brim to brim—a noise so continuous and so amorphous that hearkening from my high window it was almost, after a time, as though there were no noise at all, but a new kind of silence, in which the tinkling of the infant Boccherini's minuet, the patriotic air, and the fragmentary symphonies had become for some obscure reason utterly inaudible.

And after sunset the white flares of acetylene and the red flares of coal-gas scooped out of the heart of the night a little private day, in which the fun went on more noisily than ever. And the gas-light striking up on to the towers mingled half-way up their shafts with the moonlight from above, so that to me at my window the belfries seemed to belong half to the earth, half to the pale silence overhead. But gradually, as the night wore on, earth abandoned its claims; the noise diminished; one after another the flares were put out, till at last the moon was left in absolute possession, with only a few dim greenish gas-lamps here and there, making no attempt to dispute her authority. The towers were hers down to the roots, the booths and the hooded roundabouts, the Russian mountains, the swings—all wore the moon's livery of silver and black; and audible once more the bells seemed in her honour to sound a sweeter, clearer, more melancholy note.

But it was not only from my window that I viewed the kermesse. From the moment that the roundabouts began to turn, which was as soon as the eleven o'clock Mass on the last Sunday but one in August was over, to the moment when they finally came to rest, which was at about ten or eleven on the night of the following Sunday, I moved almost unceasingly among the delights of the fair. And what a fair it was! I have never seen its like in England. Such splendour, such mechanical perfection in the swings, switchbacks, merry-go-rounds, towers, and the like! Such astonishing richness and variety in the sideshows! And withal such marvellous cheapness.

When one was tired of sliding and swinging, of being whirled and jogged, one could go and see for a penny the man who pulled out handfuls of his skin, to pin it up with safety-pins into ornamental folds and pleats. Or one could see the woman with no arms who opened a bottle of champagne with her toes and drank your health, lifting her glass to her lips with the same members. And then in another booth, over whose entry there waved—a concrete symbol of good faith—a pair of enormous female pantaloons, sat the Fat Woman—so fat that she could (and would, you were told, for four sous extra), in the words of the Flemish notice at the door, which I prefer to leave in their original dialectical obscurity, 'heur gezicht bet heur tiekes wassen'.

Next to the Fat Woman's hutch was a much larger tent in which the celebrated Monsieur Figaro, with his wife and seven children, gave seven or eight times daily a dramatic version of the Passion of Our Saviour, at which even the priesthood was authorized to assist. The Figaro family was celebrated from one end of the country to another, and had been for I do not know how many years—forty or fifty at least. For there were several generations of Figaros; and if seven charming and entirely genuine children did indeed still tread the boards, it was not that the seven original sons and daughters of old Monsieur Figaro had remained by some miracle perpetually young; but that marrying and becoming middle-aged they had produced little Figaros of their own, who in their turn gave rise to more, so that the aged and original Monsieur Figaro could count among the seven members of his supposititious family more than one of his great-grandchildren. So celebrated was Monsieur Figaro that there was even a song about him, of which unfortunately I can remember only two lines:

'*Et le voilà, et le voilà Fi-ga-ro,*
Le plus comique de la Belgique, Fi-ga-ro!"

But on what grounds and in what remote epoch of history he had been called 'Le plus comique de la Belgique', I was never able to discover. For the only part I ever saw the venerable old gentleman play was that of Caiaphas in the *Passion of Our Saviour*, which was one of the most moving, or at any rate one of the most harrowingly realistic, performances I ever remember to have seen; so much so, that the voices of the actors were often drowned by sobs and sometimes by the piercing screams of a child who thought that they were really and genuinely driving nails into the graceful young Figaro of the third generation, who played the part of the Saviour.

Not a day of my first kermesses passed without my going at least once, and sometimes two or three times, to see the Figaros at their performance; partly, no doubt, because, between the ages of nine and thirteen, I was an extremely devout broad churchman, and partly because the role of the Magdalene was played by a little girl of twelve or thereabouts, with whom I fell in love, wildly, extravagantly, as one only can love when one is a child. I would have given fortunes and years of my life to have had the courage to go round to the back after the performance and talk to her. But I did not dare; and to give an intellectual

---

* And there he is, and there he is, Figaro,

The most comical of Belgium, Figaro!

justification for my cowardice, I assured myself that it would have been unseemly on my part to intrude upon a privacy which I invested with all the sacredness of the Magdalene's public life, an act of sacrilege like going into church with one's hat on. Moreover, I comforted myself, I should have profited little by meeting my inamorata face to face, since in all likelihood she spoke nothing but Flemish, and besides my own language I only spoke at that time a little French, with enough Latin to know what my Uncle Spencer meant when he said, '*Similia similibus curantur.*'* My passion for the Magdalene lasted through three kermesses, but waned, or rather suddenly came to an end, when, rushing to the first of the Figaros' performances at the fourth, I saw that the little Magdalene, who was now getting on for sixteen, had become, like so many young girls in their middle teens, plump and moony almost to the point of grossness. And my love after falling to zero in the theatre was turned to positive disgust when I saw her, a couple of mornings later before the performance began, walking about the Grand' Place in a dark blue blouse with a sailor collar, a little blue skirt down to her knees, and a pair of bright yellow boots lacing high up on her full-blown calves, which they compressed so tightly that the exuberant flesh overflowed on to the leather. The next year one of old Monsieur Figaro's great-grandchildren, who could hardly have been more than seven or eight, took her place on the stage. My Magdalene had left it—to get married, no doubt. All the Figaros married early: it was important that there should be no failure in the supply of juvenile apostles and holy women. But by that time I had ceased to take the slightest interest either in her, her family, or their

---

* Likes are cured by likes.

sacred performance; for it was about the time of my fifth kermesse, if I remember rightly, that my period of atheism began—an atheism, however, still combined with all my Uncle Spencer's cheerful optimism about the universe.

My Uncle Spencer, though it would have annoyed him to hear anyone say so, enjoyed the kermesse almost as much as I did. In all the year, August was his best month; it contained within its thirty-one days less cause for anxiety, impatience, or irritation than any other month; so that my Uncle Spencer, left in peace by the malignant world, was free to be as high-spirited, as gay and kind-hearted as he possibly could be. And it was astonishing what a stock of these virtues he possessed. If he could have lived on one of those happy islands where nature provides bananas and coco-nuts enough for all and to spare, where the sun shines every day and a little tattooing is all the raiment one needs, where love is easy, commerce unknown, and neither sin nor progress ever heard of—if he could have lived on one of these carefree islands, how entirely happy and how uniformly a saint my Uncle Spencer would have been! But cares and worldly preoccupations too often overlaid his gaiety, stopped up the vents of his kindness; and his quick, nervous, and impulsive temperament—in the Augusts of his life a bubbling source of high spirits—boiled up in a wild impatience, in bilious fountains of irritation, whenever he found himself confronted by the passive malignity of matter, the stupidity or duplicity of man.

He was at his worst during the Christmas holidays; for the season of universal good-will happened unfortunately to coincide with the season of sugarmaking. With the first frosts the beetroots were taken out of the ground, and every day for three or four months three hundred thousand kilograms of roots went floating down the labyrinth of little canals that led to the washing-machines and the formidable slicers of my Uncle Spencer's factory. From every vent of the huge building issued a sickening smell of boiled beetroot, mingled with the more penetrating stink of the waste products of the manufacture—the vegetable fibre drained of its juice, which was converted on the upper floors of the building into cattle food and in the back-yard into manure. The activity during those few months of the beetroot season was feverish, was delirious. A wild orgy of work, day and night, three shifts in the twenty-four hours. And then the factory was shut up, and for the rest of the year it stood there, alone, in the open fields beyond the fringes of the town, desolate as a ruined abbey, lifeless and dumb.

During the beetroot season my Uncle Spencer was almost out of his mind. Rimmed with livid circles of fatigue, his eyes glittered like the eyes of a madman; his thin face was no more than pale skin stretched over the starting bones. The slightest contrariety set him cursing and stamping with impatience; it was a torture for him to sit still. One Christmas holidays, I remember, something went wrong with the machinery at the factory, and for nearly five hours the slicers, the churning washers were still. My Uncle Spencer was almost a lost man when he got back to the Grand' Place for dinner that evening. It was as though a demon had possessed him, and had only been cast out as the result of a horrible labour. If the breakdown had lasted another hour, I really believe he would have gone mad.

No, Christmas at Uncle Spencer's was never very cheerful. But by the Easter holidays he was beginning to recover. The frenzied making of sugar had given place to the calmer selling of it. My Uncle Spencer's good nature began to have a chance of reasserting itself. By August, at the end of a long, calm summer, he was perfect; and the kermesse found him at his most exquisitely mellow. But with September a certain premonitory anxiety began to show itself; the machinery had to be overhauled, the state of the labour market examined, and when, about the twentieth of the month, I left again for school, it was a frowning, melancholy, and taciturn Uncle Spencer who travelled with me from Longres to Brussels, from Brussels to Ostend, and who, preoccupied with other thoughts, waved absentmindedly from the quay, while the steamer slowly slid out through the false calm of the harbour mouth towards a menacing and equinoctial Channel.

But at the kermesse, as I have said, my Uncle Spencer was at his richest and ripest. Enjoying it all as much as I did myself, he would spend long evenings with me, loitering among the attractions of the Grand' Place. He was sad, I think, that the dignity of his position as one of the leading citizens of Longres did not permit him to mount with me on the roundabouts, the swings, and the mountain railways. But a visit to the side-shows was not inconsistent with his gravity; we visited them all. While professing to find the exhibition of freaks and monsters a piece of deplorable bad taste, my Uncle Spencer never failed to take me to look at all of them. It was a cardinal point in his theory of education that the young should be brought as early as possible into contact with what he called the Realities of Life. And as nothing, it was obvious, could be more of a Reality than the armless woman or the man who pinned up his skin with safety-pins, it was important that I should make an early acquaintance with them, in spite of the undoubtedly defective taste of the exhibition. It was in obedience to the same educational principle that my Uncle Spencer took me, one Easter holidays, to see the lunatic asylum. But the impression made upon me by the huge prison-like building and its queer occupants—one of whom, I remember, gambolled playfully around me wherever I went, patting my cheeks or affectionately pinching my legs—was so strong and disagreeable, that for several nights I could not sleep; or if I did, I was oppressed by hideous nightmares that woke me, screaming and sweating in the dark. My Uncle Spencer had to renounce his intention of taking me to see the anatomy room in the hospital.

Scattered among the monsters, the rifle-ranges, and the games of skill were little booths where one could buy drink and victuals. There was one vendor, for instance, who always did a roaring trade by selling, for two sous, as many raw mussels as any one could eat without coughing. Torn between his belief in the medicinal qualities of shellfish and his fear of typhoid fever, my Uncle Spencer hesitated whether he ought to allow me to spend my penny. In the end he gave his leave. ('It's the phosphorus, you know.') I put down my copper, took my mussel, bit, swallowed, and violently coughed. The fish were briny as though they had come out of the Dead Sea. The old vendor did an excellent business. Still, I have seen him sometimes looking anxious; for not all his customers were as susceptible as I. There were hardy young peasants who could put down half a pound of this Dead Sea fruit without turning a hair. In the end, however, the brine did its work on even the toughest gullet.

More satisfactory as food were the apple fritters, which were manufactured by thousands in a large temporary wooden structure that stood under the shade of the Hôtel de Ville. The Quality, like Uncle Spencer and myself, ate their fritters in the partial privacy of a number of little cubicles arranged like loose-boxes along one side of the building. My Uncle Spencer walked resolutely to our appointed box without looking to the left hand or to the right; and I was bidden to follow his example and not to show the least curiosity respecting the occupants of the other loose-boxes, whose entrances we might pass on the way to our own. There was a danger, my Uncle Spencer explained to me, that some of the families eating apple fritters in the loose-boxes might be Blacks—Blacks, I mean, politically, not ethnically—while we were Liberals or even, positively, Freemasons. Therefore— but as a mere stranger to Longres I was never, I confess, quite able to understand the force of this conclusion—therefore, though we might talk to male Blacks in a café, have business relations and even be on terms of friendship with them, it was impossible for us to be known by the female Blacks, even under a booth and over the ferial apple fritters; so that we must not look into the loose-boxes for fear that we might see there a dear old friend who would be in the embarrassing situation of not being able to introduce us to his wife and daughters. I accepted, without understanding, this law; and it seemed to be a perfectly good law until the day came when I found that it forbade me to make the acquaintance of even a single one of the eleven ravishing daughters of Monsieur Moulle. It seemed to me then a stupid law.

In front of the booths where they sold sweets my Uncle Spencer never cared to linger. It was not that he was stingy; on the contrary, he was extremely generous. Nor that he thought it bad for me to eat sweets; he had a professional belief in the virtues of sugar. The fact was that the display in the booths embarrassed him. For already at the kermesse* one began to see a sprinkling of those little objects in chocolate which, between the Feast of St. Nicholas and the New Year, fill the windows of every confectioner's shop in Belgium. My Uncle Spencer had passed a third of a lifetime at Longres, but even after all these years he was still quite unable to excuse or understand the innocent coprophily of its inhabitants. The spectacle, in a sweet-shop window, of a little *pot de chambre*† made of chocolate brought the blush of embarrassment to his cheeks. And when at the kermesse I asked him to buy me some barley-sugar or a few *bêtises de Cambrai*,‡ he pretended not to have heard what I asked, but walked hastily on; for his quick eyes had seen, on one of the higher shelves of the confectioner's booth, a long line of little brown pots, on whose equivocal aspect it would have been an agony to him if, standing there and waiting for the barley-sugar to be weighed out, I had naïvely commented. Not that I ever should have commented upon them; for I was as thoroughly English as my Uncle Spencer himself— more thoroughly, indeed, as being a generation further away from the Flemish mother, the admixture of whose blood, however, had availed nothing against my uncle's English upbringing. Me, too, the little brown pots astonished and appalled by their lack of reticence. If my companion had been another schoolboy of my own age, I should have pointed at the nameless things and sniggered. But since I was with my Uncle Spencer, I preserved with regard to them an eloquent

---

* Village fair.

† Chamber pot.

‡ French boiled sweets ("stupid mistakes from the town of Cambrai").

and pregnant silence; I pretended not to have seen them but so guiltily that my ignoring of them was in itself a comment that filled my poor Uncle Spencer with embarrassment. If we could have talked about them, if only we could have openly deplored them and denounced their makers, it would have been better. But obviously, somehow, we could not.

In the course of years, however, I learned, being young and still malleable, to be less astonished and appalled by the little chocolate pots and the other manifestations of the immemorial Flemish coprophily. In the end I took them almost for granted, like the natives themselves, till finally, when St. Nicholas had filled the shops with these scatological symbols, I could crunch a pot or two between meals as joyously and with as little self-consciousness as any Belgian child. But I had to eat my chocolate, when it was moulded in this particular form, out of my Uncle Spencer's sight. He, poor man, would have been horrified if he had seen me on these occasions.

On these occasions, then, I generally took refuge in the housekeeper's room—and in any case, at this Christmas season, when the sugar was being made, it was better to sit in the cheerful company of Mademoiselle Leeauw than with my gloomy, irritable, demon-ridden Uncle Spencer. Mademoiselle Leeauw was almost from the first one of my firmest and most trusted friends. She was a woman of, I suppose, about thirty-five when I first knew her, rather worn already by a life of active labour, but still preserving a measure of that blonde, decided, and regular beauty which had been hers in girlhood. She was the daughter of a small farmer near Longres, and had received the usual village education, supplemented, however, in recent years by what she had picked up from my Uncle Spencer, who occupied himself every now and then, in his erratic and enthusiastic way, with the improvement of her mind, lent her books from his library, and delivered lectures to her on the subjects that were at the moment nearest to his heart. Mademoiselle Leeauw, unlike most women of her antecedents, felt an insatiable curiosity with regard to all that mysterious and fantastic knowledge which the rich and leisured keep shut up in their libraries; and not only in their books, as she had seen herself (for as a girl had she not served as nursery-maid in the house of that celebrated collector, the Comte de Zuitigny?) not only in their books, but in their pictures too—some of which, Mademoiselle Leeauw assured me, a child could have painted, so badly drawn they were, so unlike life (and yet the count had given heaven only knew how much for them), in their Chinese pots, in the patterns of the very carpets on the floor. Whatever my Uncle Spencer gave her she read with eagerness, she listened attentively to what he said; and there emerged, speck-like in the boundless blank ocean of her ignorance, a few little islands of strange knowledge. One, for example, was called homœopathy; another the Construction-of-Domes (a subject on which my Uncle Spencer was prepared to talk with a copious and perverse erudition for hours at a time; his thesis being that any mason who knew how to turn the vaulted roof of an oven could have built the cupolas of St. Peter's, St. Paul's, and Santa Maria del Fiore, and that therefore the praises lavished on Michelangelo, Wren, and Brunelleschi were entirely undeserved). A third was called Anti-Vivisection. A fourth Swedenborg. . . .

The result of my Uncle Spencer's teaching was to convince Mademoiselle Leeauw that the knowledge of the rich was something even more fantastic than she had supposed—

something unreal and utterly remote from life as it is actually lived, artificial and arbitrary, like the social activities of these same rich, who pass their time in one another's houses, eating at one another's expense, and being bored.

This conviction of the complete futility of knowledge did not make her any the less eager to learn what my Uncle Spencer, whom she regarded as a mine and walking compendium of all human learning, could offer her. And she enchanted him by her respectful attentiveness, by the quickness of her understanding—for she was a woman of very great natural intelligence—and her eagerness for every fresh enlightenment. She did not confide to him her real opinion of knowledge, which was that it was a kind of curious irrelevant joke on the margin of life, worth learning for precisely the same reasons as it is worth learning to handle the fork at table—because it is one of the secrets of the rich. Admiring my Uncle Spencer sincerely, she yet took nothing that he taught her seriously, and though, when with him, she believed in million-of-a-grain doses and high spiritual potencies, she continued, when she felt out of sorts or I had overeaten, to resort to the old tablespoonful of castor oil; though with him she was a convinced Swedenborgian, in church she was entirely orthodox; though in his presence she thought vivisection monstrous, she would tell me with gusto of those happy childish days on the farm, when her father cut the pig's throat, her mother held the beast by the hind-legs, her sister danced on the body to make the blood flow, and she held the pail under the spouting artery.

If to my Uncle Spencer his housekeeper appeared as he liked to see her, and not as at ordinary times she really was, it was not that she practised with him a conscious insincer-

ity. Hers was one of those quick, sensitive natures that adapt
themselves almost automatically to the social atmosphere in
which at the moment they happen to be. Thus with well-bred
people she had beautiful manners; but the peasants from
whose stock she had sprung found her as full of a hearty
Flemish gusto, as grossly and innocently coarse as them-
selves. The core of her being remained solidly peasant; but
the upper and conscious part of her mind was, so to speak,
only loosely fastened to the foundation, so that it could turn
freely this way and that, without strain or difficulty, accord-
ing to changing circumstances. My Uncle Spencer valued
her, not only as a competent, intelligent woman, which she
always was in every company, but also because she was, con-
sidering her class and origins, so remarkably well-mannered
and refined, which, except with him and his likes, she was
not.

With me, however, Mademoiselle Leeauw was thor-
oughly natural and Flemish. With her quick and, I might
say, instinctive understanding of character, she saw that my
abashed reaction to coprology, being of so much more recent
date than that of my Uncle Spencer, was much less strong,
less deeply rooted. At the same time, she perceived that I
had no great natural taste for grossness, no leaning to what
I may call Flemishism; so that in my presence she could
be her natural Flemish self and thus correct an absurd ac-
quired delicacy without running the risk of encouraging to
any undue or distressing degree a congenital bias in the op-
posite direction. And I noticed that whenever Matthieu (or
Tcheunke, as they called him), her cousin's boy, came into
town and paid a call on her, Mademoiselle Leeauw became
almost as careful and refined as she was with my Uncle

Spencer. Not that Tcheunke shared my uncle's susceptibilities. On the contrary, he took such an immoderate delight in everything that was excrementitious that she judged it best not in any way to indulge him in his taste, just as she judged it best not to indulge my national prejudice in favour of an excessive reticence about these and similar matters. She was right, I believe, in both cases.

Mademoiselle Leeauw had an elder sister, Louise—Louiseke, in the language of Longres, where they put the symbol of the diminutive after almost every name. Louiseke, like her sister, had never married; and considering the ugliness of the woman—for she resembled Mademoiselle Leeauw as a very mischievous caricature resembles its original, that is to say, very closely and at the same time hardly at all, the unlikeness being emphasized in this case by the fact that nature had, for the shaping of certain features, drawn on other ancestral sources, and worse ones, than those from which her sister's face had been made up—considering her ugliness, I repeat, it was not surprising. Though considering her dowry, perhaps it was. Louiseke was by no means rich; but she had the five hundred francs a year, or thereabouts, which her sister also had, after their father died and the farm was sold, together with another two hundred inherited from an old aunt of her mother's. This was a sufficient income to allow her to live without working in a leisure principally occupied by the performance of religious exercises.

On the outskirts of Longres there stands a small béguinage, long since abandoned by its Béguines, who are now all over Belgium a diminishing and nearly extinct community, and inhabited by a colony of ordinary poor folk. The little old gabled houses are built round the sides of a large grassy square, in the centre of which stands an abandoned church. Louiseke inhabited one of these houses, partly because the rent was very low, but also because she liked the religious associations of the place. There, in her peaked high house, looking out across the monastic quadrangle to the church, she could almost believe herself a genuine Béguine. Every morning she went out to hear early Mass, and on Sundays and days of festival she was assiduous in church almost to the point of supererogation.

At my Uncle Spencer's we saw a great deal of her; on her way to church, on her way home again, she never failed to drop in for a word with her sister Antonieke. Sometimes, I remember, she brought with her—hurrying on these occasions across the Grand' Place with the quick, anxious tread, the frightened, suspicious glances to left and right, of a traveller crossing a brigand-haunted moor—a large bag of green baize, full of strange treasures: the silver crown and sceptre of Our Lady, the gilded diadem of the Child, St. Joseph's halo, the jewelled silver book of I forget which Doctor of the Church, St. Dominick's lilies, and a mass of silver hearts with gilded flames coming out of them. Louiseke, whose zeal was noted and approved of by Monsieur le Curé, had the rare privilege of being allowed to polish the jewellery belonging to the images in the church. A few days before each of the important feasts the painted plaster saints were stripped of their finery and the spoil handed over to Louiseke, who, not daring to walk with her precious burden under her arm as far as her own house in the béguinage, slipped across the Grand' Place to my Uncle Spencer's. There, on the table in Antonieke's room, the green baize bag was opened, and the treasures, horribly dirty and tarnished after their weeks or months of neglect, were spread out in the light. A kind of paste was then made out of French chalk mixed with gin, which the two sisters applied to the crowns and hearts with nail-brushes, or if the work was fine and intricate, with an old tooth-brush. The silver was then wiped dry with a cloth and polished with a piece of leather.

A feeling of manly pride forbade me to partake in what I felt to be a womanish labour; but I liked to stand by with my hands in my pockets, watching the sisters at work among these regal and sacred symbols, and trying to understand, so far as my limited knowledge of Flemish and my almost equally limited knowledge of life would admit, the gossip which Louiseke poured out incessantly in a tone of monotonous and unvarying censoriousness.

I myself always found Louiseke a little forbidding. She lacked the charm and the quality, which I can only call mellowness, of her sister; to me she seemed harsh, sour-tempered, and rather malevolent. But it is very possible that I judged her unfairly; for, I confess, I could never quite get over her ugliness. It was a sharp, hooky, witch-like type of ugliness, which at that time I found particularly repulsive.

How difficult it is, even with the best will in the world, even for a grown and reasonable man, to judge his fellow-beings without reference to their external appearance! Beauty is a letter of recommendation which it is almost impossible to ignore; and we attribute too often the ugliness of the face to the character. Or, to be more precise, we make no attempt to get beyond the opaque mask of the face to the realities behind it, but run away from the ugly at sight without even trying to find out what they are really like. That feeling of instinctive dislike which ugliness inspires in a grown man, but which he has reason and strength enough of will to suppress, or at least conceal, is uncontrollable in a child. At three or four years old a child will run screaming from the room at the aspect of a certain visitor whose face strikes him as disagreeable. Why? Because the ugly visitor is 'naughty', is a 'bad man'. And up to a much later age, though we have succeeded in preventing ourselves from screaming when the ugly visitor makes his appearance, we do our best—at first, at any rate, or until his actions have strikingly proved that his face belies his character—to keep out of his way. So that, if I always disliked Louiseke, it may be that she was not to blame, and that my own peculiar horror of ugliness made me attribute to her unpleasant characteristics which she did not in reality possess. She seemed to me, then, harsh and sour-tempered; perhaps she wasn't; but, in any case, I thought so. And that accounts for the fact that I never got to know her, never tried to know her, as I knew her sister. Even after the extraordinary event which, a year or two after my first visit to Longres, was to alter completely the whole aspect of her life, I still made no effort to understand Louiseke's character. How much I regret my remissness now! But, after all, one cannot blame a small boy for failing to have the same standards as a man. To-day, in retrospect, I find Louiseke's character and actions in the highest degree curious and worthy of study. But twenty years ago, when I knew her, her ugliness at first appalled me, and always, even after I had got over my disgust, surrounded her, for me, with a kind of unbreathable atmosphere, through which I could never summon the active interest to penetrate. Moreover, the event which now strikes me as so extraordinary, seemed to me then almost normal and of no particular interest. And since she died before my opinion about it had had time to change, I can only give a child's impression of her character and a bald recital of the facts so far as I knew them.

It was, then, at my second or third kermesse that a side-show, novel not only for me (to whom indeed everything—fat women, fire-swallowers, elastic men, and down to the merest dwarfs and giants—was a novelty), but even to the oldest inhabitants of Longres, who might have been expected to have seen, in their time, almost everything that the world had ever parturated of marvels, rarities, monsters, and abortions, made its appearance on the Grand' Place. This was a troupe of devil-dancers, self-styled Tibetan for the sake of the name's high-sounding and mysterious ring; but actually made up of two expatriated Hindus and a couple of swarthy meridional Frenchmen, who might pass at a pinch as the Aryan compatriots of these dark Dravidians. Not that it mattered much what the nationality or colour of the dancers might be; for on the stage they wore enormous masks—huge false heads, grinning, horned, and diabolic, which, it was claimed in the announcement, were those in which the ritual dances were performed before the Dalai Lama in the principal convent of Lhasa. Comparing my memories of them with such knowledge of Oriental art as I now possess, I imagine that they came in reality from the shop of some theatrical-property-maker in Marseilles, from which place the devil-dancers had originally started. But they were none the less startling and bloodcurdling for that; just as the dances themselves were none the less salaciously symbolical, none the less typically and conventionally 'Oriental' for having been in great measure invented by the Frenchmen, who provided all the plot and dramatic substance of the ballets, while the astonished and admiring Indians contributed only a few recollections of Siva worship and the cult of the beneficent *linga.*[*] This cooperation between East and West was what ensured the performance its success; the western substance satisfied by its perfect familiarity, while the eastern detail gave to the old situations a specious air of novelty and almost a new significance.

Charmed by the prospect of seeing what he supposed would be a few characteristic specimens of the religious rites of the mysterious East, and ambitious to improve my education by initiating me into the secrets of this Reality, my Uncle Spencer took me to see the dancers. But the dramatic pantomime of the Frenchmen represented a brand of Reality that my uncle did not at all approve of. He got up abruptly in the middle of the first dance, saying that he thought the circus would be more amusing; which, for me, it certainly was. For I was not of an age to appreciate either the plastic beauty or the peculiar moral significance of the devil-dancers' performance.

'Hinduism,' said my Uncle Spencer, as we threaded our way between the booths and the whirling machines, 'has sadly degenerated from its original Brahministic purity.' And he began to expound to me, raising his voice to make itself heard through the noise of the steam organs, the principles of Brahminism. My Uncle Spencer had a great weakness for Oriental religions.

'Well,' asked Mademoiselle Leeauw, when we got back for dinner, 'and how did you enjoy the dancers?'

I told her that my Uncle Spencer had thought that I should find the circus more amusing. Antonieke nodded with a significant air of understanding. 'Poor man,' she said,

---

* Hindu symbol representing energy and strength.

and she went on to wonder how Louiseke, who was going to see the dancers that evening, would enjoy the show.

I never knew precisely what happened; for a mystery and, as it were, a zone of silence surrounded the event, and my curiosity about everything to do with Louiseke was too feeble to carry me through it. All I know is that, two or three days later, near the end of the kermesse, young Albert Snyders, the lawyer's son, came up to me in the street and asked, with the gleeful expression of one who says something which he is sure his interlocutor will find disagreeable: 'Well, and what do you think of your Louiseke and her carryings on with the black man?'

I answered truthfully that I had heard nothing about any such thing, and that in any case Louiseke wasn't our Louiseke, and that I didn't care in the least what she did or what might happen to her.

'Not heard about it?' said young Snyders incredulously. 'But the black man goes to her house every evening, and she gives him gin, and they sing together, and people see their shadows dancing on the curtains. Everybody's talking about it.'

I am afraid that I disappointed young Snyders. He had hoped to get a rise out of me, and he miserably failed. His errors were two: first, to have supposed that I regarded Louiseke as our Louiseke, merely because her sister happened to be my Uncle Spencer's housekeeper; and, secondly, to have attributed to me a knowledge of the world sufficient to allow me to realize the scandalousness of Louiseke's conduct. Whereas I disliked Louiseke, took no interest in her actions, and could, moreover, see nothing out of the ordinary in what she was supposed to have done.

Confronted by my unshakable calm, young Snyders retired, rather crestfallen. But he revenged himself before he went by telling me that I must be very stupid and, what I found more insulting, a great baby not to understand.

Antonieke, to whom I repeated young Snyders's words, merely said that the boy ought to be whipped, specifying with a wealth of precise detail, and a gusto that were entirely Flemish how, with what instrument, and where the punishment ought to be applied. I thought no more about the incident. But I noticed after the kermesse was over and the Grand' Place had become once more the silent and empty Grand' Place of ordinary days, I noticed loitering aimlessly about the streets a stout, coffee-coloured man, whom the children of Longres, like those three rude boys in *Struwwelpeter*, pursued at a distance, contorting themselves with mirth. That year I went back to England earlier than usual; for I had been invited to spend the last three weeks of my holidays with a school friend (alas, at Hastings, so that my knowledge of the earth's surface was not materially widened by the visit). When I returned to Longres for the Christmas holidays I found that Louiseke was no longer mere Louiseke, but the bride of a coffee-coloured husband. Madame Alphonse they called her; for nobody could bother with the devil-dancer's real name: it had an Al- in it somewhere— that was all that was known. Monsieur and Madame Alphonse. But the news when I heard it did not particularly impress me.

And even if I had been curious to know more, dense silence continued to envelop the episode. Antonieke never spoke to me of it; and lacking all interest in this kind of Reality, disapproving of it even, my Uncle Spencer seemed to take it silently for granted. That the subject was copiously discussed by the gossips of Longres I do not doubt; and remembering Louiseke's own censorious anecdotage, I can imagine how. But in my hearing it was never discussed; expressly, I imagine—for I lived under the protection of Antonieke, and people were afraid of Antonieke. So it came about that the story remained for me no more remarkable than that story recorded by Edward Lear of the

> '. . . old Man of Jamaica
> Who casually married a Quaker;
> But she cried out, "Alack,
> I have married a black!"
> Which distressed that old Man of Jamaica.'

And perhaps, after all, that is the best way of regarding such incidents—unquestioningly, without inquisitiveness. For we are all much too curious about the affairs of our neighbours. Particularly about the affairs of an erotic nature. What an itch we have to know whether Mr. Smith makes love to his secretary, whether his wife consoles herself, whether a certain Cabinet Minister is really the satyr he is rumoured to be. And meanwhile the most incredible miracles are happening all round us: stones, when we lift them and let them go, fall to the ground; the sun shines; bees visit the flowers; seeds grow into plants, a cell in nine months multiplies its weight a few thousands of thousands of time, and is a child; and men think, creating the world they live in. These things leave us almost perfectly indifferent.

But concerning the ways in which different individuals satisfy the cravings of one particular instinct, we have, in spite of the frightful monotony of the situation, in spite of the one well-known, inevitable consummation, an endless and ever-fresh curiosity. Some day, perhaps, we may become a little tired of books whose theme is always this particular instinct. Some day, it may be, the successful novelist will write about man's relation to God, to nature, to his own thoughts and the obscure reality on which they work, not about man's relation with woman. Meanwhile, however . . .

By what stages the old maid passed from her devoutness and her censorious condemnation of love to her passion for the Dravidian, I can only guess. Most likely there were no stages at all, but the conversion was sudden and fulgurating, like that upon the road to Damascus—and like that, secretly and unconsciously prepared for, long before the event. It was the sheer wildness, no doubt, the triumphant bestiality and paganism of the dances that bowled her over, that irresistibly broke down the repressive barriers behind which, all too human, Louiseke's nature had so long chafed. As to Alphonse himself, there could be no question about his motives. Devil-dancing, he had found, was an exhausting, precarious, and not very profitable profession. He was growing stout, his heart was not so strong as it had been, he was beginning to feel himself middle-aged. Louiseke and her little income came as a providence. What did her face matter? He did not hesitate.

Monsieur and Madame Alphonse took a little shop in the Rue Neuve. Before he left India and turned devil-dancer, Alphonse had been a cobbler in Madras—and as such was capable of contaminating a Brahmin at a distance of twenty-four feet; now, having become an eater of beef and an outcast, he was morally infectious at no less than sixty-four feet. But in Longres, luckily, there were no Brahmins.

He was a large, fat, snub-faced, and shiny man, constantly smiling, with a smile that reminded me of a distended accordion. Many a pair of boots I took to him to be soled—for Antonieke, though she was horrified at having what she called a negro for her brother-in-law, though she had quarrelled with her sister about her insane and monstrous folly, and would hardly be reconciled to her, Antonieke insisted that all our custom should go to the new cobbler. That, as she explained, 'owed itself'. The duty of members of one family to forward one another's affairs overrode, in her estimation, the mere personal quarrels that might arise between them.

My Uncle Spencer was a frequent caller at the cobbler's shop, where he would sit for hours, while Monsieur Alphonse tapped away at his last, listening to mythological anecdotes out of the 'Ramayana' or 'Mahabharata', and discussing the Brahministic philosophy, of which, of course, he knew far more than a poor Sudra like Alphonse. My Uncle Spencer would come back from these visits in the best of humours.

'A most interesting man, your brother-in-law,' he would say to Antonieke. 'We had a long talk about Siva this afternoon. Most interesting!'

But Antonieke only shrugged her shoulders. *'Mais c'est un nègre,'** she muttered. And my Uncle Spencer might assure her as much as he liked that Dravidians were not negroes and that Alphonse very likely had good Aryan blood in his veins. It was useless. Antonieke would not be persuaded, would not even listen. It was all very well for the rich to believe things like that, but a negro, after all, was a negro; and that was all about it.

---

* "But he's a negro."

Monsieur Alphonse was a man of many accomplishments; for, besides all the rest, he was an expert palmist and told fortunes from the hand with a gravity, a magisterial certainty, that were almost enough in themselves to make what he said come true. This magian and typically Oriental accomplishment was learnt on the road between Marseilles and Longres from a charlatan in the travelling company of amusement-makers with whom he had come. But he did the trick in the grand prophetic style, so that people credited his chiromancy with all the magical authority of the mysterious East. But Monsieur Alphonse could not be persuaded to prophesy for every comer. It was noticed that he selected his subjects almost exclusively from among his female customers, as though he were only interested in the fates of women. I could hint as much as I liked that I should like to have my fortune told, I could ask him outright to look at my hand; but in vain. On these occasions he was always too busy to look, or was not feeling in the prophetic mood. But if a young woman should now come into the shop, time immediately created itself, the prophetic mood came back. And without waiting for her to ask him he would seize her hand, pore over it, pat and prod the palm with his thick brown fingers, every now and then turning up towards his subject those dark eyes, made the darker and more expressive by the brilliance of the bluish whites in which they were set, and expanding his accordion smile. And he would prophesy love—a great deal of it—love with superb dark men, and rows of children; benevolent dark strangers and blond villains; unexpected fortunes, long life—all, in fact, that the heart could desire. And all the time he squeezed and patted the hand—white between his dark Dravidian paws—from which he read these secrets; he rolled his eyes within their shiny blue enamel setting, and across all the breadth of his fat cheeks the accordion of his smile opened and shut.

My pride and my young sense of justice were horribly offended on these occasions. The inconsistency of a man who had no time to tell my fortune, but an infinite leisure for others, seemed to me abstractly reprehensible and personally insulting. I professed, even at that age, not to believe in palmistry; that is to say, I found the fortunes which Monsieur Alphonse prophesied for others absurd. But my interest in my own personality and my own fate was so enormous that it seemed to me, somehow, that everything said about me must have a certain significance. And if Monsieur Alphonse had taken my hand, looked at it, and said, 'You are generous; your head is as large as your heart; you will have a severe illness at thirty-eight, but your life after that will be healthy into extreme old age; you will make a large fortune early in your career, but you must beware of fair-haired strangers with blue eyes,' I should have made an exception and decided for the nonce that there must be something in it. But, alas, Monsieur Alphonse never did take my hand; he never told me anything. I felt most cruelly offended, and I felt astonished too. For it seemed to me a most extraordinary thing that a subject which was so obviously fascinating and so important as my character and future should not interest Monsieur Alphonse as much as it did me. That he should prefer to dabble in the dull fates and silly insignificant characters of a lot of stupid young women seemed to me incredible and outrageous.

There was another who, it seemed, shared my opinion. That was Louiseke. If ever she came into the shop from the little back sitting-room—and she was perpetually popping out through the dark doorway like a cuckoo on the stroke of noon from its clock—and found her husband telling the fortune of a female customer, her witch-like face would take on an expression more than ordinarily malevolent.

'Alphonse!' she would say significantly.

And Alphonse dropped his subject's hand, looked round towards the door, and, rolling his enamelled eyes, creasing his fat cheeks in a charming smile, flashing his ivory teeth, would say something amiable.

But Louiseke did not cease to frown. 'If you must tell somebody's fortune,' she said, when the customer had left the shop, 'why don't you tell the little gentleman's?' pointing to me. 'I'm sure he would be only too delighted.'

But instead of being grateful to Louiseke, instead of saying, 'Oh, of course I'd like it,' and holding out my hand, I always perversely shook my head. 'No, no,' I said. 'I don't want to worry Monsieur Alphonse.' But I longed for Alphonse to insist on telling me about my exquisite and marvellous self. In my pride, I did not like to owe my happiness to Louiseke, I did not want to feel that I was taking advantage of her irritation and Alphonse's desire to mollify her. And, besides pride, I was actuated by that strange nameless perversity, which so often makes us insist on doing what we do not want to do—such as making love to a woman we do not like and whose intimacy, we know, will bring us nothing but vexation—or makes us stubbornly decline to do what we have been passionately desiring, merely because the opportunity of doing what we wanted has not presented itself in exactly the way we anticipated, or because the person who offered to fulfil our desires has not been sufficiently insistent with his offers. Alphonse, on these occasions, having no curiosity about my future and taking no pleasure in kneading my small and dirty hand, always took my refusals quite literally and finally, and began to work again with a redoubled ardour. And I would leave the shop, vexed with myself for having let slip the opportunity when it was within my grasp; furious with Louiseke for having presented it in such a way that the seizing of it would be humiliating, and with Alphonse for his obtuseness in failing to observe how much I desired that he should look at my hand, and his gross discourtesy for not insisting even in the teeth of my refusal.

Years passed; my holidays and the seasons succeeded one another with regularity. Summer and the green poplars and my Uncle Spencer's amiability gave place to the cold season of sugar-making, to scatological symbols in chocolate, to early darkness and the moral gloom of my Uncle Spencer's annual neurasthenia. And half-way between the two extremes came the Easter holidays, pale green and hopefully burgeoning, tepid with temperate warmth and a moderate amiability. There were terms, too, as well as holidays. Eastbourne knew me no more; my knowledge of the globe expanded; I became a public schoolboy.

At fifteen, I remember, I entered upon a period of priggishness which made me solemn beyond my years. There are many boys who do not know how young they are till they have come of age, and a young man is often much less on his dignity than a growing schoolboy, who is afraid of being despised for his callowness. It was during this period that I wrote from Longres a letter to one of my school friends, which he fortunately preserved, so that we were able to reread it, years later, and to laugh and marvel at those grave, academic old gentlemen we were in our youth. He had written me a letter describing his sister's marriage, to which I replied in these terms:

'How rapidly, my dear Henry, the saffron robe and Hymen's torches give place to the nænia, the funeral urn, and the cypress! While your days have been passed among the jocundities of a marriage feast, mine have been darkened by the circumambient horrors of death. Such, indeed, is life.'

And I underlined the philosophic reflection.

The horrors of death made more show in my sonorous antitheses than they did in my life. For though the event made a certain impression upon me—for it was the first thing of the kind that had happened within my own personal orbit—I cannot pretend that I was very seriously moved when Louiseke died, too old to have attempted the experiment, in giving birth to a half-Flemish, half-Dravidian daughter, who died with her. My Uncle Spencer, anxious to introduce me to the Realities of Life, took me to see the corpse. Death had a little tempered Louiseke's ugliness. In the presence of that absolute repose I suddenly felt ashamed of having always disliked Louiseke so much. I wanted to be able to explain to her that, if only I had known she was going to die, I would have been nicer to her, I would have tried to like her more. And all at once I found myself crying.

Downstairs in the back parlour Monsieur Alphonse was crying too, noisily, lamentably, as was his duty. Three days later, when his duty had been sufficiently done and the conventions satisfied, he became all at once exceedingly philosophic about his loss. Louiseke's little income was now his; and, adding to it what he made by his cobbling, he could live in almost princely style. A week or two after the funeral the kermesse began. His old companions, who had danced several times backwards and forwards across the face of Europe since they were last in Longres, reappeared unexpectedly on the Grand' Place. Alphonse treated himself to the pleasure of playing the generous host, and every evening when their show was over the devils unhorned themselves, and over the glasses in the little back parlour behind Alphonse's shop they talked convivially of old times, and congratulated their companion, a little enviously, on his prodigious good fortune.

In the years immediately preceding the war I was not often in Longres. My parents had come back from India; my holidays were passed with them. And when holidays transformed themselves into university vacations and I was old enough to look after myself, I spent most of my leisure in travelling in France, Italy, or Germany, and it was only rarely and fleetingly—on the way to Milan, on my way back from Cologne, or after a fortnight among the Dutch picture-galleries—that I now revisited the house on the Grand' Place, where I had passed so many, and on the whole such happy, days. I liked my Uncle Spencer still, but he had ceased to be an admired being, and his opinions, instead of rooting themselves and proliferating within my mind, as once they did, seemed mostly, in the light of my own knowledge and experience, too fantastic even to be worth refuting. I listened to him now with all the young man's intolerance of the opinions of the old (and my Uncle Spencer, though only fifty, seemed to me utterly fossilized and antediluvian), acquiescing in all that he said with a smile in which a more suspicious and less single-hearted man would have seen the amused contempt. My Uncle Spencer was leaning during these years more and more towards the occult sciences. He talked less of the construction of domes and more of Hahnemann's mystic high potentials, more of Swedenborg, more of Brahministic philosophy, in which he had by this time thoroughly indoctrinated Monsieur Alphonse; and he was enthusiastic now about a new topic—the calculating horses of Elberfeld, which, at that time, were making a great noise in the world by their startling ability to extract cube roots in their heads. Strong in the materialistic philosophy, the careless and unreflecting scepticism which were, in those days, the orthodoxy of every young man who thought himself intelligent, I found my Uncle Spencer's mystical and religious preoccupations marvellously ludicrous. I should think them less ridiculous now, when it is the easy creed of my boyhood that has come to look rather queer. Now it is possible—it is, indeed, almost necessary—for a man of science to be also a mystic. But there were excuses then for supposing that one could only combine mysticism with the faulty knowledge and the fantastic mental eccentricity of an Uncle Spencer. One lives and learns.

With Mademoiselle Leeauw, on these later visits, I felt, I must confess, not entirely at my ease. Antonieke saw me as essentially the same little boy who had come so regularly all those years, holiday after holiday, to Longres. Her talk with me was always of the joyous events of the past—of which she had that extraordinarily accurate and detailed memory which men and women, whose minds are not exercised by intellectual preoccupations and who do not read much, always astonish their more studious fellows by possessing. Plunged as I then was in all the newly-discovered delights of history, philosophy, and art, I was too busy to take more than a very feeble interest in my childish past. Had there been skating on the canals in 1905? Had I been bitten by a horse-fly, the summer before, so poisonously that my cheek swelled up like a balloon and I had to go to bed? Possibly, possibly; now that I was reminded of these things I did, dimly, remember. But of what earthly interest were facts such as these when I had Plato, the novels of Dostoevski, the frescoes of Michelangelo to think of? How entirely irrelevant they were to, shall we say, David Hume! How insipid compared with the sayings of Zarathustra, the Coriolan overture, the poetry of Arthur Rimbaud! But for poor Antonieke they were all her life. I felt all the time that I was not being as sympathetic with her as I ought to have been. But was it my fault? Could I re-become what I had been, or make her suddenly different from what she was?

At the beginning of August 1914 I was staying at Longres on my way to the Ardennes, where I meant to settle down quietly for a month or so with two or three friends, to do a little solid reading before going south to Italy in September. Strong in the faith of the German professor who had proved, by the theories of ballistics and probabilities, that war was now out of the question, my Uncle Spencer paid no attention to the premonitory rumbles. It was just another little Agadir crisis and would lead to nothing. I too—absorbed, I remember, in the reading of William James's *Varieties of Religious Experience*—paid no attention; I did not even look at the papers. At that time, still, my Uncle Spencer's convictions about the impossibility of war were also mine; I had had no experience to make me believe them unfounded, and, besides, they fitted in very well with my hopes, my aspirations, my political creed—for at that time I was an ardent syndicalist and internationalist.

And then, suddenly, it was all on top of us.

My Uncle Spencer, however, remained perfectly optimistic. After a week of fighting, he prophesied, the German professor would be proved right and they would have to stop. My own feeling, I remember, was one of a rather childish exhilaration; my excitement was much more powerful than my shock of horror. I felt rather as I had felt on the eve of the kermesse when, looking from my window, I gazed down at the mountebanks setting up their booths and engines in the square below. Something was really going to happen. That childish sense of excitement is, I suppose, the prevailing emotion at the beginning of a war. An intoxicating Bank Holiday air seems to blow through the streets. War is always popular, at the beginning.

I did not return immediately to England, but lingered for a few days at Longres, in the vague hope that I might 'see something', or that perhaps my Uncle Spencer might really—as I still believed—be right, and that, perhaps, the whole thing would be over in a few days. My hope that I should 'see something' was fulfilled. But the something was not one of those brilliant and romantic spectacles I had imagined. It consisted of a few little troops of refugees from the villages round Liége—unshaven men, and haggard women with long tear-marks on their dusty cheeks, and little boys and girls tottering along as though in their sleep, dumb and stupid with fatigue. My Uncle Spencer took a family of them into his house. 'In a few days,' he said, 'when everything's over, they'll be able to go home again.' And when indignantly Antonieke repeated to him their stories of burnings and shootings, he wouldn't believe them.

'After all,' he said, 'this is the twentieth century. These things don't happen nowadays. These poor people are too tired and frightened to know exactly what they are saying.'

In the second week of August I went back to England. My Uncle Spencer was quite indignant when I suggested that he should come back with me. To begin with, he said, it would all be over so very soon. In the second place, this was the twentieth century—which was what the Cretans said, no doubt, when in 1500 B.C., after two thousand years of peace, prosperity, and progressive civilization, they were threatened by the wild men from the north. In the third place, he must stay at Longres to look after his interests. I did not press him any further; it would have been useless.

'Good-bye, dear boy,' he said, and there was an unaccustomed note of emotion in his voice, 'goodbye.'

The train slowly moved away. Looking out of the window, I could see him standing on the platform, waving his hat. His hair was white all over now, but his face was as young, his eyes as darkly bright, his small spare body as straight and agile as when I had known him first.

'Good-bye, good-bye.'

I was not to see him again for nearly five years.

Louvain was burnt on the 19th of August. The Germans entered Brussels on the 20th. Longres, though farther east than Louvain, was not occupied till two or three days later—for the town lay off the direct route to Brussels and the interior. One of the first acts of the German commandant was to put my Uncle Spencer and Monsieur Alphonse under arrest. It was not that they had done anything; it was merely to their existence that he objected. The fact that they were British subjects was in itself extremely incriminating.

'Aber wir sind,' my Uncle Spencer protested in his rather rudimentary German, 'im zwanzigsten jahrhunderd. Und der—or is it das?—krieg wird nicht lang* . . .' he stammered, searched hopelessly for the word, 'well, in any case,' he concluded, relapsing into his own language and happy to be able to express his astonished protest with fluency, 'it won't last a week.'

'So we hope,' the commandant replied in excellent English, smiling. 'But meanwhile I regret . . .'

My Uncle Spencer and his fellow-Briton were locked up for the time being in the lunatic asylum. A few days later they were sent under escort to Brussels. Alphonse, my Uncle Spencer told me afterwards, bore his misfortune with exemplary and Oriental patience. Mute, uncomplaining, obedient, he stayed where his captors put him, like a large brown bundle left by the traveller on the platform, while he goes to the buffet for a drink and a sandwich. And more docile than a mere bundle, mutely, obediently, he followed wherever he was led.

'I wish I could have imitated him,' said my Uncle Spencer. 'But I couldn't. My blood fairly boiled.'

And from what I remembered of him in the sugar-making season I could imagine the depth, the fury of my Uncle Spencer's impatience and irritation.

'But this is the twentieth century,' he kept repeating to the guards. 'And I have nothing to do with your beastly war. And where the devil are you taking us? And how much longer are we to wait in this damned station without our lunch?' He

---

* "But we are in the twentieth century. And the war will not last long."

spoke as a rich man, accustomed to being able to buy every convenience and consideration. The soldiers, who had the patience of poor men and were well used to being ordered hither and thither, to waiting indefinitely in the place where they were told to wait, could not understand this wild irritation against what they regarded as the natural order of things. My Uncle Spencer first amused them; then, as his impatience grew greater instead of less, he began to annoy them.

In the end, one of his guards lost patience too, and gave him a great kick in the breech to make him hold his tongue. My Uncle Spencer turned round and rushed at the man; but another soldier tripped him up with his rifle, and he tumbled heavily to the ground. Slowly he picked himself up; the soldiers were roaring with laughter. Alphonse, like a brown package, stood where they had put him, motionless, expressionless, his eyes shut.

In the top floor of the Ministry of the Interior the German authorities had established a sort of temporary internment camp. All suspicious persons—dubious foreigners, recalcitrant natives, anyone suspected by the invaders of possessing a dangerous influence over his neighbours—were sent to Brussels and shut up in the Ministry of the Interior, to remain there until the authorities should have time to go into their case. It was into this makeshift prison that my Uncle Spencer and his Dravidian compatriot were ushered, one sweltering afternoon towards the end of August. In an ordinary year, my Uncle Spencer reflected, the kermesse at Longres would now be in full swing. The fat woman would be washing her face with her bosom, the Figaros would be re-enacting amid sobs the Passion of Our Saviour, the armless lady would be drinking healths with her toes, the vendor of raw mussels would be listening anxiously for the first hoarse sound that might be taken for a cough. Where were they all this year, all these good people? And where was he himself? Incredulously he looked about him.

In the attics of the Ministry of the Interior the company was strange and mixed. There were Belgian noblemen whom the invaders considered it unsafe to leave in their châteaux among their peasantry. There were a Russian countess and an anarchist, incarcerated on account of their nationality. There was an opera-singer, who might be an international spy. There was a little golden-haired male impersonator, who had been appearing at a music hall in Liége, and whose offence, like that of my Uncle Spencer and the Dravidian, was to have been a British subject. There were a number of miscellaneous Frenchmen and Frenchwomen, caught on the wrong side of the border. There was an organ-grinder, who had gone on playing the 'Brabançonne' when told to stop, and a whole collection of other Belgians, of all classes and both sexes, from every part of the country, who had committed some crime or other, or perhaps had contrived merely to look suspicious, and who were now waiting to have their fate decided, as soon as the authorities should have time to pay attention to them.

Into this haphazardly assembled society my Uncle Spencer and the Dravidian were now casually dropped. The door closed behind them; they were left, like new arrivals in hell, to make the best of their situation.

The top floor of the Ministry of the Interior was divided up into one very large and a number of small rooms, the latter lined, for the most part, with pigeon-holes and filing cabinets in which were stored the paper products of years of bureaucratic activity.

In the smaller chambers the prisoners had placed the straw mattresses allotted to them by their gaolers; the men slept in the rooms at one end of the corridor, the women in those at the other end. The big room, which must once have housed the staff of the Ministry's registry, still contained a number of desks, tables, and chairs; it served now as the prisoners' drawing-room, dining-room, and recreation ground. There was no bathroom, and only one washing-basin and one *chalet de nécessité*,* as my Uncle Spencer, with a characteristic euphemism, always called it. Life in the attics of the Ministry of the Interior was not particularly agreeable.

My Uncle Spencer noticed that those of the prisoners who were not sunk in gloom and a sickening anxiety for the future, preserved an almost too boisterous cheerfulness. You had, it seemed, either to take this sort of thing as a prodigious joke, or brood over it as the most horrible of nightmares. There seemed to be no alternative. In time, no doubt, the two extremes would level down to the same calm resignation. But confinement had still been too short for that; the situation was still too new, dreamlike, and phantasmagorical, and fate too uncertain.

The cheerful ones abounded in japes, loud laughter, and practical jokes. They had created in the prison a kind of private-school atmosphere. Those whose confinement was oldest (and some had been in the Ministry for nearly a week now, almost from the day of the German entry into Brussels) assumed the inalienable right of seniors to make the new arrivals feel raw and uncomfortable. Each freshman was subjected to a search-

---

* Outhouse.

ing cross-examination, like that which awaits the new boy at his first school. Sometimes, if the latest victim seemed particularly ingenuous, they would play a little practical joke on him.

The leader of the cheerful party was a middle-aged Belgian journalist—a powerful, stout man, with carroty red moustaches and a high crimson complexion, a huge roaring voice and a boundless gift for laughter and genial Rabelaisian conversation. At the appearance of the meek Dravidian he had fairly whooped with delight. So great, indeed, was his interest in Alphonse that my Uncle Spencer escaped with the most perfunctory examination and the minimum of playful 'ragging'. It was perhaps for the best; my Uncle Spencer was in no mood to be trifled with, even by a fellow-sufferer.

Round poor Alphonse the journalist immediately improvised a farce. Sitting like a judge at one of the desks in the large room, he had the Dravidian brought before him, giving him to understand that he was the German commissary who had to deal with his case. Under cross-examination the Dravidian was made to tell his whole history. Born, Madras; profession, cobbler—a clerk took down all his answers as he delivered them. When he spoke of devil-dancing, the judge made him give a specimen of his performance there and then in front of the desk. The question of his marriage with Louiseke was gone into in the most intimate detail. Convinced that his liberty and probably his life depended on his sincerity, Alphonse answered every question as truthfully as he possibly could.

In the end, the journalist, clearing his throat, gravely summed up and gave judgement. Innocent. The prisoner would forthwith be released. On a large sheet of official paper he wrote *laissez-passer,** signed it Von der Goltz, and, open-

---

* A pass.

ing a drawer of the desk, selected from among the numerous official seals it contained that with which, in happier times, certain agricultural diplomas were stamped. On the thick red wax appeared the figure of a prize shorthorn cow with, round it, the words: 'Pour l'amélioration de la race bovine.'*

'Here,' roared the journalist, handing him the sealed paper. 'You may go.'

Poor Alphonse took his *laissez-passer*† and, bowing at intervals almost to the ground, retreated backwards out of the room. Joyously he picked up his hat and his little bundle, ran to the door, knocked and called. The sentry outside opened to see what was the matter. Alphonse produced his passport.

'Aber was ist das?'‡ asked the sentry.

Alphonse pointed to the seal: for the amelioration of the bovine race; to the signature: Von der Goltz. The sentry, thinking that it was he, not the Dravidian, who was the victim of the joke, became annoyed. He pushed Alphonse roughly back through the door; and when, protesting, propitiatively murmuring and smiling, the poor man advanced again to explain to the sentry his mistake, the soldier picked up his rifle and with the butt gave him a prod in the belly, which sent him back, doubled up and coughing, along the corridor. The door slammed to. Vainly, when he had recovered, Alphonse hammered and shouted. It did not open again. My Uncle Spencer found him standing there—knocking, listening, knocking again. The tears were streaming down his cheeks; it was a long time before my Uncle Spencer could make him understand that the whole affair had been nothing but a joke. At last,

---

* For the improvement of the cattle breed.

† A pass.

‡ "But what is that?"

however, Alphonse permitted himself to be led off to his mattress. In silence he lay down and closed his eyes. In his right hand he still held the passport—firmly, preciously between his thick brown fingers. He would not throw it away; not yet. Perhaps if he went to sleep this incident at the door would prove, when he woke up, to have been a dream. The paper would have ceased to be a joke, and when, to-morrow, he showed it again, who knew? The sentry would present arms and he would walk downstairs; and all the soldiers in the courtyard would salute and he would walk out into the sunny streets, waving the signature, pointing to the thick red seal.

Quite still he lay there. His arm was crossed over his body. From between the fingers of his hand hung the paper. Bold, as only the signature of a conquering general could be, Von der Goltz sprawled across the sheet. And in the bottom right-hand corner, stamped in the red wax, the image of the sacred cow was like a symbol of true salvation from across the separating ocean and the centuries. *Pour l'amélioration de la race bovine.** But might it not be more reasonable, in the circumstances, to begin with the human race?

My Uncle Spencer left him to go and expostulate with the journalist on the barbarity of his joke. He found the man sitting on the floor—for there were not enough chairs to go round—teaching the golden-haired male impersonator how to swear in French.

'And this,' he was saying, in his loud, jolly voice, 'this is what you must say to Von der Goltz if ever you see him.' And he let off a string of abusive words, which the little male impersonator carefully repeated, distorted by her drawling English intonation, in her clear, shrill voice: 'Sarl esspayss

---

* For the improvement of the cattle breed.

de coshaw.' The journalist roared with delighted laughter and slapped his thighs. 'What comes after that?' she asked.

'Excuse me,' said my Uncle Spencer, breaking in on the lesson. He was blushing slightly. He never liked hearing this sort of language—and in the mouth of a young woman (a compatriot too, it seemed) it sounded doubly distressing. 'Excuse me.' And he begged the journalist not to play any more jokes on Alphonse. 'He takes it too much to heart,' he explained.

At his description of the Dravidian's despair, the little male impersonator was touched almost to tears. And the journalist, who, like all the rest of us, had a heart of gold whenever he was reminded of its existence—and, like all the rest of us, he needed pretty frequent reminders; for his own pleasures and interests prevented him very often from remembering it—the journalist was extremely sorry at what he had done, declared that he had no idea that Alphonse would take the little farce so seriously, and promised for the future to leave him in peace.

The days passed; the nightmare became habitual, followed a routine. Three times a day the meagre supply of unappetizing food arrived and was consumed. Twice a day an officer with a little squad of soldiers behind him made a tour of inspection. In the morning one waited for one's turn to wash; but the afternoons were immense gulfs of hot time, which the prisoners tried to fill with games, with talk, with the reading of ancient dossiers from the files, with solitary brooding or with pacing up and down the corridor—twenty steps each way, up and down, up and down, till one had covered in one's imagination the distance between one loved and familiar place and another. Up and down, up and down. My Uncle Spencer sometimes walked along the poplar-lined high road between Longres and Waret; sometimes from Charing Cross

top-hat, and carrying in her hand a little cane—did two or three rattling clog dances and sang a song with the chorus:

> 'We are the nuts that get the girls
>   Ev-ery time;
> We get the ones with the curly curls,
> We get the peaches, we get the pearls—
>   Ev-ery time.'

And when, at the end of the turn, she took off her top-hat, and, standing rigidly at attention, like a soldier, her childish snubby little face very grave, her blue eyes fixed on visions not of this world, sang in her tuneless street-urchin's voice an astonishingly English version of the 'Brabançonne', then there was something more than enthusiasm. For men would suddenly feel the tears coming into their eyes, and women wept outright; and when it was over, everybody violently stamped and clapped and waved handkerchiefs, and laughed, and shouted imprecations against the Germans, and said, 'Vive la Belgique!' and ran to Emmy Wendle, and took her hand, or slapped her on the back as though she had really been a boy, or kissed her—but as though she were not a girl, and dressed in rather tight striped trousers at that—kissed her as though she were a symbol of the country, a visible and charming personification of their own patriotism and misfortunes.

When the evening's entertainment was over, the company began to disperse. Stretched on their hard mattresses along the floor, the prisoners uneasily slept or lay awake through the sultry nights, listening to the steps of the sen-tries in the court below and hearing every now and then through the unnatural silence of the invaded town, the heavy beat, beat, beat of a regiment marching along the deserted street, the rumble and sharp, hoofy clatter of a battery on the move towards some distant front.

The days passed. My Uncle Spencer soon grew accustomed to the strange little hell into which he had been dropped. He knew it by heart. A huge, square room, low-ceilinged and stifling under the hot leads. Men in their shirt-sleeves standing, or sitting, some on chairs, some on the corner of a desk or a table, some on the floor. Some leaned their elbows on the window-sill and looked out, satisfying their eyes with the sight of the trees in the park across the street, breathing a purer air—for the air in the room was stale, twice-breathed, and smelt of sweat, tobacco, and cabbage soup.

From the first the prisoners had divided themselves, automatically almost, into little separate groups. Equal in their misery, they still retained their social distinctions. The organ-grinder and the artisans and peasants always sat together in one corner on the floor, playing games with a greasy pack of cards, smoking and, in spite of expostulations, in spite of sincere efforts to restrain themselves, spitting on the floor all round them.

'Mine!' the organ-grinder would say triumphantly, and plank down his ace of hearts. 'Mine!' And profusely, to emphasize his satisfaction, he spat. 'Ah, pardon!' Remembering too late, he looked apologetically round the room. 'Excuse me.' And he would get up, rub the gob of spittle into the floor with his boot, and going to the window would lean out and spit again—not that he felt any need to, having spat only a moment before, but for the sake of showing that he had good manners and could spit out of the window and not on the floor when he thought of it.

Another separate group was that of the aristocracy. There was the little old count with a face like a teapot—such shiny round cheeks, such a thin, irrelevant nose; and the young count with the monocle—the one so exquisitely affable with every one and yet so remote and aloof under all his politeness; the other so arrogant in manner, but, one could see, so wistfully wishing that his social position would permit him to mingle with his spiritual equals. The old count politely laughed whenever the journalist or some other member of the cheerful party made a joke; the young count scowled, till the only smooth surface left in his corrugated face was the monocle. But he longed to be allowed to join in the horse-play and the jokes. With the two counts were associated two or three rich and important citizens, among them during the first days my Uncle Spencer. But other interests were to make him abandon their company almost completely after a while.

On the fringes of their circle hovered occasionally the Russian countess. This lady spent most of the day in her sleeping apartment, lying on her mattress and smoking cigarettes. She had decided views about the respect that was due to her rank, and expected the wash-house to be immediately evacuated whenever she expressed a desire to use it. On being told that she must wait her turn, she flew into a rage. When she was bored with being alone, she would come into the living-room to find somebody to talk to. On one occasion she took my Uncle Spencer aside and told him at great length and with a wealth of intimate detail about the ninth and greatest love-affair of her life. In future, whenever my

Uncle Spencer caught sight of her turning her large, dark, rather protruding eyes round the room, he took care to be absorbed in conversation with somebody else.

Her compatriot, the anarchist, was a Jewish-looking man with a black beard and a nose like the figure six. He associated himself with none of the little groups, was delighted by the war, which he gleefully prophesied would destroy so-called civilization, and made a point of being as disagreeable as he could to everyone—particularly to the countess, whom he was able to insult confidentially in Russian. It was in obedience to the same democratic principles that he possessed himself of the only arm-chair in the prison—it must have been the throne of at least a *sous-chef de division*[*]—refusing to part with it even for a lady or an invalid. He sat in it immovably all day, put it between his mattress and the wall at night, and took it with him even into the wash-house and the *chalet de nécessité*.

The cheerful party grouped itself, planet-fashion, round the radiant jollity of the journalist. His favourite amusement was hunting through the files for curious dossiers which he could read out, with appropriate comments and improvised emendations, to the assembled group. But the most relished of all his jokes was played ritually every morning, when he went through the papers of nobility of the whole Belgic aristocracy (discovered, neatly stowed away, in a cupboard in the corridor), selecting from among the noble names a few high-sounding titles which he would carry with him to the chalet of necessity. His disciples included a number of burgesses, French and Belgian; a rather odious and spotty young English bank-clerk caught on his foreign holiday; the Russian

---

[*] Second in command of the division.

countess in certain moods; the male impersonator, on and off; and the opera-singer.

With this last my Uncle Spencer, who was a great lover of music and even a moderately accomplished pianist, made frequent attempts to talk about his favourite art. But the opera-singer, he found, was only interested in music in so far as it affected the tenor voice. He had consequently never heard of Bach or Beethoven. On Leoncavallo, however, on Puccini, Saint-Saëns, and Gounod he was extremely knowledgeable. He was an imposing personage, with a large, handsome face and the gracious, condescending smile of a great man who does not object to talking even with you. With ladies, as he often gave it to be understood, he had a great success. But his fear of doing anything that might injure his voice was almost as powerful as his lasciviousness and his vanity; he passed his life, like a monk of the Thebaid, in a state of perpetual conflict. Outwardly and professedly a member of the cheerful party, the opera-singer was secretly extremely concerned about his future. In private he discussed with my Uncle Spencer the horrors of the situation.

More obviously melancholy was the little grey-haired professor of Latin who spent most of the day walking up and down the corridor like a wolf in a cage, brooding and pining. Poor Alphonse, squatting with his back to the wall near the door, was another sad and solitary figure. Sometimes he looked thoughtfully about him, watching his fellow-prisoners at their various occupations with the air of an inhabitant of eternity watching the incomprehensible antics of those who live in time. Sometimes he would spend whole hours with closed eyes in a state of meditation.

When someone spoke to him, he came back to the present as though from an immense distance.

But, for my Uncle Spencer, how remote, gradually, they all became! They receded, they seemed to lose light; and with their fading the figure of Emmy Wendle came closer, grew larger and brighter. From the first moment he set eyes on her, sitting there on the floor, taking her lesson in vituperation from the journalist, my Uncle Spencer had taken particular notice of her. Making his way towards the pair of them, he had been agreeably struck by the childishness and innocence of her appearance—by the little snub nose, the blue eyes, the yellow hair, so stubbornly curly that she had to wear it cut short like a boy's, for there was no oiling down or tying back a long mane of it; even in her private feminine life there was a hint—and it only made her seem the more childish—of male impersonation. And then, coming within ear-shot, it had been 'sarl esspayss de coshaw' and a string besides of less endearing locutions proceeding from these lips. Startling, shocking. But a moment later, when he was telling them how hardly poor Alphonse had taken the joke, she said the most charming things and with such real feeling in her Cockney voice, such a genuine expression of sympathy and commiseration on her face, that my Uncle Spencer wondered whether he had heard aright, or if that 'sarl coshaw' and all the rest could really have been pronounced by so delicate and sensitive a creature.

The state of agitation in which my Uncle Spencer had lived ever since his arrest, the astonishing and horrible novelty of his situation, had doubtless in some measure predisposed him to falling in love. For it frequently happens that one emotion—providing that it is not so powerful as to make us unconscious of anything but itself—will stimulate us to feel another. Thus danger, if it is not acute enough to cause panic, tends to attach us to those with whom we risk it, the feelings of compassion, sympathy, and even love being stimulated and quickened by apprehension. Grief, in the same way, often brings with it a need of affection and even, though we do not like to admit it to ourselves, even obscurely a kind of desire; so that a passion of sorrow will convert itself by scarcely perceptible degrees, or sometimes suddenly, into a passion of love. My Uncle Spencer's habitual attitude towards women was one of extreme reserve. Once, as a young man, he had been in love and engaged to be married; but the object of his affections had jilted him for somebody else. Since then, partly from a fear of renewing his disappointment, partly out of a kind of romantic fidelity to the unfaithful one, he had avoided women, or at least taken pains not to fall in love any more, living always in a state of perfect celibacy, which would have done credit to the most virtuous of priests. But the agitations of the last few days had disturbed all his habits of life and thought. Apprehension of danger, an indignation that was a very different thing from the recurrent irritability of the sugar-making season, profound bewilderment, and a sense of mental disorientation had left him without his customary defences and in a state of more than ordinary susceptibility; so that when he saw, in the midst of his waking nightmare, that charming childish head, when he heard those gentle words of sympathy for the poor Dravidian, he was strangely moved; and he found himself aware of Emmy Wendle as he had not been aware of any woman since the first unfaithful one of his youth had left him.

Everything conspired to make my Uncle Spencer take an interest in Emmy Wendle—everything, not merely his own emotional state, but the place, the time, the outward circumstances. He might have gone to see her at the music hall every night for a year; and though he might have enjoyed her turn—and as a matter of fact he would not, for he would have thought it essentially rather vulgar—though he might have found her pretty and charming, it would never have occurred to him to try to make her acquaintance or introduce himself into her history. But here, in this detestable makeshift prison, she took on a new significance, she became the personification of all that was gracious, sweet, sympathetic, of all that was not war. And at the end of her performance (still, it was true, in poorish taste, but more permissible, seeing that it was given for the comfort of the afflicted) how profoundly impressive was her singing of the 'Brabançonne'! She had become great with the greatness of the moment, with the grandeur of the emotions to which she was giving utterance in that harsh guttersnipe's voice of hers—singing of exultations, agonies, and man's unconquerable mind. We attribute to the symbol something of the sacredness of the thing or idea symbolized. Two bits of wood set cross-wise are not two ordinary bits of wood, and a divinity has hedged the weakest and worst of kings. Similarly, at any crisis in our lives, the most trivial object, or a person in himself insignificant, may become, for some reason, charged with all the greatness of the moment.

Even the 'sarl coshaw' incident had helped to raise my Uncle Spencer's interest in Emmy Wendle. For if she was gentle, innocent, and young, if she personified in her small, bright self all the unhappiness and all the courage of a country, of the whole afflicted world, she was also fallible, feminine, and weak; she was subject to bad influences, she might be led astray. And the recollection of those gross phrases, candidly, innocently, and openly uttered (as the most prudish can always utter them when they happen to be in an unfamiliar language, round whose words custom has not crystallized that wealth of associations which give to the native locutions their peculiar and, from age to age, varying significance), filled my Uncle Spencer with alarm and with a missionary zeal to rescue so potentially beautiful and even grand a nature from corruption.

For her part, Emmy Wendle was charmed, at any rate during the first days of their acquaintance, with my Uncle Spencer. He was English, to begin with, and spoke her language; he was also—which the equally English and intelligible bank-clerk was not—a gentleman. More important for Emmy, in her present mood, he did not attempt to flirt with her. Emmy wanted no admirers, at the moment. In the present circumstances she felt that it would have been wrong, uncomely, and rather disreputable to think of flirtation. She sang the 'Brabançonne' with too much religious ardour for that; the moment was too solemn, too extraordinary. True, the solemnity of the moment and the ardour of her patriotic feelings might, if a suitable young man had happened to find himself with her in the attics of the Ministry of the Interior, have caused her to fall in love with a fervour having almost the religious quality of her other feelings. But no suitable young man, unfortunately, presented himself. The bank-clerk had spots on his face and was not a gentleman, the journalist was middle-aged and too stout. Both tried to flirt with her. But their advances had, for Emmy, all the impropriety of a flirtation in a sacred place. With my Uncle Spencer, however, she felt entirely safe. It was not merely that he had white hair; Emmy had lived long enough to know that that symbol was no guarantee of decorous behaviour—on the contrary; but because he was, obviously, such a gentleman, because of the signs of unworldliness and mild idealism stamped all over his face.

At first, indeed, it was only to escape from the tiresome and indecorous attentions of the bank-clerk and the journalist that she addressed herself to Uncle Spencer. But she soon came to like his company for its own sake; she began to take an interest in what he said, she listened seriously to my Uncle Spencer's invariably serious conversation—for he never talked except on profitable and intellectual themes, having no fund of ordinary small talk.

During the first days Emmy treated him with the respectful courtesy which, she felt, was due to a man of his age, position, and character. But later, when he began to follow her with his abject adoration, she became more familiar. Inevitably; for one cannot expect to be treated as old and important by someone at whom one looks with the appealing eyes of a dog. She called him Uncle Spenny and ordered him about, made him carry and fetch as though he were a trained animal. My Uncle Spencer was only too delighted, of course, to obey her. He was charmed by the familiarities she took with him. The period of her pretty teasing familiarity (intermediate between her respectfulness and her later cruelty) was the happiest, so far as my Uncle Spencer was concerned, in their brief connection. He loved and felt himself, if not loved in return, at least playfully tolerated.

Another man would have permitted himself to take liberties in return, to be sportive, gallant, and importunate. But my Uncle Spencer remained gravely and tenderly himself. His only reprisal for 'Uncle Spenny' and the rest was to call her by her Christian name instead of 'Miss Wendle', as he had always solemnly done before. Yes, Emmy felt herself safe with Uncle Spenny; almost too safe, perhaps.

My Uncle Spencer's conversations were always, as I have said, of a very serious cast. They were even more serious at this time than usual; for the catastrophe, and now his passion, had brought on in his mind a very severe fit of thinking. There was so much that, in the light of the happenings of the last few weeks, needed reconsidering. From the German professor's theory to the problem of good and evil; from the idea of progress (for, after all, was not this the twentieth century?) to the austere theory and the strange new fact of love; from internationalism to God—everything had to be considered afresh. And he considered them out loud with Emmy Wendle. Goodness, for example, was that no more than a relative thing, an affair of social conventions, gauged by merely local and accidental standards? Or was there something absolute, ultimate, and fundamental about the moral idea? And God—could God be absolutely good? And was there such a vast difference between the twentieth and other centuries? Could fact ever rhyme with ideal? All these disturbing questions had to be asked and answered to his own satisfaction once again.

It was characteristic of my Uncle Spencer that he answered them all—even after taking into consideration everything that had happened—on the hopeful side, just as he had done before the catastrophe; and what was more, with a deeper conviction. Before, he had accepted the cheerful idealistic view a little too easily. He had inherited it from the century in which he was born, had sucked it in from the respectable and ever-prospering elders among whom he had been brought up. Circumstances were now making that facile cheerfulness seem rather stupid. But it was precisely because he had to reconsider the objections to optimism, the arguments against hopefulness, not theoretically in the void, but practically and in the midst of personal and universal calamity (the latter very bearable if one is comfortably placed oneself, but real, but disturbing, if one is also suffering a little), that he now became convinced, more hardly but more profoundly, of the truth of what he had believed before, but lightly and, as he now saw, almost accidentally. Events were shortly to disturb this new-found conviction.

Emmy listened to him with rapture. The circumstances, the time, the place, inclined her to the serious and reflective mood. My Uncle Spencer's discourses were just what she needed at this particular moment. Naturally superstitious, she lived at all times under the protection of a small gold lucky pig and a coral cross which had once belonged to her mother. And when luck was bad, she went to church and consulted crystal-gazers. That time she broke her leg and had to cancel that wonderful engagement to tour in Australia, she knew it was because she had been neglecting God in all the prosperous months before; she prayed and she promised amendment. When she got better, God sent her an offer from Cohen's Provincial Alhambras, Ltd., in token that her repentance was accepted and she was forgiven. And now, though she had seemed to belong to the cheerful party in the attics of the Ministry of the Interior, her thoughts had secretly been very grave. At night, lying awake on her mattress, she wondered in the darkness what was the reason of all this—the war, her bad luck in getting caught by the Germans. Yes, what could the reason be? Why was God angry with her once again?

But of course she knew why. It was all that dreadful, dreadful business last June when she was working at Wimbledon. That young man who had waited for her at the stage door; and would she do him the honour of having supper with him? And she had said yes, though it was all against her rules. Yes: because he had such a beautiful voice, so refined, almost like a very high-class West End actor's voice. 'I came to see the marionettes,' he told her. 'Marionettes never seem to get farther than the suburbs, do they? But I stayed for you.'

They drove in a taxi all the way from Wimbledon to Piccadilly. 'Some day,' she said, pointing to the Pavilion, 'you'll see my name there, in big electric letters: EMMY WENDLE.' A hundred pounds a week and the real West End. What a dream!

He had such beautiful manners and he looked so handsome when you saw him in the light. They had champagne for supper.

In the darkness, Emmy blushed with retrospective shame. She buried her face in the pillow as though she were trying to hide from some searching glance. No wonder God was angry. In an agony she kissed the coral cross. She pulled at the blue ribbon, at the end of which, between her two small breasts, hung the golden pig; she held the mascot in her hand, tightly, as though hoping to extract from it something of that power for happiness stored mysteriously within it, as the power to attract iron filings is stored within the magnet.

A few feet away the Russian countess heavily breathed. At the stertorous sound Emmy shuddered, remembering the wickedness that slumbered so near her. For if she herself had ceased to be, technically, a good girl, she was—now that her luck had turned—ashamed of it; she knew, from God's anger, that she had done wrong. But the countess, if sleep had not overtaken her, would have gone on boasting all night about her lovers. To middle-class Emmy the countess's frankness, her freedom from the ordinary prejudices, her aristocratic contempt for public opinion, and her assumption—the assumption of almost all idle women and of such idle men as have nothing better to do or think about—that the only end of life is to make love, complicatedly, at leisure and with a great many people, seemed profoundly shocking. It didn't so much matter that she wasn't a good girl—or rather a good ripe widow. What seemed to Emmy so dreadful was that she should talk about it as though not being good were natural, to be taken for granted, and even positively meritorious. No wonder God was angry.

To Emmy my Uncle Spencer—or shall I call him now her Uncle Spenny?—came as a comforter and sustainer in her remorseful misery. His wandering speculations were not, it was true, always particularly relevant to her own trouble; nor did she always understand what he was talking about. But there was a certain quality in all his discourses, whatever the subject, which she found uplifting and sustaining. Thus my Uncle Spencer quoting Swedenborg to prove that, in spite of all present appearances to the contrary, things were probably all right, was the greatest of comforts. There was something about him like a very high-class clergyman—a West End clergyman, so to say. When he talked she felt better and in some sort safer.

He inspired in her so much confidence that one day, while the journalist was playing some noisy joke that kept all the rest of the company occupied, she took him aside into the embrasure of one of the windows and told him all, or nearly all, about the episode on account of which God was now so angry. My Uncle Spencer assured her that God didn't see things in quite the way she imagined; and that if He had decided that there must be a European War, it was not, in all human probability, to provide an excuse for getting Emmy Wendle—however guilty—locked up in the attics of the Ministry of the Interior at Brussels. As for the sin itself, my Uncle Spencer tried to make her believe that it was not quite so grave as she thought. He did not know that she only thought it grave because she was in prison and, naturally, depressed.

'No, no,' he said comfortingly, 'you mustn't take it to heart like that.'

But the knowledge that this exquisite and innocent young creature had once—and if once, why not twice, why not (my Uncle Spencer left to his own midnight thoughts feverishly speculated), why not fifty times?—fallen from virtue distressed him. He had imagined her, it was true, surrounded by bad influences, like the journalist; but between being taught to say 'sarl coshaw' and an actual lapse from virtue, there was a considerable difference. It had never occurred to my Uncle Spencer that Emmy could have got beyond the 'coshaw' stage. And now he had it from her own lips that she had.

Celibate like a priest, my Uncle Spencer had not enjoyed the priest's vicarious experience in the confessional. He had not read those astonishing handbooks of practical psychology, fruit of the accumulated wisdom of centuries, from which the seminarist learns to understand his penitents, to classify and gauge their sins, and, incidentally—so crude, bald, and uncompromising are the descriptions of human vice that they contain—to loathe the temptations which, when rosily and delicately painted, can seem so damnably alluring. His ignorance of human beings was enormous. In his refinement he had preferred not to know; and circumstances, so far, had wonderfully conspired to spare him knowledge.

Years afterwards, I remember, when we met again, he asked me after a silence, and speaking with an effort, as though overcoming a repugnance, what I really thought about women and all 'that sort of thing'. It was a subject about which at that time I happened to feel with the bitterness and mirthful cynicism of one who has been only too amply successful in love with the many in whom he took no interest, and lamentably and persistently unsuccessful with the one being in whose case success would have been in the least worth while.

'You really think, then,' said my Uncle Spencer, when I paused for breath, 'that a lot of that sort of thing actually does go on?'

I really did.

He sighed and shut his eyes, as though to conceal their expression from me. He was thinking of Emmy Wendle. How passionately he had hoped that I should prove her, necessarily and *a priori*, virtuous!

There are certain sensitive and idealistic people in whom

the discovery that the world is what it is brings on a sudden and violent reaction towards cynicism. From soaring in spheres of ideal purity they rush down into the mud, rub their noses in it, eat it, bathe and wallow. They lacerate their own highest feelings and delight in the pain. They take pleasure in defiling the things which before they thought beautiful and noble; they pore with a disgusted attention over the foul entrails of the things whose smooth and lovely skin was what they had once worshipped.

Swift, surely, was one of these—the greatest of them. His type our islands still produce; and more copiously, perhaps, during the last two or three generations than ever before. For the nineteenth century specialized in that romantic, optimistic idealism which postulates that man is on the whole good and inevitably becoming better. The idealism of the men of the Middle Ages was more sensible; for it insisted, to begin with, that man was mostly and essentially bad, a sinner by instinct and heredity. Their ideals, their religion, were divine and unnatural antidotes to original sin. They saw the worst first and could be astonished by no horror—only by the occasional miracle of sweetness and light. But their descendants of the romantic, optimistic, humanitarian century, in which my Uncle Spencer was born and brought up, vented their idealism otherwise. They began by seeing the best; they insisted that men were naturally good, spiritual, and lovely. A sensitive youth brought up in this genial creed has only to come upon a characteristic specimen of original sin to be astonished, shocked, and disillusioned into despair. Circumstances and temperament had permitted my Uncle Spencer to retain his romantic optimism very much longer than most men.

The tardy recognition of the existence of original sin disturbed my Uncle Spencer's mind. But the effects of it were not immediate. At the moment, while he was in Emmy's pretty and intoxicating presence, and while she was still kind, he could not believe that she too had her share of original sin. And even when he forced himself to do so, her childish ingenuous face was in itself a complete excuse. It was later—and especially when he was separated from her—that the poison began slowly to work, embittering his whole spirit. At present Emmy's confession only served to increase his passion for her. For, to begin with, it made her seem more than ever in need of protection. And next, by painfully satisfying a little of his curiosity about her life, it quickened his desire to know all, to introduce himself completely into her history. And at the same time it provoked a retrospective jealousy, together with an intense present suspiciousness and an agonized anticipation of future dangers. His passion became like a painful disease. He pursued her with an incessant and abject devotion.

Relieved, partly by my Uncle Spencer's spiritual ministrations, partly by the medicating power of time, from her first access of remorse, depression, and self-reproach, Emmy began to recover her normal high spirits. My Uncle Spencer became less necessary to her as a comforter. His incomprehensible speculations began to bore her. Conversely, the jokes of the cheerful ones seemed more funny, while the gallantries of the journalist and the bank-clerk appeared less repulsive, because—now that her mood had changed—they struck her as less incongruous and indecorous. She was no longer, spiritually speaking, in church. In church, my Uncle Spencer's undemonstrative and unimportunate devotion had seemed beautifully in place. But now that she was emerging again out of the dim religious into the brightly secular mood, she found it rather ridiculous and, since she did not return the adoration, tiresome.

'If you could just see yourself now, Uncle Spenny,' she said to him, 'the way you look.'

And she drew down the corners of her mouth, then opened her eyes in a fishy, reverential stare. Then the grimace in which my Uncle Spencer was supposed to see his adoration truly mirrored, disintegrated in laughter; the eyes screwed themselves up, a little horizontal wrinkle appeared near the tip of the snub nose, the mouth opened, waves of mirth seemed to ripple out from it across the face, and a shrill peal of laughter mocked him into an attempted smile.

'Do I really look like that?' he asked.

'You really do,' Emmy nodded. 'Not a very cheerful thing to have staring at one day and night, is it?'

Sometimes—and this to my Uncle Spencer was inexpressibly painful—she would even bring in some third person to share the sport at his expense; she would associate the bank-clerk, the opera-singer, or the journalist in her mocking laughter. The teasing which, in the first days, had been so light and affectionate, became cruel.

Emmy would have been distressed, no doubt, if she had known how much she hurt him. But he did not complain. All she knew was that my Uncle Spencer was ridiculous. The temptation to say something smart and disagreeable about him was irresistible.

To my Uncle Spencer's company she now preferred that of the journalist, the bank-clerk, and the opera-singer. With the bank-clerk she talked about West End actors and actresses, music-hall artists, and cinema stars. True, he was not much of a gentleman; but on this absorbing subject he was extremely knowledgeable. The singer revealed to her the gorgeous and almost unknown universe of the operatic stage—a world of art so awe-inspiringly high that it was above even the West End. The journalist told her spicy stories of the Brussels stage. My Uncle Spencer would sit at the fringes of the group, listening in silence and across a gulf of separation, while Emmy and the bank-clerk agreed that Clarice Mayne was sweet, George Robey a scream, and Florence Smithson a really high-class artist. When asked for his opinion, my Uncle Spencer always had to admit that he had never seen the artist in question. Emmy and the bank-clerk would set up a howl of derision; and the opera-singer, with biting sarcasm, would ask my Uncle Spencer how a man who professed to be fond of music could have gone through life without even making an attempt to hear Caruso. My Uncle Spencer was too sadly depressed to try to explain.

The days passed. Sometimes a prisoner would be sent for and examined by the German authorities. The little old nobleman like a teapot was released a week after my Uncle Spencer's arrival; and a few days later the haughty and mon-ocled one disappeared. Most of the peasants next vanished. Then the Russian anarchist was sent for, lengthily examined and sent back again, to find that his arm-chair was being occupied by the journalist.

In the fourth week of my Uncle Spencer's imprisonment Alphonse fell ill. The poor man had never recovered from the effects of the practical joke that had been played upon him on the day of his arrival. Melancholy, oppressed by fears, the more awful for being vague and without a definite object (for he could never grasp why and by whom he had been imprisoned; and as to his ultimate fate—no one could persuade him that it was to be anything but the most frightful and lingering of deaths), he sat brooding by himself in a corner. His free pardon, signed Von der Goltz and sealed with the image of the Sacred Cow, he still preserved; for though he was now intellectually certain that the paper was valueless, he still hoped faintly in the depths of his being that it might turn out, one day, to be a talisman; and, in any case, the image of the Cow was very comforting. Every now and then he would take the paper out of his pocket, tenderly unfold it and gaze with large sad eyes at the sacred effigy: *Pour l'amélioration de la race bovine*[*]—and tears would well up from under his eyelids, would hang suspended among the lashes and roll at last down his brown cheeks.

They were not so round now, those cheeks, as they had been. The skin sagged, the bright convex high-lights had lost their brilliance. Miserably he pined. My Uncle Spencer did his best to cheer him. Alphonse was grateful, but would take no comfort. He had lost all interest even in women; and when, learning from my Uncle Spencer that the Indian was something of a prophet, Emmy asked him to read her hand, he looked at her listlessly as though she had been a mere male and not a male impersonator, and shook his head.

One morning he complained that he was feeling too ill to get up. His head was hot, he coughed, breathed shortly and with difficulty, felt a pain in his right lung. My Uncle Spencer tried to think what Hahnemann would have prescribed in the circumstances, and came to the conclusion that the thousandth of a grain of aconite was the appro-

---

[*] For the improvement of the cattle breed.

priate remedy. Unhappily, there was not so much as a millionth of a grain of aconite to be found in all the prison. Inquiry produced only a bottle of aspirin tablets and, from the Russian countess, a packet of cocaine snuff. It was thought best to give the Dravidian a dose of each and wait for the doctor.

At his midday visit the inspecting officer was informed of Alphonse's state, and promised to have the doctor sent at once. But it was not, in point of fact, till the next morning that the doctor came. My Uncle Spencer, meanwhile, constituted himself the Dravidian's nurse. The fact that Alphonse was the widower of his housekeeper's sister, and had lived in his city of adoption, made my Uncle Spencer feel somehow responsible for the poor Indian. Moreover, he was glad to have some definite occupation which would allow him to forget, if only partially and for an occasional moment, his unhappy passion.

From the first, Alphonse was certain that he was going to die. To my Uncle Spencer he foretold his impending extinction, not merely with equanimity, but almost with satisfaction. For by dying, he felt, he would be spiting and cheating his enemies, who desired so fiendishly to put an end to him at their own time and in their own horrible fashion. It was in vain that my Uncle Spencer assured him that he would not die, that there was nothing serious the matter with him. Alphonse stuck to his assertion.

'In eight days,' he said, 'I shall be dead.'

And shutting his eyes, he was silent.

The doctor, when he came next day, diagnosed acute lobar pneumonia. Through the oppression of his fever, Alphonse smiled at my Uncle Spencer with a look almost of triumph. That night he was delirious and began to rave in a language my Uncle Spencer could not understand.

My Uncle Spencer listened in the darkness to the Dravidian's incomprehensible chattering; and all at once, with a shudder, with a sense of terror he felt—in the presence of this man of another race, speaking in an unknown tongue words uttered out of obscure depths for no man's hearing and which even his own soul did not hear or understand—he felt unutterably alone. He was imprisoned within himself. He was an island surrounded on every side by wide and bottomless solitudes. And while the Indian chattered away, now softly, persuasively, cajolingly, now with bursts of anger, now loudly laughing, he thought of all the millions and millions of men and women in the world—all alone, all solitary and confined. He thought of friends, incomprehensible to one another and opaque after a lifetime of companionship; he thought of lovers remote in one another's arms. And the hopelessness of his passion revealed itself to him— the hopelessness of every passion, since every passion aims at attaining to what, in the nature of things, is unattainable: the fusion and interpenetration of two lives, two separate histories, two solitary and for ever sundered individualities.

The Indian roared with laughter.

But the unattainableness of a thing was never a reason for ceasing to desire it. On the contrary, it tends to increase and even to create desire. Thus our love for those we know, and our longing to be with them, are often increased by their death. And the impossibility of ever communicating with him again will actually create out of indifference an affection, a respect and esteem for someone whose company in life seemed rather tedious than desirable. So, for the lover, the realization that what he desires is unattainable, and that every possession will reveal yet vaster tracts of what is unpossessed and unpossessable, is not a deterrent, is not an antidote to his passion; but serves rather to exacerbate his desire, sharpening it to a kind of desperation, and at the same time making the object of his desire seem more than ever precious.

The Indian chattered on, a ghost among the ghosts of his imagination, remote as though he were speaking from another world. And Emmy—was she not as far away, as unattainable? And being remote, she was the more desirable; being mysterious, she was the more lovely. A more brutal and experienced man than my Uncle Spencer would have devoted all his energies to seducing the young woman, knowing that after a time the satisfaction of his physical desire would probably make him cease to take any interest in her soul or her history. But physical possession was the last thing my Uncle Spencer thought of, and his love had taken the form of an immense desire for the impossible union, not of bodies, but of minds and lives. True, what he had so far learned about her mind and history was not particularly encouraging. But for my Uncle Spencer her silliness, love of pleasure, and frivolity were strange and mysterious qualities—for he had known few women in his life and none, before, like Emmy Wendle—rather lovely still in their unfamiliarity, and if recognized as at all bad, excused as being the symptoms of a charming childishness and an unfortunate upbringing. Her solicitude, that first day, about poor Alphonse convinced him that she was fundamentally good-hearted; and if she had proved herself cruel since then towards himself, that was more by mistake and because of surrounding bad influences than from natural malignity. And, then, there was the way in which she sang the 'Brabançonne'. It was noble, it was moving. To be able to sing like that one must have a fine and beautiful character. In thinking like this, my Uncle Spencer was forgetting that no characteristic is incompatible with any other, that any deadly sin may be found in company with any cardinal virtue, even the apparently contradictory virtue. But unfortunately that is the kind of wisdom which one invariably forgets precisely at the moment when it might be of use to one. One learns it almost in the cradle; at any rate, I remember at my preparatory school reading, in Professor Oman's *Shorter History of England*, of 'the heroic though profligate Duke of Ormonde', and of a great English king who was, none the less, 'a stuttering, lolling pedant with a tongue too big for his mouth'. But though one knows well enough in theory that a duke can be licentious as well as brave, that majestic wisdom may be combined with pedantry and defective speech, yet in practice one continues to believe that an attractive woman is kind because she is charming, and virtuous because she rejects your first advances; without reflecting that the grace of her manner may thinly conceal an unyielding ruthlessness and selfishness, while the coyness in face of insistence may be a mere device for still more completely ensnaring the victim. It is only in the presence of unsympathetic persons that we remember that the most odious actions are compatible with the most genuinely noble sentiments, and that a man or woman who does one thing, while professing another, is not necessarily a conscious liar or hypocrite. If only we could steadfastly bear this knowledge in mind when we are with persons whom we find sympathetic!

Desiring Emmy as passionately as he did, my Uncle Spencer would not have had much difficulty in persuading himself—even in spite of her recent cruelty towards him— that the spirit with which he longed to unite his own was on the whole a beautiful and interesting spirit; would indeed have had no difficulty at all, had it not been for that unfortunate confession of hers. This, though it flattered him as a token of her confidence in his discretion and wisdom, had sadly disturbed him and was continuing to disturb him more and more. For out of all her history—the history in which it was his longing to make himself entirely at home as though he had actually lived through it with her—this episode was almost the only chapter he knew. Like a thin ray of light her confession had picked it out for him, from the surrounding obscurity. And what an episode! The more my Uncle Spencer reflected on it, the more he found it distressing.

The brutal practical man my Uncle Spencer was not would have taken this incident from the past as being of good augury for his own future prospects. But since he did not desire, consciously at any rate, the sort of success it augured, the knowledge of this incident brought him an unadulterated distress. For however much my Uncle Spencer might insist in his own mind on the guiltiness of external circumstance and of the other party, he could not entirely exonerate Emmy. Nor could he pretend that she had not in some sort, if only physically, taken part in her own lapse. And perhaps she had participated willingly. And even if she had not, the thought that she had been defiled, however reluctantly, by the obscene contact was unspeakably painful to him. And while the Indian raved, and through the long, dark silences during which there was no sound but the unnaturally quick and shallow breathing, and sometimes a moan, and sometimes a dry cough, my Uncle Spencer painfully thought and thought; and his mind oscillated between a conviction of her purity and the fear that perhaps she was utterly corrupt. He saw in his imagination, now her childish face and the rapt expression upon it while she sang the 'Brabançonne', now the sweet, solicitous look while she commiserated on poor Alphonse's unhappiness, and then, a moment later, endless embracements, kisses brutal and innumerable. And always he loved her.

Next day the Dravidian's fever was still high. The doctor, when he came, announced that red hepatization of both lungs was already setting in. It was a grave case which ought to be at the hospital; but he had no authority to have the man sent there. He ordered tepid spongings to reduce the fever.

In the face of the very defective sanitary arrangements of the prison, my Uncle Spencer did his best. He had a crowd of willing assistants; everybody was anxious to do something helpful. Nobody was more anxious than Emmy Wendle. The forced inaction of prison life, even when it was relieved by the jokes of the cheerful ones, by theatrical discussions and the facetious gallantry of the bank-clerk and the journalist, was disagreeable to her. And the prospect of being able to do something, and particularly (since it was war-time, after all) of doing something useful and charitable, was welcomed by her with a real satisfaction. She sat by the Dravidian's mattress, talked to him, gave him what he asked for, did the disagreeable jobs that have to be done in the sick-room, ordered my Uncle Spencer and the others about, and seemed completely happy.

For his part, my Uncle Spencer was delighted by what he regarded as a reversion to her true self. There could be no doubt about it now: Emmy was good, was kind, a ministering angel, and therefore (in spite of the professor's heroic though profligate duke), therefore pure, therefore interesting, therefore worthy of all the love he could give her. He forgot the confession, or at least he ceased to attach importance to it; he was no longer haunted by the odious images which too much brooding over it evoked in his mind. What convinced him, perhaps, better than everything of her essential goodness, was the fact that she was once more kind to him. Her young energy, fully occupied in practical work which was not, however, sufficiently trying to overtax the strength or set the nerves on edge, did not have to vent itself in laughter and mockery, as it had done when she recovered from the mood of melancholy which had depressed it during the first days of her imprisonment. They were fellow-workers now.

The Dravidian, meanwhile, grew worse and worse, weaker and weaker every day. The doctor was positively irritated.

'The man has no business to be so ill as he is,' he grumbled. 'He's not old, he isn't an alcoholic or a syphilitic, his constitution is sound enough. He's just letting himself die. At this rate he'll never get past the crisis.'

At this piece of news Emmy became grave. She had never seen death at close quarters—a defect in her education which my Uncle Spencer, if he had had the bringing up of her, would have remedied. For death was one of those Realities of Life with which, he thought, everyone ought to make the earliest possible acquaintance. Love, on the other hand, was not one of the desirable Realities. It never occurred to him to ask himself the reason for this invidious distinction. Indeed, there was no reason; it just was so.

'Tell me, Uncle Spenny,' she whispered, when the doctor had gone, 'what *does* really happen to people when they die?'

Charmed by this sign of Emmy's renewed interest in serious themes, my Uncle Spencer explained to her what Alphonse at any rate thought would happen to him.

At midday, over the repeated cabbage soup and the horrible boiled meat, the bank-clerk, with characteristically tasteless facetiousness, asked, 'How's our one little nigger boy?'

Emmy looked at him with disgust and anger. 'I think you're perfectly horrible,' she said. And, lowering her voice reverently, she went on, 'The doctor says he's going to die.'

The bank-clerk was unabashed. 'Oh, he's going to kick the bucket, is he? Poor old blacky!'

Emmy made no answer; there was a general silence. It was as though somebody had started to make an unseemly noise in a church.

Afterwards, in the privacy of the little room, where, among the filing cabinets and the dusty papers, the Dravidian lay contentedly dying, Emmy turned to my Uncle Spencer and said, 'You know, Uncle Spenny, I think you're a wonderfully decent sort. I do, really.'

My Uncle Spencer was too much overcome to say anything but 'Emmy, Emmy,' two or three times. He took her hand and, very gently, kissed it.

That afternoon they went on talking about all the things that might conceivably happen after one were dead. Emmy told my Uncle Spencer all that she had thought when she got the telegram—two years ago it was, and she was working in a hall at Glasgow, one of her first engagements, too—saying that her father had suddenly died. He drank too much, her father did; and he wasn't kind to mother when he wasn't himself. But she had been very fond of him, all the same; and when that telegram came she wondered and wondered. . . .

My Uncle Spencer listened attentively, happy in having this new glimpse of her past; he forgot the other incident which the beam of her confession had illumined for him.

Late that evening, after having lain for a long time quite still, as though he were asleep, Alphonse suddenly stirred, opened his large black eyes, and began to talk, at first in the incomprehensible language which came from him in delirium, then, when he realized that his listeners did not understand him, more slowly and in his strange pidgin-French.

'I have seen everything just now,' he said, 'everything.'

'But what?' they asked.

'All that is going to happen. I have seen that this war will last a long time—a long time. More than fifty months.' And he prophesied enormous calamities.

My Uncle Spencer, who knew for certain that the war couldn't possibly last more than three months, was incredulous. But Emmy, who had no preconceived ideas on war and a strong faith in oracles, stopped him impatiently when he wanted to bring the Dravidian to silence.

'Tell me,' she said, 'what's going to happen to us.' She had very little interest in the fate of civilization.

'I am going to die,' Alphonse began.

My Uncle Spencer made certain deprecating little noises. 'No, no,' he protested.

The Indian paid no attention to him. 'I am going to die,' he repeated. 'And you,' he said to my Uncle Spencer, 'you will be let go and then again be put into prison. But not here. Somewhere else. A long way off. For a long time—a very long time. You will be very unhappy.' He shook his head. 'I cannot help it; even though you have been so good to me. That is what I see. But the man who deceived me'—he meant the journalist—'he will very soon be set free and he will live in freedom, all the time. In such freedom as there will be here. And he who sits in the chair will at last go back to his own country. And he who sings will go free like the man who deceived me. And the small grey man will be sent to another prison in another country. And the fat woman with a red mouth will be sent to another country; but she will not be in prison. I think she will be married there— again.' The portraits were recognizably those of the Russian countess and the professor of Latin. 'And the man with car- buncles on his face' (this was the bank-clerk, no doubt) 'will be sent to another prison in another country; and there he will die. And the woman in black who is so sad . . .'

But Emmy could bear to wait no longer. 'What about me?' she asked. 'Tell me what you see about me.'

The Dravidian closed his eyes and was silent for a moment. 'You will be set free,' he said. 'Soon. And some day,' he went on, 'you will be the wife of this good man.' He indicated my Uncle Spencer. 'But not yet; not for a long time; till all this strife is at an end. You will have children . . . good fortune . . . .' His words grew fainter; once more he closed his eyes. He sighed as though utterly exhausted. 'Beware of fair strangers,' he murmured, reverting to the old familiar formula. He said no more.

Emmy and my Uncle Spencer were left looking at one another in silence.

'What do you think, Uncle Spenny?' she whispered at last. 'Is it true?'

Two hours later the Indian was dead.

My Uncle Spencer slept that night, or rather did not sleep, in the living-room. The corpse lay alone among the archives. The words of the Indian continued to echo and re-echo in his mind: 'Some day you will be the wife of this kind man.' Perhaps, he thought, on the verge of death, the spirit already begins to try its wings in the new world. Perhaps already it has begun to know the fringes, as it were, of secrets that are to be revealed to it. To my Uncle Spencer there was nothing repugnant in the idea. There was room in his universe for what are commonly and perhaps wrongly known as miracles. Perhaps the words were a promise, a statement of future fact. Lying on his back, his eyes fixed on the dark blue starry sky beyond the open window, he meditated on that problem of fixed fate and free will, with which the devils in Milton's hell wasted their infernal leisure. And like a refrain the words repeated themselves: 'Some day you will be the wife of this good man.' The stars moved slowly across the opening of the window. He did not sleep.

In the morning an order came for the release of the journalist and the opera-singer. Joyfully they said good-bye to their fellow-prisoners; the door closed behind them. Emmy turned to my Uncle Spencer with a look almost of terror in her eyes; the Indian's prophecies were already beginning to come true. But they said nothing to one another. Two days later the bank-clerk left for an internment camp in Germany.

And then, one morning, my Uncle Spencer himself was

sent for. The order came quite suddenly; they left him no time to take leave. He was examined by the competent authority, found harmless, and permitted to return to Longres, where, however, he was to live under supervision. They did not even allow him to go back to the prison and say goodbye; a soldier brought his effects from the Ministry; he was put on to the train, with orders to report to the commandant at Longres as soon as he arrived.

Antonieke received her master with tears of joy. But my Uncle Spencer took no pleasure in his recovered freedom. Emmy Wendle was still a prisoner. True, she would soon be set free; but then, he now realized to his horror, she did not know his address. He had been released at such startlingly short notice that he had had no time to arrange with her about the possibilities of future meetings; he had not even seen her on the morning of his liberation.

Two days after his return to Longres, he asked permission from the commandant, to whom he had to report himself every day, whether he might go to Brussels. He was asked why; my Uncle Spencer answered truthfully that it was to visit a friend in the prison from which he himself had just been released. Permission was at once refused.

My Uncle Spencer went to Brussels all the same. The sentry at the door of the prison arrested him as a suspicious person. He was sent back to Longres; the commandant talked to him menacingly. The next week, my Uncle Spencer tried again. It was sheer insanity, he knew; but doing something idiotic was preferable to doing nothing. He was again arrested.

This time they condemned him to internment in a camp in Germany. The Indian's prophecies were being fulfilled with a remarkable accuracy. And the war did last for more than fifty months. And the carbuncular bank-clerk, whom he found again in the internment camp, did, in fact, die. . . .

What made him confide in me—me, whom he had known as a child and almost fathered—I do not know. Or perhaps I do know. Perhaps it was because he felt that I should be more competent to advise him on this sort of subject than his brother—my father—or old Mr. Bullinger, the Dante scholar, or any other of his friends. He would have felt ashamed, perhaps, to talk to them about this sort of thing. And he would have felt, too, that perhaps it wouldn't be much good talking to them, and that I, in spite of my youth, or even because of it, might actually be more experienced in these matters than they. Neither my father nor Mr. Bullinger, I imagine, knew very much about male impersonators.

At any rate, whatever the cause, it was to me that he talked about the whole affair, that spring of 1919, when he was staying with us in Sussex, recuperating after those dreary months of confinement. We used to go for long walks together, across the open downs, or between the grey pillars of the beech-woods; and painfully overcoming reluctance after reluctance, proceeding from confidence to more intimate confidence, my Uncle Spencer told me the whole story.

The story involved interminable discussions by the way. For we had to decide, first of all, whether there was any possible scientific explanation of prophecy; whether there was such a thing as an absolute future waiting to be lived through. And at much greater length, even, we had to argue about women—whether they were really 'like that' (and into what depths of cynicism my poor Uncle Spencer had learned, during the long, embittered meditations of his prison days and nights, to plunge and wallow!), or whether they were like the angels he had desired them to be.

But more important than to speculate on Emmy's possible character was to discover where she now was. More urgent than to wonder if prophecy could conceivably be reliable, was to take steps to fulfil this particular prophecy. For weeks my Uncle Spencer and I played at detectives.

I have often fancied that we must have looked, when we made our inquiries together, uncommonly like the traditional pair in the stories—my Uncle Spencer, the bright-eyed, cadaverous, sharp-featured genius, the Holmes of the combination; and I, moon-faced and chubby, a very youthful Watson. But, as a matter of fact, it was I, if I may say so without fatuity, who was the real Holmes of the two. My Uncle Spencer was too innocent of the world to know how to set about looking for a vanished mistress; just as he was too innocent of science to know how or where to find out what there was to be discovered on any abstracter subject.

It was I who took him to the British Museum and made him look up all the back numbers of the theatrical papers to see when Emmy had last advertised her desire to be engaged. It was I, the apparent Watson, who thought of the theatrical agencies and the stage doors of all the suburban music halls. Sleuth-like in aspect, innocent at heart, my Uncle Spencer followed, marvelling at my familiarity with the ways of the strange world.

But I must temper my boasting by the confession that we were always entirely unsuccessful. No agency had heard of Emmy Wendle since 1914. Her card had appeared in no paper. The porters of music halls remembered her, but only as something antediluvian. 'Emmy Wendle? Oh yes, Emmy Wendle . . .' And scratching their heads, they strove by a mental effort to pass from the mere name to the person, like palæontologists reconstructing the whole diplodocus from the single fossil bone.

Two or three times we were even given addresses. But the landladies of the lodging-houses where she had stayed did not even remember her; and the old aunt at Ealing, from whom we joyfully hoped so much, had washed her hands of Emmy two or three months before the war began. And the conviction she then had that Emmy was a bad girl was only intensified and confirmed by our impertinent inquiries. No, she knew nothing about Emmy Wendle, now, and didn't want to know. And she'd trouble us to leave respectable people like herself in peace. And, defeated, we climbed back into our taxi, while the inhabitants of the squalid little street peered out at us and our vehicle, as though we had been visitors from another planet, and the metropolitan hackney carriage a fairy chariot.

'Perhaps she's dead,' said my Uncle Spencer softly, after a long silence.

'Perhaps,' I said brutally, 'she's found a husband and retired into private life.'

My Uncle Spencer shut his eyes, sighed, and drew his hand across his forehead. What dreadful images filled his mind? He would almost have preferred that she should be dead.

'And yet the Indian,' he murmured, 'he was always right . . .'

And perhaps he may still be right in this. Who knows?

BOOKS BY ALDOUS HUXLEY

BRAVE NEW WORLD

Available in Paperback and E-book

A fantasy of the future that sheds a blazing critical light on the present—considered to be Aldous Huxley's most enduring masterpiece.

BRAVE NEW WORLD REVISITED

Available in Paperback and E-book

In one of the most important and fascinating books of his career, Aldous Huxley uses his tremendous knowledge of human relations to compare the modern-day world with his prophetic fantasy as portrayed in *Brave New World*.

ISLAND

Available in Paperback and E-book

Huxley transports us to a Pacific island where, for 120 years, an ideal society has flourished. Inevitably, this island of bliss attracts the envy and enmity of the surrounding world.

EYELESS IN GAZA
A Novel

Available in Paperback

The story of one man's quest to find a meaningful life, which leads him from blind hedonism to political revolution to spiritual enlightenment

THE GENIUS AND THE GODDESS
A Novel

Available in Paperback and E-book

A lost novella from Aldous Huxley now available in print: The story of a brilliant physicist, his beautiful wife, and the young man who tears their world apart.

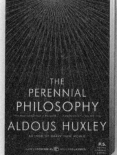
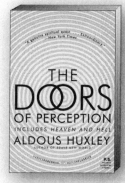
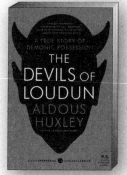